Arianne Richmonde's full-length novels in the Pearl Series, *Shades of Pearl*, *Shadows of Pearl*, *Shimmers of Pearl*, *Pearl* and *Belle Pearl* follow the tumultuous and heart-rending love story between Pearl Robinson and Alexandre Chevalier. All five books are bestsellers in erotic romance. The first three books are also available as one book: *The Pearl Trilogy*.

What people are saying about Pearl and Belle Pearl:

"I have to say that *Belle Pearl*—the conclusion for this series—was definitely a roller coaster ride! I was shocked, I was surprised, and I was ultimately floored with the turn of events! It was that interesting and unexpected!! I absolutely LOVED this book and devoured every minute."

—*Kawehi Book Blog*

"Can Pearl and Alexandre really have their HEA? You must read to find out. But I PROMISE you, it is a truly amazing ride and finale. One you will never see coming!"

—*Sam Stettner*

"5 Stars. I've loved Alexandre since book 1. Reading the series from his POV just made me love him more."

—*Nade Ferrabee*

"Five stars because Alexandre is worth every one of them."

—*Cindy at The Book Enthusiast*

"I LOVE LOVE LOVE Alexandre! I have been looking forward to reading these books and I can say without a doubt…it was worth the wait!"

—*The Literary Nook*

"I went completely crazy over Alexandre in *The Pearl Trilogy* and I fell even more crazy in love with him in *Pearl.*"

—*Books, Babes and Cheap Cabernet*

"Don't miss out on this amazingly hot and smoldering read…you will love it!"

—*Two Crazy Girls With A Passion For Books*

"I devoured this book and loved every second of it."

—*The Book Blog*

"CALL THE FIRE BRIGADE my house is burning down from Alexandre's sexpertise!!"

—*Island Lovelies Book Club*

"This is a 'MUST READ'!!!!"

—*Sugar and Spice Book Review*

"Alexandre is one of my original Book Boyfriends right up there with Fifty… this new look at him only solidified that crush."

—*Mommy's A Book Whore*

Pearl

Belle Pearl

by

Arianne Richmonde

About these novels.

Pearl and ***Belle Pearl*** follow Arianne Richmonde's bestselling books in *The Pearl Trilogy*: *Shades of Pearl*, *Shadows of Pearl* and *Shimmers of Pearl*; the tumultuous and heart-rending love story between forty-year-old documentary producer, Pearl Robinson, and French Internet billionaire, Alexandre Chevalier, fifteen years her junior.

Pearl and ***Belle Pearl*** are written from Alexandre's point of view, from the moment he and Pearl first meet on a rainy summer's day in a coffee shop in New York City. In any relationship details are hidden; things are left unsaid. Not all conversations are remembered in the same way. And not all actions are disclosed—especially to the one you love most.

In ***Belle Pearl*** the story is continued beyond *Shimmers of Pearl* and has a completely different ending than the trilogy.

At only twenty-five, Alexandre Chevalier is a billionaire. His social media site, HookedUp, is more popular than Twitter, more global than Facebook. With his devastating looks, alluring charm, and his immense wealth, he has women falling at his feet, desperate for his attention—ex girlfriends and an ex-fiancée who simply *cannot* let him go. Although his heart is set on only Pearl, she tests him to his limits and proves that she is even more damaged than he first believed.

Alexandre's dark and dysfunctional past makes him crave a normal relationship with Pearl but he soon finds out that she is not your average woman. However, he believes that they are both two peas in the same dysfunctional pod, made to 'disfunction' together, and is determined to make their union work. But Pearl puts Alexandre in a position where he is made to choose. His loyalties are split, his patience torn.

After many trials, misunderstandings, and revelations of dark secrets, finally their wedding ensues and it looks as if their happily ever after is sealed.

Until something unforeseen rips their world apart.

Cover design © by: Arianne Richmonde

About the Author

Arianne Richmonde is an American writer and artist who was raised in both the US and Europe. She lives in France with her husband and coterie of animals.

As well as ***The Pearl Series*** she has written a suspense novel, *Stolen Grace.*

The Pearl series:

The Pearl Trilogy bundle (the first three books in one)

Shades of Pearl
Shadows of Pearl
Shimmers of Pearl
Pearl
Belle Pearl

To be advised of upcoming releases, sign up:
ariannerichmonde.com/email-signup

For more information on the author visit her website:

www.ariannerichmonde.com

Acknowledgements

To every one of my amazing readers who demanded more of Pearl and Alexandre. Thanks for all your love and feedback. ***The Pearl Series*** would not have been possible without you. Thank you to all the bloggers and readers who recommended my books to their friends and followers. Your tireless support and enthusiasm have me in awe. Thank you so much.

Pearl

1

It was raining in New York City. The sort of rain that felt vaguely tropical because it was summertime and the muggy heat was broken by a glorious downfall. Very welcome, because my sister and I had just given a talk at an I.T. conference and she was feeling hot and bothered—really getting on my case.

The rain eased the tension.

Sophie was driving me nuts that day. It wasn't easy going into business with a sibling, but if it hadn't been for her shrewd business savvy, I wouldn't have had the same luck. Sophie inhaled HookedUp. Exhaled HookedUp. Being as obsessed with money as she was, she wouldn't rest until we'd practically taken over the world. And, as everyone now knows, social media really *has* taken over the world so she was onto something big. Clever woman.

Sophie had moved our conference talk forward by an hour because she was in a foul mood—wanted to get it over and done with—get the hell out of there. I, on the other hand, felt bound by some odd sense of duty to share our success story; inspire people to jump into the deep end as we had done. To go for it.

At the conference, someone in the audience asked me how I would describe myself and I replied: "I'm just a nerd who found programming fascinating. With a keen eye for patterns and codes, I pushed it to the limit and got rich. I'm a lucky geek, that's all." People laughed as if what I said was a silly joke. But I meant it.

I'm still not used to being a billionaire. Even now, if I ever see an article written about the power of social media and HookedUp, it's as if I'm taking a glimpse into someone else's life; a driven, ambitious, 'ruthless businessman' (as I've often been described), when I'm still just a guy who likes surfing, rock climbing and hanging out with his family and dogs. Just an ordinary man. Others don't perceive me that way—at all. I suppose I should be flattered by their attention, although I'm a private man and hate the limelight.

I took a chance, worked hard, and got lucky. A Frenchman living the American Dream.

That's what I love about American culture. Everybody gets a shot if you get off your ass and have the will to succeed. Not so in France. It's hard to break away from the mold; people don't like to see others rise above their station. Maybe I'm being hard on my country, judgmental, but all I know is if I'd stayed there, HookedUp wouldn't be the mega-power it is today. Not even close. The USA has given us all we have and I'm grateful, even though having this much money still feels sinful at my age. Or any age, for that matter.

Funny how Fate pans out; you never know what life has in store for you.

I nearly didn't go into the coffee shop that day. Sophie needed a shot of caffeine and I really wasn't in the mood to argue, so we dashed in from the rain and stood in line.

Our conversation had been heated, to say the least. We'd been discussing the HookedUp meeting we had scheduled in Mumbai in a couple of weeks time. It was a mega-deal that she'd been feverishly working on all year. I didn't think HookedUp could get any more global and powerful than it already was, but I was wrong. That deal was going to make us silly money. Really silly money. I knew I was going to be able to buy that Austin Healey I had my eye on. Hell, I could have bought a fleet of them. Aircrafts too. Whatever I wanted.

Sophie took out her Smartphone from her Chanel purse and said in French—her voice low so that nobody would overhear, "Look, Alexandre, this is the guy we're meeting in Mumbai." She scrolled down to a photo of a portly man with a handlebar mustache. "This is the son of a bitch who's squeezing us for every dime. He's our enemy. He's the one we need to watch."

"But I thought you said he's the one we're signing with—"

"He is," she interrupted. "Keep your enemies close." She brushed her dark hair away from her face and narrowed her eyes with suspicion—a habit I had myself. I remember thinking how elegant and beautiful she looked; yet in 'predator mood,' she was also formidable. I was glad to have her on my side.

Half listening to my sister gabble on about the Mumbai deal, I noticed a woman rush through the door—a whirlwind of an entrance. She was flustered, her blonde hair damp from the summer rain, her white T-shirt also damp, clinging to her body, revealing a glimpse of perfectly shaped breasts through a thin bra. I shouldn't have noticed these sorts of things, but being your average guy, I did. She was battling with an enormous handbag—what was it with women and those giant handbags? What did they carry in those things—bricks?

"Arrête!" Sophie snapped and proceeded for the next couple of minutes to berate me for not paying attention. She was rolling her eyes and puffing out air disapprovingly. Ignoring her, I wondered, again, why I had gone into business with her because she was really bugging me. She added, "If you want to fuck that girl you're staring at, you can you know—American women put out on the first date."

I hated it when my sister talked like that to me—it made me cringe—especially her sweeping generalizations about other countries and civilizations.

"She doesn't strike me as that type," I mumbled back in French. The pretty lady was now closer and I couldn't take my eyes off her. She had her head cocked sideways and was staring at the coffee menu, chewing her lower lip in concentration. She was beautiful, like a modern version of Grace Kelly—she looked about thirty or so.

My eyes raked down her perfectly formed body. She was dressed in a tight, gray skirt which accentuated her peachy butt. The slit on the pleat revealed a pair of elegant calves, but her chic outfit was marred by sneakers. Somehow, it made her all the more attractive as if she didn't give a damn. As my gaze trailed back up to her breasts, I saw that she was wearing an *InterWorld* button. *Good,* I thought, *we have something in common—I can chat her up.*

I cleared my throat and moved a step closer. "So how did you enjoy the conference?"

She jumped back in surprise; her eyes fixed on my chest. I felt as if I was towering above her, although she was a good five foot six. I looked a mess—T-shirt and old jeans with holes in the knee. So far, she was not responding. I knew that New Yorkers could be just as rude as Parisians so I wasn't fazed.

She flicked her gaze at me but said nothing. I was right—she hadn't answered my question, just continued to look at me; stunned, as if she really didn't want to have a conversation at all.

I smiled at her. I felt like a jerk, but dug myself in deeper. "Your name tag," I said. "Were you at that conference around the corner?" I decided that she obviously thought I was a total jackass as her response was clipped, terse.

"Yes I was," is all she said and then cast a glance at Sophie.

I realized that this woman—her nametag said **Pearl Robinson**—must have assumed that Sophie was my girlfriend—the perils of hanging out with my beautiful sister. Or maybe Pearl Robinson wasn't smiling simply because she wanted me to shut the hell up and leave her alone.

But I didn't back off. "I'll pay for whatever the lady's having, too," I told the girl serving our coffee. I wanted to say, 'Whatever Pearl's having' but thought that Pearl would peg me for some kind of stalker. Why I continued to pursue her I wasn't sure, since she was clearly not interested. But I couldn't help myself. "For Pearl," I added, wondering why I was not getting the response I was after. Not to be arrogant, but women did normally smile at me, if not give me the eye. They still do. Daily. But Pearl was not buying it. I wanted her to flirt, brighten up my dull day.

I went on, undeterred—for some reason I didn't feel like giving up; she had really piqued my interest. "Pearl. What a beautiful name." *Jesus what did I sound like? A typical French gigolo type, no doubt.* "I've never heard that before. As a name, I mean."

In my peripheral vision, I caught Sophie rolling her eyes, again, and she whispered in French, "Bet you anything you'll have that woman on her back in no time." *Shut up!*

Pearl Robinson finally reciprocated with a beautiful big smile. *Nice.* Pretty teeth. Sexy, curvy lips. She told me about her parents being hippies or something—explaining her name. I wasn't listening. I'd got her attention, that's all I cared about. I could tell she liked me. *Took long enough for her to warm up, though—all of forty seconds.* I felt triumphant. Why? I met pretty women all the time. But there was something about this one that really captured my attention. She was poised and elegant, yet unsure of herself. There was a childish, vulnerable quality about her which I found disarming, even beguiling. She was rifling through her enormous handbag, trying to find her wallet. Why are American women so keen on paying for themselves? Was she embarrassed because I was buying her a coffee?

"What's your name?" she asked, while simultaneously staring at my nametag.

Good...ironic sense of humor, I thought. I laughed and introduced myself. Introduced Sophie, too.

Pearl went to shake Sophie's hand and her wristwatch caught on my T-shirt. I looked down at her other hand. No wedding ring. *Good.* I felt my heart quicken with the physical contact of her delicate wrist brushing against my chest—the intimacy—and I knew….in that nanosecond, I knew; I was going to have to fuck this girl.

The way she was looking at me was giving me the green light. Yet her big blue eyes were unsure of me. She looked down at the floor, and then up again at me. She may not have even known it herself at that point—women rarely do—but she wanted me to claim her. I could almost hear her screaming my name. I pictured myself pinning her up against a wall, all of me inside her.

I wanted her. And I was going to have her. You bet. Every last inch of her.

"Remember to use protection," Sophie whispered in French, "she may look like an nice Upper East side WASP, but you never know."

I retorted, also in French. "Get your coffee, or whatever you're drinking, and *leave* because I've had enough of your snippy conversation for one day."

Sophie cocked her eyebrow at me and smirked. I turned my attention back to Pearl Robinson and prayed that her French was limited or non-existent. I gazed at her, right into her clear blue eyes. *Yes,* I decided, *I want this woman.*

And she wanted me. I was pretty damn sure. She was jittery, nervous, tongue-tied—couldn't get her sentences out straight. Why? Because I was running my eyes up and down her body, mentally undressing her, and she could sense the electricity. The heat. She was all flustered. She could read my mind. She was fumbling for something in her monster-bag again. Her apartment keys, she told me. Was she planning on inviting me over?

"Nice to meet you, Pearl," Sophie said, giving her the once-over. "Maybe see you around some time?" The innuendo was so thick you could have cut it with a machete.

Sophie sashayed out of the coffee shop and I exhaled with relief. *Thank God, now I can get down to business. Real business.*

"I got the drinks to go, but do you want to sit down?" I suggested to Pearl. She nodded.

Why I was so taken with this New Yorker, apart from her obvious good looks, I wasn't quite sure—she had a quirky kind of charm. I liked her. And I decided right there and then—I didn't just want to fuck Pearl, I wanted to get to know her, too.

She eased her way into an armchair but was unsure whether to cross or uncross her legs. Like a schoolboy, I found my eyes wandering to her crotch and imagining what lay beneath, but she was too demure for that. Her legs crossed closed, and she smoothed that sexy pencil skirt over her thighs. I thought about fucking her again—I couldn't stop myself. I wondered if what Sophie said was true: that Pearl would put out on a first date. I'd have to find out….

We were interrupted by a phone call from my assistant, Jim, telling me to snap up the Austin Healy I'd had my eye on—they'd accepted my offer. So the conversation with Pearl swung around to cars. I felt like a jerk. I knew what women were like; feigning interest about bits of machinery when they really couldn't give a damn. Pearl was no different. Still, she did a good job of pretending. She nodded and smiled and widened her pretty eyes. Meanwhile, I had one thing on my mind: to get her into the sack ASAP.

But then she took me off guard. She started talking about re-runs of old sitcoms, classic novels, and old songs and I began to think we had something in common besides physical attraction. Then, when I mentioned my black Labrador, Rex, that was it. I began to mentally tuck my tackle back into my pants, so to speak, because she admitted that she was crazy for dogs, too. She loved the fact that I could take Rex to restaurants in Paris and a flash of our future ran before my eyes. I swear. I had a vision of us together eating something delicious, Rex at our side, and something told me that Pearl and I would make the grade. It does sound crazy, that. Call it a premonition—I think it was.

She was telling me about her childhood Husky.

"My dog was called Zelda," she said, her liquid eyes flashing with happy memories.

"Like Zelda Fitzgerald?" I asked. "Scott Fitzgerald's wife?"

She looked up at me, surprised. "Yeah, you know about her?"

"Of course I do. She was a little bit crazy, wasn't she? *The Great Gatsby* was partly inspired by her."

"Well, like Zelda Fitzgerald, our Zelda was a little out to lunch. I mean, literally. She loved chickens. Went on several murderous escapades."

"The way you say that with a little smile on your face makes me believe you didn't have much sympathy for the innocent, victimized chickens," I teased.

"They were going to be slaughtered anyway, poor things." She put her hand on her mouth as if she'd put her foot in it. "Sorry, Alexandre, are you a vegetarian?"

I loved the way she said *Alexandre* with her cute American accent, trying to accentuate the *re*. "No, you?"

"No red meat. Only organic chicken. I know...kind of

ironic considering what Zelda did. I do have a conscience—I'm against intensive farming, you know, animals spending their lives in tiny cages, so small they can't even turn around. Cows being forced to eat grain, not grass—being pumped full of antibiotics. People don't like inviting me to dinner. I'm a tricky customer."

"Not for me, you're not," I found myself saying. "I'd be delighted if you came for dinner. I'll cook you something wonderful." I narrowed my eyes at her. Fuck she was sexy.

Her eyes, in return, widened and her lips clamped around her straw, as she sipped her iced cappuccino, seductively. Jesus, I felt my cock harden watching her mouth. I shifted in my seat and leaned forward to hide my bulge. As I leaned down, I let my hand brush against her golden calf. Smooth, soft legs. *Nice.* This unexpected coffee date was getting too hot to handle so I tried to turn the conversation around to stop myself from mentally undressing her. She got there first, asking me why I chose to live in New York.

"France is a great country," I began. "Beautiful. Just beautiful. Fine wine, great cuisine, incredible landscape—we really do have a rich culture. But when it comes to opportunity, especially for small businesses, it's not so easy there."

"You own a small company? What do you do?"

Interesting. This woman has no idea who I am. Refreshing. She won't be after my money—she doesn't have an agenda. Good.

"That's why I was at that conference," I explained.

I expanded a bit, gave her the usual blab about 'giving back,' and how I liked to share a few tricks of the trade with others.

"And you?" I asked, wondering what the hell this unlikely

sexpot was doing at an I.T. conference. She so didn't look the type. "What were *you* doing there?"

She flushed a little, slid down into her chair as if she wanted to disappear and shifted her gaze to her feet. She looked acutely embarrassed. Maybe she had a very boring job, I reasoned, and didn't want to spoil the mood. I dropped the subject. So we brought the conversation back to me again, and she *had* heard of HookedUp, after all. Of course she had. Who hadn't? Everyone and his cousin hooked up with HookedUp, even married couples. But Pearl didn't seem particularly impressed by me, even when I let it slip that I was the CEO.

"So when you're not working or zipping about in your beautiful classic cars, or hanging out with Rex, what do you do to relax?"

"I rock-climb," I replied, already having planned in my head that rock climbing would be the perfect first date for us. Not too 'date-like,' not typical—she'd go for it.

"Oh yeah? I swim. Nearly every day. It's what keeps me sane."

Ah, so that accounts for her tight peachy ass and sculpted legs. We discussed the benefit of sports—how it was good for one's mental state of mind as well as keeping your body fit. This woman had me intrigued. I was getting more than a hard-on talking to her. She made me laugh. She was bright, opinionated. Had read the classics, loved dogs and sure, I couldn't deny it, she had a body like a pin-up and the face of an angel. Besides, with all her straw-sucking, I knew what was going through her mind. She wanted to see me with my shirt off. Yes, damn it, I could tell. She couldn't take her eyes off my chest. She even licked her luscious lips while she was ogling me, and then said—her eyes all baby-doll…all come-and-fuck-me-now:

"I tried rock climbing once. I was terrified but I could really understand the attraction to the sport."

On the word, *attraction*, I swear to God, she looked at my chest, then my groin, and back again to my chest before she finally fastened her gaze on my face. Oh yeah, believe me, I knew what was going on in Pearl's mind. Her smart attire, educated voice and expensive handbag didn't fool me. Still, her come-on would have been imperceptible to an un-trained eye—not slutty, not over-flirtatious…just a split second of wanton lust on her part, which I bet she thought I hadn't clocked onto.

But…Miss Pearl Robinson, daughter of hippies, lover of dogs, quasi-vegetarian temptress….I had your number.

I knew everything there was to know—instinctively.

I wanted her quirky ass and I was going to have it. And everything that went with it, too. All of it. I was going to put my mark on that peachy butt.

I presumed I had her all worked out. Clever me.

Little did I know that I was dead wrong.

Things weren't going to be quite so simple.

So there we were chatting about this and that, still drinking our coffees, lingering over them, trying to make our drinks last, because neither of us wanted our tête-à-tête to end.

During the conversation that followed, it struck me that Pearl was damaged goods. But it was too late. *I was invested.* I invited her rock climbing—feeling smug about all the things I was going to do to her, picturing her having multiple orgasms as I fucked her senseless in several different ways. How I'd take her to a hotel the night before, we'd have passionate sex, and by the next day, she probably wouldn't even want to go rock climbing anyway, because let's face it, when she told me she'd once been, she was obviously lying.

"Would it seem too forward to invite you to come with me for the weekend?" I suggested.

Her eyes lit up, *at first,* "Not at all!" she said with enthusiasm. But suddenly, she froze. *Froze.* She was like a beautiful flower closing its petals. I saw horror flash across her face. She was even eyeing the front door as if she planned to make a dash for it. Why? She was stunning, had a great body (so must have felt confident in that department), fancied the pants off me, obviously wasn't playing the hard-to-get-I'm-so-virtuous game, so why was she freaking out about us spending the night together?

I read her expression: she was terrified of sex.

"Don't worry, Pearl. I can arrange for us to have separate bedrooms," I said.

But it only made things worse: she looked even more panicked; her face paled, her mouth fell open. She mumbled—her disappointment deeper than a well, "Yes, of course. Separate bedrooms."

I understood, then and there, that she wanted me, but would be too traumatized for anything more than a peck on the cheek.

How did I know all this at the tender age of twenty-five? I won't go into it now, but trust me, I know women. I've been intimate with the female species—because they *are* a 'species' unto their own—since the age of fourteen, when I lost my virginity to a friend of my sister's, a 'colleague' of hers. Women have always revealed to me their deepest secrets, fears, loves and passions. How many women have I 'known' in my life? I lost count a long, long time ago. Because I started young, by the time I was college age, I really was *au fait* with the physical and physiological machinations of the female sex. Not that I went to college. Not for long, anyway. I was too busy plotting to take over the world, shut in my man cave. Coding. Being a nerd. Designing HookedUp. But as most people know, nerds get their revenge. One day I'd be a rich man, I told myself.

And I was right.

So by the time I was the grand old age of twenty, I'd played the field so much that all I wanted was a safe, stable relationship with a normal girl. I ended up in the arms of someone less than stable and swore I wouldn't make the same mistake twice. But here I was again, being drawn to somebody with *issues. Major issues,* I suspected.

And that somebody was Pearl Robinson.

I was a rich, powerful man used to getting what I wanted. And ironically, I wanted her.

So I suggested I'd pick her up the following day. No hotel. I'd play it safe.

"Actually, I know another place that we can go rock climbing closer to the city. It's only ninety miles upstate—we can drive there early and come back late, all in one day. What do you say?"

"Great," she answered. And I saw both relief and regret flicker in her blue eyes.

I wouldn't fuck her, after all. I'd wait. Bide my time. Because something told me that this woman hadn't been fucked properly for a very long while. Maybe never.

Most guys like the chase. They love it when girls spurn them and play hard to get. I guess they have something to prove to themselves, like going hunting. But I don't operate that way. I don't want a woman to be with me because of my own powers of persuasion, or because I've 'bulldozed' her into it. I'm not the bulldozing type. I don't want to tread over anyone's sensibilities, least of all a female's. You know how children and dogs can be? Curious but wary? You can't force them. Let them come to you, I say. Pique their interest. Don't be overbearing or over-possessive. It makes for a good story in a romance novel (I know, my mother devours them, one a day), but in reality, a woman wants a man to be a man, not some insecure wreck wondering where she is every second, or having a jealous fit if her top's too revealing. A woman desires a *confident* man—that's another thing I've learned over the years from listening to their woes: be confident.

And if you aren't feeling that way?

Fake it.

Besides, I believe in love at first sight, or at least, *lust* at first sight. If the magic isn't there for both parties within the first twenty seconds of meeting each other, you can be sure it never will be. Of course, many people would disagree with that, but for me, I've found this to be true. With Pearl that connection was there. Has it ever been there before or since? No, never. Not in that twenty-second kind of way.

I didn't let Pearl know how I felt. Another rule: Don't scare a woman off by being too keen or pushy. Because if she succumbs to you, you'll never know if it's because she genuinely loves you or because you've worn her down. There are a lot of worn-down women out there. They think it's easier to give in. Some men are foolish enough to mistake that for lust, or even love.

Also, I'm French. Pride is in my DNA. I can't help it. So when Pearl made it obvious that she had second thoughts about spending the night with me, I held back.

Our rock climbing date was interesting, to say the least. I picked her up at 7 am from her Upper East Side apartment, and we drove upstate to the Shawangunk Mountains. During the car ride, I knew I was giving her double messages but I couldn't help myself. One minute I was talking about falling in love with my Corvette because of the LeMans blue, adding, "Same color as your eyes," and the next I was acting like a strict Victorian father, telling her how certain types of sex play didn't do it for me—namely whipping. (Fantasy is one thing, reality is another. Seriously, what woman wants to be physically hurt?) Pearl was confused. I was confused. How the hell did the conversation veer off in that direction? Was it normal for two people to talk about sex on a first date? Talk about it, but not do it? I didn't think so, but nothing was normal about the pair of us. We were two misfits trying to slot our jiggled bits of puzzle into the right place, hoping that somehow, at least *our* pieces would fit together.

When I alluded to her LeMans blue eyes, she replied, "*My* eyes? You should talk with your tiger-green eyes set off against your dark hair."

At that point, on Date One, I wasn't quite sure what Pearl's deal was. What kind of Life Cards she'd been dealt. So far, I had learned that her hippy, surfer father abandoned her family when Pearl was young and he now lived in Hawaii. She told me that her mother died of cancer—they'd been very close. And her gay brother, Anthony (who sounded like a jerk, reading between the lines), lived in San Francisco with his boyfriend, Bruce. All this I gleaned, and yet I felt I was no closer to knowing why there was a shadow of fear in her eyes, a shimmer of benign mistrust.

Men. They can be pigs. I know, I've heard women complain about them all my life. Besides, there had been no truer hog than my father. On one of his bad days, he was a monster.

I contemplated Pearl's past. What man/men had hurt her? (Because, let's face it, it usually is a man). I studied her quietly all day. While she was climbing, she was brave and very focused. Even though she had never been rock climbing before, she embraced that rock-face with gusto. I got to enjoy great views of her slender legs doing their stuff, her nimble fingers hooking into tiny crevices, her glorious ass in all sorts of uncompromising positions. I heard myself calling her *chérie* and that's when I knew that I must have wanted to date her seriously. Chérie? I had never called *anyone* that before, not even my ex fiancée, Laura.

"You've passed the second test," I teased on the drive back home. My 1968 Corvette was humming away beautifully, and I didn't want Pearl to fall asleep. I saw exhaustion in her eyes after such a long, physical day. Her golden legs were stretched out, scratched by the rocks; there were little bloody nicks all over her limbs. I liked that. I may not have fucked her yet, or even kissed her, but I felt I'd made my mark on her. Yes, just like the bulldozer guys, I was guilty. Even on Date One, I wanted others to know that Pearl Robinson was mine.

She jolted from her sleepy reverie and shifted her weight in the car seat. "Second test? I didn't know I was being tested!" She laughed. "I'm assuming going climbing was the second test. What was the first test, then?"

"You have no idea?" I said, thinking it was obvious after our detailed conversation about Rex and Zelda, and dogs in general. Actually, come to think of it, this wasn't Date One but

Date 1.5. We'd been through all the preliminaries in the coffee shop. Had she turned her nose up at the mention of Rex, it would have been an instant deal breaker. I didn't, and don't, trust people who are not animal lovers. *Must love dogs.* No ifs or buts about it. I'd made that mistake once before.

"Go on, give me a clue," Pearl pleaded, raising her legs onto my dashboard, her bare feet revealing perfect, slender toes, set off by delicate ankles. I wanted to suck those pretty toes, then move my mouth further northward up her body.

"Give me a hint," she said with a pout. That pouting mouth. *Very sexy!* I had not-so-pure visions of things I wanted to do to that mouth, and things I wanted *it* to do to me.

I said nothing, just gave a cocky little smirk. I wanted to intrigue her, make her think about me. Dream about me when she got home that night. Make her want me. I could tell that, so far, it was working. I changed the music...*Can't Get Enough of Your Love Baby* by Barry White—a sexy song with a rhythmical drum beat. It set the scene. She jiggled about in her seat and I was curious. I wanted to know if she was moist between her legs. I wanted to know, for sure, if she was feeling as horny as I was.

I put my hand on her bare thigh and let it rest there, tapping my finger *very* lightly to the beat of the music. She whimpered. Very, very quietly. Almost imperceptibly but I caught it. I had her. But I still wouldn't fuck her that night. No, I'd make her wait. Make her wonder. I let my fingers wander higher. I had my eyes on the road, but in my peripheral vision, I noticed she licked her lips and fluttered her eyelashes. So very subtly, I let my fingers creep closer to her panties. I could sense her chest heaving with hot desire. Her nipples were erect—I saw that through her skimpy outfit. *Good,* I thought. I so wanted to plunge my fingers inside her, but instead, I took my hand away and put it back on the steering wheel. She sighed with frustration. I was getting to her—getting under her skin.

3

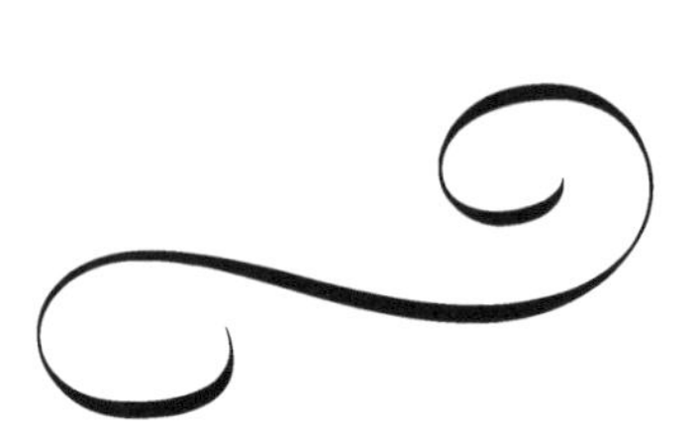

My cell had been switched off all day; I didn't want any interruptions. I had ten messages on my voicemail, more than half of which were from various women in my life: three from Sophie, all business calls except the last—she was curious as to where I'd been all day, and wondered who the lucky woman was. It seemed that it was my karma to attract jealous women, even my *sister* was possessive of me, and that's one of the reasons Pearl appeared so different; she was vaguely aloof, even though I could tell she liked me.

The next calls were from Laura, my ex, telling me that she would be coming to my house in Provence. I listened to the messages with half an ear, her Queen's English more pronounced than ever.

"Hi Alex, darling. Just to say that my plans have changed a bit. James doesn't seem to want to come this year, so it'll just be little old me. Is that okay? Of course it's okay. But I'll be really miffed if you're not there at the same time. I mean, I'll get bored all alone. Speak later, Alex, darling."

Then another:

"Oh yes, I almost forgot, just to let you know my physiotherapy sessions are going really well. I mean *really* well. I haven't been using the wheelchair for six whole months now. I'm a bit wobbly still, but it's all looking good. I mean, *I'm* looking good, though I say it myself! Call me, darling, and let me know when you'll be in France and I'll make plans."

If Laura said she was looking good, I believed her. She had been a model once, before she had a nasty accident with some concrete steps and ended up in a wheelchair. She had been a sailor, too—practically Olympic standard. Why I felt that the accident was somehow my responsibility, I don't know. But I did. Guilt has a way of grabbing you by the throat. Hence, my unfounded belief that I was responsible for Laura's happiness, despite her being married to another man.

The next message was from Indira, the woman I was fucking. I'd be seeing her the following week in Mumbai. Her Indian accent was husky and breathy, laced with desperation and desire.

"Baby, I can't wait to see you. I'm going crazy. Crazy, I tell you. I can't wait to lie with you. I've been dreaming of you every night. I need you so badly. See you next week."

Lie with you. What a quaint, polite way of saying, 'fuck.'

Indira was a movie star. A Bollywood legend, even though she was only thirty-three. She had long, dark, wavy hair and pale gray eyes, set against her caramel-colored skin. Stunning. She was a real beauty, gracing magazine covers and cherry-picking leading roles. She was also a widow. Her husband had died a few years before, leaving her a small fortune, not that she needed it—she was wealthy in her own right. He'd been a film producer, and was a good thirty years older than Indira. She had one grown-up teenager who was also making her name in movies. Women in India were generally treated like second-class citizens, except in two key areas where they really had clout: politics and cinema. Indira was a powerful woman, and used to getting what she wanted.

And she wanted me. Or rather, she wanted my cock.

I needed to end it with Indira but it was going to be tricky, because the grease-ball bastard with whom Sophie and I were signing our upcoming deal, was her first cousin. Indira was also investing a large chunk of her own money into HookedUp in India. Something I begged her not to do—I never mix business with pleasure—but she was insistent, and Sophie would have never forgiven me if I'd bungled the deal.

Meanwhile, I had Pearl Robinson on my mind.

Hmm...could get complicated. With Pearl Robinson now on the horizon, I wasn't sure how I'd organize my time. It depended on Pearl, really. Would she want me as a full-time boyfriend? I assumed so. Another thing I'd learned about women over the years: the exclusivity factor. Even Laura, who was married to someone else, wanted exclusivity. Not that I was fucking Laura, but I got the feeling from her flirtatious demeanor, that she was keen for our old candle to be re-lit.

The last voicemail was from Claudine. An ex from my teenage years. Uh oh. I'd be seeing her the next day. Now, Claudine was so fucked-up, that to *not* see her could be dangerous. I really didn't want a suicide on my conscience.

I listened to the message: "Alex? Mon amour?" She talked

into the receiver as if she were speaking to a live person. As if voicemails had only been invented yesterday. "Alex, tu es là?" I heard her TV on, a cackling noise in the background, her heavy breathing, as if she was waiting for me to magically say something. Then she hung up.

The last time I'd seen Claudine, she had gotten her hands on a Colt.45 and was threatening to shoot herself if I didn't fuck her. She told me that no other man could give her an orgasm. Claudine, like Laura, was a model.

Every man's fantasy seems to be to date a model, but believe me, models can be psychotic. You'd think that by being so beautiful they'd be brimming with self-confidence, but no. They can be the most neurotic women in the world. No matter how gorgeous they are, they feel they're too fat, or their forehead isn't high enough, or their lips are too thin or…whatever—the list goes on.

Claudine was like that. Very neurotic. Very high-maintenance. In order to get the gun away from her for good, I had to give her a mercy fuck. It wasn't exactly a punishment for me, but I was trying so hard to limit the complications in my life—e.g. limit the amount of women. Hone it down to just one.

I didn't consider myself a 'multi-tasker' by nature—not even when it came to women.

Quality, not quantity, was what I was aiming for.

But it was proving to be a tough call.

I was beginning to realize that my mantra of treating women well was backfiring on me.

You see I have a code:

• No woman is a 'slut'. Ever. I do not use that word in my

vocabulary. If a woman is sleeping around or being promiscuous it's because she is searching: for love, for a good time, for a good orgasm, for an escape. Or maybe even for money. For whatever reason it may be, no man (or woman) has a right to judge her.

- Always call a woman after a date. Even if you never want to see her again. Why? Because it's polite. Tell her you had a nice time. Treat others as you would like to be treated yourself, especially women.
- Don't bullshit a woman. Don't say, "I'll call you," if you don't mean it. If you just want sex, make that clear from the beginning. Don't make promises you can't keep.
- Always walk her home at night, drive her home or call a cab. Pay for the cab yourself. Make sure she has unlocked her door before you drive away.
- Don't invite yourself into her house. Like a vampire, let yourself be invited.
- Don't fuck another man's girl, no matter how tempting.
- The most important rule of all: When you fuck her, let her come first.

You see, it's no good just having sex for your own pleasure. Where's the fun in that? A real man needs to know that a woman *needs* him. Even if it's for just one night, you want her remembering you for being a good fuck, not a fuck-up. Your cock is a tool that must be used carefully. As with any tool, you, the *artisan,* need to deploy it with precision. Trust me, the rewards are worth it.

Women are experts at faking orgasms and a lot of men are too dumb to tell the difference, or too proud to acknowledge that it has ever happened to them. But in that department, believe me, most women could win an Oscar.

However, having said all this, I was, at that point in my life, beginning to realize that by *not* being an asshole and caring too much, I was creating a 'backlog' of women: ex-girlfriends, and exes of every kind. It was dawning on me: *Women don't forget.* I guess there are so many assholes out there, that by being halfway decent, a man can earn big brownie points.

I'd earned too many brownie points.

And it was getting out of control.

The next day, I got up early and cadged a lift to Paris with Sophie in her jet. I had business there and wanted to drop in on my mother and see Rex. I decided that I wouldn't pick him up that time around, because of the Mumbai trip coming up, but that I'd make arrangements for him to come and live with me in New York as soon as I could. After all, he was the one I bought my huge apartment for, with its views of Central Park and its rooftop garden. Only the best for Monsieur Rex!

Sometimes, I try to imagine a world without dogs, and I can't. Rex has seen me through no end of strife. He helped me set up HookedUp. That's not a joke, it's a fact.

So Sophie and I were on the plane, about to fly to Paris. She was dressed immaculately (as always), stretching out her slim legs as she carefully tucked a tendril of dark hair into her chignon while looking into her powder compact, or whatever it is that women use. She eased herself back into her airplane seat: we were taking off. I could tell she was in 'personal' mode, not 'business' mode by the look on her face, when she began, "So you actually *like* the American?"

I frowned at her. I wasn't in the mood.

"How *is* she?" she added.

I knew what she meant by that. She wanted me to give her intimate details. I replied, "She's a very friendly, fun girl."

"Watch out."

"Why, you think she's *dangerous?"* I said with a dry smile.

"You can't risk everything by playing about with American gold-diggers."

I languidly stretched out my arms. I wasn't even going to reply to her inane comment, but found myself mumbling, "Get a life, Sophie, and stop meddling with mine."

"I'm only looking out for you."

"I can look out for myself, thanks."

"Well, when I have a moment, I'm going to get her checked out," she warned.

"Don't you dare! I hate all this Googling shit and cyber-spying. I know *we* can't talk, with *HookedUp* and stuff, but I miss the old days when you found out about someone little by little, face to face, not from the Internet. It's so bloody unromantic."

"You see *romance* on the cards with that woman?"

That woman. She sounded like Bill Clinton. I closed my eyes. "Shame you turned gay, Sophie. Because you know what? You sound frustrated. You obviously need a good seeing to."

"Oh, you think a man's penis is the answer to everything, do you, you sexist jerk."

I smirked. "You'd be surprised." *Touché.*

Sophie had a girlfriend. Fine. But Sophie was also married. Married, and with a stepdaughter, Elodie, who was eighteen.

Sophie's predilection for women was a deep secret. Didn't want her husband or Elodie finding out. I had no idea whom Sophie was seeing, though. Asking my sister about her sex life didn't interest me.

"She is pretty, though—" Sophie continued, "—the American in the coffee shop. Must be in her early thirties, I'd say—a tad younger than me."

I could see that my sister was bordering on obsession.

"Very sexy. Very fuckable," she said.

"Drop it, Sophie."

"Am I right? Is she good, then?"

"I don't know."

"Ah, so she's playing hard to get, is she? Clever girl."

I put on my headphones and turned on my iPod, glad to let Al Green's *Let's Stay Together* drown out Sophie's drivel.

I always stay in the Presidential Suite at the George V when I go to Paris, and this time was no exception. My mother was disappointed, but I preferred to come and go when I pleased, not worry about offending anyone by turning up late to dinner and so forth. The hotel let me bring Rex, too—a bonus for clocking up a large bill and being such a good, repeat customer.

I was ensconced in my suite. My loyal Labrador-mix lay patiently by my side while I had various meetings with people who were keen to take a slice of the HookedUp pie. A couple of government officials dropped by; embarrassed by the fact that it had been America, not France that propelled HookedUp forward. Too late, now—they'd missed the boat for real investment.

Then, just as I was winding things up, Claudine called. I'd forgotten about her. *Christ.*

"Mon amour," she began in a sweetie voice.

"Claudine. Everything okay?" I asked, dreading what was to come.

"Look, I want to clear the air first," she said ominously. *Fuck, what did that mean?* I had a vision of her with a razorblade poised at her doll-like wrist. "I can't involve myself with you sexually anymore," she explained.

"Wow," was all I could muster. I took a deep breath. Was there a catch? *This was too good to be true!*

"I have a boyfriend now."

Poor bastard, I nearly said, but answered, "That's wonderful, Claudine."

"You're not jealous?"

"No, not at all."

"Why not?" she asked suspiciously. "Have you turned gay?"

I laughed. "I've met someone." I told her about Pearl, immediately wondering if that was a mistake. I wouldn't have put it past Claudine to stalk her, Glenn Close style.

To my surprise, she said. "I'm happy for you, I really am. Truce then? No sex, is that a deal?"

This was getting better by the second. "No sex," I agreed.

"Then I can trust you to accompany me to Delphine Aimée's *vide grenier* at her house? You won't try to seduce me or anything?"

The ego of some models, I thought, but ignored her little quip. "You're joking? *A vide grenier?*" I said. Delphine Aimée resided in one of the oldest and most beautiful mansions of Paris. She had recently died; the papers were full of her obituaries, celebrating her colorful life as one of the great Parisian beauties and fashion setters of her time.

"Her children are selling some of her furniture and belongings and I have a private invitation. A friend of a friend," Claudine went on. "You have no idea how much string-pulling I had to do to wangle this. Only a few select people are being invited to see her treasures."

"Is the house itself for sale, too?" I'd always had my eye on that mansion. A real gem. Or as the French expression goes: a rare pearl.

"If it were, it would be fifty million euros, at least."

I didn't flinch at the price. It was an old Parisian mansion and I was damned if some Russian oligarch was going to get his hands on it.

"But no," Claudine said, "the house isn't for sale, as far as I know. Just some of its contents—the family needs the money. Meet me there in an hour."

I met Claudine outside the gates of the house. She looked less pale than usual, as if she had finally had a good, hot meal. She was dressed in a pair of shorts, her long legs going on forever, her auburn hair hanging down to her waist. She looked happy, for once, less Gothic. Her dark eyes, usually coal-lined, were free of make-up.

Delphine Aimée's mansion was even more beautiful than I had remembered. It sat like a giant doll's house, not attached (a rarity in Paris), with a large garden in front, flanked by a perfectly trimmed hedge and ornate, wrought-iron railings.

The interior was no less impressive. A grand marble staircase swept up the center of the house. Above was a sort of rotunda: a dome of glass letting in streams of light, with rooms leading off a circular, balconied walkway. The floors were oak herringbone, polished to a high shine. Each room was decorated with antique furniture and great drapes that pooled on the floor in swathes of red, gold or pink damask. There were Persian rugs, and original paintings by Corot, Cézanne, and even Picasso. Delphine Aimée's daughter, a wobbly woman of eighty with a large hook nose, showed us around. She said little, just smiled and nodded, until we arrived at the great woman's bedroom. Being a man, I felt it was intrusive to enter this legend's private quarters. I stood at the doorway, but the old daughter insisted I come in. I gingerly followed her into the spacious bedroom, with high ceilings and Italian mirrors gracing the walls.

"My mother loved going to balls," she revealed in an almost inaudible whisper. "Even the most famous jewelers of her day fought to be chosen as her designers. She had the best collection of jewelry in the whole of Paris. My father was hopelessly in love with her, you know. It's always best if the man is that teensy-weensy bit more in love with his wife than the other way around, don't you agree?"

I mulled over what this woman had just said. Had I ever been *that* in love? No, I hadn't. So in love that my heart missed a beat, so in love that I thought about the other person while I breathed? It almost brought a tear to my eye just contemplating that kind of passion. Here I was, embroiled with all these different women: Claudine, Laura, Indira (and there were others, too), all wanting a piece of me, yet all I wished for was just one woman, one stable relationship, just one person who would make sense to me.

The old lady led us to her mother's dressing-table, topped with old-fashioned perfume bottles, silver hairbrush sets and miniature paintings. On top of the table, sat a black, leather jewelry box.

"Would you mind, young man, helping me with that box? It's extremely heavy. You can lay it on the bed for me."

I took the box carefully in my grip and laid it on a vast, four-poster bed. The box sank into a silk eiderdown as I laid it down.

"Some of the best pieces are in the bank vault," she told us. "The diamonds, emeralds and such. These were some of my mother's daytime choices, the ones we're willing to let go. It's somebody else's turn to give life to them. Your wife, perhaps, Monsieur Chevalier?"

She remembered my name. I was about to tell her that I wasn't married, but stopped myself. Why, I wasn't sure. Perhaps I didn't want to spoil her image of me as a happily married, family man. Because I, too, had secret longings to be a happily married family man. With children running about. Walks in the park with my beautiful wife, my little ones, and my dog. So I didn't correct the lady.

"Be my guests. Take a peek," she urged, her hooded green eyes sparkling with excitement.

"May I?" Claudine asked, taking out an elaborately carved, jade necklace.

"Of course, my dear."

Claudine looked as if she was about to pass out. "My heart's palpitating. Have you ever seen anything so exquisite in your life? And look at these earrings to match. What a gorgeous set."

"Buy it if you like it so much," I said.

"Don't be silly." And she whispered hoarsely, "Have you any idea how much this would *cost?* I'm just *window-shopping,* silly."

I suddenly felt ashamed. This kind old lady was opening up her museum of a house to us, her *heart* to us, and Claudine was admitting to just *window-shopping?* I knew I had to do something. Fast.

"I'd love to buy something," I said, glaring at Claudine. I turned to the lady. "What else do you have?"

"What's your wife's name?" the eighty-year-old asked.

I hesitated. I've never been fond of lying, but not putting the facts straight wasn't a *lie* exactly… just a little…*white* lie. "Her name is Pearl," I blurted out without even thinking, and in that second, crazy as it sounds, I had another premonition—one day, Pearl, would indeed, be my wife.

The lady grinned, her wrinkly mouth revealing a naughty yellow fang, and she said, "I have just the piece for you, Monsieur." She shuffled back to the dressing table and opened a drawer. She brought out a pale blue leather box which was scuffed and had seen better days, but still, was obviously once from one of the best jewelry houses in Paris. "This is from one of the jeweler's in La Place Vendôme," the lady said. "Open it."

I carefully opened the box. Inside, was an unusual-looking, double-strand of pearls. The pearls graduated subtly in size. It was more a choker than a necklace, with a diamond and platinum, Art Deco-style clasp. It was beautiful. I had a flash of it around Pearl's elegant neck, her blonde hair setting off the golden-pink, honey-colored pearls. I had just planned on getting Pearl some little thing, just a token gift from Paris—I didn't want to come on too strong—but the second I saw the choker, I knew that it had Pearl's name written all over it. *Pearls for Pearl.* Perfect. "I'll take it," I said without hesitating.

"It will be expensive, Monsieur," she warned.

"I don't care about the price, I'd like to buy it, please. If that's alright with you, of course, madame."

"My father had them especially designed for my mother. It was her wedding present. There are eighty-eight pearls. They brought her good luck whenever she wore them."

"Eighty-eight is a lucky number," I said. "The number of infinity, the double directions of the infinity of the Universe, the period of revolution—the days it takes for Mercury to travel around the sun." *Only a nerd can know these things.* I smiled to myself, wryly, thinking back to my schoolboy years when I spent hours reading the encyclopedia, memorizing whole chunks by heart of facts that interested me.

"It's the number of keys on a piano, too," the woman replied. "My mother played so, so beautifully."

"It's an untouchable number," Claudine added. "Whoever this Pearl chick is, I'm envious of her. She's gonna flip out when she sees that choker."

4

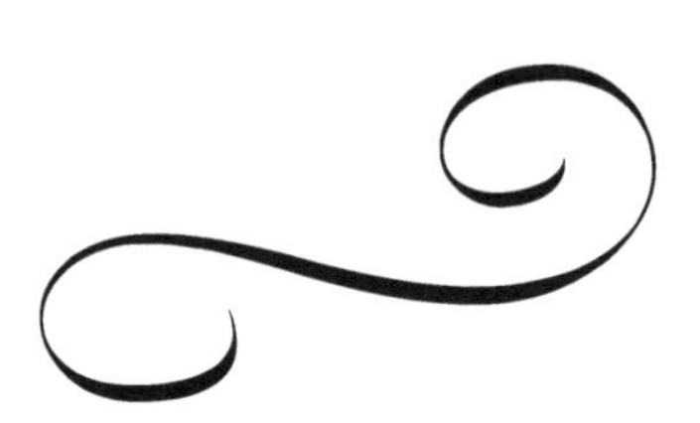

But Pearl didn't flip out. She didn't even call. I'd had the pearl choker delivered by hand to her apartment; the box within another box, within a huge box with her name on it. It couldn't have gone missing. Nothing. No reply. Not a word.

I began to ponder the reason for her silence. My interest was piqued. It should have been a warning sign, telling me, *She's an ungrateful, ill-mannered brat.* But it made me wonder about her. Did she have a boyfriend? Worse, maybe, *she was married.* Shit, that possibility hadn't occurred to me. *The husband was probably having a jealous fit!* Maybe, he'd found the box first and chucked it away. *Fuck, I should have thought of that.* Duh! On our date and at the coffee shop, I had never actually ascertained whether Pearl Robinson was attached!

My mind flipped back to all our conversations. Yes, I remembered her asking *me* if I had a girlfriend. But did I ask *her* if she had a boyfriend or husband? NO, I DID NOT!

It was obvious by that point. This woman, whom I was fantasizing about, was bloody well married!

That's why she freaked out about spending the night at a hotel with me! *That's* why she looked terrified of having sex. A little flirtation, fine. But cheating on her husband? It obviously wasn't her style. He must have been out of town on business and she was up for having a little fun. That's why she accepted going on a date. My mind wandered back again to our conversations. I did remember asking her about her family and she didn't mention a husband, but had I asked her directly, *Are you single?* No, I had not!

I thought of one of my golden rules: *Don't fuck another man's girl.* I felt like a fucking idiot.

By the time a week had gone by, piqued interest had morphed into near obsession. I should have called, should have just said, *Hey, Pearl, did you get the necklace?* But my pride got the better of me.

I couldn't get her out of my mind. Her ass. Her pert breasts which I'd noticed through her light, summertime dress. Just thinking about her was giving me a hard-on. Why hadn't she called me? She had my business card—I'm sure I'd given it to her. Hadn't I?

All these thoughts were spinning about my head. I was trying to concentrate on work, but all I could do was think about fucking Pearl Robinson.

So by the time, one whole week later, I got a message from her on my voice-mail, saying 'thank you' and apologizing for taking so long about it (the doorman had apparently forgotten to give her the box), my dick was behaving as if it had a brain of its own and propelled me to get in a cab and head straight over to her apartment. If she wasn't single, I told myself, I'd soon find out. Her apartment would give me instant clues.

If she was attached, I'd walk away.

But if she wasn't, I'd fuck her.

I took a risk and bought champagne and flowers. If I was greeted by the husband....

Well, I'd have to cross that bridge when I came to it.

The doorman opened the door for me and I sauntered into the lobby, trying to look casual but realizing that I was feeling edgy. I gripped the chilled bottle of Dom Pérignon in my hand and tightly held the bunch of roses I'd bought.

"Good evening sir," the uniformed doorman said.

"Good evening. Pearl Robinson, please."

"Ah, Mrs. Robinson," he replied with a knowing smile.

Mrs? Fuck! So *she is bloody married,* I mumbled to my dick, which had been, up until now, *so* cocky, *so* confident that he was going to score. "*Mrs.* Robinson?" I repeated.

"Mrs. Robinson is upstairs, sir."

"Is her husband in?" I asked weakly.

"Husband?"

"Yes, her husband." My dick was seriously disappointed. I felt like a fucking fool standing there with flowers and a bottle of Dom Pérignon.

"No, no husband," the doorman answered, his thick moustache twitching above his inanely happy grin.

"But she is *Mrs.* Robinson?"

"She *was* Mrs. Robinson, now she's Mzzzz. Robinson," the

doorman replied, still smiling. "She is a very modern woman. I call her now."

The Ms. Made me feel more relaxed. Although, a lot of American women prefer Ms. even if they are married so that was no guarantee. Or, if not married, Ms. meant Pearl could be dating on a regular basis. But I figured that if Pearl was busy, otherwise occupied with another man, she'd tell me to piss off.

I waited, trying to look patient while the doorman called on the landline.

"No answer," he told me.

"But you say she's in?"

"Yes, she's definitely at home."

I realized that I was about to be just as guilty as the 'bull-dozer' types I despised. I wanted Pearl Robinson and I wasn't going to let this go. I called her myself, on my cell.

She finally picked up. "Yes?"

"I'm downstairs," I said, forgetting to say who I even was.

"I'm in the bathtub," she replied.

And my dick (because I swear it wasn't me) answered, "Good, I'll join you."

"Pass me onto Dervis, the doorman," she said.

Uh oh. This is the moment that she's about to get me flung out of the building.

Dervis listened, nodded, smiled into the receiver and said, "Okay, Mrs. Robinson."

So it *was* ***Mrs.*** Robinson, after all. I turned on my heel to go, but the doorman shouted after me, "Mrs. Robinson's expecting you. You can go up." He buzzed open the elevator door for me and pressed the button for her floor. "Enjoy your evening, sir," he said, beaming.

When Pearl opened the door, my heart missed a beat. *Fuck!* She was wearing the choker, and all she had on was a towel draped about her hot, sexy body. She had just gotten out of the tub and smelled like heaven, sweet and tender and…*Jesus.* She looked so gorgeous, so fucking fuckable. Her eye make-up was slightly smudged, giving her a sleepy, bedroom look. I could feel my cock expand in my jeans. I *had* to have her. Right there, right then. Mrs. or Ms. I didn't care, I'd have to break my code, if need be. Pearl Robinson was going to get my attention that very night.

I moved in on her like the bulldozer I was morphing into. "I've missed you, Pearl," I said, putting down the champagne and flowers on the hall table.

Her mouth opened and her eyelids started fluttering. Sex was so thick in the air that neither of us could hardly breathe. "You're wearing the necklace," I said, raking my eyes down her body, knowing that I was about to rip that towel off her.

"The necklace is stunning," she whispered, then caught her bottom lip between her teeth.

She started protesting about how she shouldn't accept such a gift. Women always do that. They don't want you to believe they're greedy but they have no intention of *not* accepting your gift. Pearl was no different. I saved her by saying something like:

"That necklace was made for you, Pearl. Nobody else has the right to wear it." Did I tell her that she was beautiful? I must have, because she did look incredible. Like a classical painting. Elegant, even half-naked. Poised, even though wanton.

I couldn't stop myself. My cock was on fire. I pushed her

up against the wall, right there by the elevator door, and start licking her lips slowly, softly. She moaned. I growled like a beast, ripping that towel off her, as I probed her mouth with my tongue, kissing her deeply, passionately.

"Fuck, you're beautiful," I murmured into her mouth, and I meant every word. She closed her big blue eyes and yielded to me completely, returning the kiss with everything she had. I let my mouth wander down to her neck as my lips brushed softly over her sweet skin. The choker accentuated every delicate curve, every tiny muscle. I noticed how she swallowed as if she was about to drown in her own desire.

My tongue traced across her collarbone, down her chest, to her tits. Her beautiful, pert tits that turned upwards, but were full and hard. I slid my tongue over to one nipple, swirling it around till her rosebud turned taut, and I sucked greedily. I groaned again and grazed my fingers down the crack of her butt, trailing them further down between her thighs. She was soaking wet. Already, and I'd hardly even begun. I could feel her nails in my back, then clawing softly across my biceps, they made their way over my pecs and the muscled ridges of my abdomen. Her touch was driving me crazy. She cupped my huge, throbbing cock through my jeans.

"Not yet," I said. "Ladies first."

She splayed her legs apart a touch, thrust her hips forward, trailed her hands from my back, up the nape of my neck and then dug her fingers into my hair.

"Fuck, baby, I'm going to have to do all sorts of things to you," I whispered in her ear, before nipping her gently on her lobe, then along her jawline. She shuddered. I was burning with unprecedented desire, every cell in my body awakened. Her skin was so soft and unblemished and she smelled like an exotic flower. I breathed her in, ran my thumb over her full lips, taking a moment to appreciate all that was before me. *Sugar and spice and all things nice.* I remember thinking, in that second, how women really were the best invention. Ever. God must have been particularly inspired on that extremely creative day.

I palmed her pussy with one hand and slipped a finger inside her. Her hot flesh was deliciously slick. "You're really asking for it, aren't you, Pearl Robinson?"

She said nothing, just whimpered and circled her hips. She was so ready to be fucked by me, but I'd make her wait. Make her beg for it.

"Ooh, chérie, so perfect, so wet," I said, spinning her around so her ass was up against me. That peachy round ass that was doing things to my brain. I felt it press against my groin; my erection was screaming at me to fuck her, right there. Pound into her, hard. Push her down on the floor and fuck her senseless. But I needed to control myself. With one hand, I rolled her hardened nipple between my fingers, and with the other, I slipped my thumb inside her, with all my fingers cupping her mound, tautly. I had her, all of her, in my contained grip.

"So juicy, so designed for me," I rumbled into the nape of her neck. I could feel the swell of her wet clit, hard and pulsating. So ready for me. I was driving her to distraction but I wanted her to be totally and utterly relaxed, so I said, "Let's have some champagne, shall we?"

With my other hand I grabbed the champagne and flowers from where I'd set them on the hall table, earlier. I steered her forward while I walked behind her, my thumb still inside, her pussy all mine in my hand, while I simultaneously massaged her clit, her moisture hot on my fingers. I loved it. This woman was mine. All fucking mine. After a little while, I took my hand away, trailing a finger up her butt crack again, and letting my hand rest on the small of her back.

I said, "Come on. Champagne time. We need a drink. The flowers also need a drink."

I was still fully dressed. She was nude, with only the pearls about her pretty neck. The whole scenario made me feel amused. And very in control. Pearl was utterly undone.

She spun around to face me. "Is this what you always do, Alexandre Chevalier? *Manhandle* women like this? You were holding me like a six-pack!"

"But you loved it," I said, getting down on my knees. I whispered light kisses on her taut belly and flickered my tongue downwards. I could feel her quivering as I nuzzled my head in between her thighs. She gasped. I rested my tongue quietly on her clit and she pushed herself closer with a moan. I licked her in great sweeps and tasted her honeyed juices as I explored her wetness with my tongue. She tasted delicious, her sweet nectar making me so fucking hard it was almost painful. Hot. Welcoming.

"Sexy little pearlette," I mumbled into her pussy, coining a new word that suited her perfectly; fucking her with my tongue, flicking it on and around her sensitive nub. *My Pearl and her little pearlette.* Pearl was groaning out loud. As for my part, this was giving me so much pleasure, I was literally about to come myself.

"Oh, God," she murmured, fisting and clawing her hands in my mussed-up hair. "This feels incredible."

But I taunted her again. Stopped what I was doing and led her to the kitchen. She got up onto a chair to retrieve some champagne glasses from a cupboard. They were vintage, crystal ones, the kind you didn't often see anymore. She mentioned that they were a wedding present from her mother and I realized that, *oh shit*, I *was* fooling around with a married woman, after all. I decided that, as long as I didn't actually penetrate her, I could get away with this.

My rule was, *Don't fuck another guy's girl,* not, *Don't play around with another guy's girl.*

I made excuses for myself.

I liked having her up on that chair. She was vulnerable and couldn't escape from me. She had the delicate glasses in her hands so her wrists were as good as bound, because she didn't want the glasses to drop. I held her hips still so she couldn't move. I began with her ass—what was it about that ass that had me so fucking mesmerized? The fact that it was round and firm? Maybe. Whatever…I was transfixed. And hard as a fucking diamond.

I started licking up and down her butt crack, something I never usually did to women. But Pearl had me drooling for her like a horny devil. I could feel her ease herself into the situation, her body heaving with yearning desire. I looked up and noticed her erect nipples as I controlled her hips with both my hands. I pressed the small of her back forward so she was bending over slightly, slid my thumb inside her wet warmth and located the magic spot that I knew would drive her wild.

My thumb pressed this erogenous zone while I circled her clit with my palm. I went back to licking her butt crack again. Slowly. Deliberately. Up. And then down. Up. And then down. I could feel her center throbbing. She was panting and thrusting, and pumping her clit hard against my firm hand.

"Alexandre!" she screamed "Oh, sweet Jesus, what are you doing to me?"

I probed my tongue into her sweet ass, tunneling deep inside, flicking and licking. She was all clean and fresh, oiled up from her bath. She smelled of orange blossom or vanilla, or something that sent my head spinning. Simultaneously, my fingers continued the rhythmical massage on her clit, my thumb still circling inside her. She couldn't take it anymore—she was about to detonate. I could hear her screaming while she contracted around my large thumb, her orgasm coming in a hot rush. "Oh, my God! It's like triple pleasure….oh fuck….I'm coming," she yelled out, still gyrating against my hand. "I'm coming so deep…so deep from inside!" She sounded shocked, surprised as hell.

Was *I* surprised?

Not one bit. I knew exactly what I was doing. I'd zapped her G-spot. Hit the jackpot.

And this was just the beginning.

The beginning of something beautiful.

Something inevitable.

I never did get to fuck Pearl that night, but I did learn all about her. Well, about her sexuality, anyway. While we were drinking the champagne, I asked her about her first orgasm. She was lying seductively on her chaise-longue in the living room, wearing nothing but my shirt, while I stroked her long, lean legs, kissed her, licked her, and generally absorbed the wonder of her, letting her very being seep into my every pore. She struck me as so intrinsically beautiful, not just physically, but there was a sweetness about her, an innocence, as if she was completely unaware of her splendor. Even though she was blonde, her lashes were thick and dark and her skin a sun-kissed gold. She was a genuine, star-spangled, American girl. Wholesome but elegant. All in one, sexy, very fuckable package.

I caressed her gently, enjoying her softness, the delicacy of her smooth skin, while she revealed to me that she couldn't come from penetrative sex; at least hadn't since she was twenty-two, when she dated her best friend's brother. It seemed as if all this time she had been alone, although I finally asked her *the question,* which I had been avoiding, probably because I was nervous of the answer.

"Pearl, this may come as a stupid question….a little late, I know, but—"

"What?"

"You mentioned that those crystal glasses were a wedding gift, and your doorman calls you *Mrs.* Robinson. Are you *married,* by any chance?"

She laughed. "You think I'd be lying here, now, in this un-compromising position if I were married?"

I shrugged my shoulders. "Maybe."

"No, that's not my style. I *was* married but got divorced a couple of years ago."

I could hear my lungs heave out a sigh of relief.

That's when, I guess, most men would have fucked her. And yes, I was tempted. Of course I was.

But I wanted to wait. Why? Because I realized that I was dealing with a neo-virgin. A woman who hadn't had an orgasm with anyone in all those years? I'd need to take it slow, I decided. Make her first time with me special. Something she'd never forget.

As she lay there, slightly tipsy, she said, "Really, Alexandre, I'm too much of a head-case. You should be with someone much younger than me. Someone more receptive."

I thought she was kidding. She was the most receptive woman I had been with in ages. She was honest, vulnerable. When she came, I thought she might collapse she seemed so affected. I didn't want some sassy college girl who'd experienced very little of the world, who'd never had any real knocks or bruises to call her own. I needed, I understood in that moment, a damaged bird. I wanted to repair her wing and help her fly again. Set her free. Hope that she would fly back to me of her own accord.

Pearl was that bird with the broken wing.

The more she tried to convince me that I was wasting my time even trying with her, the more I was determined to fix her.

She stroked me tenderly on the cheek. "I don't want you to be disappointed with me, Alexandre. I can't come with sex, not even oral sex. I haven't been able to for years. You're gorgeous and everything but—"

"There are no buts, chérie," I told her. "An orgasm isn't just physical. It's all about your mental state of mind. The biggest sex organ of all is your brain. Think of the Big O as an orchestra that needs a conductor. I want to be that conductor, to conduct sweet, mind-blowing music that climaxes....right—" I trailed my finger down her stomach over her mound of Venus and tapped her gently between her legs—"here," I said.

She closed her eyes blissfully but shook her head as if to say that what I was describing was impossible.

But impossible is not a word in my vocabulary.

I had a mission:

To be the best fuck that Pearl Robinson had ever had in her life.

6

I was still thinking about Pearl while I navigated my way around the capital city of Mumbai. It was hot and sticky. Traffic everywhere. The streets were seething with ramshackled activity: cows dodging rickshaws (because cows are holy in India so they hang out, loose on the streets), scooters, diesel-belching trucks, cars, all ebbing and flowing as people tried to cross jam-packed roads without getting mowed down. Although India was still a third world country, it was innovative and ahead when it came to I.T. Not to mention the sheer volume of inhabitants. That's why Sophie and I were keen to establish HookedUp there. But it was proving to be less than straightforward because of government corruption. So we decided that the best approach was to keep ourselves out of running the show in India. Sell them our company's franchise and let them deal with it. There was no way either of us wanted to get embroiled in the day-to-day bribery and fraud that was an evil necessity there.

We'd take the money and run, so to speak.

Not in cash. But in precious stones and gems.

Sophie and I had several specialists on our team because we didn't trust a soul. Especially, the baggy, boozy-eyed bastard who was procuring the gems: Indira's cousin.

Indira…

I was on my way to see her. We'd always meet at the Leela Hotel: a lavish, five-star piece of heaven that sits on the outskirts of the city, amidst the chaos that is Mumbai. We'd spend a relaxed day together swimming in the pool, having massages or a long lunch, although in India you can never feel completely at ease, knowing how the other half live; one-armed beggars, hungry children and mangy, half-starved dogs. Living beings that make you feel guilty with all you own, yet their problems are so bottomless you don't know where to begin.

Don't get me wrong; there's magic in India, too. Real beauty. But every time I visit, it always takes a while to adjust to its inequality: the uber-rich and dirt-poor living side by side.

I had employed Indira to set up a charity for me in Mumbai. That's how we became acquainted in the first place. Being such a high-profile star, she could garner lots of interest and attention. She'd done an amazing job, so far. I admired her for her tenacity. She had gathered a lot of other Bollywood actors on the board of directors, and they were doing so much good. But I wanted to pull out completely. I was keen to extricate myself and let her get on with it herself, without me.

The charity was for children and their education. It incorporated schools and means for training them for professions where they could get real jobs. It was very hands-on, and the Bollywood stars made personal appearances every month or so. That made the kids turn up, because they were fearful of missing out on the action. Attendance was great. Movie stars have so much power in India—even more so than in the USA.

Indira was lying on the bed in the hotel, waiting for me. Red rose petals led like a carpet from the door to the bed, sprinkled about like confetti, spelling out our names and arranged in the form of hearts. She had a pink sari draped about her which set off her caramel-colored skin and her dark, cascading hair. I entered the room and gazed at her. She was stunning, no doubt, but there was someone else who had taken precedence. Someone else who had stolen my attention: Pearl Robinson. As I mentioned before, multi-tasking wasn't my strong point.

"Hi baby," Indira said, batting her coal-rimmed eyes. She wore a sparkling, red *bindi* between her eyebrows and looked very exotic. She licked her lips to wet them. "Come to me. I've been so lonely. Come and lie beside me."

"You're looking good, Indira," I said. "How's it been going?" I came over to the bed, and sat down. I held her hand the way a brother or father would. She pulled me toward her and began to unravel her sari. She started to fondle her breasts, her lips parting. She cupped one hand around my groin. I could feel my cock twitch beneath my jeans. I took her hand away and clasped it again.

Alarm flashed in her gray eyes like a warning siren. "What's wrong?"

"I'm very, very tired," I lied.

But she rolled over onto her stomach, jiggled down the bed and pressed her head into my crotch. She started biting me along the ridge of my dick, through my jeans. I had to admit it was turning me on, but I wasn't in the mood to go through with it. My dick didn't agree, though. What she was doing felt really good.

She began to unbutton my pants, frantically, making mewing sounds like a cat in heat.

"I'm wet," she breathed hoarsely. "All I've been thinking about twenty-four hours a day is you. Is *this*. This beauty," she groaned, as she grappled with the material of my jeans, freeing my cock so it sprang up against her lips. I didn't have underwear on. It was too goddamn hot. I noticed how Indira hadn't kissed me on the mouth yet. It was my cock that had her obsessed. I was relieved—a kiss was the last thing on my mind—too intimate.

"You know you have the most beautiful penis in the world," she purred between kissing and nibbling its crest. "Big, hard, thick, pulsating, en….ORmous. So thick…so huge. Proud like a cobra. So enormous…so smooth…so magnificent. It's like a work of art." She started licking her tongue up and down my erection.

I held her head still, restraining her movements. "No, Indira. This isn't a good idea."

She looked up at me from beneath her long lashes, shock flashing across her face. "Don't you fucking deny me this!" she lashed out, her mouth half full. "What the hell is wrong with you? Do you know how many men fantasize about me doing this to them? They dream about me while they masturbate every night, my poster on their wall. And you are telling me to *stop?"* Her large mouth stretched over my throbbing crown and she sucked hard. I lay back, yielding to her, my dick telling me how good it felt, as if it had a brain of its own. She took my huge erection to the back of her throat, focusing on suction, greedy for it as if her life depended on it. But still, it wasn't right. It felt wrong to me. Very wrong. I forced myself to shuffle my ass away from her and sit up. My cock was throbbing with desire, but my head was telling me this all had to end.

"You're so beautiful, Indira. You're such a special lady, you really are, but I can't do this anymore. I don't want to use you, you're worth more than that." I tucked my unwieldy tackle back into my jeans.

Horror drained the color from her face. She stared at me, incredulous.

"I've met someone else, I'm sorry," I explained, getting up and going to the bathroom. I locked the door. I could hear her screaming, her abusive tirade ricocheting about the room. She was throwing things about like a small child having a tantrum. God knows who could have heard; they must have believed I was beating her up.

I had to finish off what she started. I took my cock in a tight vice of a grip and began moving it up and down ferociously. I had Pearl's hot, wet pussy in my mind's eye, her glorious ass. I was on rewind, remembering my tongue exploring all her crevices, her screams when I reached her G-spot. *Her amazing scent. Her taste. Her wet….*I clenched my cock tighter*….wet….pussy…her hot, wet, horny, tight….her mouth…her lips…her ass…her big blue eyes…her smooth skin…her wet….*I could feel myself coming hard. Semen burst from me in a thick, scalding rush. It spurted all over the bathroom mirror as my hips drove forward in one last thrust. I groaned quietly, my release felt fucking great.

As I cleaned up my mess, I could hear Indira's screeching

curses. She was yelling, "Who the fuck is she? Who IS she?!" I knew I was in big trouble and I hoped it wouldn't screw things up with the charity or with her cousin.

But all I could think about was what it was going to be like when I fucked Pearl.

Actually, I didn't want to just fuck Pearl, I wanted to make love to her, too.

I called Sophie to warn her about how I'd spurned Indira and the backlash that could follow with the grease-ball cousin. My sister was quick to act. She organized a high-class sex worker to sweeten him up. The girl admitted that it was the best gig she'd ever had—she was paid handsomely for her service. Sophie, you see, used to be in the game herself. She knew about Pussy Power. I managed to steer clear of the cousin and let my sister take control of this delicate situation with Indira. But Sophie was as furious with me as Indira was. *Furious.*

On the plane back to New York, as Sophie was counting out the uncut emeralds, rubies and sapphires, her slim fingers fondling every nuance, every dimple of the precious stones—our illegal booty—she spat out:

"You fucking moron, that's the last time I bail you out, fuckhead!"

I was used to Sophie's tirades—I took them with a pinch

of salt.

"What the fuck did you think you were doing snubbing such a powerful woman like Indira Kapoor?" she hissed. "Fuckwit jerk behaving like a fucking schoolboy!"

Sometimes I'd say nothing, just wait for whatever abusive adjective Sophie would come up with next. She had a good imagination. "A schoolboy would have seen the blowjob through," I said with a wry smile. "A schoolboy wouldn't have walked off halfway through, the way I did."

"A fucking dillock, wanking, fuckface fool, that's what you are!" She brought a sapphire to her lips and kissed it. I burst out laughing.

"It's not funny. Who is this silly bitch that's got you so fucking obsessed with her? What is *so special* about her? Eh? What's so great about her that you couldn't even fuck beautiful Indira Kapoor? It's that blonde, isn't it? That fucking girl-next-door?"

I took a glug of cold beer and relaxed into my airplane seat. "You said she was sexy, if I remember correctly," I goaded.

"Nobody's so sexy they have the power to jeopardize a multi-million dollar business deal."

"I don't know," I answered, thinking about a Skype-sex-session Pearl and I had enjoyed, just a while earlier. "Cleopatra stirred things up a bit."

Sophie narrowed her eyes threateningly. "Fuck off."

I'd managed to avoid Sophie earlier that day—we'd taken separate limos to Mumbai Airport, but now, I had no choice but to ride in this plane with her. I put on my headphones. This was getting to be a habit: flying about with Sophie on private jets, listening to music, in order to drown out her gibberish. I selected *Sexbomb* by Tom Jones on my iPod, closed my eyes and thought of all the things I was going to do to Pearl the second I got back. I wouldn't even go home; I'd go straight to her apartment.

7

Just rapping at Pearl's apartment door had me hard. It was about 5 a.m. She opened the door slowly, knowing it was me because I'd just phoned, but she was obviously being cautious.

"Hi," she said. There was surprise in her tone but also relief. I was hoping she'd just been dreaming about me.

She stood there in a crimson, silk satin robe. More beautiful than I remembered. Her hair was bedroom hair, wild and slept in. I went to kiss her; her mouth tasted of mint and was cool and welcoming. I ripped off her robe which shimmied to the floor, and I stepped back in order to admire her perfect body. Her legs were strong but lean, worked-out but the muscles long and elegant. I noticed her tiny waist, her feminine curves; not too slim but not an ounce of fat. Her tits were, literally, perfect. The kind any man wants to pop into his mouth and suck—ample, very full, but not too big—they didn't need a bra and the nipples lifted upwards. Pert. I had her just how I wanted her: naked.

"Come here, beauty," I whispered.

I caught both of her wrists in my right hand, pinning them behind her back. I had her captive. My other hand trailed around her breasts, circling each nipple until they stiffened. I stroked her along her neck and pulled her face to mine, cupping the back of her head. She moaned and leaned in close to me, her measured breath showing me that she was aching to be kissed.

"I've been waiting for this, Pearl. You have no idea how much," I murmured into her mouth.

I explored her curvy lips with my tongue as my erection pressed hard against her abdomen. "All I've been thinking about is all the different ways I'm going to make you come, chérie."

She opened her mouth wider and nipped me on my lower lip like a kitten. Then she fluttered her eyes as if she were in a mesmerized trance, and drew in a sharp breath to steady her nerves. I probed my tongue hard into her welcoming mouth. Greedily. Devouring her taste, my tongue lashing at hers as they tangled in a passionate dance. My hand traced down her neck to her stiff nipples as I played with each one in turn before grazing my fingers down her belly to her clit, where I rested my finger languidly. She groaned. Then I let it slide, oh so slowly, a little further, finding its way inside. As I expected, she was drenching wet. I could feel my cock swell even more. I cupped her whole core with my hand and eased my finger deep into her soaking, velvet cave. A place where I couldn't wait to call home, call my own. My dark man-cave. Because once I'd entered, I knew I'd want to return over and over again.

"I'm going to have to fuck you," I whispered in her ear. "So wet already. So. Beautifully. Wet." I thrust my finger further up inside her and felt her juices.

She was obviously enjoying the moment but was impatient for more—wanting all of me. She shook her hands free from my vice behind her back and growled like the little tigress she was. "Alexandre, let me free to do what I want—"

She went down on her knees before me and frantically unbuttoned my jeans. She ripped them down my legs and I stepped out of them. She was as hungry for this as I was. My erection slapped her in the face as it sprang free, so solid, so fucking horny for her lips. She cupped my balls in one hand and guided one into her pretty mouth. *Jesus fucking Christ!* I rocked my hips forward. It felt amazing. So hot. The thermometer was rising fast. I pulled off my shirt. My heart started racing. I gently held her head and laced my fingers through her golden mass of hair as she sucked gently on me, sending my head spinning.

"Oh Pearl. Oh Pearl, baby, you're so beautiful."

She got up from her knees to get better leverage, and bending down, started to run her lips along my shaft, teasing me, then lashing her tongue up and down along its pulsating length. I looked down at her, her lips at work with luscious concentration. Fuck this was sensual. She teased my sensitive crest, rimming the broad head round and round with the tip of her pink tongue—I swear to God, I felt it all the way down to my toes. This wasn't just turning me on, this was an *experience,* somehow different than it had been with other women. The way she was doing it with such care made me believe that there was more than just lust dancing between us. It felt as if there were molecules of love filling the air.

She looked up at me, her blue eyes full of wonder and awe and she closed them again. Did I see a tear fall? I think so. This meant something *big* to her (didn't mean to sound crass there). But seriously, this was an intimacy that was not only electric, but strangely poetic. What she was doing meant the world to her in that moment. My pleasure was her pleasure because she was moaning while she had me in her mouth and lost in a kind of reverie.

With all the women I had been with (and there have been far, far too many) this one was different. I could tell that she was already hopelessly in love with me, and I wanted to protect her, nourish her (again, no joke intended). But I saw her as so vulnerable, my cock in her mouth as she was feasting on me. Her head was bobbing up and down and she clawed my ass with her nails, pulling me closer to her, hungry for every inch of me.

"Pearl, cherié, this is what I've been dreaming of. This feels incredible."

And I meant every word. *What I had been dreaming of.* Not just lately, but for years. Someone who was truly in *love* with me. Not only for what I could offer her, but also for what she could offer *me*. Pearl was giving me her all. Here was a woman who was no expert, but because she cared so much about pleasing me, I found it the most erotic thing in the world. She was moving fast by now, my massive length in her mouth, touching the back of her throat. She was jerking her head speedily up and down, up and down, sucking hard, her lips like a vacuum. *It felt fucking amazing.*

"Pearl. Oh you beautiful, rare pearl," I breathed, exploding as I fucked her luscious mouth, coming like a train, hard and mercilessly into her. There was a lot bursting from within me; she'd fucking aroused me. In fact, I came twice in a row, spurting like a fountain into her sexy mouth, clamped tightly about me.

And I still wasn't finished with her. Oh no. This woman had me hooked. I wanted to see her face when I fucked her—see what she'd do when I made her come.

"That's maybe the best blowjob I've ever had in my life," I said, still tingling from all that intense pleasure, as she licked my cum from her lips.

I meant it as a compliment but Pearl looked, for just a second, as if she was about to burst into tears. I suddenly realized why. I'd basically said (in women's language): *I've fucked loads of women.* Foolishly, I used the word, 'maybe.' That was *maybe* (Jesus you have to choose your words carefully with the female sex) the best blowjob…e.g. *there's competition out there. I am comparing you with others.* Bad choice of word: maybe.

I had to dig myself out of my *faux pas*, fast.

But I couldn't help smiling. She was so sweet. So vulnerable. I pulled her up from her position and drew her close to my beating heart. I tilted her head up to me and looked into her eyes, and to reassure her I said, "Come here you gorgeous creature and give me a kiss. You know I want to make love to you, don't you?"

Her countenance changed from fear of rejection to ease. Better choice of word: *make love*, not *fuck*. There is a difference.

You see, women like the *fantasy* of being fucked. Rough. Hard. With no mercy. They even like to imagine being tied up, whipped and chastised. But in reality, they're just looking for one true thing.

And that one true thing's called *love.*

It's easy for a guy to fuck. Easy to play the rough and tough bastard that women often fall for. What's hard is to *not* be a bastard. *Not* to be a jerk.

Call me a fool, but I've always liked a challenge.

There I was, feeling on top of the world. I felt cocky and self-assured after that mind-blowing blowjob. It was obvious Pearl Robinson was crazy about me. I kissed her and she slowly, teasingly, kissed me back.

"Oh Alexandre," she groaned into my mouth.

Suddenly my tune changed. Her lips felt as if they no longer belonged to the sweet little neo-virgin who needed to be guided, but were part of a over-confident, cool, I've-fucked-a-lot-of-people-too, woman of the world. What was it? The way her tongue flickered over my top lip and made me instantly hard again, my cock throbbing for Round Two? I couldn't tell, but a jealous rage soared through my hot veins. The idea of Pearl ever having been touched by another man filled me with absolute fury. *Ridiculous!*

"Who else has fucked you before me?" *What the hell kind of question was that?* Women either lie or tell you the truth. Either way, you'll never know for sure.

She gazed at me, her look pure as a puppy. "It's been so long, I feel like a virgin," she said, her lips parting in a let-me-suck-your-cock-but-I'm-a-schoolgirl kind of way. I stared her down. Was she lying? Now I was flummoxed. I just couldn't read her.

I narrowed my eyes. "I don't believe you. The way you made me come in your mouth was too good. Too expert. Who taught you how to do that?"

"Instinct," she blurted out, her big blue eyes as innocent as a lying teenager who has just been caught with a big sack of weed. "It's you, Alexandre. You make me want to be sexy like this."

"Who else has been fucking you?" I thought I said it in a quiet voice but it came out as a roar. I jealously sucked her tits and palmed her pussy. *Mine. All mine.* My heart slowed to a normal beat as I understood how absurd I was being. I never showed jealousy. Hell, I never even felt it. How this woman already held me so tightly under her spell after such a short time of knowing her, I couldn't fathom.

"I swear," she promised, "I haven't had sex for two years. Not since my divorce."

No sex in all that time = *tight,* I thought, and my cock got hard thinking about how I was going to be her first in so long. Divorce meant vulnerability. My cock twitched again at the thought of her needing me to care for her, protect her. For some reason that really aroused me. And if she was telling the truth about not having had an orgasm, then boy, I was going to really make her head spin.

"Good girl," I said, feeling convinced, after all, that she was telling the truth. Then I whispered in her ear, "I don't want you involved with anyone else, is that clear? I want you for myself. I'm not a jealous man but I am possessive of my treasures. You and your tight, hot pearlette are both mine, do you understand?" Choice of words, again. Not *pussy* or *cunt* or anything else that can make a woman feel like a tramp. But *pearlette.* Pearl deserved to feel treasured and loved. She'd obviously had a shit time of it in the sex department, and probably in the general male department. I could change that for her, I decided.

At the time, I would have said that I was telling her all this to put her mind at rest; let her know that I wanted to 'go steady' with her, to date exclusively. But the truth was that I was scared for the first time in my life when it came to the opposite sex. I was scared of losing her.

Because, God damn it, I realized that I was falling in love.

8

Okay, love is a very strong word. Although, lust just didn't quite cover it. Yes, I was feeling horny as the Devil himself, but I felt so much more. Yet I hardly knew Pearl. I hadn't asked her about her dreams and aspirations, whether she wanted children and a family like I did, hadn't discussed her career with her in depth. I knew nothing about her ex-husband, except for the fact he was obviously lousy in bed. I wasn't even sure how old she was, not that it mattered to me.

It felt as if I was in one of my sports cars going from 0-60 in 4.3 seconds. It was all going so ridiculously fast.

She loved dogs, she was adventurous enough to go rock climbing. She was sexy, smart, beautiful, independent, and although I very much liked what I saw, I needed to get to know her better.

I'd start by fucking her. Or rather, making love to her.

"On the bed," I ordered, leading her into the bedroom and

adding, pokerfaced, "where you belong." I'd test her sense of humor.

Her lips curled up into a subtle smile. She thought I was kidding. But I wasn't. I did want to dominate her. Control her body. But willingly. Not with whips or handcuffs, but with my sexual prowess. Make her need me, make her body lose control and have her begging for more. Give her mind-blowing orgasms, every time. I guess you could say that was pretty narcissistic but I think it was more out of insecurity on my part. I'm a pretty cocky bastard, very self-assured on the outside, but on the inside I'm just a regular guy looking for approval. I wanted Pearl to think me the hottest thing that had come along since the sauna.

"Seriously, Pearl, get on the bed. It's about time you got fucked properly."

She lay on her rather ornate, four-poster bed, nervously waiting on her back. Her breath was shallow, her breasts rising and falling, her moist folds already glistening with anticipation. I straddled her, my cock proud, rock-hard against my abdomen. I cupped her with my hand and slipped my middle finger inside her warm core, locating that sweet spot. I picked her up like a six-pack again, and she whimpered, giving herself over to me readily. I could see she had a submissive streak in her and it turned me on.

I whispered in her ear, "You really want me to fuck you, don't you?"

She could hardly speak. Just moaned and nodded her head. Her nipples were stiff, her tongue was licking lasciviously along her lips. She looked like a fucking centerfold and I wanted to plunge into her. But I had to remain focused. I lifted her up higher. She loved me taking control. I lifted that sweet pussy to my face. Her back arched and I supported her ass with both my hands. I let my tongue rest against her clit and she started bucking her hips at me. I didn't do anything—just let her feel my wet tongue pressing against her. Then I started long, sweeping strokes up and down. Up and down, along her slit. Up. And down. Slowly. Up. And down. *Oh yeah.* She tasted deliciously sweet and salty. And horny as hell; my taste buds were laced with her sexy nectar.

"Please fuck me, Alexandre. Please."

But I wanted to make her wait. Part of my plan, my history of success with the female sex: *Make women beg for it. Make them want more. Control yourself.*

I began a slow, torturous tease, fucking her with my tongue. In and out, careful not to touch her clit, which was swelling with desperation for me to play with it. Pearl was moaning, clawing her fingers in my hair, and yelling out.

"I can't take this anymore. Please. Please Alexandre, I *need* you to fuck me!"

I laid her ass back down on the bed and fished a condom out of my jeans' pocket. Lambskin. Better sensation. The only ones that fit properly and didn't pinch me. I rolled it onto my solid length. I wanted her to feel every tiny nuance, every little movement as I stretched her open. So I'd go slow. Little by little. I couldn't overwhelm her or my whole game plan would be spoiled.

I lay my naked body carefully on top of her, my erection poised at her wet entrance, throbbing and twitching a millimeter away from her. She was flexing her hips at me again; her legs open wide. Every time she pushed forward, she could feel my hardness, her clit slapping against me. She was moaning, her tongue lashing out at my mouth and I kissed her hard. Deep. Hungrily. She was getting the kiss she wanted but I wasn't going to fuck her yet, as most men would have done at that point. This took willpower, believe me.

I let myself dip into her, with tiny, shallow thrusts. Only my tip was fucking her. She was going wild.

"Oh God," she moaned. "Please, oh God. Don't stop. This is incredible."

Then I stopped. I pulled back a touch.

"Alexandre! What are you doing to me? Why are you torturing me?"

My lips flickered into a gentle smirk. "Torture can lead to heaven," I murmured. I started fucking her clit. Again, just tiny, almost imperceptible thrusts, as my hard cock massaged her between her wet folds. She was screaming. *Screaming.*

"Ssh, baby. Quiet now. So juicy. I love your hair, your soft skin, your incredible body, your Big. Blue. Eyes. On each of those words I thrust inside her, rolled in little circles to massage her clit with my pubic bone, and then pulled back out. I was huge. Swollen as fuck. I was counting in my head. *One, one thousand, two, one thousand, three….*I had to stop myself from coming. This was getting too hot to handle.

"Are you ready for all of me?" I said with a low groan.

"You're so big. It's so *huge.* Oh God!"

What she told me was the truth. What I said about your cock being a tool—that was no joke. Tools can do wonders but tools can also do damage, depending on how you use them. I had to go easy. If I pounded into her now, it would be uncomfortable for her; there was no way she'd come.

"Jesus, you're tight. Like a virgin," I said, entering her a millimeter more.

I still didn't feel she was ready to be fucked yet so I carried on teasing her with tiny thrusts, my crown feeling incredibly sensitive, even though I was wearing a condom. Then I withdrew completely, took my cock in my hand and slapped it back and forth on her hard nub. From the noises she was making and her movements, I saw she was on the verge of coming. Her eyelids started fluttering, her legs stiffened and she looked as if she was entering another zone. I pushed my cock halfway inside her and she started shuddering, her inner contractions pulsating and quivering all over me. I held it there, not even all the way in. She was moaning again, her back arched, her fingers clawing and gripping my ass like she never wanted our groins to part. Ever. She was coming hard, her hands clutching my buttocks to bring me closer.

"Alexandre, I.... Jesus, *aahh... aahh...*oh my freaking *God!*"

I stopped my *one, one thousand* and let myself go. Fuck, this girl was hot. I imploded inside my sweet, hot pearlette, luxuriating in her as we both came together, united in our carnal frenzy: our greedy, insatiable feast. "I'm coming baby, I'm coming hard," I groaned into her mouth, lashing my tongue all over her, thrusting into her with abandon at last, as my orgasm ripped right through me.

She lay there panting. Satiated. Fulfilled, with me still inside her. "I came with penetrative sex," she meowed, releasing her claws from my ass. She was shocked. Amazed. She couldn't believe what had just happened.

Was I shocked?

Not a bit. I knew what I was doing.

I started young, remember? I'd made more women come by the time I was twenty-five than most men could even fantasize about doing over an entire lifetime, even if only in their wet dreams.

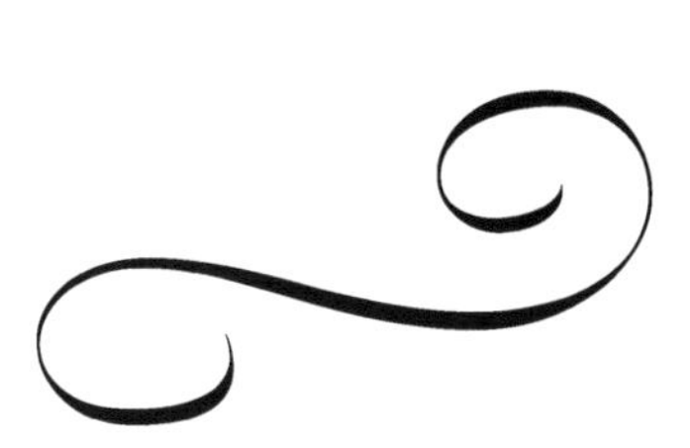

By the time I hit my fourteenth birthday, I was already physically mature. My balls had dropped and my voice had broken to a deep baritone. I was getting tall, muscular; my Alsation roots from my mother's side of the family began to really show. Compared to other guys my age, I was pretty developed. I was masturbating constantly. All I could think of were pussies, asses and tits. But I was shy and had no intention of doing anything about my obsession.

One of Sophie's co-workers took a shine to me. She took me under her wing.

Her name was Hélène.

Sophie had been in the game since we left home when she was seventeen. But she was picky. She started out as just as an escort, refusing for a full two years to have penetrative sex. Wouldn't even blow the guys. No, she was educated, she maintained—she had more to offer. She could hold an intelligent conversation and she looked like a top model. She was ambitious, too. It wasn't long before she was the darling of several politicians and men in extremely high places. Sex was not her thing. She hooked them in a different way.

She was a Dominatrix.

They'd get off on being whipped and scolded. She'd set the scene, sometimes playing mommy, nanny or a wicked step-mother, sending them to bed with no supper or dripping hot wax onto their chests. They loved it. Some wanted golden showers. One, she even dressed up in giant diapers and spanked when he cried. It was all pretty sick but she was making a fortune. The more insane it got, the richer she became. There was one, though, who became obsessed with her. Set us up in a luxurious apartment in the Champs-Elysées, and wouldn't share Sophie with anyone. He paid handsomely for exclusivity. She became his official mistress. We were still both going under false names. She had read *The Three Musketeers* and liked the name of the author. So she chose Dumas. I was fascinated with chivalry and jousting knights so I chose Chevalier—Knight when translated into English.

We were the *Two* Musketeers, fighting to survive.

She then got bored of having to cow-tow to the politician, but before she left him, she managed to extract enough money from his coffers to set herself up in business. She became a Madame. He was furious, but her *Little Black Book* with all the names and phone numbers of some of the most powerful men in Europe spelled Doom for anyone foolish enough to mess with her. She was above the law because, guess what? She had them in her pocket: politicians, government aids, heads of police, big business men married with children, with too much at stake to lose face. Sophie was practically running Paris, not to mention her British and German contacts. She had it all sewn up very nicely.

What I later told Pearl about our stepfather helping us set up HookedUp with his piddly 15,000 euros? Bullshit. It was *Sophie* who funded HookedUp. She needed to launder money, needed to put all that cash somewhere legitimate. That's where I came in.

But back to my fourteenth birthday, several years before…

Hélène knew that I was obsessed with her. She wore black stockings, held up with garters, and a gray schoolgirl uniform. She also had a lot of powerful clients and they loved that dirty-sweet look. She was thirty but looked a lot younger. Slim, but with a curvy ass. I could smell her every time she walked by me. Vanilla, or something that smelled like candy. All I thought about was burying my cock inside her. I could hardly sleep nights I was so infatuated.

On my birthday, she knocked on my bedroom door at five in the morning. She was laughing, had been up all night and was tipsy.

She leaned back against the wall and splayed her legs apart, her high heels digging into the wooden parquet floor, her skimpy, silk panties flashing a scarlet red. "Come on then, big boy. Come and show me what you've got. I saw that huge great cock of yours bulging in your pants the other day. I have a feeling that big boy has a crush on me, doesn't it?"

I was mortified. My face was burning like a scalding iron but what she was saying was giving me a hard-on.

"You see? I just look at you and you get a stiffy." She burst out laughing again and then got down on her knees and pulled down my pajama bottoms.

When I told Pearl, "That was maybe the best blowjob I ever had," the *maybe* bit was a clue to the truth. Because Hélène's blowjob was iconic. Unforgettable.

It was my *first*. And being a green fourteen-year-old, you can imagine what it felt like.

The fuck that followed was even more incredible for me, but disastrous for Hélène. I clawed and panted and came instantly. How could I stop myself? That's when she decided I needed 'training.' I became her 'valet,' her sort of Action Man doll. She trained me, all right. She taught me almost everything I know.

After about six months, I began to get the hang of it. She wouldn't let me fuck her until she was soaking wet first. I learned to *earn* my fuck and enjoy foreplay as much as the act itself. Lubricant was banned. That was a curse word. "Any man who uses that shit isn't worth the time of day, and certainly isn't worth the time of night," she sneered. She taught me that it wasn't a race. And woe betide if I ever came before she did. Not. Allowed. Ever. If I did that, she wouldn't let me fuck her for a week.

Word got out that I had a big dick so her friends got curious and she began to share me. I was insatiable, wanting it several times a day, so I sure as hell wasn't complaining.

There were several in the game who were inorgasmic. They put on a great act, though—could have fooled anyone. And did. Fooled me, till I was shown how to read the signs: the fake screams and eye-rolls. Hélène explained that all women were natural born actresses in the bedroom, and not to be taken in by the Big Lie. They taught me how to understand women's bodies. Really know them. *Feel* them. One was even into

Tantric sex, so we did it without hardly even moving. I learned to detect the tiniest twitch in her pussy and make her come by not even fucking her. Teasing her with my stillness. Making her beg for the smallest movement, which could send her over the edge. That's when I learned about the power of the brain, and that sexual organs were no more than the brain's tools.

"Don't get cocky about having a big penis," Hélène warned. "It's useless unless you know how to use it properly. God gave you a big dick for one reason only: to give us women pleasure. Don't abuse that gift. One day you'll find someone special, want to get married and have a family. The rule will still apply; you'll want to make your wife happy. If she's happy, you'll be happy. Trust me on this."

Just one woman? Marry? The idea seemed inconceivable to me at the time. I wanted every pretty woman I laid my eyes on, and that's the way it continued for many years.

But Hélène's words had an impact on me and have lived with me ever since.

Naught to sixty and I was still cruising.

I invited Pearl to dinner that very same day. To celebrate her Big O, if you like. Not that I made a big deal of it to her. I wanted her to know how special she was to me. When a woman lets a man enter her, she feels an extraordinary vulnerability afterwards, partly because so many guys start acting like assholes once they've got what they wanted. They see women as vessels for their own pleasure. That's not the way I operate. I want a woman to feel ecstatic after I have been with her, not deflated.

Besides, I couldn't get enough of Pearl.

I spent the whole afternoon preparing for her visit. I went food shopping and got gourmet treats delivered to my apartment: sea bream, hot peppers from the Pays Basque in France, black truffles, razor clams from Galicia in Spain, Cornish cream from England. I wanted to impress Pearl as much in the cuisine as I had in the sack. They say the way to a man's heart is through the stomach. Believe me, it works the other way, too. Prepare a woman a home-cooked meal and you score major brownie points.

I had conquered the business world. People needed HookedUp, or at least thought they did. It dawned on me that I liked feeling needed. Perhaps that's what came of coming from a dysfunctional family; a desire to feel accepted, needed, wanted. My mother fled when she should have stayed. She left me when I was only seven years old. So I knew all about rejection and being abandoned.

Something I still secretly feared. Yes, I wanted women—in general—to need me.

And as for Pearl? I wanted her to feel she *really* needed me.

I called Elodie, my niece, to come and help me prepare the feast. Elodie was eighteen and your typical surly teenager. However, she was bright and had an aptitude for numbers and figures so I had her working for me at the offices of HookedUp for the summer. She'd dropped out of college and was floating about, luxuriating in the fact that she was only eighteen and had all the time in the world to screw-up her life.

We stood in the kitchen, drinking cold beers, listening to Elvis Presley sing *Can't Help Falling In Love.* I had Elodie reluctantly chopping vegetables, pouting and rolling her eyes every time I asked something of her.

I raised my brows and said, "You think eighteen's young, don't you?"

She shrugged. Her dark brown hair flopped over her beautiful, heart-shaped face that was so delicate and adorable, you felt it could break.

I went on, "First kitchen rule, Elodie: hair up. Go to the bathroom and tie that horse's mane into a nice, neat ponytail or bun. I don't want strands of hair in the food."

She made a face at me. "Who is this chick that's got you into, like, Mr. Perfection mode and listening to corny love songs?"

"When you make a gourmet meal you have to pull out all the stops—get thee to the bathroom, young lady. Now!" Of course, all this conversation was in French. Elodie's English was still, at that point, floundering. I'd enrolled her in intensive classes—she needed them.

"And after this can I go to my room?" she asked, spearing a tomato.

"What? And hide behind video games, wasting your life online? No, you cannot go to your room. You stay here with me while I show you how to cook properly. Then, an hour before my guest is due to arrive, go take a shower and make yourself look pretty and presentable. Take off that dark coal around your eyes, those silly fuck-me heels that you go tottering about in, and make yourself look like a lady. There is a lady somewhere deep down inside there, isn't there? Just dying to get out?" I teased.

She jokingly wielded a large stainless-steel knife at me. "I'll go back to Paris if you keep bossing me about like this."

"What? And get driven crazy by your mother? What will you live on?"

Elodie pouted air, puckering up her lips like a model on a fashion shoot. Sophie wasn't giving her a dime. I, at least, had her on my payroll. She was learning how HookedUp operated in New York. Learning a trade. "Bathroom," I ordered. "Hair out of face. Hair out of food."

She sloped off.

"And shoulders back. Stop looking like an angry teenager and get your shit together."

I was being tough on Elodie but it was the only way to bring her out of her shell. The more I treated her with kid gloves, the more she withdrew. So I was playing dad, although she did have a real father, Sophie's husband. Sophie was Elodie's stepmother, but she had still taken her on as her own. Elodie's mom died when she was six, or so. But right now, things weren't going well between Elodie and Sophie. Elodie had clammed up and Sophie was hurting with the rejection. The usual mother/daughter stuff. I didn't ask too many questions.

Elodie thought I didn't know about her secret but I had a pretty good idea. Something bad had happened to her. Whatever it was, it wasn't pretty. It didn't seem as if it was the usual, teenage heartbreak trouble. As far as I knew, Elodie had never even had a boyfriend. No. Some shit had gone down that had broken her. Changed her from a giggly, bubbly girl into a very angry person. She looked as if she had been deceived. Destroyed. I wanted to help. I loved Elodie as my own and I felt protective towards her. To me, she felt like my flesh-and-blood daughter. I'd tried, various times, to get her to open up to me. Not easy.

Elodie clicked back into the kitchen, her hair up in a messy, ragamuffin bun. I gave her a C for effort.

"You'd be more comfortable taking off those heels," I remarked.

"I know."

"Well then?"

"I like to feel tall. Makes me feel stronger. If anyone fucks with me I can take one off and stab him in the eye."

"Ah, a weapon," I observed with a wry smile. "Interesting."

Elodie was petite. Tiny. She had wrists that looked as if you could crack them in two. Her skin was translucent, as if she had been living in a dark cave all her life. She used to be bronzed and healthy-looking, spending summers diving in and out of my pool in Provence, but now she shied away from sunlight like a vampire.

"Have you had any lunch today?" I asked her.

"An apple."

"Right. I'm going to prepare you a *steak au poivre* and French fries."

"I'm not eating meat anymore."

"No, of course not," I said, my eyes taking in the bloodless pallor of her thin skin, as I gathered some ingredients out of the fridge. "A nice, big, hearty bowl of pasta, then, with *a lot* of Parmesan on top? You need some protein, my girl."

"Whatever," she said listlessly. Then she muttered, "Who is this Pearl Robinson, anyway?"

I narrowed my eyes suspiciously. "How do you know her

name?"

"Maman mentioned her. She's getting her checked out."

I sucked in a lungful of air. "Of course she is," —and I exhaled with a long, exasperated groan— "of course she fucking is."

The dinner with Pearl went beautifully. It was the perfect date. The meal impressed her, and the delicious wines I'd chosen had her as loosened-up as a young teenager left alone at home for the very first time; innocently wicked. Her eyes sparkled; her body language spoke to me in tones of abandoned curiosity. I felt that I had her in the palm of my hand.

After dinner, we relaxed in a bath laced with lavender oil—the lavender from my very own fields. Then I played Dom, albeit with a kingfisher feather. I tied her up with some neckties of mine; her legs splayed apart, each ankle knotted to the bedpost of my big, brass bed. Her wrists I'd bound together with the pearl necklace I'd given her, which she arrived wearing, setting off a chic, black dress which was neither overtly sexy nor too smart. The sort of dress which although stunning, gives you hints to what lies beneath and invites you to rip it off as soon as you feasibly can. I surprised myself with my Dom game. It wasn't something I'd planned. It was all very spontaneous. But Pearl got off on it. She liked to be dominated. Strike that. She *loved* being dominated. And I was finding, more and more, that I liked being in control, too. Especially with her.

Mission number 2: make her come through oral sex. That was another thing I'd learned from my tutors. Don't zero in on the clitoris. It can get numb and lose all sensitivity if too much attention is paid to it. Make the clit beg. Tease it. Brush past it with light whispery kisses. Taunt it and you'll have your woman coming hard when you finally let it get its lustful way.

So I played all sorts of games with Pearl that night. I'd sent Elodie out on a date—didn't like the idea of her being in my apartment, especially as I realized Pearl was a screamer, even though my apartment was vast—still, I wanted Elodie out for the evening.

I blindfolded Pearl, dribbled honey all over her torso, smeared her tits in cream and Nutella and licked it off her curves and valleys. Her wrists remained bound as I teased her, swirling my tongue around her nipples, getting her so worked up, that by the time I pressed my tongue flat against her clit, she was ripe for a big, pounding orgasm. I didn't even have to do anything; just had to keep that pressure up and let her fuck my tongue at her own pace. She brought herself to climax, bucking her hips up and down against me. I felt triumphant, feeling her quivering quim ripple into a pulsating, tremulous orgasm right into my mouth. She was writhing about, screaming my name.

By that point, I knew she'd really fallen for me hook, line, and sinker.

Or so I thought.

A big shock was about to prove me wrong.

Pearl slept like an angel all night. The next morning, I don't know why or how, but the conversation had somehow veered itself around to my childhood. Something I never discussed with anyone. In fact, I painted it to be better than it actually was. I told Pearl that my mother returned to us a year after Sophie and I left and she stayed with my father, too chicken to come with us. But she didn't return a year later. It was *several* years later.

Pearl was shocked enough that my mother had abandoned her own son. She was less concerned about her not being there for Sophie because Sophie was my mom's stepdaughter and she was already seventeen. But I was just seven.

I let Pearl know about how my sister and I had plotted to kill my father, mixing rat poison with his food and how Sophie attacked him with a knife to his groin. After that, we had to get the hell away from him for good. My mom stayed. She was too co-dependent. Too in love. Or too browbeaten to gather the strength to leave him.

I didn't want Pearl knowing the true story; that Sophie and her sex worker friends were my real family. Still, I lay my heart open to Pearl—told her my deepest secrets. Or at least, a couple of them. Enough anyway, to be as vulnerable as a gaping wound. She, in return, told me about her brother, John, who had died ten years before of a drug overdose. I felt that Pearl and I had shared vulnerable parts of ourselves, and our jigsaw puzzle pieces were slotting together perfectly.

I was about to be proved otherwise.

We were enjoying a beautiful breakfast spread at The Carlyle. It was only 7 a.m. Pearl was wearing her elegant black dress from the night before, and high heels. She looked like a million dollars. Happy. Orgasmed-out. The way every woman should look every morning of the week. How every woman should feel.

I was spouting off a load of nonsense; something about the differences between French and American culture. Pearl was listening intently. I thought how pleasant it was that we were able to engage in interesting conversation—our relationship was not just about sex.

My cell had already buzzed a couple of times and I let it go to voicemail, but when the caller—Sophie, Claudine, Indira, Laura?—insisted, I thought that perhaps there was some kind of emergency, so I picked it up and listened to two frantic messages.

Both from Sophie.

The first:

"I was right. I knew there was something fishy about Pearl Robinson. Guess what, buddy? Your sweet little baby-doll-eyed-girlfriend is forty years old! Oh yes, fucking forty! You might be happily thinking that you are her *boyfriend* but she has other ideas: you are her TOY BOY! She's playing with you, Alexandre. She's out to get what she's after and then she'll dump you like a hot potato, you watch."

Second message:

"Sorry, forgot to explain myself. Pearl Robinson was stalking us, like the cougar she is, when we met her in that coffee shop. Coincidence, my ass! Do you remember how she pretended she just so *happened* to be there? She works for Haslit Films, the ones who were hounding us to take part in their fucking documentary! She's their producer! Do you remember that? The film company who were hassling us, wanting to do a piece about us? She was bloody well following us! Why the fuck aren't you picking up your phone, Alexandre?"

I called Sophie back, my eyes on Pearl. I couldn't believe what I'd heard but I knew my sister; she would have done her homework. Sophie never made mistakes. Wow, Pearl had me fooled. First of all, she looked not a day older than thirty, with that tight, smooth body that even a twenty-five year old would have been proud of. I'd been dumb. I was so wrapped up in the romance of our relationship, I hadn't bothered to find out who she really was, what she did for a living. Damn it, I probably could have known everything within ten minutes, just by Googling her.

Pearl was gazing back at me, her face ashen. She knew something was wrong. My eyes had turned as cold as two sharpened flints—I could feel it myself. I never had been good at hiding my anger.

I looked at her. *Pearl Robinson, you've fucking betrayed me. I trusted you.*

Sophie picked up on the first ring and continued her rant without even saying hello. "Fucking Americans! They always have an ulterior motive. Always out to get something from you. Pearl Robinson is a fucking snake in the grass! I suppose you're shagging her as we speak!"

"No, I'm not, actually," I said coolly, my heart feeling as if it had been ripped out of my chest. Talk about a good performance. Pearl had me conned. Really fooled. There I was imagining that she had desperately fallen for me. I was the one who had fallen. Fallen hard.

Fallen on my goddamn face.

Sophie went on, "I hadn't put two and two together because it was her boss, Natalie something-or-other who'd sent me all those emails, begging us for an interview, to take part in their fucking spy-film. What have you told her, Alexandre?"

"Nothing," I lied.

"Because if you've spilt the beans about our business, it will be all over the papers, soon enough, or edited into some bloody documentary for the whole world to see!"

"Don't worry about it," I said, my heart pounding. Fuck! Pearl knew so much about my past. About Sophie stabbing my father in the groin. Me, trying to kill him off with rat poison…a fascinating story it would make: the CEOs of HookedUp both belonging in a loony bin.

"Does she know about the gems? Does she know about our highly illegal Mumbai deal?" Sophie screamed at me.

"Of course not."

"Get the fuck away from that scheming, lying bitch and never, ever see her again."

"Sure," I answered sadly, my eyes still fixed on Pearl's beautiful face. My insides were churning like a cement mixer. "Bye, Sophie, I'll call you later."

I pressed 'end' and let out a disappointed sigh. I shook my head, "Oh Pearl, oh Pearl." I was wondering how I'd be able to bear it—how I'd be able to stand not having her in my arms, not be able to fuck her, make love to her, see her face when she came, hear her moan with desire.

Her big blue yes widened with guilty innocence. Damn, she was a good actress. "What?" she asked.

"Why didn't you tell me? Why didn't you tell me who you were?" I was waiting for her to admit what she did, to offer me a reasonable explanation, but she just dug her grave deeper.

"What do you mean?" she said, her finger touching her nose. *Such a giveaway.*

That was her fucking response—that's the best she could come up with.

My lips pressed tightly together, my body tensed. I'd given her a chance to wriggle out of her deceit, but she'd blown it. I hissed between gritted teeth, "Is this what all this means to you? Having breakfast with me, spending time, making love? All this so you can go back to your fucking editing suite and plot out the next scene? The scene where Alexandre Chevalier and Sophie Dumas's pasts are revealed? Was *that* what it meant to you when we were in bed together? A ploy to get intimate with me and make me spill the beans about my private life?"

"NO! I mean…I…let me explain, Alexandre—"

"Explain what? That you lied to me? Oh no, not lied, that would have been too obvious. You omitted information. Omitted to tell me what your game plan was. Why didn't you just come out with it?" I lower my voice, "Because if you wanted to fuck me as part-and-parcel of your deceitful little package deal, I would have done that for free. The only difference is I would have fucked you harder, cared a little less," and I leaned down and whispered in her ear, "I would have fucked your ass off, pounded into you ruthlessly like you fucking deserved, so you couldn't walk for several days afterwards."

The people in the hotel restaurant were staring at us now. Fascinated by our domestic scene. Pearl's eyes were brimming over with tears—mascara running down her cheek. But she still couldn't come up with a decent excuse. She did what every woman does when they are caught out—she pulled out the sympathy card. But I wasn't falling for it.

"Don't fucking cry on me now," I said coldly.

"Please Alexandre," she whimpered, dabbing her tears with a linen napkin. The sympathy card wasn't working, so she laid out her next card on the table: The Queen of Hearts. "I love you," she sobbed.

Her words pinched my heart but I took a big breath and muttered, "Good try, baby."

She babbled on incoherently about the coffee shop—how she'd missed our talk, something about not giving a toss about HookedUp but wanting to focus on important things, like exposing arms dealers.

More important stuff. My point exactly. Sophie and I were just pawns to her.

I stood up, heat flushing through me, not wanting to listen to her bullshit, lame excuses anymore. She'd proven to me that she was your typical, ambitious, ball-busting career woman. Tough. Ruthless. Trampling over others at any cost to get what she wanted. I slapped a couple of hundred dollar bills on the table to more than cover the check. "Keep the change," I snapped. "Oh yeah, you left your gifts at my place—the pearl necklace, the kingfisher feather. I'll have them delivered to you—a little keepsake, a souvenir," I said bitterly, "so you can remember our time together." I turned on my heel and strode out of the room, not looking behind.

Pride before a fall.

10

That fall came a good week or so later.

Meanwhile, I had Laura on my case, not to mention Indira.

"Darling," Laura purred into the phone, "please let me know about France. I want to book my holiday but I also want you to *be* there. Like I told you, James won't be coming this year. I miss you. A lot. Call me."

Next voicemail: Indira. "Alexandre, please forgive me. I was behaving like a banshee. I don't know what got over me. Of course you're seeing other women, it's natural. We live thousands of miles apart from each other. I can completely understand. You were such a gentleman the other day, not wanting to take advantage of me. Please don't hate me because I flipped out. Water under the bridge? Anyway, I'm coming to New York to promote my next film and I'd love it if we could have dinner or something. Call me."

Next message: just tears and sniffling down the line. It

must have been Elodie because I didn't recognize the number. She'd changed it so many times in the last six months, I couldn't keep count. Was there someone she was trying to avoid? I called the number back. No answer. I was tempted to set up a GPS tracking system on her phone. Something I didn't feel good about—I hated spyware of any kind, but Elodie was eighteen years old, new in New York with limited English, and so stunning that people stared at her when she walked by, despite her sneer, her black Goth make-up and her fuck-me-fuck-you-or-I'll-stab-you-in-the-eye-heels.

Women. They really were a handful.

I called Elodie back.

"Where are you, sweetheart?" I asked. I was sitting at my desk in my apartment, looking at a framed photo of Rex. I made a mental note of going to Paris to get him ASAP.

Elodie spluttered as if a drink had gone down the wrong way. "How did you know it was me?"

"Only about ten people have my number and I figured that if a number comes up I don't recognize, it has to be you. Are you okay?"

"I'm fine. By the way, do you still have that bodyguard who works for you sometimes?"

"Of course," I said, my jaw ticking at her out-of-the-blue, very worrying question.

"Can I borrow him for a while?"

"Elodie, what's up? Is someone following you?"

There was a long pause. I could hear street noises, her clicking heels. Then she answered, "No. No, of course not. I'd just feel safer, you know. I don't know this city so well."

"I'll put him back on the payroll full-time, then," I told her.

"What about the new apartment? Will you be scared without a man in the house?" I had just bought her a two-bedroom apartment in Greenwich Village. She was going to get a roommate to share it with her: an old friend from Paris. "Maybe you should carry on staying at my place?" I suggested.

"No, it's fine. I love my new flat. Can't wait to move in. Listen I've got to go. Speak later." She ended the call and I sat there wondering what was going on. I got up and started pacing the room. I'd try and find out without compromising her privacy too much, but if my niece felt she needed a bodyguard, I sure as hell wanted to find out why.

The week dragged on. I tried to concentrate on work but everywhere I looked I saw signs of Pearl. I hadn't returned her gifts, mostly because I couldn't bear to let go of her memory. I didn't wash the shirts I'd worn because I could still smell her on the fabric. She was everywhere—even on my bloody iPad—in one of my goddamn lists.

Being a nerd, I write lists, something I have always done to make sure I'm on top of any situation. As I said, multi-tasking has never been my strong point by nature, so all thoughts, all ideas get written down. So being as busy as I was, with so many fingers in pies (and other places), I had to be on the ball.

I read the bullet points I had written about Pearl:

Problems to be solved concerning Pearl: needs to reach orgasm during penetrative sex. (My big challenge).
Needs confidence boosted—age complex due to American youth worship culture.
Need to get her pregnant ASAP due to clock factor—need to start family.

The list just went to show how hard I'd fallen for her and how much I had invested myself in her.

I expected her to call and apologize, the way Indira had. Pearl was in the wrong, and yet still, each day went by with no news. It was beginning to really irk me. How dare she fuck me over and then not even say she was sorry?

Then I started worrying about her, the way you do about members of your family. Was she alright? Had she died in some freak car accident? Then Sophie called and put my mind at rest. At least, for all of five minutes, until I started obsessing about Pearl again—pacing the room, wringing my fingers through my hair.

Sophie was in Paris. But even from long distance, I could feel her whiskers twitching, her claws sharpened.

"The gems are in Amsterdam," she started off by saying. "All good. They're with the best cutters, the best jewelers. We're going to make a mint. We'll need to buy some more real estate with the cash…distribute. I'd like to buy a brownstone on the Upper East Side, you know, for when I visit New York."

"Good idea, we should launder a bit."

"Launder. I hate that word—it's so crass. By the way, speaking of laundry, of your *dirty* laundry, we don't need to worry about Pearl Robinson anymore; she doesn't seem to be a threat. Looks like she's got bigger fish to fry."

"What do you mean?" I asked, ignoring her dirty laundry jibe.

"She's turned her attention to that Russian billionaire, that arms dealer."

"What Russian arms dealer?"

"You know, the handsome one, that young thirty-year-old Adonis-Casanova guy who's always strutting about on red carpets with supermodels. What's-his-face, you know, Mikhail Prokovich."

A stab of jealousy pierced my gut. Pearl was turning her attention elsewhere? "That blond guy? He's an arms dealer? I thought he was in real estate. He's an *arms* dealer?" I repeated, incredulous.

"A clandestine one. I doubt Pearl knows whom she's dealing with. He's very black market. He mixes with war criminals, soldiers of fortune, crooked diplomats and small-time thugs who keep militaries and mercenaries loaded with arms. But he's powerful. Very powerful. Pearl was seen having dinner with him just last night. All smiles, apparently."

I hated him already. I felt my fists clench into tight knots. What was Pearl *doing*? She hated arms dealers, was talking about exposing them in her next documentary. And now she was *hanging out* with one?

"What else do you know?" I pressed my sister, blood bubbling in my veins, jealousy rippling through every muscle in my body. This guy was sickeningly good-looking. Even as a man I could tell you that. Dashing, one of those square-jawed types that look like they've walked straight out of a cartoon strip.

Blondish hair, searing blue eyes. Sophie was right; he was a red carpet kind of guy—liked to be seen. Cocky. With beautiful women hanging on his arm, and probably hanging onto his every word, as well. Jets. A fleet of flashy cars, some of them enviably cool. Houses all over the world. Every woman's fantasy.

"Sophie, what else do you know?" I demanded again in a low growl.

"That Pearl's been out to dinner with him, that's all. Him and some important guy from the United Nations. She's not just some sweetie-pie, naive American chick with big blue eyes and luscious lips, you know, Alexandre. She's a smart little operator, a user. She knows people in high places. Knows what she's doing. Obviously loves mixing business with pleasure. Anyway, at least she's off our case now, onto the next fool who'll fall for her innocent little act. Oh wait, before I go, how's Elodie getting on?"

"I think you'd better ask her that yourself," I said, not wanting to betray Elodie's confidence in any way. But my mind was now focused on Pearl, not Elodie. Sophie's words rang cruel in my ear… *"Pearl likes mixing business with pleasure."*

The more I thought about it, the adrenaline surged through me. Fuck her! Flirting and smiling with that fuck, Mikhail Prokovich? She was *mine!* I could hear my breathing getting more unsteady by the second. I was feeling hot and very bloody bothered. I loosened my tie; I'd been in a meeting earlier that day and was wearing a suit.

The idea of her being anywhere near another man was making blood rush to my head. Especially one as powerful Mikhail Prokovich. I got up from my desk and counted to ten to calm myself. But then I did the reverse, I started counting *down* from ten, and by the time I hit zero, I was out the door and into the elevator. I had to fuck her.

Before the Russian got his clammy hands on her.

I just hoped it wasn't already too late.

By the time I reached Pearl's apartment, my heart rate had doubled. Tripled. She hadn't apologized. She'd been using me. Using me to further her career. And now she was onto the next guy (her next project) without even a blink of one of her big, baby-blue eyes! Her whole "I haven't had an orgasm forever" was bullshit, obviously. Her little ploy to draw sympathy, to get gullible men like me all worked up and horny. To bring out our macho side—be *the one* to make her come, be *the one* to fuck her properly. Clever girl. Clever, clever girl. She'd hooked me in. Now she was moving onto the next guy.

She deserved a fucking Oscar.

Perhaps she won't even be home. Maybe she's on that son-of-a-bitch arms dealer's yacht by now, her lips clamped around a straw sipping cocktails, or worse…her lips clamped around his….ugh! The thought made my brain burn. But my dick was propelling me to her. Just thinking about her was getting me hard. I couldn't bear the idea of that cocky-faced shit touching her ass—that sexy, curvy ass, or kissing her beautiful lips. Maybe I was jumping to conclusions, maybe I was being paranoid, but I didn't want to let the distance between us encourage some gatecrashing jerk to push his way into her life.

The doorman let me in, and as he was reaching for the

landline to call her to announce me, I dashed through the lobby to the service elevator, thought twice and legged it up the back stairs, instead. I couldn't risk Pearl instructing him not to let me up, or halting the elevator between floors. I'd bang on her kitchen door until she answered—goddamn it, I *had* to have her. *Had* to fuck her. Remind her how good we felt together. Remind her that she didn't want any other man bulldozing his way into her panties. The fact that I, myself, was acting like the biggest bulldozer of all, escaped my one-track mind.

By the time I reached her floor, I was sweating. My tailored suit didn't help my frantic climb. I banged on her back door outside her kitchen. I stood by the trash bins, my heart pumping as adrenaline surged through me like a lion hunting its prey.

Pearl answered the door. James Brown's *Sex Machine* was blaring. *Good. She probably hasn't even heard the phone which is still ringing—the doorman trying to announce me.* She stood there, and I swear to God, my dick flexed hard within seconds. I was like an untamed animal. All decorum lost, all manners out the window.

I heard myself actually panting. "That'll be the doorman on the phone telling you that a rapist is on his way up to fuck you," I blurted out, not even thinking how crass I sounded.

She looked fucking beautiful, all poised in her business outfit: white shirt and navy blue pencil skirt and high heels. She must have just gotten home from work. My eyes raked her up and down and I even rearranged my crotch—that obvious—I had a hard rod in my pants. She looked down at my groin and bit her bottom lip. *Right, that's it—she wants to get fucked, alright.* My foot was wedged in the doorway so she couldn't kick me out. I pushed the door open further.

"Aren't you going to invite me in," I said, moving forward. She didn't have much choice.

"I don't know." *Oh yes you do know, you cock-teaser.*

"I have to fuck you, Pearl," was my answer.

I pushed my way inside and pressed her against the wall. *Sex Machine* pumping away was making me even hornier. I start kissing her, my erection pressed hard up against her, my hand fisting her hair so she couldn't move and had no choice but to get devoured by me. My tongue was licking her mouth and she started moaning quietly. I could see her nipples harden even though it was hot. No bra. I had to have those tits in my mouth. I pushed her arms up and pulled her shirt over her head with ravenous intent. I nipped her hard buds between my teeth, one and then the other, my hand up her skirt, the other cupping her round ass. I slipped my finger inside her saturated folds and surprise, surprise, her body was begging me to do anything I wanted to it. And I intended to. You bloody bet.

"You want to get fucked, Pearl? The way you fucked me over? The way you fuck men over to further your career?"

"No," she moaned, her eyelids fluttering in carnal stupor.

"No, you don't want to get fucked? I think you do. So. Horny. And. Wet. So ready for me to fuck you senseless, aren't you?"

I rammed my fingers up her higher, and she gasped. Her skirt was in the way so I unzipped it and ripped it down her thighs. The little harlot was wearing scarlet panties that screamed out, *fuck-me.* How fitting. I unbuttoned my fly opening. My cock was throbbing to get inside her. I got down on my knees. I had to taste that hot pussy. Had to stick my tongue inside her. I took those moistened panties between my teeth and peeled them aside, my teeth gripping them with lustful ardor. I could smell her, smell her sweet, fruity odor. My tongue darted inside her wet cunt.

"You want to fuck, Pearl? Because you're so much better at fucking than you pretend. Fucking people over, especially."

I so nearly didn't bother with sheathing myself with a condom. My instinct—like one of those soldiers using rape as a war weapon—was to impregnate her. Make her mine, even if it was against her will, and feel every juicy cell in her pussy without any barrier between us, but I relented, reminded myself how fucked-up that was, and rolled the condom reluctantly on my raging-hard erection. I didn't even take off my jacket, let alone my pants.

I pushed her red panties to one side and rammed myself into her ruthlessly, fucking her against the wall. I was half expecting her to try and stop me, but she was groaning with pleasure, relishing being 'raped' by me.

God, she felt good. I realized that this was something I couldn't do without. I had to have Pearl Robinson on a regular basis even if she *was* using me. By now, I didn't even care.

"I love. Fucking. You." I was growling, pounding her so hard I could feel myself ripping her open. She'd never had so much of me inside her before. I was holding nothing back this time.

She was loving every second, though.

"You like to get used, Pearl, or you just like using!" I said in a deep, angry voice, my mouth all over hers.

"I wanted to get to know you, Alexandre. I want to get to know you. All of you....every...beautiful...inch of you," she said, flexing her hips at me. "All…oh God…oh wow…oh God…" She could hardly speak as I thrust into her over and over, slamming her against that kitchen wall. She was clawing me, her mouth on mine, greedy for my lust.

"Is this what you want to get to know?" And I grabbed her ass in both hands so I could bring her closer, fuck her harder. "So. Tight. This. Tight. Pussy. Clenching. My. Hard. Cock." I felt her contractions like a pair of skin-tight gloves pressuring my erection. The red panties were also grazing back and forth against it, adding to my arousal.

Her nails were digging into my back—she didn't want to let me go. "You're so huge. Oh my…so enormous! I love you, Alexandre. I love you…fucking me."

"You love me, Pearl Robinson? Is that what you're saying?" I asked with irony. I was going to come any second. That *love* word went straight to my dick, even if it was a bold-faced lie. I burst inside her, my giant orgasm ripping through my center, and hers, with abandon, breaking my golden rule—not caring that I was coming first. I was moaning like a child, not a grown man. I felt weakened by my desire for her. She had me hooked—her smell, her pussy, like an exotic fruit. Her taste. Everything was driving me wild and had me spellbound.

The pulse of my orgasm faded to a tingle and I pulled out, but seconds later, literally seconds, I felt myself flex again. I had a flashback of our Skype sex phone call the week before—when I was in the limo on my way to Mumbai Airport—and I got her to fuck the sofa. Pearl and her sweet pearlette pressed up against the arm of the couch as she rocked back and forth in her white, schoolgirl panties. I wanted more of that, and I was going to get more. You bet. But with me 'live,' this time, not just us on screen.

I grabbed a cushion off a kitchen chair and pressed it onto the corner of the table. "Fuck the table," I told her. I peeled her red panties down her thighs so I could see her moistness, hot between her legs, and pressed my erection against the soft flesh of her round butt. "Push that hot little pussy up against that cushion," I ordered.

She did as she was told. A wave of desire shot through my whole torso. "Press harder," I said, putting on a fresh condom in haste. "Massage your clit back and forth against that table."

She obeyed me. Telling her what to do gave me a thrill and I gloated, *Eat your heart out you Russian cocksucker; this girl's mine!* I pushed the tip of my cock against her entrance—I could see her glistening gate to Heaven with my eyes. Every time she moved back, her wet slit bumped up against the crown of my cock. I was letting her tease me as it dipped in an out of her a couple of centimeters on each movement. She was moaning on every thrust.

"Gotta love this pussy," I growled like the horny lion I was. "It's warm and wet and shiny pink—like a beautiful shell. No wonder the Spanish call it a *concha.* Little sexy *conchita.*"

Her ass was high in the air as she was bent over, her torso flat on the table. I cupped her ass with one hand and with the other, took my cock in my closed fist and teased her, up and down, up and down her butt crack, then sometimes plunging all the way into the wet warmth of her folds, then pulling almost all the way out. She was writhing before me, her arms steadying her torso, flat-out on the table.

"Please Alexandre. Oh God. This feels incredible. Oh God!"

Then I started thrusting. I reminded myself that, this time, I didn't have to go easy on her. I had to remember that she was a selfish, career-getting operator out to *use* me. So I drove into her hard again, to remind her that two could play at the using game.

"Little. Career-getting. Pussy. Using. Me. And. Getting. Off. On. It." On each word I thrust into her and held myself still for a second. Pulled most of the way out then thrust back inside her. But this was no punishment for her, I soon realized. No, she started coming, moaning like the little tigress she was, her tight velvet glove contracting around me, which tipped me over the edge. I could feel myself thicken and I slowed way down, letting my climax surge through me in a blissful, throbbing rush. I moved languidly inside her, both of us coming simultaneously, something we seemed to do with ease. I was like a switch with her. Her gratification aroused me instantly, so when she climaxed, I did, too. Hard.

I collapsed on top of her, my body blanketing her smooth back, her glorious ass. "Pearl, baby, what am I going to do? I just can't keep away from you. I have to keep fucking you. Over and over. I just have to, I can't stop."

The problem was, that however much I tried to stay furious with her, I couldn't. When I spun her around to face me, she had tears in her eyes. A look of love. A look that said, *We are meant to be together, you and I. Please don't hurt me.*

And I melted.

The Russian flashed through my mind again. I couldn't risk it. I knew his playboy reputation, his bulldozer mentality. I had to get Pearl out of New York City for a few days. Just in case he came sniffing about.

Make her irrevocably mine.

If any other man even thought of coming near her, I'd fucking flatten him.

11

I took Pearl to my house in Provence. The ultimate test. Does it travel well?

It did travel well, *very well indeed.*

In fact, she traveled so well that we both joined, for the first time ever, the Mile High Club. We hitchhiked a ride on a French government jet—they owed me a few favors and I thought I'd cash in on one. No point contributing to global warming by taking a private jet ourselves—cadging a lift seemed like a good option.

Sex on a plane (there should be a cocktail named after that) was better than I had ever imagined. Of course, most mere mortals have to suffice with doing it in the toilet. Not us. We did it in full view, so to speak. Now Pearl and I were fully-fledged members. Not only that, but I found myself coming inside her without using a condom, without even consulting her first. What was that all about? A stake to claim? My dick acting as if it had a brain of its own, again? A mixture of the two, I guessed. I felt such relief to have her back in my arms after that week of lonely torture without her, that claiming her as mine in every way I possibly could, felt natural. The beast in me. The instinct to mark her as my property took over. Making her pregnant was the surest way, I supposed. Although, I truly *was* acting on instinct. The logical side of my brain was AWOL.

Did I forgive Pearl for not having come clean with me when we first met? Yes, I did. We spoke about it briefly on this flight. She told me that before she met me, she had imagined that I was a computer-nerd-geek. So when she bumped into me in the coffee shop, she was taken off guard—surprised by her beating heart and the powerful physical attraction we shared within the first few seconds of setting eyes on one another. She didn't want to blow it (that sounds like a bad joke, doesn't it?) She didn't want to jeopardize a possible romantic liaison because of a work project (which Sophie and I never would have agreed to anyway—and I think Haslit Films had cottoned on our reluctance by that point). So Pearl kept quiet about who she was. I understood. She presented herself, not as Pearl Robinson-documentary-producer, but as Pearl Robinson-look-into-my-eyes-and-tell-me-what-you-see. And what I saw was a woman needing attention. Lots of attention.

Besides, I wasn't the type of person to milk a grudge with a woman. I realized that during the week I hadn't seen her, I'd been climbing the walls.

Yes, I was falling in love with Pearl Robinson, despite her faults. Maybe even *for* her faults.

Although it was obvious that Pearl was in control when it came to her career, she certainly wasn't when it came to her heart. I had captured her heart and that thrilled me. It was instantaneous for both of us. Cupid was in a good mood that day in the coffee shop and decided to zap us with his arrow. I had her tongue-tied, confused, disarmed.

It was evident that neither of us could keep away from each other.

Love is not logical. If it were, we would all be able to follow the rules and live in a nice, neat, square box. Love is a hurricane or a tsunami. It hits you when you least expect it. And what you have to work out…is how to survive it.

With Pearl, I had a premonition that I was up for a roller coaster ride with her, but I also had a very strong feeling, even then, that if I tried to get off, I'd fall flat on my face.

I knew that when Pearl woke up the following day in our bedroom in Provence (note how I say *our* bedroom—yes, it was getting that serious), she would be enchanted. The lavender fields were in full bloom, the scent of jasmine was also wafting through the French doors that looked out onto the stunning view below.

Who wouldn't fall in love with an old stone farmhouse in the middle of the French countryside? In the olden days in the South of France, people built their own houses stone by stone, getting friends and family to help them. A far cry from the multi-million dollar properties they have become nowadays. When I restored my house, I wanted to pay attention to each stone, bring out the beauty and detail of the workmanship—the sheer labor of what they had achieved by hand (no machines), all that time ago. I left it exactly the way it was originally; crooked walls, wobbly oak beams, wonky floors. I kept all of its charm, just added a swimming pool. Not a Hollywood-style pool—no bright blue or anything. I wanted it to look as if it had always been there and blend in with the landscape, organically.

I woke up early that morning as I had house business to attend to—I wanted to ensure that the elderly couple (who look after it when I'm away) had everything under control, and that the garden was in order. I wanted to let Pearl rise and shine on her own— soak up her new surroundings. I'd instructed Madame Menager to take her up some breakfast, while I took care of a few business and personal phone calls.

Last but not least, Laura, my ex. As I stood by the pool, white butterflies darting by me, the gentle sound of water tinkling from the fountain, I called her on my cell.

As I expected, she was not too thrilled.

"Laura," I began, "how are things?"

She had ears like a bat. "Is that your fountain I hear by the pool? Are you in Provence?"

"Yes, I am," I replied evenly.

"Alex, you promised!"

"No, actually, I didn't."

"I said you should wait for me! How long are you there for? I'll get on a flight today."

"Laura. No." I walked slowly from the pool area into the house and sat down on the sofa in the living room, where coffee, fresh-baked *brioche* and croissants awaited me. I spread some homemade jam I'd concocted myself (from my very own cherry trees) onto a croissant and took a large bite. I was half listening to Laura and her protestations and wondering what

Pearl's reaction would be when she woke up here, in this beautiful, peaceful haven.

Laura droned on, "What do you mean, *no?* I told you I was planning a visit, I told you—"

I cut her short. "I've met someone, Laura, and I wanted to tell you directly."

Why I even felt I owed Laura an explanation, I have no idea. But I did. I suppose it was the whole wheelchair thing, the guilt I felt about her having suffered for so long. As silence rang in the air, my eyes strayed to the bookshelves where several of Laura's hardback books still lined the shelves. I needed to return them to her. Now that I had met Pearl, it didn't seem right to have my ex's belongings in my house. There was something else in those shelves I needed to deal with, too. Something Top Secret, hidden inside a multi-volume encyclopedia. I had cut out the middle and buried the incriminating evidence inside. Now that we had Wikipedia online, nobody used encyclopedias anymore—the stuff was safe, I decided.

Laura's silence still echoed down the line. I knew that the words, *I've met someone* would be a blow to her, even though she was married.

"Who is she?" she finally asked.

"I'll tell you when we're really serious." *Damn, that came out wrong.*

I didn't feel inclined to tell Laura Pearl's name because I didn't want her sniffing about my personal affairs. But at the same time, I wanted to nip any fantasy Laura might have had about rekindling our relationship…in the bud. Inferring that my relationship with Pearl wasn't yet serious was a mistake. It gave Laura false hope.

"Well, I'm sure you're having great fun but it won't last." She tittered knowingly. "Is she a local French girl from the village?"

"No, she's American." *Shit, why couldn't I keep my mouth shut?*

Laura's lighthearted tone changed several octaves. "So you brought her over specially? Imported her from *America?*"

"Listen, Laura, I have to dash. Take care. Send my best to James. You're both welcome to come for your vacation in a couple of weeks, when I'm not here. Bye."

Pearl and I spent the day by the pool, wandering about my lavender fields, lingering over a long lunch and drinking too much chilled rosé wine, pale as rainwater; the grapes from my own vineyard. I took her to visit my local villages, or rather, she took me. I let her drive my electric blue, 1964 Porsche Coupé, sunroof open, as we soaked up the sun and Nina Simone singing a song that reflected our moods, *Feeling Good*, as we sped by open lavender fields, and rolling hills of wheat and sunflowers—the summer landscape dotted with farmhouses and hilltop villages.

I can't remember the order of things that day, or exactly where and when each conversation took place, but we discussed a few important issues; namely the pregnancy topic. Knowing that Pearl was forty put our relationship on a sort of fast-forward. At least in my mind—there wasn't time to dither about. I'm a practical man. I'm also impatient for outcomes. I'd met Pearl, I couldn't bear to be without her, and she was forty.

We didn't have the luxury of waiting around to find out if we were a hundred percent perfect for each other—we simply had to get on with it.

She didn't know that I knew she was forty. I was brought up to never ask a woman her age or discuss it with her. I was told it was bad manners. Pearl, however, berated me for having come inside her when we had sex on the plane. I guess she felt her freedom of choice had been tampered with. I didn't blame her. Talk about bad manners! The bulldozer had momentarily taken me over—I couldn't help it. But the upshot of it was (I know...*upshot*...does sound crude) that she admitted she did want a family.

There was another topic I'd been meaning to talk to her about: the Russian.

While she managed the steering wheel of my Porsche, I steered the conversation in another direction. "So," I began, "how are things in the documentary department, now that Haslit Films has given up on my company?"

Pearl's eyes were on the road. "Fine. Great. Natalie and I want to do a special about child trafficking in the sex trade. What's going on is really despicable. You'd think it would be getting better with so much publicity and so many arrests, but it's worse than ever."

"I really admire what you do, Pearl. Didn't you mention something about arms dealers the other day?"

"I sure did. That's another thing Natalie and I are focusing on."

"Oh yeah? Any leads?"

"My contact at the UN is pulling a few strings for me."

I turned to look at her. To gauge her expression. "What

kind of strings?"

Pearl swerved a little too fast around a hairpin bend. I pressed my foot on an imaginary brake and sucked in a breath.

"Oh, you know, just organizing a few contacts," she said, with a nonchalant wave of her hand. *Keep your hand on the steering wheel!*

Was it my imagination or was she being cagey? "Anyone in particular?" I asked, trying to keep my voice casual.

"Oh, you know, just *contacts*. I prefer not to jinx things. Not discuss them till I have the goods in the bag."

The goods in the bag?? What bloody goods? "Have you met any of these arms dealers, personally?" I pried.

She just shrugged her shoulders. By this point, I could feel my pulse pick up; blood pumping hard. I felt aroused by jealousy, which in turn, made me feel possessive. Possessive, jealous, horny, irritated—all the sort of traits in myself I wanted to keep under control. I can't remember how I did it, but I veered the conversation toward Laura. I'd mentioned Laura earlier that day. I wanted to let Pearl know that there was an ex in the picture, be honest about it. Just in case Laura called and Pearl picked up the phone or something. But now I decided to toy with the situation; I just wanted to keep Pearl on her toes…let her feel that same stab of jealousy that was spiking my Latin veins.

"I'll show you some photos of Laura when we get home," I told Pearl, "and some letters she wrote me. When you see the pictures you'll understand why she left me for someone else." I knew what was going through Pearl's mind and she fell for the bait.

"Was Laura a *supermodel*, or something?"

"She was beautiful, both inside and out." *Outside, yes. Inside….A grand exaggeration on my part.* But I continued, blithely, "Yeah, she did do some modeling."

At least, I *thought* Pearl had fallen for the bait, but she coolly, not only changed gear, but changed the conversation back to the subject of my Porsche like she didn't give a fuck. Couldn't give a toss about my exes. Yet *I* was burning up. Why was she insisting on not mentioning that she'd had dinner with Mikhail Prokovich? My pride wouldn't let me delve any further, so I dropped the subject. But my curiosity had been whetted and the possessive gene in my DNA got the better of me.

What was I to do with a cool, independent woman like Pearl Robinson? She was forty. She had her own money, an amazing career, owned her own apartment; men no doubt, were desperate to date her and falling at her feet. She didn't *need* a man like me. Was my sister right? Was I just a sort of *Toy Boy* to her? Was she taking me seriously or just enjoying great sex? Women often confuse great sex with love. Maybe Pearl would wake up and smell the coffee. Find out about my fucked-up past and screwed-up head, not to mention my nutty family.

Not only did I want Pearl to think me the hottest thing since the sauna, but also the coolest thing since Mount Everest.

I was balancing a difficult act.

That night, one of my fears materialized. We went to a party nearby, given by my friend Ridley. Sophie appeared like a bat out of hell, wearing a black slinky dress, her hair loose and sleek. I had an ominous feeling she might show up.

Everybody's eyes were on Pearl in her sexy red dress. I mean, *everybody,* including my sister. As we walked in they were playing *Can't Take My Eyes off of You* by Franki Valli & The Four Seasons—the perfect song for Pearl. Charlize Theron was there, and people were getting them confused—that's how good Pearl looked. Some movie star was chatting her up, without any qualms at all—some blond guy, Ryan, who had been in a romantic, Kleenex type of tear-jerker movie—female film goers wailing with emotion at every scene. I knew this because of Elodie; she'd taken me to see it. That was before Elodie had become an Angry Young Woman. Now, it seemed, she eschewed the male sex in general, so I doubt even this Ryan character would have done it for her. And there he was now, brazenly hitting on *my* Pearl.

It was obvious to me that Pearl could get any man she chose. She didn't look a day over thirty. When I say thirty, I mean a beautiful, hot, sexy thirty. She looked amazing: tall and slim, but with killer curves in all the right places. Her skin and body glowed with health and fuckability. I know fuckability isn't even a word but it should have been coined just for Pearl because she oozed it from every pore. She was confident, self-assured, elegant. Despite her hot little dress.

Then *Wonderful Tonight* by Eric Clapton was playing and it couldn't have been a better song to describe how I felt about her.

But I knew I had to get her out of that party ASAP. Away from Ryan the megastar, and away from Sophie and her sharpened claws.

While Pearl was being flirted with, I located my sister,

grabbed her by the wrist and pulled her into the kitchen, where I hoped we could be masked by a little privacy.

"What the fuck are you doing here, Sophie?" I demanded, with a smile on my face. *The HookedUp CEOs. My what a lovely sibling team they are! They get on so well.*

"Ridley invited me," she said in a singsong voice.

"Where are you staying?"

"At your place, of course."

"You can't just turn up to my house whenever you feel like it! Especially when I'm there with company."

"Company? I can't believe you're still fucking that cougar! In her slutty red dress, drawing so much attention. You *have* seen her, haven't you, Alexandre, doing the rounds, 'networking' as the Americans like to call it." She added in a whisper: "Four-tee. A cougar if ever there was one—I wonder what poor creature she'll hunt down tonight."

"Sophie, let me tell you something," I enunciated, pinning her against the fridge. "40 is just a number, forty is just a word. In five year's time *you* will be forty. In several year's time, every single young woman *out there* will be forty—that is, if she's lucky enough, and doesn't get run over by a bus, first. And most of these women, I guarantee you, will not look as hot as Pearl *ever* during their whole lifetime, let alone when they're forty. Stop pigeonholing people, especially Pearl. She's my girlfriend and that's final. Do. You. Understand?" I glared at her, my eyes burning through her and the smirk on her face. I had never felt this protective about a girlfriend before.

"Ooh, the Toy Boy's getting touchy! Have I hit a nerve?" She threw her head back and cackled.

No, but Pearl has. Pearl has hit a nerve. Every single nerve in my body.

I answered, "Sophie, I haven't felt this wide awake for years." It was true; every emotion of mine had been stirred. Anger, jealousy, fury, passion, desire, sympathy, compassion… Pearl had done that to me. Pearl had woken me right up.

"It's just a faze, Alexandre; you're just in lust with her, that's all. Mark my words… Oh look, there's Ridley; I must go and say hello. Please, dear brother, could you kindly unleash my wrist?"

"With pleasure," I said. And I got the hell out of her way.

I exited the kitchen and went on the prowl for Pearl. The party was in full gear. Glamorous people glittered everywhere. Champagne was flowing. A wild boar was being roasted on a spit in the garden; the aroma wafting through the open doors. Everybody seemed delighted, chatting in French or English, even Frenglish, clinking glasses and blowing air kisses. Everyone, except me, that was.

I located Pearl through a sea of floating gowns and penguin suits, marched over to her and pulled her away from the blue-eyed movie star. I nodded at him in a gallant, *This is my woman, move aside,* type of way.

I took her gently by her hand. "Pearl, we have to leave."

She shrugged her smooth, golden shoulder. My eyes scanned down to her peachy ass, accentuated by her red silk dress. *I'd have that ass, later.*

Meanwhile, I was hatching a plan in my head. We couldn't go home because of Sophie. We'd drive to a hotel. In fact, I'd take her somewhere really special—the French Riviera, the Côte d'Azur. To a stunning place on the southern tip of the Cap d'Antibes: the Hotel du Cap-Eden-Roc.

And I'd fuck her senseless.

12

My plan to fuck Pearl out of her mind backfired. By mistake, I got her drunk. We enjoyed too many vintage wines with dinner, and by the time we were finished, I had to carry her to bed. The wine, I think, was Pearl's way of blotting out the unpleasantness of last night: as we were leaving Ridley's party, Sophie appeared at the doorway, vampire fangs out. Pearl hadn't even recognized her but knew something was up when my sister practically spat at her: "Cougar!"

I felt so ashamed. Embarrassed. I suppose I hadn't understood the extent of Sophie's possessiveness toward me. She had attacked Laura in the same way, but when Laura and I split up, Sophie suddenly decided that the sun shone out of Laura's ass. Very convenient. But I hadn't felt the same sense of fury with Sophie concerning Laura that I was now feeling with Pearl. Pearl was bringing out my protective side.

I needed to deal with my sister, fast. Before she really

fucked up my love life for good.

The wine, plus the long drive, made Pearl woozy. The hotel prepared us a candlelit dinner under the stars. Crickets were singing, and the Mediterranean waves lapped soporifically, inducing an intoxicating scent of sea and fresh air that had Pearl in a trance. She leaned back in her chair, sipping her Châteauneuf-du-Pape.

"Am I in Heaven?" she asked drowsily.

"I'm afraid so," I said with a guilty smile. "I've got you a bit tipsy."

"I'm tipsy on the aroma of wild thyme and lavender and France, not to mention this wine which is out of this world."

"I'm glad you appreciate it. A good Châteauneuf-du-Pape is like a beautiful work of art that takes you by surprise. It's not for everybody. It's earthy and sometimes fierce, the proverbial 'brooding' wine."

"Like you, you're a brooder," she said, pointing her finger at me, almost toppling over in her chair.

She has my number. "Why do you think I'm broody, Ms. Robinson?"

"Oh, Mr. Broody, Mr. Moody…you think I haven't worked you out? There's more to you, Monsieur Chevalier, than meets the eye."

"Honestly Pearl, I'm very basic. Boringly so." I tipped her a wry smile.

"Yeah, right, Michael Corleone with your illegal empire." She closed her eyes and inhaled the saline breeze as if it were her last breath. *My illegal empire? Did she know about the gems? And what lengths I would go to, to protect my loved ones? Michael Corleone, huh?…I always did respect that man.*

When Pearl opened her eyes again—her pupils dark like pools of fathomless ultramarine—she gazed at me questioningly, and asked, "Why, Alexandre, don't you just throw in the towel with HookedUp? You have more money than you need for several lifetimes. You said you wanted to get back to being creative, not just making deals."

My throat felt suddenly dry. Perhaps if Pearl hadn't been so tipsy, I wouldn't have admitted my failings so readily. "The problem, Pearl, is that making money has become addictive—the more I make, the more I feel I need. Power does corrupt, no doubt. I've created a kingdom, and like any king...." I trailed off. Pearl was rocking in her chair, about to pass out. I took her hands to steady her and thought about what I'd just said. I, like Pearl now, could topple. I was afraid to lose my crown. Sophie was part of my kingdom—the queen to my king, as it were. We were equal partners in HookedUp, so it would have been tricky to extricate myself. Her obsession with making money, and more money, and more, had rubbed off on me. But our relationship wasn't healthy—we were too entwined with each other mentally, as well as being business associates. A 'marriage' made in hell.

I was beginning to want out completely.

I got up from my chair and walked over to my beautiful Pearl. Her red dress reflected against the glass of deep wine, like blood, glinting under the moonlight. I took the glass from her hand and set it on the table—she'd had enough to drink for one night. "And you, Pearl? Do you care about money?" I asked, scooping her up in my arms and turning in the direction of our suite.

Her head flopped back and she grinned. "If I did, I'd be

doing a different job, don't you think? Being a producer of controversial documentaries isn't going to bring me millionzz," she slurred. "I love what I do. I've had a lot of headhunters knock at my door offering me almost double but, you know, I'm not motivated by money." She nuzzled her head into my neck and kissed me there. I took in the sweet smell of her hair, of her sun-kissed skin, and carried her, like a baby, to bed.

It was true what Pearl said. I could tell that she really didn't give a toss that I was so wealthy. So if she didn't care, why did *I?* I *could* wind down HookedUp. Sell my share to Sophie—go back to being more creative. Sophie was meddling with my life, and without realizing it, destroying my happiness. I'd lay my cards on the table, I decided. Tomorrow.

So the next day, while poor Pearl was suffering from a morning-after-the-night-before hangover from consuming champagne, plus two different vintage wines (each paired with a different course of the meal), I started by explaining to her a little about my past. I told her that Sophie had once been a sex worker, that she was fearful of being poor again, and that she was like a mother to me after we left home when I was seven. I didn't get into the nitty-gritty details about her being a Dominatrix, nor about her eventually running the show and being a *Madame* with her own highly illegal 'house,' hiring other women to work for her. Too much information at once could have scared Pearl off. I tried to explain to Pearl Sophie's motivations but I think it came out wrong. It sounded as if I was defending my sister, putting her before all else.

Putting her before Pearl.

The look on Pearl's face after I'd admitted that Sophie was a sex worker made me snap, "Don't be judgmental, Pearl. Have you any idea how tough it was for Sophie? She was only seventeen when we left home. She was doing her best."

"I guess life has never gotten that....*tough* for me," Pearl replied, choosing her words carefully in an undertone which said, *I would never do something like that—never stoop so low.*

"*You* should understand, Pearl. Your brother, John, got involved with drugs and alcohol—it was his demise. People don't always do the right thing for themselves or others but it's right for them in that particular moment. You can never judge someone else's life or their choices—the path they take, because there are always two sides to every story. Or more. Sometimes there are multiple sides to someone's story."

"I guess you're right," Pearl answered, her eyes welling up.

I hadn't meant to bring her down by mentioning John's death, but I wanted to put us on the same par. I held her hand and we sat there silently for a while, both of us what-if-ing about our individual histories.

I thought of my mother, what she'd done, and my own shady past and wondered if Pearl would stick with me if she knew my whole story. Probably not. She was a wholesome, star-spangled, American girl who, after the initial novelty of great sex wore off, might decide she didn't want some screwed up Frenchman in her life. Was that why I had come inside her—to get her pregnant? So she couldn't get away from me, even if she tried? So that we'd always have a bond even if she left me?

We went for a swim in the sea and I watched Pearl in awe. She dipped and dived, her toes pointed like a dancer, and when she swam, she sliced the water like a sharp blade. Watching her do the crawl made my chest fill with pride, knowing that she was my girlfriend, knowing that this interesting, sexy, independent American woman had chosen me as her mate.

Still, there were undulations of bad feeling about Sophie, rippling between us. I sensed that Pearl had reservations; that there would be only so much she could take. I needed her close to me. Needed to be buried inside her. So after the swim, I took her to our suite. The more hooked on sex she was, I reasoned, the more likely it would be that she would never leave me, despite my crazy family history, despite Sophie's uncontrollable jealousy. Despite my dark side. I'd fuck her senseless. Literally. Make it so she couldn't see straight. Couldn't think straight.

Outside our suite, the cicadas were singing their summer song, thick in the pine trees. From our open balcony, the blue sea glittered beyond, and an aroma of pine and oleander, sweet as cake, wafted into the room, blowing perfume in the air. But the view that caught my attention was Pearl, herself. We Europeans are used to seeing topless women on the beach. So when Pearl took off her bikini and revealed two vanilla breasts, begging to be sucked they looked so tasty, I was instantly hard—instantly aroused by the forbidden, American fruit.

I gazed at my beautiful Pearl lying on the sumptuous bed, as she teased me—trailing ice cubes about those full tits; making the nipples pucker up into stiff buds that I wanted to stroke with my rock-hard cock. Yes, I wanted to fuck those tits.

"You're asking for it again, Pearl Robinson," I said.

She lay there seductively, her lips curved into a knowing smile, her smooth legs splayed open. She slid the ice cube down her stomach, then up and down her slick cleft, slowly inserting it inside herself. She gasped. My dick flexed, as it prepared itself to fuck her, throbbing with desire. I took off my swim-shorts—there was no more room and they were getting uncomfortable. I could feel how big I was—huge. I sauntered up to her, my cock proud against my abdomen, and straddled her on the bed, pinning her beneath me. She had hunger in her eyes; a look of lust that matched mine. I took a sip of champagne, and fed her with the liquid, letting it trickle into her luscious mouth.

I studied her oval face. Her blue eyes shone the same color as the Mediterranean Sea, with glints of turquoise, and faint freckles had appeared about her nose and cheeks. It gave her the air of a teenager. I still couldn't believe that she was forty—she looked so young, so fresh. And, as I appeared several years older than I was, we were an ideal match. We must have looked exactly the same age to anyone seeing us walk about, arm in arm.

The perfect couple in love.

"You're so beautiful, Pearl. So, so exquisitely *beautiful.* Your eyes…"

"*My* eyes? What about yours? They're green, but not really green, at all. They're like tiger's eyes with flecks of gold in them. *You're* the beautiful one, Alexandre. You take my breath away—every time I wake up with you next to me, every time you catch my eye, and when you touch me?"—she whispered in my ear and licked my lobe. I shivered, electricity coursing through my body, making my dick swell even more—"I can hardly—" she continued, with another swipe of her tongue—"function. And when you fuck me?"

Her attention switched from my earlobe to the rest of me.

First, my mouth, which she kissed with fervor, exciting me so much that I couldn't take the ache in my groin anymore. I edged my way up the bed and slipped my throbbing erection between her lips. It was as if I were entering the twilight zone. Having her pouting mouth suck on me was the most erotic thing in the world. She flickered her tongue, moaning as she licked off my pre-cum, and I pushed my hips forward, rocking slightly, languidly, fucking her mouth. Damn, it felt good. I could smell her sweet taste of sex as it lingered in the air with the scent of pine and sea. I needed to lick her all over; explore every crevice, every secret place. So I did.

I started under her arms, then I swirled my tongue about her breasts and aroused nipples. I listened to her groan as I trailed my tongue over her salty, tanned body, down her pretty stomach and then between her legs, fluttering my tongue on her clit, but taking it away again so I knew she'd be begging for more. I sucked her toes, licked her delicate ankles, up her calves, behind her knees and along her thighs…up, up, up to her core, pale against her tan because, like her tits, that part of her had been hidden from the sun. She was writhing on the bed, wet and wanton, her pussy glistening like the little pearl it was. I circled my tongue around her engorged nub and tasted her nectar.

"Please Alexandre. Please fuck me." She bucked her hips into my mouth as I sucked and teased her, and she murmured something about a dream she'd had the night before, featuring a big, black stallion.

"You want to ride me, baby? Is that what you want? Ride me like a stallion?"

Now that I'd made Pearl come in several different ways, it

was time for something a little more experimental. I could have carried on and had her come in my mouth, but she wanted to ride? Sure, why not. Let her ride my cock. The *Reversed Cowboy, hmm…nice.* I put myself beneath her, and maneuvered her so that she slipped her wet warmth onto my pounding erection, her head facing my feet, so my view was of her glorious, round ass.

"Show me what you've got, cowgirl. You call the shots with your pussy pistol." I grinned. I had her exactly where I wanted her, and it felt great. My hands were either side of her little waist as I guided her up and down. Up and down. She was stroking my ankles at the same time—so sensual. Mixed with the image of her behind, I was a happy man, indeed.

"Love that peaches and cream ass, Pearl. Love that. Tight. Wet. Pearlette."

I still hadn't worked out if Pearl was full of it, or not, about her orgasm (or lack of) history. Sometimes, I felt suspicious.

a) because she was bloody good in bed and…

b) because she seemed to come every single time with me.

Every time, except when I practically raped her and fucked her so hard against her kitchen wall—but even then, I got her on Round 2. Here she was again, going crazy for me. Moaning while she fucked me, her hands cupping my balls (where did she learn that?), easing me out of her, and then slapping the tip of my cock about her clit. Driving me fucking crazy. Teasing me. Nobody had ever turned me on so much as Pearl.

"That's right baby," I breathed, "lasso my cock with your tight, tight pussy, you cowgirl."

My hands played with her nipples, rolling them between my fingers as Pearl continued her horny ride, rocking back and forth. I grabbed her ass, and feeling myself about to come, started my *one, one thousand* count. Luckily, I didn't have to keep it up for long, because when I tilted my hips forward, she started moaning. Tiny beads of sweat broke out on the small of her back, and her contractions told me that I could break free and let myself go—hard. Fuck, I was coming like the bloody Niagara Falls; my cum bursting inside her, as she slammed down on me, swallowing me deep.

"Oh Pearl, oh Pearl, you beautiful thing," I murmured as she sank all the way down, grinding herself into me.

"I'm coming Alexandre." *Yeah, babe, I know.* "Oh God, oh...."

She started twiddling her clit with her hand and it brought on another rush from me. And her.

"Fuck, Alexandre, I'm coming again. This has never happened to me. Ever! I thought it was impossible to come twice in a row."

A crooked smile played on my lips. "*Mission Impossible*," I said, and started humming the tune, as my hands roamed around Pearl's small waist and then over the curves of her ass. Was she lying?

Or was I a fucking *god* in bed?

Whatever, I was on fire. I had to keep fucking this woman. I felt like an animal and needed more. Had to get her pregnant. Had to have more, more, more! More of my seed inside her. More of everything. Pearl was my life tonic. My elixir.

Once her orgasm had calmed, I pushed her off me and spun her around so she was on all fours.

"Hold onto the headboard, baby. I have to keep fucking you." I grasped her ass with my hands as I slid into her—she held on, her head leaning against the soft headboard as I consumed her. Not in her ass, no, but entering her from behind. Her. Sweet. Hot. Addictive. Pussy.

She was groaning. I knew I was being unreasonable. Dominating. Bestial. But I couldn't stop.

"Love. Fucking. You. Fucking. This. Sweet….Jesus, Pearl, what is it about you? All I want to do is make you come, come inside you." I kept pumping her. Fucking her relentlessly. I knew she must have been sore as hell but I had to admit, I liked that idea. I wanted her to feel me. Raw. Untamed. A man who at times, would lose control. A man that had to have her. Own her. Take all of her. All *mine*.

But I slowed down. A voice inside my head told me I was acting like a dick. I pulled out slowly and went to 'kiss it better.' Kiss that sweet pearlette that I'd been treating like a hot, juicy cunt. Pearl was too special for me to be losing control like this. I flickered the tip of my tongue around her bruised center and she whimpered with pleasure…but I could taste myself, taste her, taste sex and it got me ravenous again.

The beast was back. I had to come inside her, once more. I entered her again.

She cried out, "Oh God Alexandre, I love this!"

"This ass is…oh fuck…this creamy, peachy, hot ass has got me hooked…your hot, sweet pussy…" Pearl had me beside myself. I cupped both butt cheeks with my hands and carried on with my assault as I drove myself into her. In. And. Out. In. And. Out. She was tight like a glove around me. The sensation was incredible. "This ass belongs to me. *All of it* belongs to me," I heard myself growling. I eased up and stilled myself, knowing I'd gone too far. Knowing I'd pushed poor

Pearl to her limits, my Neanderthal instincts had taken me over.

But what do you know? My rock-hard, throbbing cock, still inside her, had her contracting all over it. She started moaning, her nipples as hard as cherry pips, her golden hair flopped like bands of silk over her shoulders.

She moaned, "Oh God…Alexandre, I'm coming again. This is insane. What are you doing to me?"

I flooded into her. I was coming again, too. Every sweet sensation was in my cock. As if every brain molecule was there. It was ruling me. Ruling her. This was my true queen: Pearl Robinson. I wanted her to reign with me; run my empire by my side.

"Je t'aime, Pearl. Je t'aime," I whispered, my climax surging through me like flashes of white lightening.

She didn't reply.

I just told her I loved her. That was a huge thing for me. But she said nothing.

I wished I knew what she was thinking.

Wished I knew what was going through her mind.

13

I guess I should have known that when things seem too good to be true, they usually are.

Sophie really outdid herself this time. She had made me so furious that I began to have fantasies of having her shipped off to a desert island and dumped there, with no means of communication. I'd have care packages flown in by parachute but she'd have to survive on her own. Because boy, was she being one hell of a Megabitch.

I was happily basking in the sun on the hotel rocks by the sea, having sex flashbacks of Pearl, when I discovered Pearl had done a runner on me. While I was busy being Master of the Universe; taking care of business calls and making more money that I didn't need, Pearl had taken herself to Nice airport, alone, and never wanted anything to do with me again. I listened for the forth time to her phone message on my voicemail (the message had come in when I was otherwise engaged). It was too late to catch up with her. More fool me.

"Alexandre—what can I say? I've left. Obviously. I received a message on my cell from Sophie who seemed to know every intimate detail of my sex life. I'm glad your 'challenge' worked out for you. And for me, too. It was a real eye-opener—an experience of a lifetime. It was beautiful. Beautiful because I believed in it. But now I've found out that it was just a game for you. I know that it could never be the same between us again. You said it yourself: the biggest sex organ is your brain. And my brain is shot to pieces right now. Goodbye, Alexandre. Good luck with Rex—shame that cute dog and I will never meet. Bon voyage."

Never meet? What the fuck had happened?

I called my sister.

"Alright, what have you done this time?" I demanded when she picked up.

"You'll get your share of the rubies and stuff, don't be impatient, Alexandre."

"I'm not talking about the fucking rubies, I'm talking about a rare pearl—more important than any gem. Pearl. What did you say to her?"

"Nothing she doesn't already know."

"You told her stuff about our sex life, didn't you? Stuff I have never, ever discussed with you. Why did you spin her a load of lies, Sophie?" I shouted, my voice on fire.

"Not lies. The truth. She's a stalker. A cougar-stalker almost twice your age. I found things on your iPad, too. You should lock it with a password, you know."

"My iPad is private, for fuck's sake. I had no idea you'd be gatecrashing my house. Plus, I write stuff down in English so people like *you* can't snoop. More fool me, obviously."

"Google Translate is my new best friend, Alexandre. Sorry, but I couldn't resist taking a peek."

My stupid list about Pearl, I remembered. *That's what freaked Pearl out and made it look as if I'd betrayed her confidence.*

I said coldly, "You and I are over, Sophie. From now on, speak to my attorney because I can't deal with you anymore. I'll find a solution to HookedUp. Meanwhile, stay out of my fucking life."

"She's too old for you, Alexandre. What's more, she was trying to stalk you. I was just looking out for you."

"You, yourself, know that Pearl doesn't look her age, Sophie. And Pearl and I have moved forward. She was not *stalking* us, per se. The past is the past and I want that woman *in my life.* As I said, stay out of my affairs. You and I are DONE."

Sophie was silent. I could hear her hitched breaths on the line. "Shit, you're really in love with Pearl Robinson, aren't you?" she said in a shaky voice.

"Yes, I am and I'm choosing her over you, Sophie. So either get with the fucking program, apologize to Pearl, be nice to her for *evermore,* or get the fuck OUT of my life for good, because not only are you making Pearl miserable, you are making *me* miserable, too."

"Okay," she muttered in a quiet voice.

"You mean it?"

"Yes, I do. I'm sorry Alexandre, I didn't know she meant *that* much to you. I don't want my little brother to be unhappy, I really don't. I care for you too much."

"The damage may be too great. She might not even take me back. She's a nice girl, Sophie. A nice, wholesome girl who doesn't need a couple of dysfunctional French nutcases in her life. I'm hanging up now. You'd *so* better make it up to her in the future. That is, if she and I even *have* a future. She might not want me now."

I clicked end and dialed Pearl's number. I suspected her cell would be off, but still, I just wanted to hear her voice. I left three messages in a row, explaining things and I prayed to God, Jesus, even (my *Personal Jesus)*, that I could make things right again, and that Pearl hadn't given up on me for good.

I flew by helicopter to Paris. I *had* planned to do this with Pearl, of course, so she could meet my mother and we could collect Rex and take him back to New York with us. That part of the plan still stood; I needed my dog with me now more than ever, not just for myself and for Rex, but as bait to catch Pearl. Even if she hated me by now, and loathed Sophie's guts, surely she wouldn't be able to resist my loving black Lab? I refused to give up.

I *would* win Pearl back, no matter what.

When I saw my mother, I took a double take. People say that the woman you end up choosing will resemble your mom, and I laughed to myself. I *could* see Pearl in her. Tall, elegant, poised. Beautifully dressed. Blonde hair and large blue eyes—her complexion flawless. What lay beneath her cool exterior, though, nobody would have guessed. I had still kept her dark, dark secret; hadn't told a soul, not even Sophie.

Maman was reading a book in the living room, a romance, no doubt—she was hooked on them. She loved the dominant alpha male, the type that rode up on horseback and swept a lady off her feet and galloped off with her into the sunset, the lady protesting but secretly delighted that the hero wouldn't take no for an answer. I slipped in quietly and observed her lying back on the sofa, shoes off, her feet up, and I wished that her real hero, my father, hadn't turned out to be such a demon. Wished that she could have been stronger, more resilient, because what happened in the end—the finale—could have been a scene right out of a horror story. She was smiling as she read, and as I stepped closer, I realized that it wasn't a book she was holding in her hands, but an e-reader.

"You're very modern, I didn't think e-readers had caught on yet in France," I remarked.

She jumped up and hid the thing behind her back. She looked mortified, her cheeks flushing a deep pink. "Alexandre. Darling! How wonderful to see you."

I came up to her and kissed her on both cheeks. "Did I interrupt something, Maman?"

She quickly switched off the contraption and composed herself. "No, of course not. Just a non-fiction, non-descript book, you know. Quite dull, actually."

Yeah, right.

She smoothed her hands over her skirt. "Where's your friend? The girl you said you were bringing to meet us?"

"She had an important meeting in New York, sadly. Had to get back early."

"Oh. How disappointing. This is the first time you've asked a woman to come here to meet us so I was all excited. I figured it must be someone very special to you. I've got all sorts of delicious treats for dinner."

"Yes. Yeah, she is special to me. Look, Maman, I'm so sorry but I can't stay long. I *also* need to get back to New York. I just came by to say hi and pick up Rex. I'm sorry you went to so much trouble for dinner, I feel terrible. But we have a jet waiting for us; I'll need to get going any minute."

"A jet? A *private* jet?"

"Yes, I didn't want Rex to travel in the hold."

"I know you're doing very well, Alexandre, but a private jet for an *animal?*"

"Sure, why not? Speak of the little devil!" Rex came bounding in from his walk with my stepfather who stood in the doorway awkwardly holding his leash. Ever since I had started making so much money, my stepfather felt redundant. *As if a man's merit is measured by his wallet.* But I guess that's how he felt. I stroked Rex's soft black ears and kissed him on the nose. "Thanks for looking after him so well."

Silence was thick in the air, save the tick-tock of a grandfather clock in the hallway. The house was replete with antiques and Persian rugs which gave the atmosphere an even more somber air. More reminders, I supposed, that I had furnished this house with these luxuries. You can't buy love. Only fear, respect, and resentment. My stepfather smiled at me uneasily and came over to shake my hand, and patted me on the back.

"Still in flip-flops and jeans even when you can afford the best shoes and suits that money can buy," he quipped, eyeing my feet disdainfully. It was only a matter of time before he suggested I get a haircut.

He was a tidy, attractive man but he lacked charm and charisma, something my father had oozing from every pore. That was when he wasn't carrying his dark passenger about with him—the character who took him over at any unexpected second. If only my stepfather knew my mother's secret. *If only he knew.* He'd probably pick up the phone and call the police, I suspected. No wonder she stashed her erotic romance behind her back when I walked through the door. He would have been shocked. He saw her as perfect. The man had no idea whom he was married to. Not *a damn clue.*

Still, he wasn't beating her up, so in my mind, he was worth his weight in platinum.

"Look, I feel so rude to do this to you, but the jet, even though it's private still gets a slot, you know, a take off time. Rex and I really need to get going. Come and visit me in New York. Any time. There are some great Broadway shows, fabulous restaurants—"

My stepfather cut me short with a chuckle. "We have the best food in the world in Paris, why would we be tempted by foreign cuisine?"

"Whatever," I answered. "But you know what? You'd be surprised what you discover when you scratch beneath the surface. When you dig deep, you never know what you may find."

My mother gave me a look that was more potent than a poison dart. "Bye darling, she said. "You'll need to *leave* now so you don't miss your private jet. Bye, Rex, baby," she said, cupping Rex's head and giving him a kiss—and she added with dry sarcasm, "Do send us a postcard from New York, sweet doggie, and let us know how you're getting on with the American cuisine."

I winked at her and smiled. My stepfather eyed up my mother—her seamless perfection—my comments flew right over his head.

Good. I wanted it to stay that way.

On the flight back to New York, I nodded off. Perhaps it was the hum of the plane—whatever, something reminded me…

I'm entangled in this web of ferocious filth. Fifteen years old and seeing stuff that no person could ever imagine in the span of a whole lifetime. I'm a cog in this wheel of destruction that I brought upon myself. Round and round—there's no end. The woman is pleading with me, "If the president says no to the peace deal and the French leave, the Rebels will kill us all. The French can't leave. We owe you our lives."

She's on her knees now, trembling, her hands clutching the material of my combat pants.

I look down at her, a specter of a woman, her hair matted with dirt, dried blood on her makeshift dress, as mosquitoes buzz around us in the hazy, dusty heat. She has been witness to horror. Her uncle was chopped up into tiny pieces in front of her, her younger sister decapitated, but she's grateful to be alive after ten rebels raped her consecutively at gunpoint. I hold her hand. What else can I do? What can I tell her? I can't assure her that everything will be okay, because it won't. These little villages are swollen with pain, each on the frontline of terror and war. A country broken and maimed. No matter how many rebels I kill, they double in droves. Like angry, maddened wasps. Fearless. Relentless. Some of them even younger than I am. Just children. Children! Young boys wielding machetes and rifles almost half their bodyweight. It's them or me. It's kill or be killed.

But still, some of these 'Rebels' are children.

"I'm sorry," I say to the woman. Behind her I see the smoke and

ashes of what was her house, burned to the ground. Yet she is still grateful. Grateful to be alive.

A man who must be in his late twenties, his eyes hollow graves, tells me, "My youngest cries herself to sleep every night. They took my wife from us, dragged her into the street and shot her. Like a wild animal, they shot her in the head. My daughter sees images of blood before she goes to bed at night. Please help us. You have to stop the Rebels. Please don't abandon us."

I jerked up in my seat, sweat dripping on my back and brow. The memories had snuck up, unexpected. The shadows of war. The horror that had been buried in some dark corridor of my mind had been unleashed once more, letting in the demons which were keen to knock at my brain's back door.

The words tumbled out of my mouth as I rolled them on my tongue, "The Ivory Coast," I mumbled to myself. It sounded so romantic—just the name conjured up a tableau of elephants, yawning sandy beaches, and thick forests. But for me it was one long nightmare, not the glamorous dream I had conjured up. Joining the French Foreign Legion had been a wild impulse. I lied about my age. I was just a lad of fifteen bursting to explore the world. An idealist. How are boys meant to know that fantasies will crumble to dust right before their very eyes?

I got up, ambled rockily to the airplane toilet and splashed my face and the back of my neck with cold water, trying to shake the cruel pictures from my mind, imbedded there like crimson etchings. I replaced the graphics of blood and gore with fields of lavender, the undulating waves of the Mediterranean—anything to let a sliver of peace ease its way into my assaulted brain. I splashed more water into my eyes, on my chest, my stomach, in the hope that it would help wash away the ghosts intent on sneaking into my soul. Because when you've been in war, your soul is seeped in black, however hard you may pretend it isn't. It's your secret. A secret you don't share with your loved ones because the pain, the dark knowledge of the truth, would be too great for them to bear. You have to convince yourself you did the right thing. You can even believe it. But your soul will never lie to you.

The adoration shimmering in Rex's eyes was tonic to my battered psyche. Dogs are great forgivers. Dogs don't care who you are, what you've done, if you haven't had a shower (the stinkier the better, right?), or how much money you have. As long as they get fed and watered, walked and loved, they'll stick by you. Rex was traveling in style but he was oblivious. He was about to live in one of New York's swankiest districts with a private roof terrace which boasted a lawn and trees and a view to Central Park. I had even hired a dog walker-nanny for him, Sally, who'd need to stay over sometimes if I was away on business. I didn't want Rex to be alone. Spoiled much? You bet.

Rex…my buddy. The one who could forgive all. Because as far as he was concerned, there was nothing to forgive in the first place.

He was excited by his new home, rushing and sniffing about, exploring the three floors of my apartment as if there was buried treasure somewhere. The staff had even bought him treats and toys. I guess they knew their way into my heart was through my dog.

Everything was almost perfect. I was setting myself up with the ideal family situation. Beautiful home, people to help me run it, money galore, dog….but the most important ingredient of all was missing: Pearl.

She hadn't responded to a single one of my messages. Text, voice messages, emails. Zilch. She had obviously had enough. I'd have to work really hard to win her back. But I was confident I had a good chance. *Feelings like that don't count for nothing.* With all the women I'd been with, it *felt* to me as if Pearl was genuinely in love with me, more than any of them. But who knew? She hadn't said the words, even though I had laid my heart out to her.

It was nine a.m., New York time. I was sitting by my desk at home, listening to *Miss You* by The Rolling Stones, trying to do something other than obsess about Pearl. She'd be at work by now, I imagined. Rex and I had arrived at my apartment at 3 a.m. I didn't feel tired, so we walked around Central Park. I practiced some Taekwondo moves—I needed to keep my black-belt polished, so to speak.

I still like to do that sort of thing—toy with dangerous situations, walk about in dodgy places at night under the cover of darkness. Places where muggers and drug addicts could be hanging out. Keep myself alert. Sharp. When you've been in war zones the way I have, you've got eyes in the back of your head. Forever. The fear, like an author's sharpened pencil on a page poised to write, needing to write, never abandons you. You don't want it to because it's what you trust, what you rely on, even though it once nearly broke you. Fear is your friend. I'm a man who obviously needs adrenaline. Rock climbing. Surfing. Sex. Taekwondo. Hanging out in Central Park at 4 a.m. These things keep me alive. Keep me sharp as that pencil.

Besides, I had a Pit-Bull cross by my side; Rex's secret. He could pin a person down at a moment's notice if I gave the signal. His gentle Labrador side had people fooled.

I must have checked my cell twenty times. Nothing. Pearl. Pearl. Pearl. Her name rang in my head so many times, that by the end of the morning, the word 'pearl' sounded surreal, as if *my* Pearl was disconnected somehow, as if our relationship had been just a dream.

I wondered what direction I should take to win her back. Then again, she deserved better—*maybe I should just leave her in peace.* My mind was in turmoil, vacillating between the two extremes. I wanted her back. But if I pursued her, I didn't want to just show up at her work or apartment. I'd played that card.

I was going crazy. Lack of sleep…the memories swirling about my brain…my dark past telling me to let her go—to allow her get on with her life without me. But my burning heart and the hole in my gut couldn't bear to even entertain that thought. I needed to convince her to stay with me; not run away anymore. I didn't want to hound her but I did want, at the very least, to know how she was doing. I'd need to talk to her and explain, but right at that moment, I knew she was sick of the sight of me. Sick of Sophie. Pearl would need time to simmer down. I needed to keep the bulldozer at bay.

At least for a while.

First, I needed to sort out the tangled web of madness that Sophie had spun us into. No, I wouldn't turn up at Pearl's work. I'd write her a letter and have it hand-delivered to her apartment, with the pearl necklace that she'd left behind.

I found the choker in my bedroom, tore off my T-shirt which I wrapped around it. Only afterwards did I realize that the T-shirt was two days old and must have stunk of my sweat, but I didn't have time to do everything with decorum. Rex watched my every move, following me around my apartment, as if to make sure I did the right thing. I strode into my office, grabbed a piece of paper from my desk and hastily wrote a note:

Darling, precious Pearl,

You are my pearl, you are my treasure. Don't deny me this. Don't deny me the love I have for you.
When you left my heart broke in two. The Spanish describe their soul-mate as 'media naranja'–the other half of the same orange. And that is what you are to me, the other half of me, the perfect half that matches me. I have never felt this way before about anybody. Ever.
You think I betrayed your trust. No, I would never do that. Sophie snooped at my iPad and saw my personal notes. They were written in English so I never imagined she would bother to translate them. Call me a jerk, call me a nerd for making notes concerning you. But here they are. (I have copied and pasted this). This is what she saw:

I printed out the nerd-notes I had on my iPad (how shameful, how embarrassing!) and attached it to the hand-written part. It was the only solution. *Better for her to think me a geek who wrote everything down than a liar:*

Problems to be solved concerning Pearl:
Needs to reach orgasm during penetrative sex. (My big challenge).
Needs confidence boosted – age complex due to American youth worship culture.
Need to get her pregnant ASAP due to clock factor. (Want to start a family with her.)

I scribbled on:

I feel embarrassed showing this to you but it is the only way I know how to explain myself. I write lists and notes – I write them for everything – you know that.
When I first set eyes on you in that coffee shop, I was smitten, instantly. I remarked to Sophie how beautiful you were. Sophie commented on how easy American girls are, how they jump into bed with anybody at the drop of a hat. I told her, that in your case, I thought I stood very little chance – that you looked sophisticated and classy. (Given that I had never been with an American woman, I had no idea if what she said was true). It was disrespectful of me to discuss this in French with her while you were standing right there before us when we were all waiting in line. I apologize.
But that was then.
This is now.
Now I have found my Pearl I do not want to let her go.
I will fight for you. I want you in my life.

I have made a decision. I am giving over HookedUp to Sophie. I will still keep shares but will no longer be involved in the daily decisions of running it. I'd like to start up a new enterprise – a film production company and I will be looking for someone to run it (production skills mandatory). I wondered if you would consider yourself for the job?
Here is the necklace. It belongs to you, and only you.
A squadron of kisses,

Your Alexandre

P.S Rex has arrived and wants to meet you.

P.P.S For the present time my family members will no longer be staying at my apartment when they visit New York.

I decided I'd deliver this to Pearl's apartment myself. I called Sophie. I knew she'd still be having her 'power nap', six hours ahead, Paris time, but I didn't care; she owed me one.

She picked up but didn't even speak, just shuffled about, breathing into the receiver.

"It's me," I said curtly.

"What is it? Is Elodie okay?" she asked in a weary voice.

"Fine. Just fine. Listen. I know you did all that super-sleuthing about Pearl so I'm assuming you know everything there is to know about her."

Sophie groaned. "I told you I'd get off her case and I will, Alexandre. I've even been thinking of ways to make it up to her. Just to keep you happy."

"I appreciate that. Sophie, I need her best friend Daisy's phone number or contact address. The redheaded British girl who lives in New York. Do you have it?"

"Somewhere, I guess," she replied in a bored drawl.

"I need it now."

"Can't you find it yourself?" she said with a long noisy yawn.

"Yes, I *could* but I thought you were trying to make things right, Sophie."

"Okay, okay, I'll call you right back, I'll need to locate it."

I went into the kitchen, opened the fridge, which suddenly struck me as being absurdly large, especially for a bachelor, as I now hopelessly was. Would I be living alone forever with this massive thing, stuffed with enough food to feed several families? With no family of my own to feed? It didn't matter how much money I had. It didn't—as Hélène pointed out—matter how big my dick was, if I didn't have the right person to share it with, to create a family with.

I brought out a bowl from the fridge and Rex wagged his tail, expecting a treat. Would it be just Rex and me, then, if Pearl decided she's had enough? Two, tough, single males, roaming Central Park at night, daring anyone to fuck with us? I dug my hand into the bowl of blueberries and stuffed a handful into my mouth. Rex seemed to be interested in the blueberries, too, so I threw him a couple which he caught mid-air. My cell buzzed. It was Sophie, with Daisy's home phone and cellphone numbers. Even her address. Christ, my sister was such a stalker. I was glad to have her on my side and not as my archenemy.

I called Daisy, my heart inexplicably racing.

"Hello?" she said guardedly.

"I'm sorry to disturb you, to call so early—"

"Look, please, I'm not interested in buying your product, please don't call this number any—"

"It's Alexandre Chevalier," I interrupted.

"Oh." There was a weighty silence and then, "How on earth did you get this number, is Pearl okay? I just had breakfast with her, I—"

"You just had breakfast with her?" I said with hope.

"Excuse me, Alexandre, I'm not sure why you're calling me."

"Can we meet up?" I asked, and then instantly regretted my question. She must have thought I was hitting on her. Great. That's all I bloody needed.

"No, we can't meet up. I'm busy. If you want to see Pearl, she'll be at work by now. Call her."

"Look Daisy, that's why I'm calling *you*. I'm sorry to impose but I need to talk about Pearl. I just want to know if she's alright. She won't answer my calls, my emails, my texts."

"Good girl," I heard her whisper under her breath. Was she talking to her daughter or referring to Pearl?

"And I don't feel inclined to barge my way into her office when I know she's busy and too furious to see me right now," I added. Not only was that true but I wasn't feeling my greatest, with the surge of Foreign Legion memories battering me, bashing my self-worth to a pulp, my *raison d'être*. Right now, I felt Pearl deserved better than me, but still, I couldn't let her go.

"Look, Alexandre, I'm not Pearl's keeper. I can't help you. You really shouldn't be calling me in the first place."

"I know. I'm sorry, but I just want to know if she's okay. We had an argument. About my sister. I won't go into it but I assume Pearl—you two being best friends—has already told you everything."

There was a measured beat of silence and Daisy said languidly, "No, I don't think she even mentioned you, Alexandre. I mean, in *passing*, yes. Said she just got back from France but…you know, Pearl is a very busy, *in demand* woman. She doesn't have time for any nonsense."

I paced up and down the kitchen, blood roaring in my ears. Pearl hadn't even mentioned me to her *best friend?* Or only did so *in passing?* So…she really didn't give a fuck, after all. She would just get over me in a flash. *Shit!*

Daisy went on coolly, "Look, Alexandre, Pearl is the kind of woman who has men queuing up to date her. Literally. Men go crazy for her. Extremely wealthy. Important. Interesting. Men. It won't be long before someone snaps her up. I mean, men propose marriage to her all the time."

Marriage proposals? Yes, well that would make sense. She was forty. Wanted a family. She wasn't going to hang around and watch opportunities pass her by.

Daisy carried on, "She's beautiful. Clever. She's a catch. She's extremely busy with work, too. You know, she has a project about child traffickers, and another one concerning arms dealers—both in the pipeline. Important, life-changing stuff that the world needs to know about. She doesn't have *time* for silly games, or people who dick her around."

Those two words—*arms dealers*—sent a bolt of fury through my gut. That fuck Mikhail Prokovich would be moving in on Pearl any moment.

Daisy talked on, "If you want to catch a woman like Pearl Robinson, Alexandre, you'd better pull your socks up. I know it's summer and you probably aren't even wearing any socks—" she snickered at her joke.

She was right…I looked down at my flip-flops. My bare chest. Apart from taking off my T-shirt, I still hadn't changed out of last night's clothes. I had a five o'clock shadow, dog hair all over me, and apart from brushing my teeth that morning, I felt pretty grungy. I probably looked like a backpacker about to set off for a round-the-world trip. I imagined Pearl at her office; elegant, suited-up, heels. Legs smooth and golden. Cool and relaxed, talking on the phone to clients or in the editing room. A mover. A shaker. And me? I had lost the plot. So much so, I was calling her best friend for clues. This whole situation was ridiculous.

"I'm so sorry Daisy. I haven't slept all night. I don't know what got into me to call you. I just wanted some news of Pearl and didn't want to bombard her with my presence, you know. I've kind of been there, done that—don't want overkill, you know. I just wanted news of her, I guess. I couldn't bear the silence. Please don't tell her I called you, though."

"Alright, I won't. But think about it, Alexandre. Think about it carefully. Either fuck off and leave her alone, or do something big. You know what I'm saying? If you want Pearl you'd better step up to the *big* league and do something to really impress her. I mean, *really* impress her. We'll keep this conversation between ourselves. At least for the moment. I'm sure if you get your shit together I'll hear about it from her."

Tough cookie! "Thanks, Daisy," I said, making a mental note of never crossing this fiery redhead. "Good to get your take on it. See you around." I hung up.

I stuffed another handful of blueberries into my mouth, mulling everything over thoughtfully in my mind. Rex stared up at me, his head cocked to one side, as if to say, *Well, what are you waiting for?*

"You're right, Rex," I said, patting him on the head. "I'll impress Pearl, alright. This is it. *Make or break.*"

She had teased me, calling me Michael Corleone. I wouldn't let her down:

I'd make her an offer she couldn't refuse.

14

On my way over to Pearl's apartment to deliver the necklace, I decided to call Sophie. I knew she had an important meeting that she didn't want interrupted. Too bad. Even if busy, I knew she'd pick up her cell. Sophie was one of those people who was bitten by curiosity—couldn't bear to leave a question unanswered. So even a ringing phone was too much to pass up. And she never left her cell on voicemail in case she missed out on some elusive deal. She had a team working around the clock for her: investors, hedge fund managers, people on her payroll with their noses to the ground, sniffing like pigs for truffles. Not only that, but any country could be calling her at any hour, any second. A president. A mogul. A Russian oligarch. A billionaire Indian. Even The Queen of bloody England. Yes, believe it or not, there were people out there with even more money than us, and Sophie wanted a piece of each and every juicy pie.

Just as I had announced in my letter to Pearl, I decided that

I was getting out of HookedUp. That I couldn't take the antics of my sister anymore. *I'll call her. Put her to the test.* I knew what the result would be, but I just wanted to hear the words come out of her mouth. I stopped by a deli and bought some fruit. I dialed my sister's number.

"Sophie, I need that big diamond," I demanded, when she picked up on the second ring.

"Oh it's you again," she groaned. Are you eating something?"

"An apple."

"I hate the way you can only get three or four kinds of apples these days. You know, there used to be over ten thousand varieties of apples in England, alone. Now all we have are—"

"I need the diamond now. Today," I told her with my mouth full.

She hissed into the receiver in a whisper, "Are you fucking nuts? a) the diamond's the most expensive stone out of the lot of them—we already have a buyer at seven million and b.) it's in Amsterdam with the jewelers—excuse me gentlemen, I just need two minutes to end this call—" I heard my sister's clipped footsteps and a door banging closed. She continued, "What the fuck are you doing interrupting this meeting? You know how long I've waited for this."

"I knew I shouldn't have let you do all the organizing of the gems yourself. Get that fucking diamond on a plane now! I need it for Pearl's engagement ring." I wanted to hear my sister's reaction just to test her, and I couldn't have been more spot-on.

She cackled with laughter like one of Shakespeare's Macbeth witches. "N-O," she spelled out. "No. You're *marrying* her? Oh my God, she's really got you by the balls this one, hasn't she?"

"That's all I wanted to hear. Confirmation of how impossible you are. How little you care when it comes to my wellbeing. I'm finished with HookedUp, Sophie. I'm going to start up a new venture. You can buy me out little by little—I won't squeeze you for all the money at once. Have fun in your meeting with that scheming son-of-a-bitch, Mikhail Prokovich."

"How the hell do you know he's part of this meeting?"

"Because I'm aware of how your mind works, Sophie, like billions of dollar bills wrapped about each brain cell. I've also heard from a source of mine that he's suddenly become interested in doing deals with HookedUp. Maybe he fancies you, who knows? But he seems to be all over everyone like a rash, right now." I bit an angry chunk out of my apple. "Doing business with that shifty bastard? No thanks. Another reason I'm out." I hung up.

I didn't want *that* diamond for Pearl. No. I had a better idea—something even more special. A one-off. A piece of history. Something that belonged to a princess. My museum contact who'd secured me the ancient silver stater (my 550BC coin from Greece that brought me luck), had told me about the most stunning diamond of all: something that was worth far more than seven million dollars.

That would be my engagement gift.

But first, I needed to make sure that I gained entry into Pearl's apartment. I couldn't do a re-run of last time when I dashed up the back stairs; the doorman would be onto that trick. Pearl still hadn't returned my calls or messages. The chances of her even letting me up when she was obviously still pissed at me, were slim. It seemed a lifetime ago that we'd been swimming in the sea in Cap d'Antibes, but less than twenty-four hours had passed. She was playing it cool. Maybe she'd stay that way. She might even feel inclined to send the necklace back, the box unopened. All my plans of asking for her hand, like some knight in shining armor on a quest, could be smashed if I didn't get to see her face to face.

I had to come up with something good.

Something really good.

Several hours later, I clanked my way up the fire escape of Pearl's building on the Upper East Side, carabiners jangling off my belt. Before climbing up, I had told the young doorman that someone had called 911 about smoke in the building, and he believed me.

I was clad in all the right firefighter gear but had abandoned the jacket somewhere further down below because it was still very hot from the late summer sun—I was sweating—beads of moisture trickling down my chest and abs. I felt bad for firefighters; they had to wear this stuff to work, yet not so bad that I didn't know the magic it spun. Women have always gone wild for them. I was hoping that Pearl would be no different. Perhaps, I thought, she'd just laugh at me—I looked like a cliché, Playgirl centerfold. At least I'd get her attention.

"Excuse me, ma'am, I said, peering through the kitchen window after I'd made my way up to the eleventh floor, "I heard there was a fire in this apartment." *True. The fire of Pearl's wrath.*

Pearl stared at me, her mouth dropped to the floor, but then her expression changed. She wasn't angry, nor did she laugh at me. A naughty smirk, yes, and a suppressed giggle at my outrageous outfit, but the second I laid eyes on her through the glass that separated us, I knew I was forgiven.

I pulled up the sash window and gatecrashed my way inside, surprised that the burglar alarm hadn't gone off by now; my big black boots stomping on the tile floor as she appraised my sweaty body, her melting blue eyes taking me in with approval.

"You nearly had me fooled but your accent gave you away," she said with a grin, no doubt brought on by the incongruity of the scenario: a faux French firefighter.

I wanted to ravage her she looked so beautiful: her golden arms hung cool by her side, her blonde hair loose about her shoulders, her scent of flowers and magic which always had me intoxicated. But I felt so much more than just pounding physical attraction for her. My heart was bursting through my sun-warmed chest: I was going to ask this woman to marry me. I yearned to start a family with her. All this, I was going to spell out to her.

When the moment was right.

I longed for her whole; her heart, her soul, her body, and every tiny emotion that came along with that trinity.

The good, the bad, the happy. And even the miserable. Because I knew there'd always be tough days up ahead. I'd be there for her. I wanted to wake up next to her every morning, smell her scent, hear her smooth voice. I'd even settle for a grumpy voice, as long as she was there beside me.

I was brimming over with love for Pearl Robinson. And I knew that if I carried on without her, I would only be half the man I was capable of being. Rich, powerful, successful; all those things men strive for in this world are nothing without the right mate—just sand in an egg timer that will come to an abrupt stop if you can't turn your life around.

We kissed, our mouths as one. I licked her all over, devouring her taste, her nectar, her essence, then carried her over my shoulder where I deposited her on her four-poster bed. I had to lie with her, make love to her—feel her every muscle, soak up her every cell. The firefighter garb seemed absurd by this point. It had helped me achieve my goal—to catch her attention. Get me into her apartment.

I jested with her, teased her with 'spanking' (an excuse to slap my cock against her glorious behind). I nipped her, pretending, with a sulky, downcast face, that she needed to be punished for running away from me, abandoning me. An old trick to re-balance the equilibrium of the relationship. I could feel myself falling and I needed to pick myself up.

"Get this garb off me," I said in a solemn voice. "I feel claustrophobic. I need to lie with you, Pearl. We've played enough silly games, it's time to get serious."

She was the student and I was the teacher—at least that is what I was striving for. Hoping to have some kind of command over her so she wouldn't run from me again. But in my soul, I knew that Pearl was her own person. She would never truly be mine. How can you own a free spirit like Pearl?

She put on some music which answered my question. *Je T'aime, Moi Non Plus*—I love you….Me Neither. *The 'me, neither'* said it all. Yes, she loved me, but I knew she wouldn't take any crap from me. I had a vision of her by the sea in France, looking over her smooth tanned shoulder, which she shrugged as if to say, *Catch me if you can*, and with a toss of her blonde mane, she dove into the water like a mermaid from the rock where she was perched.

Here I was, coming to catch her, but a presentiment, deep down inside told me, that in the end, Pearl would never be completely mine.

But I soldiered on, determined. I stroked her soft, golden hair and laid all my cards on the table, face up, "You're unique, Pearl, I've fallen in love with you." There—she had my vulnerability, my weakness laid out before her like a crudely woven carpet for her to walk all over if she wished, each thread visible, each weave part of my soul.

She smiled serenely and took in a long breath, but didn't answer me. She still hadn't told me she loved me yet. I did what came naturally when I felt insecure: my cock flexed at the softness of her velvet skin, her erotic scent, and I entered her, stretching into her wet, welcoming warmth. My power, my security: my big cock that had never let me down. It was the only tool I had that I knew how to use with precision. Everything else was new to me. I was ill equipped in the art of love. I hadn't known *true,* burgeoning love before—how it can burst your chest open and bring tears to your eyes. How it can sneak up on you and take hold of your gut and twist it into a pit of fear and loneliness when you think it has escaped you. Those twenty-four hours without Pearl had me as vacuous as a shooting star on impact—reduced to a particle of pale dust.

I controlled her sexually but in every other respect she held all the cards in her realm. She was the Queen of Hearts, the

Queen of Cups. All I could do was fill her in the way I knew how. I pushed myself into her until I felt her tightness cling to me, my security returning like a welcome friend.

I punctuated each word with a thrust, "Will. You. Marry. Me. Pearl. Robinson?"

As usual, she deflected the love question. I hadn't meant to ask for her hand in marriage this way. It was cheating. Using my sexual prowess to reach my goal. My insecurity had me thrusting harder inside her, grinding my hips slowly; making small figures of eight. The number eighty-eight. Infinity. A number that would keep going infinitum and would last forever, unbroken. I could feel myself expand as her walls gripped about my throbbing cock—she was on the brink. I sucked her hard nipples which I knew would push her over the edge, and then slammed my mouth on hers, my tongue ravishing her as I fucked her slowly, pulling out so my crown massaged her sweet clit, and then pushing back inside again, rolling back into the figure of eight, my hands like a vice about her smooth shoulders. She started screaming, writhing about beneath me. I had her, yet I *didn't* have her, and it was killing me.

So I asked her again, "Will you marry me, Pearl?"

She was coming hard, her orgasm so intense that I felt her unraveling beneath me, her fingers knotted in my hair, her tongue lashing on mine with so much carnal desire that she couldn't even speak—she just moaned. She bucked her hips at me, her skin misted with sweat, and hooked her legs about my calves as she dug her nails into my ass. Christ, she was like a tigress with her prey. Her climax was consuming her so intensely that her mind was blank.

I silently begged for an answer. I needed to know that she wanted me in other ways, too; spiritually, mentally. My cock was a fucking double-edged sword. But her folds, so snug around every stiff inch of me, clenching me like a fist, pushed me over the precipice. I let myself go, the rush of climax spurting hard inside her as her extended orgasm kept rippling through her beautiful body, uniting us in one detonating, fire-cracking explosion. She quivered and trembled under me as I groaned with deep, carnal satisfaction.

Only to be replaced with a flutter of insecurity, seconds later. *Say yes, God damn it, say the word,* I willed her silently.

"Oh yeah, oh yeah, baby," she whimpered, "this is….oh my God…oh…YES!"

That wasn't a 'yes' in my book! Then again, asking a woman to marry you while you're fucking her was hardly playing it by the rules. "What are you saying yes to, Pearl?" I breathed into her mouth as her orgasm wavered through her quiet moans, her body still writhing, her kisses still wet on my tongue.

But she still wouldn't reply coherently, only languid, brain-numbed moans escaped her lips.

I decided I'd ask her properly the following night. I'd just have time to buy the piece of jewelry that had been put aside for me: a vintage pendant that belonged to a white Russian princess. I'd have it adapted into a ring, especially for Pearl. Big bucks shout. If I paid the jeweler silly money, maybe he could have it done in time. I'd set up a dinner à deux at the top of the Empire State: king of all skyscrapers worldwide, at least in my opinion. I knew the owners and I was sure they'd do me that favor.

And if that didn't bloody well give me a bona fide 'Yes,'

then I'd be lost like a wayward ship on a stormy ocean about to go down.

I *had* to have Pearl.

For my own sanity.

15

Pearl was so busy at work that it took me three days to pin her down for our rendezvous. She was free for dinners but I needed to know that she could take a day off, too—I wanted her to be reeling, delirious, drunk on love for me.

I was nervous about popping the question—as my old friend Shakespeare so rightly put it: *There's many a slip twixt cup and lip.* Those three days crawled by, my heart jumpy, my solar plexus churning with anticipation.

Edgy as I was, it gave the jeweler time to do a beautiful job on the ring. It shimmered brightly, its myriad hues and unusual oval cut made it glitter, even in the dark, and it was so huge that it almost looked vulgar. *Eat your heart out Elizabeth Taylor*—this was a rock to be reckoned with.

Although they will tell you that it is 'impossible to accommodate requests to close down the Observatory at the Empire State for proposals,' when you pay the right person the right price, anything is possible. Pearl and I had the rooftop to ourselves.

It was perfect. The sirens and sounds of the city were muted by distance, the buildings, in a panoramic sweep below were almost like glittering pieces of Lego. The cars were just toys, smaller than my thumbnail, and the lights of Manhattan, Queens, Brooklyn, and New Jersey twinkled as far as the eye could see. The breeze was cool because we were so high up, but not chilly; the summer evening caressed our skin amidst a cloudless night, the stars blinking with swathes of the Milky Way dusted above the skyline like a pastel painting. The Empire State's saxophone player was there, playing haunting jazz tunes that set the mood.

Pearl was wearing a long, flowing gown in silk chiffon. Pale pink. I was wearing a Nehru jacket and suit that I'd had tailored in India. I kept dinner simple; I didn't want it to distract from the evening; champagne throughout—Dom Pérignon1953 with fresh strawberries and a selection of endless hors d'oeuvres (prepared by a French chef I'd hired), that kept arriving at our table—treats to nibble on while we gazed at each other, or walked about admiring the glorious view. Pearl looked exquisite. I hadn't seen her in a long gown before. I was glad that I was giving her a diamond that belonged to a princess because she looked every bit the part. We wandered about the observatory, peering down to the nuggets of light below, glittering, shimmering—the way Pearl glittered and shimmered.

A whoosh of breeze blew Pearl's thick blonde hair, making it billow behind her like swathes of gold, and in that moment I took her hand and got down on one knee. Her lips quivered into a knowing smile.

"My knight," she said. "The name Chevalier does you justice."

Still on one knee, I kissed her hand and said, "Pearl Robinson, will you do me the honor of being my damsel, of sharing the Chevalier name, of being my wife?"

Tears sprang to her eyes and she didn't answer. *Was she about to reject me?* I asked again, third time lucky, "Pearl, will you marry me?"

"I thought you'd forgotten, gone back on your word," she whispered, choking back tears.

I stood up and laid my arms about her shaking shoulders. *Note, she still hadn't bloody well answered my question!* "What do you mean?" I said bewildered.

"You asked me to marry you when we were making love and I said 'Yes,' and then you didn't mention it again. I thought you'd changed your mind."

I laughed. "Oh, Pearl, what am I going to do with you?" And then I put it to her once more, "Pearl Robinson, "Will you marry me, goddamn it?"

She squeezed me close and I smelled the sweetness of her hair, her breath. She leaned back and I kissed her in the hollow of her neck, on her lips, and on the tears that were flowing down her cheeks. "Of course I will, you fool," she told me with a little laugh, "I've wanted to marry you forever."

"I'm afraid I don't have a ring," I said. "Things are a little tight with HookedUp, right now. Do you mind waiting?"

She wrinkled her nose and gazed at me, love dancing in her blue eyes, "I'd be happy with a ring made of tin as long as the world knew that I belonged to you. And as for HookedUp going through a rough patch? I make enough money for us both to live on. We won't starve, don't worry."

You see, that's why I wanted to marry this girl. She didn't care about money. She was genuine and true. She did not show even a flicker of disappointment about not being given a ring.

I led her back to our table and poured us both some more champagne. I looked over to the saxophone player and gave him a quiet nod. He began to play *Manhattan Serenade,* and then the waiter brought out a tall, tiered cake, covered in fresh white lilies.

"Cake?" Pearl exclaimed. "And such a grand one? This beautiful evening has me speechless."

"It's not just any cake," I said with a wink. "Here, I'll cut you a slice."

"Really, I'm sure it's delicious but I don't think I can eat anything more," she said, patting her stomach. "Can we do a doggie bag?" she half joked.

"What? And let Rex get his chops all over this masterpiece? Just a small slice," I insisted, cutting a large chunk.

"Really, I couldn't, I'm so full...what on earth is that inside...it looks like...Alexandre, what the...?"

I pulled out a small red box from inside her slice of cake, licking the icing from my fingers and wiping the box with a napkin. "Open it," I said. "Go on, it won't bite."

Pearl gingerly took the box and bit her bottom lip in concentration, bracing herself—maybe for a ring made of tin. She looked at me, and then at the box again. She opened it and gasped. It was almost the sort of gasp she made when she came—blown away, as if in shock, as if that sort of thing could never happen to her.

"You like it?" I asked with a sideways grin. How could she

not? But then again, after what I'd said about HookedUp being in trouble, she might have imagined this ring was from a Cracker Jack box. It was so flashy, so ridiculously sparkly that it could have been fake.

"Alexandre Chevalier," she said. "Alexandre Chevalier…what am I going to do with you?"

"You're going to marry me," I said.

16

In the next couple of months that followed, I got to know a new facet of Pearl's nature: her stubbornness.

She was refusing virtually every offer of mine.

"Pearl," I said, as we strolled through Central Park with Rex, golden orange leaves falling before our feet, "please be reasonable. See sense. I don't want to do a bloody pre-nup." I took her by the hand and stood in front of her. She needed to look into my eyes. She wanted to sign this unromantic contract, stating that if we were to ever split up, she would take nothing that wasn't hers before the wedding.

She sighed and said, "Alexandre, I'm just being practical. You've worked so hard for your money."

"I've worked hard so I can share it with someone special, have a family, live a real life. I don't give a shit about the money itself."

"Ah, you say that, but what about your fancy classic cars, your house in Provence that needs looking after, your apartment and Rex's nanny? That stuff doesn't come for free."

She was right. I'd gotten so used to having money I didn't even think about it. "*Our* apartment," I corrected her. I laced my fingers through her thick mane and drew her close to my face. "Anyway," I said with a brooding look in my eye. "I will. Not. Hear. Another. Fucking. Word. About. A. Pre-nup. Is that crystal clear?"

She threw her head back and laughed as Rex jumped up on me, concerned about the raucous I was making. "You see? You're upsetting Rex when you're so bossy!"

I walked along, silently brooding. Furious with her stubbornness. I'd have to fuck that out of her later, when we got home from work that evening. Make her acquiesce to my wishes. Worse than the pre-nup nonsense, was the wedding itself. She'd decided to wait until winter—had always, she told me, fantasized about a white wedding. But I knew the real reason. She was testing me. Using our engagement as a trial period to make sure she was doing the right thing. Fair enough, but it did little to ease my anguish....*Many a slip twixt cup and lip.* Why, I asked myself, couldn't we just get on with it? She was stalling and I didn't know the real reason behind her breezy, casual façade.

"White wedding," I mumbled, knowing, at least, that Sophie had made amends and was paying for a designer wedding gown that was going to cost her a cool seventy grand. "We could get married right here, today. Have a *golden* wedding—all these autumnal colors—wouldn't that be beautiful? In the boathouse, right here in the park? I could serenade you in one of those little boats like a Venetian gondola man and sing you that Italian aria. And Rex could be our witness."

Pearl laughed again and nuzzled her head into the side of my neck. Hmm, she smelled so wonderful; the essence of woman, of sweet, sensual delight. The sort of smell that cannot be described however hard you try. She was sensual, all right, but as stubborn as a wild rose.

She stroked her hand over the bicep of my arm and nipped her bottom lip between her teeth. I could feel my cock flex. Yup, I'd really fuck her good and hard when we got home. I couldn't wait.

"You know, Alexandre," she said squeezing my arm, "you must be about the fittest male specimen I have ever laid eyes on." Then she slapped her hand on her mouth and cried, "No! How can I say that? There is someone, who, I have to admit *does* have a better body than you. Is even more toned than you. Maybe stronger. I know it's cruel to be honest…but…" She winced with a pitiful, sympathetic look on her face.

Slam! A wave of jealousy surged through me. I squinted my eyes at her and asked coolly, "Who?" I imagined my leg swinging into this character's chest and knocking him down flat in one, easy, Taekwondo kick—I'd show him who was stronger.

She burst out laughing again. "So easily roused with envy, aren't you?"

"Who is this buffed-up character?"

"Well," she began, "he's black."

"A black guy?"

"Black and very beautiful. Younger than you. Loves running. Very active. Friendly. Handsome. Adorable. Actually, it was love at first sight. The second I saw him I knew he was special. Stole my heart, really. Definite competition for you,

Alexandre. I mean, I know I shouldn't be saying this to my own fiancé but it *is* the truth."

I finally twigged. I pinched her butt, teasingly. "So wicked, aren't you? So *femme fatale* to get me worked up about my own bloody dog! I knelt down and Rex came bounding up to me, skidding along the wet leaves, careening into me like a block of concrete. "Black and beautiful, friendly, adorable and very…" I slapped my hand against his rock-hard thigh muscles, "*very* compact."

Pearl knelt down, too. She was dressed for work, wearing a navy blue suit. She kissed me lightly on my nose and whispered, "I love to provoke you, love it when you get just that *little* bit jealous."

"What, me? Jealous? Don't be silly," I said. "I knew you we're kidding all along,"—I winked at her— "I'm far too self-assured to let envy get in my way. You'd better get yourself to work, chérie, or you'll be late. I'll walk you there."

We made our way behind the Metropolitan Museum where we could cut through the park to her new office building.

In an attempt, not only to cement Pearl's career and make her dream come true to work in feature films, but to also keep her under my wing, I'd bought out the company she worked for, Haslit Films, making it part of a new firm, HookedUp Enterprises. It was separate from HookedUp and had nothing to do with Sophie. I designed the deal so that Pearl and her ex boss, Natalie, could be equal partners.

But Pearl wouldn't accept HookedUp Enterprises as a gift. No. That stubbornness, again. Stubborn as the hook of a woman's bra on a first date. Pearl would only accept the position as director, working for a salary, refusing a share—just a percentage of future deals, instead. With me as silent partner. No special favors. She even insisted on having a contract drawn up with lawyers. She was the consummate professional—very irritating for me. I could have made her an extremely wealthy woman. But there was no way in this world I was going to convince her to take the profit and call the company her own.

She wanted to *earn* her riches, herself.

Another thing: she refused to sell her apartment. Just in case. *In case of what,* I wondered? She was renting it to someone on a one-year lease, while living with me, but *would not sell it. It was her nest egg*, she explained. I tried to convince her that she could have thousands of nest eggs. All the bloody eggs she could have dreamed of. Enough to make soufflés with. Omelets. But no. She wanted it *her* way. Financial independence from me, obviously. *Just in case.* She felt she had to prove herself.

I supposed it was from all those years of being self-sufficient. Two people had died on her: her brother, John, from an overdose, and her mother from cancer. Her surfer-dude dad had abandoned them when she was just a little girl, and Anthony, her other brother, was a self-centered jerk, or had proven himself to be, thus far.

Pearl was used to fending for herself, and however hard I tried to cajole her, to comfort her into believing that I could look after her, and *would* look after her, she was adamant that she could do it all on her own.

That should have been a warning siren but I just put it down to her pride and a reluctance to change the status quo.

I had told her that I felt more comfortable with 'a mature

woman who had lived, who had suffered knocks and bruises,' but I was beginning to pay the price; Pearl didn't trust me a hundred percent, however much in love she was.

All in good time, I told myself as I gazed at her now beside me, her golden hair shimmering in the morning autumnal sun. I needed to be patient. She had a broken wing that had not completely healed.

At that point, I still didn't know what, or who, had broken that delicate wing.

"Jesus Christ, Pearl," I groaned as I dragged myself off her; loath to break up yet another incredible session of lovemaking. Fucking? Lovemaking? Both words described what we did best. Really, sex was designed for us. Us together, anyway. With Pearl it was always delicious. Intense. Physically the best I'd ever had. Yes, and that even included Hélène.

I was still hard. "I could go on doing this all day long," I said, planting a kiss on her lips and letting my eyes celebrate her lithe, curvaceous body, still slightly tanned from summer. She moaned sleepily and took in a long, satisfied breath, her orgasm still lingering.

But I had to catch a plane to London and I was already late, so I tore myself away from her side and went to have a shower. I'd hoped that Pearl would come with me to London, show her the sights, eat in my favorite restaurants. I wished that she could just generally hang out with me on business trips, but she was a career girl and she had her own plans, her own agenda. The fact that Hookedup Enterprises was a toddler learning to walk made Pearl relentlessly busy.

Her brother Anthony was coming to stay for a few nights so I was happy, in that respect, to leave them to their family reunion.

When I sauntered back into the room and saw her lying on the bed like a classical French painter's odalisque, I stood still and absorbed my view. I never tired of observing Pearl. She had the sort of beauty that was difficult to put into words. Some women can look hard, chiseled, with a look of ambition cut into their jawbone. Pearl's face struck me as always being so gentle, even though defined. Her nose neat and straight, her cheekbones sweeping up into her perfectly shaped head which was crowned with a thick mane of blonde hair, cut in wavy layers. But it was her eyes that had me mesmerized. Clear and blue, yet the blue would change from a deep ultramarine that almost looked black sometimes, to an almost translucent sky color. Her eyes spoke of innocence and vulnerability: the eyes of a child.

"It's not too late to change your mind, you know. About coming to London with me," I cajoled. She was half asleep. I sat on the edge of the bed and whispered a kiss on her shoulder.

Pearl's eyelids fluttered and I stroked the length of her smooth back, tracing the curve down into her dip and up again over her peachy round buttocks. I could have stared at that ass all day long.

She groaned languidly and parted her legs a touch. Her eyes flicked open and she smiled lazily. Just touching her soft, silky skin and looking at her beautiful face got me hard again. I wanted to fuck her endlessly. Over and over. I leaned down to kiss her, my tongue parting her full lips, and she responded as her tongue met mine. Slowly, teasingly. I groaned into her mouth—an erotic sound of carnal need vibrated through me. I held her jaw with my hands and deepened the kiss, hungry for more, waiting for her to plead for me to ravage her again. Damn that plane, I was feeling uncontrollably horny. Insatiable. I couldn't get enough of her and felt edgy at the thought of leaving her for just a couple of days. We needed the physical closeness, the frenzied power of orgasms that always hit us simultaneously, that united us.

My eyes scanned down to her hand, flopped by her side, and I took it, feeling her engagement ring between my fingers, mollified that if other men looked at her, at least they'd know she belonged to someone else. *To me.*

"You'd better go or you'll miss your plane," she told me, and I flinched.

"Why are you tormenting me like this? You know I don't like us being apart?"

"I can't just leave Anthony alone," she murmured sleepily.

"Why not? He wouldn't care; he'd have the run of the place, get the staff darting around for him—he'd love it. I don't know why you're going so out of your way for him. He treats you like…" I trailed off—no need, I decided, to point out her brother's failings.

"He's been making more effort lately. That's why he's coming to visit. Anyway, there's another reason I can't go to London: I've got that important meeting with Samuel Myers, you know."

"Sam Myers…the big, fat, Hollywood fish who smokes too many Cuban cigars and calls everyone honey."

Pearl's lips curved into a smile. "I know, he's like a walking cliché from some bad B movie. I want to pitch my buddy movie to him. But I don't want male leads. I want to see a *woman* playing at least one of those parts, maybe both, if I can swing it. I'm so fed up of seeing actresses playing just the love interest."

I squeezed her hand. "Well let's hope he goes for it. I'm proud of you, Pearl, I really am. You're doing a great job of getting HookedUp Enterprises on its feet."

My eyes shifted back to the curves of my fiancée's divine body. I wanted to suggest that another great project would be for her to do a workout video for women over the age of thirty-five; show them that females didn't have to be in their twenties to be in great shape. With Pearl, herself, as the exercise guru—she was a good model for beauty and health. But I never mentioned age to Pearl because I knew that was a soft spot for her. I didn't want to draw attention to the fifteen-year age gap between us, mainly because I never even thought about it myself. Except on occasions like this, when she blew me away with how young she looked, and it annoyed me that people pigeonholed anybody by a number.

She took my hand and kissed it. Soon, I thought, I'd be wearing a wedding ring there. "You'll be late," she warned me again.

"Such a cool customer, aren't you? Sending me off like this when all I want to do is get right back into bed with you." I ran the top of my finger around the dimples in the small of her back again, tracing it over the mound of her behind and into the luscious, moist valley of her wet folds—a place where I'd spent so many wonderful hours of ecstasy and where I intended to visit for the rest of my life.

"What I like, though," I murmured, my cock rock-hard again, "is when the ice-princess part of you melts." And I whispered in her ear, my fingers deep inside her, "when I fuck the cool-customer nonsense out of you and you lose all self-control. When you whimper and beg me, and scream my name when you come." I eased my fingers out of her again. Let her feel what she'd be missing—have her longing for my return. "Have fun in your meeting, chérie. I'll be keeping tabs on you—just in case you get tempted by sexy Sam."

She laughed and pushed me off the bed. I walked over to my closet and got dressed, slinging on a T-shirt and jeans—I was really late—and when I turned around, Rex had somehow managed to sneak his way onto the bed. Pearl and I had nicknamed him her 'French lover.' I knew he'd be trying to usurp my place when I was gone.

I said goodbye to the pair of them and felt a rush of inexplicable adrenaline coil through my stomach. Leaving my little family behind made me feel nauseous, partly because when I got to London I knew who was waiting for me: Laura.

Like tenacious ivy entwined about an oak tree, Laura just couldn't let me go.

17

I couldn't stop thinking about Pearl. Her image, plus the jet's rumbling and vibrations on the runway before takeoff, were making me fucking horny. I locked the door of my cabin, my cock aching for an orgasm—Pearl fresh in my mind like a haunting painting or photograph that has impacted your soul. It reminded me of my teenage years when I had sex on the brain constantly. That's what Pearl was doing to me.

I undid my jeans and my cock sprang up. *Wait,* I thought, getting my iPhone out of my pocket. *I'll share this with her—make sure she thinks about me while I'm gone. She and I are in this together.*

I remembered entering her from behind, just that morning, fisting her hair to hold her where I wanted her, her soaked core welcoming me as I crammed her full with my thick, heated length, unable to control myself, fucking her probably too hard for her tight, hot kernel. But she still crumbled beneath me, her pussy clenching in a shuddering climax as she dug her nails into the mattress, pushing her butt closer against me....always closer. Both of us craved that intense proximity.

I lay back on the bed in my cabin and put my phone on record mode, holding it close to my huge erection. Then I panned up to my face so she could see my lustful expression. This wasn't going to be live; I'd send it to her when I landed—a little porn movie for her own pleasure. *A keepsake, for when we're old, doddery and gray and I won't be able to get it up any more.*

"I'm thinking of you, chérie," I began, my hand clamped around my stiff cock, "—I should have abducted you and brought you with me." I licked my lips, thinking of her mouth sucking me, flicking her teasing tongue over the broad head of my crest, making me come. "I've got your hot, wet, pearlette in my mind's eye, Pearl, and the expression on your beautiful face when you come for me. Your hard, peaked nipples when I suck them, when I lick you, when I stretch you open and fuck you really hard."

I was moving my hand up and down, tight on my massive erection, jerking it hastily and remembering how, just the day before, I'd come in her mouth, fucking it slowly, and how incredible it felt.

"When I get home, baby, I'm going to tease you with my cock, bend you over and flutter my tongue against your clit. Just the tip of my tongue. You'll be begging me for more and I'll make you wait till you're moaning with anticipation."

What I was doing in that moment felt good but nothing compared to the real thing. I imagined Pearl when she received this little film, would be sitting in her office chair, legs wide open, her fingers inside herself, her other hand massaging her clit, and how I wish I could be there to enter her slowly, the head of my thick cock pushing into her just an inch, then withdrawing and teasing her sensitized cleft, then ramming my whole length into her wet warmth, fucking her hard, then tantalizing her clit again. Over and over, I'd do this, until she was begging for me to fuck her, screaming for me, crying out for her release.

My cock twitched, its broad crown wet with lust. "I'm going to fuck your clit, Pearl, with the tip of my cock, rim it around and around and then cram you full, baby. I'll slip my way in, just an inch, no more. Then thrust it all the way, hard, and then pull almost out. Then tease you again, just a centimeter inside. You won't know when I'm going to slam you. Maybe I'll pump you good and hard, maybe I won't. You'll be screaming for me to fuck you."

My pulse quickened and my breath came heavily—I could feel my impending orgasm about to explode. My fingers squeezed like a vice around the wide crest of my cock and then all the way down to its thick root. "All I can think about is fucking you. I. Love. Fucking. You. Pearl. I love fucking you hard, fucking, you, really slow."

Semen spurted out in a hot rush as the image of Pearl's tits and ass brought harmonies, musical notes of bliss swirling about my brain in an abstract pattern. Like the crescendo of a beautiful aria. Her tits, ass, pussy, nipples, mouth, all one giant billboard in my head. A knock on my cabin door jerked my climax into a tsunami of a wave, coursing through me, and flooding over in abandon.

"I'm coming," I shouted out. *And how.*

The flight attendant said, "Sir, I need you to buckle-up for takeoff."

I was taking off, all right. Really taking off. "Coming," I said again and grinned at the irony of my words.

When I exited my cabin, I nearly had a heart attack. The person sitting right there in my line of vision, neatly and serenely in her seat, was none other than Indira bloody Kapoor, herself. She looked up from her book and said calmly, "Alexandre, how wonderful to see you."

I gazed at her, speechless. *What the fuck was she doing on this plane?* She was wearing a sky-blue sari, draped elegantly about one shoulder and her hair was braided. I had to admit, she looked great. No wonder she was such a big movie star.

"Indira. What a surprise." I walked over, bent down to kiss her on the cheek. "What brings you here on this very *private* plane?"

"I'm like you, Alexandre; I like to hitch-hike on G-5s. So much global warming—always good to spread the wealth a bit, you know, not be too greedy. You were flying to London so I thought I'd hop aboard."

"How did you know I'd be here?" I asked, not even wanting to know what strings she'd pulled.

"A little birdy told me so," she said enigmatically. "You're looking good, Alexandre Chevalier. Truly, you must be one of the most handsome men I think I've ever had the pleasure of working with, including my co-stars. Your eyes—what is it about them? They almost rival mine."

I chuckled. Indira was always good for a laugh. *To work with?* "Well, if you consider the charity work, I guess—"

"Not the charity. You signed that oh, so lucrative piece of paper giving me power of attorney in India with all things HookedUp," she said coolly, smoothing her braid. I stared at her. She was very composed, very *butter-wouldn't-melt-in-my-mouth.* Her eyes were wide with innocence. Where was this leading?

I sat down next to her, my blood rising, my mind shuffling through possible scenarios with utmost confusion. "No, Indira, I never signed anything of the sort. What are you on about?"

"Oh, but you did. HookedUp is already making waves there and I'm the director."

The flight attendant came by with some hors d'oeuvres and champagne, breaking up our conversation. *What the fuck was Indira playing at?*

"Indira, the only thing you have power of attorney of concerning me, is our charity. A charity which is a *non-profit* organization. A charity which, I hope to God, you will not exploit for your own coffers."

She leaned towards me and, putting her hand on my knee, uncomfortably close to my crotch, whispered, "It's so easy to forge a signature. All you have to do is press the original document against a window with your own on top, and trace over it. Easy peasy pudding and pie. I swear, nobody can tell the two apart. It's even been signed by a notaire, 'witnessed' by two lawyers. I have contacts in high places, as you can imagine. And it's too late now for you to turn the clock back. Of course, if you and I were *real* partners in the true sense of the word, you'd be in on it fifty/fifty."

I laughed. "You're just pulling my leg. Trying to get a reaction out of me." *The woman was nuts. Why did I attract crazy women into my life?*

She arched a dark eyebrow and smirked.

"Indira, Sophie and I sold our India rights of HookedUp to

your cousin. I'm out. You, yourself, invested your own money into the HookedUp franchise in India. You wouldn't cut your nose off to spite your own pretty face. You wouldn't jeopardize it. I don't know why you're playing this silly game. I *got* my payment," and I lowered my voice, "I got the gems. That was my deal. Even if you did forge my signature, which I doubt very much, it isn't going to help you."

"Oh, but it will. You watch. My fat little cousin doesn't have full proof of purchase. I do. The company is mine."

"Indira, you're playing with fire. He's not a man to cross." *She wouldn't be so crazy….would she?* My head told me she was spurting a load of nonsense just to rile me, but then I sat up. That cousin could really cause trouble. *Fuck, maybe I do need my bodyguard, after all!* "Really, Indira, if you did what you say you did, you will have gotten yourself into a big, tangled web of a mess."

She adjusted the folds of her sari. "My cousin loves me. In fact, he's *in* love with me. Always has been. I'm family. He'll believe me when I say I was unaware of your gem deal. Because it's true. I wasn't there. I can play dumb. He'll think you double-crossed him."

I closed my eyes in disbelief. *She must be lying.* Whatever, I had no idea what the repercussions would be, but somehow I knew I could end up embroiled in one, big, spicy, tandoori, Bollywood-style banquet of disaster.

Laura. Indira. Who knew? Maybe Claudine would be waiting for my plane to land in London.

I thanked the Lord that Pearl, at least, was normal.

But then a niggling doubt crept into my mind. I'd never had a relationship in my entire life with any woman who was 'normal'—not even my mother was normal. Especially not my mother. And certainly not Sophie.

Why, I asked myself, would Pearl be any different?

Luckily, Indira had a screen test to go to at Shepperton Studios, so we parted ways as soon as we landed. As crazy as my sister drove me, I was glad that she'd be able (I hoped) to come up with some sort of solution for Indira and deal with the cousin. Indira's story was implausible, ridiculous…

But a woman spurned is capable of revenge….history books told us so.

I had a vision of that greasy cousin of hers sending out a sniper to shoot me down, planted on a rooftop somewhere as I went out for an innocent stroll in the park. That part I believed…that he was in love with her. Those large families with cousins and aunts and great uncles and weddings that went on for a whole week, often had incestuous blood snaking through their veins.

I'd have to be alert and on the ball.

18

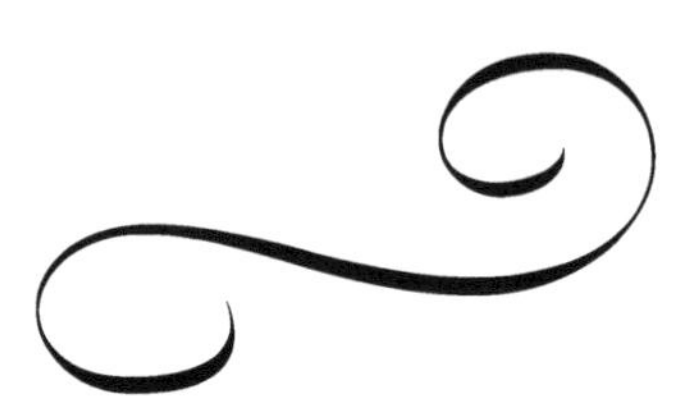

The purpose of my London visit was to meet an up-and-coming, twenty-three-year-old video game designer, and talk business. I was getting into the video games market, where budgets were bigger than blockbuster feature films and big money could be made. I was a secret player, had been since I was a young boy, although I kept that side of things under wraps. Now, at least, I could use my vice as an excuse. 'Research,' I could say. Boys will be boys. Or rather, men will be boys. When it comes to toys, no man's a grown-up, no matter how hard he pretends.

I also had a meeting with the Minister of Finance from the British government, some of his aides and Sophie. We needed more leeway in Britain. As much as I had threatened Sophie with getting out of HookedUp, I decided to hold off—give her another chance. She'd been making amends with Pearl and her effort seemed genuine. The wedding gown gift proved it. And she'd promised not to let shits like that Russian arms dealer anywhere near our business, so for the moment, I was cool with things.

But I also had other stuff to attend to in England. Of a more personal nature.

Over the last few weeks, I'd listened to several frantic messages from Laura on my voicemail. At first, I ignored them, but as time went on, I decided that I had to deal with the situation. She was threatening to come to New York and I needed to nip that possibility in the bud. She was desperate to see me face-to-face, said she needed to discuss something that couldn't be resolved by phone. She'd been on holiday to my house in Provence, expecting the whole time for me to show up. When I didn't, she really started hounding me.

Poor Laura was obviously hurting. Rationally, my brain told me that it wasn't my problem. Laura was the one who split up with me, dumped me for James—left me to nurse my broken heart. It had been years ago so I was completely over it, but she had no right to play the underdog now. Yet the sympathetic side of me was whispering a different story in my ear: reminding me that she was disabled, only just recently out of a wheelchair. She'd suffered immeasurably and she needed a friend. Since I'd met Pearl, I'd been distant; Laura rarely crossed my mind, but inexplicably I still felt a sense of guilt. So I agreed to meet up. She was going to come and see me at The Connaught where I was staying.

As I was mulling all this over, taking a shortcut through St. James's Park on my way back to the hotel, like a bolt of lightening, I remembered my niece. I'd been so wrapped up in Pearl, and Sophie's dodgy business antics over the past couple of months that I'd forgotten to check up on Elodie. I'd seen her around the office building in Manhattan but we hadn't had a chance to talk. She'd asked for security so I'd provided my bodyguard to be on call for her whenever she wanted him. I'd never actually used him for myself but had him on my payroll just for good measure. Maybe, I'd be asking for his help now, though, after Indira's shenanigans.

I called and waited for Elodie to pick up. My walk was a welcome relief, away from the city's traffic and noise. As I looked around, I noted that there was a difference between the parks in London and Paris, a clue to the discrepancy in nature between both countries. Paris was so formal; people were forbidden to loll about the grass in the parks of central Paris—but in London you saw kids play football, dogs chasing ducks and geese, and people sprawled out sunbathing, or enjoying a picnic.

It was lunch hour and office workers were eating sandwiches and basking in the crisp autumnal sunshine, away from the confines of their stuffy offices, the tyranny of their computers and petty internal politics—the perils of a nine-to-five job. As I was listening to Elodie's ring tone, I people-watched and dog-watched. Why wasn't she picking up?

She finally answered. "Elodie," I said, relieved that she hadn't changed her number. "What took you so long? And why haven't you called to check in?"

"I'm sorry," she replied in a bored drawl, "just put the roses over there, would you? I've been busy with stuff."

"Roses?"

"Just a delivery," and she added quickly, "for my roommate."

"Is everything okay?"

"Yeah, it's okay now. Things are better."

"You're not still scared? Not worried about being followed?"

"No, no," and then she said with a faint giggle, "I was imagining things. Everything's fine."

My eye caught the view of the London Eye in the distance, peeking out above the golden and russet-colored trees. "You're sure?" I checked again. There was something in her tone that I found disarming. A beat of silence at her end of the line was muffled by cries of geese near the park's small lake. I thought about the position of where I stood in that moment; Buckingham Palace at one side, and at the other, the Foreign Office and 10 Downing Street where the British Prime Minister lived. I imagined several M15 spies had their meetings right here, away from bugs and walls with ears—spyware everywhere. They, too, were spying on others for a living. And I wondered, once again, if I should do my own share of espionage; have Elodie followed for her own safety, or if that was breaching her privacy too much.

Because something made me suspect that when she said that everything was okay, she was lying.

I relaxed back into the sofa of my penthouse at The Connaught, described by the hotel as, 'London's most luxurious home.' I was enjoying a power nap. I have always been a fan of the nanosecond siesta—it can do wonders. There was a knock at the door. Odd, the concierge always called first and room service had already passed by that morning. I hadn't ordered anything, hadn't summoned the butler. I looked at my watch. Laura wasn't due for another forty minutes. I had specifically arranged for us to meet downstairs—I didn't want the intimacy of her being in my living quarters. I knew Laura, her persuasiveness, her doggedness. When she wanted something, she usually got it, and right now, I sensed she wanted me.

My heart started racing. *Fuck—Indira's cousins—the London lot—Indians always have relatives in London. Perhaps a clan of them are waiting outside my door with crowbars, ready to top me off.*

I called reception. "Hello, Mr. Chevalier here. Did anyone ask to come up and see me?"

"No, sir," the concierge replied.

Just at that moment, there was another knock at the door and a voice, which I knew well, cried out, "Alexandre, it's me. I know you're in there, let me in."

Bloody hell. It was Laura.

Being so relieved that it wasn't a bunch of furious uncles about to launch an attack, I let Laura in. She looked taller than usual, or perhaps I had just gotten used to Pearl. Laura seemed Amazonian in comparison—she was at least six foot two in heels. Her blonde hair flowed down her back and her bee-stung lips pouted at me like a small child who was determined to get her daddy's attention.

"Alex, why the look of suspicion on your face? You look like you've seen a ghost." She stepped into the room and threw her white cashmere coat onto an armchair. She looked like a supermodel: tall, skinny. Swaggering with confidence, even though she was using a cane and had a very slight limp. The cane was black with a mother-of-pearl handle, so it matched her glamorous outfit.

"How did you get past reception?"

"Oh please," she murmured, as if I'd said the dumbest thing in the world. She thrust her shoulders back and stuck out her chest. She wasn't wearing a bra and her nipples pointed sharp under her flimsy silk blouse. "Well, aren't you going to kiss me hello?"

I came over to her and offered a peck on the cheek. She responded with a soft, damp kiss. "I've missed you darling," she breathed into my ear.

"Shame Pearl couldn't be here," I said in reply, walking to the other end of the room and sitting on a couch. "She would have loved to have met you." *Not.*

"So how's your mum?" she said, totally ignoring my comment.

"Fine. I saw her in Paris a couple of months ago. Or was it just last month? Time flies."

"Yes, time does fly. Especially when you're suffering." She looked down at the floor.

"I'm sorry if things haven't turned out the way you wanted, Laura. But you're looking great. I see you're on your feet again. You should be proud of yourself. So, what was it that was so important and couldn't wait? What did you want to talk to me about?"

She flicked her long hair. "I've always been curious to see this famous penthouse apartment at The Connaught." She surveyed her surroundings with approval. "Nice. Very chic. I'll go and check out the balcony in a moment, when I've caught my breath. I have to say, it's stunning. I could quite happily move in."

"Your house is hardly a hovel," I said, realizing she was in the mood to play the beat-around-the-bush game.

"Aren't you going to offer me a drink?"

"Yes, of course. A soft drink?"

"God, no. I need a *real* drink."

"Should I call the butler? Or better still, we can go downstairs."

"No. God, no. Let's just keep it us, shall we, and stay right here."

I stood up and made my way to the bar. I turned around. "What would you like, then?"

She shuffled on the edge of the armchair and I saw a flash of her panties. Bare legs, apart from killer-heeled, thigh high, black leather boots. Probably Gucci. She loved Gucci. A mini skirt. She had modeled pantyhose once—her legs didn't seem to end.

"Something expensive," she said.

"What?"

"I don't know, you choose. A bottle of chilled Cristal? A vintage Bordeaux? Nothing too plebian. Something I don't drink at home."

"Laura, you and James have the best-stocked drinks' cabinet in London!"

"Surprise me. *Impress* me."

I had forgotten that about Laura. She was high-maintenance. I'd been constantly scrambling about to please her when we dated. Wanted to make her proud of me. Tried to treat her like the queen she felt she was. But that was when I was twenty. I had grown up a bit since then.

"I have no idea what will impress you, Laura."

"What about a Bloody Mary, how about that?"

"Okay," I agreed. "Good idea." It did seem a fitting drink for her, but in that moment I didn't know why. "Living in New York has trained my taste buds," I said. "They know how to make a kickass Bloody Mary there. Lots of horseradish sauce and the right amount of spice."

"Kickass? Ugh, you're picking up some really tacky American expressions, Alex." And then she mumbled, "Must be that....that..." She didn't finish her sentence, just sneered, and then continued, "Actually, let *me* make the Bloody Marys. I bet I can outdo those New York bartenders."

"I bet you can't, but be my guest, give it a go—I need to make some calls."

I went out onto the balcony and took in the views over Mayfair, wondering how I could get this too-cozy-for-comfort rendezvous over with as quickly as possible. I didn't often drink midday but what the hell, I thought. Maybe Laura had started self-medicating with booze because of the physical pain she was in, so no harm in joining her—my important meetings for the day were safely out of the way.

I called various work contacts. Then, as I was chatting to someone in Rome about a share in a boutique hotel I had there, Laura came out and handed me my Bloody Mary.

"Here we go," she whispered. "Don't want to interrupt your call. Don't mind me, I'll entertain myself with a magazine or something, while you take care of business."

I watched her out of the corner of my eye as she moved off toward the dining room, aided by her cane. The place was vast: a dining room with seating for ten, two bedrooms, two bathrooms and a large living room. Fresh flowers in bespoke vases, oil paintings adorning the walls, strategically placed at eye level.

Creams and pale blues and, oh, so very Laura—I knew she'd be impressed and would want to nose about. That's why she'd insisted on coming up and not meeting me in the lobby, I thought. I sipped my Bloody Mary. Actually, it was very good; she'd gotten the recipe right, after all.

I called Sophie.

"Did you deal with Indira?" I asked her when she picked up.

"She's full of shit—she was just winding you up, Alexandre. Of course she hasn't forged your signature."

"I thought as much. Did she admit that?"

"In so many words. I'm having tea with her today at The Ritz, just to smooth things over. Want to join us? We could pass by and pick you up."

"No, don't. Please, *you* deal with her, Sophie. I don't want hoards of angry relatives hunting me down. Right now, I have other issues which I need to sort out. I'll be back in New York tomorrow. I'll call you then."

I could have sworn I heard water running. I made my way to where the sound was coming from, and lo and behold, Laura was running a bath. Worse, she was *in* the bath. Nude. There, in the pristine, all-white bathroom was an oval tub, smack bang in the middle of the room. Laura was lying right in it, coated in frothy bubbles, splashing about.

"Jesus, Laura, what the fuck are you doing?"

"Ssh, Alex, don't shout. I thought I'd have a little soak, that's all. Don't get your knickers in a twist."

I don't wear knickers. I turned around, my back to her; *this* view of London, Laura nude, had not been on my agenda. "Laura, you're not even meant to be up here; we were meant to meet *downstairs*. Fine, pop by to say hello, but you can't just fucking *move* in on me!"

"Alex, I'm in pain! Why do I have to keep reminding you of this? Have you any idea what it's like…your muscles aching and pinching and throbbing all the time? I just need a hot soak to make me feel better. Will you be an angel and fetch me my Bloody Mary? I left it in the living room by mistake."

"Laura, *please*."

"Bring me my drink, Alex, and stop being such a bore. Oh yes, and a magazine. I forgot that, too. *Vogue* or *Interiors*. Nothing tacky."

"Laura, please. I'm engaged to be married! *You're* married. Fine, we can still be friends, but you *in the bath at my hotel?* This is going beyond the boundaries of friendship—this is *too fucking much!*"

"Alex darling, please stop being such a pleb. Just bring me my drink and magazine, I'll have a nice quiet soak and then I'll leave. Or better still: *join* me. This bath is big enough for two."

She was incorrigible but I knew that the only way to get her out of that bathtub would be to physically manhandle her, which I wasn't about to do. "Ten minutes," I warned. "Then it's time for you to leave. You said you had something important to discuss but that was obviously a ruse to hang out with me. I can't just *hang out* anymore, Laura. Not like this. Pearl and I are getting *married*."

"Yeah right. Winter's a long way away."

I turned around in surprise. She was sitting up, erect, with her chest out, her breasts little and pert—she was fluttering her eyelashes at me, and smiling.

"How do you know that?" I demanded, turning my back

on her again. I don't know why I even bothered—I'd seen it all before.

"Oh you know, Elodie and I chat every so often. I call her for news once in a while."

In-fucking-corrigible. I drained my Bloody Mary—the kick of alcohol felt good—I needed it to ease my irritation. "Ten minutes, Laura. I'm not bringing you your drink and any magazines because making things more comfortable for you here is *not* my intention."

"Alex, you *will* come around, darling, believe me. Because I have a little surprise for you."

I narrowed my eyes with suspicion. "Like what?"

"Ooh, that would be telling."

"I've got work to do. I'm going next door. Ten. Minutes. Only. Then I'm sending you home in a cab."

I left the bathroom, wondering how I'd forgotten about Laura's manipulative ways. Still, it was nothing I couldn't handle….

Or so I thought.

The next thing I knew, I'd fallen asleep on the sofa. I tried to shift myself but felt all floppy. I realized my arms were above my head, tied together with some sort of wire cable. In fact, *all* of me felt buzzy and floppy, except the one part of my anatomy which mattered most. When I finally focused, I saw Laura on top of me, pinning me down like a vice—her nude body straddling me, her long knees digging into the sofa either side of my hips. A scar ran down her left thigh where they'd operated on her after her accident. My eyes flicked down. The buttons of my jeans were open, my shirt, open. Fuck! My dick was mysteriously rock-hard and she was about to ease herself on top of me.

Laura, what the fuck are you doing? I thought I said the words, but all that came from my lips was a sort of incoherent groan.

She pushed back my head as I attempted to get up. "Ssh, Alex, just relax. All you have to do is lie there, darling, I'll do the work."

Madonna's *Frozen* was playing, ringing in my ears. How apt, considering every cell in my body felt numb. Laura's long blonde hair was flopping over me, her lips centimeters away from mine.

"Hmm, I'd forgotten how good you smell," she purred.

She had my cock firmly in one hand and was guiding it towards her pussy like a rocket aimed for liftoff.

Any second now, that rocket was about to be launched.

Belle Pearl

It's true what they say about muscle memory; that your body instinctively does whatever it has been trained to do, seemingly without your brain being involved.

Because right now, my brain was in a fuzzy haze. My limbs felt like the puppet, Punch, being left in a tangle of strings and broken joints, abandoned by his puppet master—gone for a coffee break. My arms were still above my head, tied tightly together. I lay there, all askew, my body in fragmented pieces, but my cock like a thick, solid, wooden rod. Laura's breath was heavy in my ear, her skin oiled and sweet as she sniffed me, her hand clamped about my dick, aiming it inside her.

"Oh yeah, Alex, I've been fantasizing about this for years. In my bloody wheelchair, in my bed, dreaming of you instead of James. Oh darling, I've been waiting for this moment."

My leg kicked up and over her as if it belonged to someone else, not me. I watched it with fascination, curl its way in front of Laura's chest, not kicking her, but the force of it pushing her off balance, knocking her hand out of its vice-like grip, freeing me from her tight hold and pushing her sideways off the sofa. She tumbled onto the floor.

"Fuck you, Alex! What the fuck? That bloody hurt!"

I tipped my head forward and brought my arms in front of me but my neck instantly fell back into the soft, feathery nest of silk cushions. I'd never felt more uncomfortable about being comfortable in my life.

Laura lurched her skinny body back on top of me. "Not so fast, Alex, I want to get my money's worth out of this Viagra!"

So that explained my erection! Again, I tried to shout and scream but only groans emanated from my cotton-wool mouth.

"I know, baby. I know. You think you have to be all Mr. Faithful to that silly American tart, but we know very well that your lusty relationship won't last, so why not nip it in the bud now, eh? You'll thank me later for this, I swear."

"Laoor….ra."

"I know, darling, I know." She gripped her knees about my hips, spat on her fingers and smeared them inside herself for lubrication. So much for her being turned on. This wasn't about love or lust; Laura had other plans, obviously. She spat on her fingers once more, and spread another glob of spittle where she felt she needed it most, thrusting her skinny frame over me, covering me like a blanket. My arms pushed forward, pressing on her collarbone. I didn't want to hurt her, I just wanted her *off* me. I saw that it was electric cable tying my wrists together. In an infallible sailor's knot.

She tumbled backwards and cried out. "Alex! Ouch!"

"Fuck ow, Laoara," my tongue managed. *Fuck off, off of me!* I pinned her down with my torso so she was locked beneath me.

She grinned as if she had won a prize. "Ooh, sexy, I like a bit of rough. Come on then, Mr. Stud, give it to me, ram it in me, baby!"

My breath was uneven. My heart pounding out of sequence. Jesus! What the hell had she put in that Bloody Mary, apart from Viagra? Qualudes? Some sort of date-rape drug? Enough to bring a horse to its knees, anyway.

We lay there panting, her arms draped about my neck, holding me close to her, her legs hooked about my calf muscles and she thrashed her groin up at me, her hands grappling, trying to find their way back to my dick. But I pressed myself even closer so there was no space between us. I almost wanted to laugh the situation was so absurd. There was something comical about Laura, and in that moment, I remembered the fights we used to have which would always end up with make-up sex and then us laughing about it afterwards. She would goad and provoke me, knowing that the only way we'd even end up speaking to each other again was after we'd fucked.

"Oh Alex, oh Alex, how I've missed this," she breathed into my ear. "You and I are destined to be together. Destined. I love you, darling."

No you don't, you nutter! "Laaoura."

If I moved from my position, she could get leverage again and I couldn't risk it. I wanted to call for help but then realized how mad it would seem. A big grown man like me being 'raped' by a beautiful ex-model? *Yeah, people would really believe that one.* My hands fumbled in front of me, trying to cup my dick to protect its 'virtue.' No, 'cup' is the wrong word, as it could not be cupped—it was like a fucking missile.

My tongue tried to wrap its way around a simple sentence: "Laaoora, pleathe."

She started inhaling me again, writhing beneath me, edging her way higher so my missile was in the perfect spot to be fired into her. "Oh yeah, Alex. Oh yeah, just a couple of centimeters lower…come on baby, give it to me."

And my dick was tempted. How do you undo centuries of male instinct? I wasn't made of stone. Except…I was—my cock, anyway. The drugs were now making me horny too. I half wanted just to fuck her and get it over with, but even in my woozy state, I knew that it was just the beginning of something more ominous. If she got away with this, who knew what was next on the cards? Besides, I was engaged to another woman. Being a cheater wasn't my style, even if I was being coerced into it.

No. Laura isn't fucking getting her insane way with me!

Except she was. Almost. I could feel her pussy poised at the crown of my cock, now soaked with her spit.

Using the arm of the sofa to maneuver myself, I pushed myself down the sofa so my head was now on her chest. My cock was free. For the moment, anyway.

"Oh yeah, baby, suck my tits, that's good."

I thrashed my head from side to side, fumbling with my butter-fingers to untie the electric cable which was digging into my wrists. But it was useless. So I dipped my head over the edge of the sofa and performed a very ungracious somersault, crashing into the coffee table—glasses and Bloody Marys tumbling to the floor—but I managed to roll myself forward with enough force that I landed on my feet in a crouch. Laura's arms slapped into my thighs as she tried to bring me down again, her hooky nails clawing at my jeans, which were half way down my thighs. But I leapt to my feet. At last, I was upright.

Stars flooded my brain as dizziness threatened to topple me over again. My head rushed with a mélange of bright colors, swirling about in dashes and flashes. I could hear Laura cackling hysterically.

You think this is funny, eh? I tried to say without words forming, just moans. But to my horror, I too, was laughing—my belly contracting in painful howls. The drugs were coursing through me. I was now doubled-up. In that second, it was as if every hilarious movie, book, play and memory was crashing into me, making me roar with uncontrollable mirth.

"You see how we're made for each other, darling? That American just doesn't have your sense of humor! No American does. They're so bloody earnest, so goody-goody. You and I are a real *team,* Alex. We're naughty, irreverent, *wild! We* break the law, *we* will stop at nothing."

I howled with hilarity at every word spoken. It was true: *Pearl is a good person. Too good for me. Too wholesome. Too honest. I'm bad. Rotten inside. Killed people. Done illegal deals with Sophie, smuggling gems and all sorts of other moneymaking schemes to get rich and powerful. Pearl deserves better. I deserve Laura. Laura knows how fucked-up I am and she still doesn't care.* I tried to button up the fly of my jeans, my wrists tied, my fingers hopelessly numb. I screamed with laughter at my ineptitude.

"Let's have another drink," suggested Laura.

I burst out laughing again. The idea that she was about to mix another Bloody Mary, lacing it with another round of drugs, was the funniest thing I'd ever heard in my life. I held out my wrists. "Undooo," I howled.

"You want me to undo that sailor's knot, darling?"

I nodded.

"Where would the fun be in that? You know very well that if I undooooo you, *I* will be undone. I think we should get back on the sofa, don't you? One more try and if it doesn't work, I'll mix another cocktail."

A cocktail of drugs. Hmm, not so amusing. My pulse was pounding in my ears. This woman could kill me! I took a deep breath and staggered towards the door. I needed air but not just air—I needed my freedom.

In my peripheral vision—a blur of flesh and limbs—I saw Laura race after me. I kept going, my heart like an old-fashioned steam train, pumping as hard as it could to gain momentum. Laura rugby-tackled me but I stepped aside and she went flying on her face. Her arms curled about my ankles but I kept moving—Laura was letting herself be dragged behind me. I dared not bend down to unlatch her, in case I lost my balance again.

"Where the fuck are you going!" she yelled. It was not a question but a command.

The scenery of paintings, smooth walls and light fittings of the hotel penthouse swam before my eyes as I lugged myself, and the limpet on my leg, to the door. Finally I reached my destination, my head flopping against the wood. I turned the handle and poked my head outside. I wedged my foot in the door and edged my body into the corridor.

Sophie was standing right there.

With Indira.

"We came by to see if you wanted to have tea with…" Sophie stopped herself mid-sentence.

Indira smiled at first, then her eyes swept down to my crotch. I followed her gaze and saw that my missile dick was poking out of my unbuttoned jeans. My hands were still tied with electric cable and groans and moans were coming from my ankles: Laura.

Indira pushed the door with a mighty thud, and Laura cried out:

"Ouch, that's my head, thank you very much! What the fuck—"

Indira's eyes scanned down to the floor where Laura was sprawled out, naked, still clinging onto my ankles.

"Jesus," Sophie said, speaking in French. "What the hell is going on?"

"Help me!" I mouthed silently. "Take Laura away, call James." But I started laughing again, clutching my stomach with bellyache howls.

Indira's hand came down hard on my face. The slap stung like twenty wasps biting me all at once. "You slut! And into dirty bondage games to boot! You disgust me!" She spat in my face and shuffled away, nearly tripping over her flowing sari. I knew what really irked her: that she had wanted to experiment with bondage one time, and I wouldn't play ball.

I rubbed my face against my shoulder to wipe off her spittle. I'd had enough female saliva for one day.

I said with a silent growl, "Sophie, please, help—it's not funny," but between a racing heart and hitched breaths, I chortled again with another round of hysteria, tears streaming down my face, my jaw sore with all the grinning.

Sophie stood there, glaring at me, her eyes two empty holes, her lips twitching.

Like a scolded schoolboy sent to a corner, her disdainful look made me roar all the more.

2

As the drugs wore off, my amusement at the situation waned. Although, the more I thought about Laura, the more I sort of admired her gusto. I had to give her an A+ for effort. But I felt as if I was wrapped up in a psychological suspense movie with the mad ex stalking me, and if I wasn't more vigilant I could wind up dead, poisoned in a back alley somewhere, Laura weeping over my dead body; the body she'd topped off.

One thing was for sure, though: you had to give her ten out of ten for an active imagination.

Once again, my sister had bailed me out of trouble. Indira stormed off in a huff and Sophie rescued me, untied the sailor's knot, and sent Laura on her way, waiting patiently while she got dressed, but not leaving my side until Laura was safely out of the hotel. Sophie called James but he still wasn't answering his cell, or returning calls.

Once I was alone again, and with my dick still Viagra-hard,

I called Pearl for some Skype sex–I had to do something to tone down my raging erection. My libido was hungry enough as it was; the last thing in the world I needed was bloody Viagra—I didn't know how long the effect would last but I needed a release.

Pearl was in the bath with the soundtrack from the beautiful 1960's film, *Un Homme et Une Femme* in the background. She wanted to chit-chat about this and that—her meeting with Samuel Myers and how they'd got the gay actress Alessandra Demarr on board, and that they'd be working together on this feature film Pearl was producing, *Stone Trooper*. I wondered if Pearl would be tempted by a gay woman? After all, her first orgasm had happened with her schoolgirl friend.

I didn't want to talk about the film; I needed a release. And fast. I conjured up girlie images of Pearl and Alessandra together, sucking each other's tits—anything to get my wooden dick to climax and then get back to normal.

"I know you have a penchant for pretty women," I breathed into my iPhone as I gazed at the screen; Pearl's beautiful breasts lathered with bubble-bath foam. "Remember when you told me about your first time? When your best friend stroked you with a feather? Fuck," I groaned, my hand moving up and down my mammoth cock. I had Pearl's wet pussy in my mind's eye, me licking her, flicking my tongue on her clit, fucking her hard. Her squirming beneath me as I thrust myself in and out of her slick wet warmth.

"I'd love to suck your cock right now." Pearl was holding her iPad, her big blue eyes staring at me as if she were right there in the flesh.

I curled my grip harder about my erection, jerking my hand

up and down vigorously. "Tell me, baby. Tell. Me. How. You'd. Suck. My. Hard. Cock."

"I'd take your big, beautiful centerpiece and guide its silkiness all over my face, licking off your pre-cum, dancing my tongue on your huge, thick crown."

"Oh, yeah…oh baby…" My hand clenched harder, pressuring my swollen tip.

"I'd breathe in the smell of you, Alexandre…the one thousand percent pure, unadulterated, all-male, luscious helping of Alexandre Chevalier."

I flinched at the word 'unadulterated' and wished it were true—wished what had happened to me as a boy hadn't been real. I focused on her other words, 'luscious helping' and imagined myself being served up at some banquet. I started laughing manically again—the drug laugh—taking my phone away from my face so Pearl couldn't see my crazy eyes; the mad Frenchman who wanted her to be his bride.

"Go on," I urged, trying to make my voice sound serious.

Her mouth was pouting and I imagined my cock deep inside it. She continued in a whisper, "I'd tease my lips along your balls and let my hot tongue flick up and down along your rock-hard, thick, throbbing cock, thinking how it makes me come when it fucks me so hard—every time. Every single time. No man has ever been able—"

"Don't *ever* put the idea of another man into my head," I interrupted her. "I don't want to know who's touched you. I don't ever want to even *imagine* that you've been with anyone else. You're *mine,* Pearl. Do you understand? You're fucking well *mine.*" My eyes flashed like two balls of fire, my jealousy surging through my veins in an emerald-green rush.

She was moaning, pleasuring herself, turned on by my outburst. For some reason, she liked it when I showed jealousy. Her iPad was all skewwhiff, balanced precariously amongst a pile of scented soaps and fluffed-up towels—maybe it would end up tumbling into the bath again. It had happened before.

"Tell me about my cock in your mouth," I growled. "About how you can't live without it, that you can't live without me fucking you, fucking your hot, tight, juicy cun—" I stopped myself "—pearlette—"

"It's so sexy, so virile, so huge, and even after that big bad boy has spurted into my mouth, he's ready for round two."

"Round three, round four," I moaned. The truth was that I could have fucked Pearl all day, every day, but I knew neither she, nor any normal woman, could have taken that much of me. I looked down at my cock. It was still swollen as fuck. "When I get back tomorrow, Pearl, I'm going to lick that clit, tunnel my tongue deep inside you, reach your G-spot with my tongue, turn you over and fuck you so hard…"

I tightened my grip, racing my hand up and down my erection until the heat rose within me, my orgasm catching up with visions of Pearl's tight pussy, hugging and climaxing all around my cock, me fucking her hard from behind and coming, fucking her mouth and coming, and in my deep, dark, secret fantasy—shamefully buried and snuffed out from my conscious mind—easing my cock very, very slowly into the forbidden part of her where I would never venture. Off limits. Not allowed, even though she'd suggested it several times.

Somewhere I dared not go because of what had happened to me. The shame. The fear. The humiliation. I had the scar to prove it really did take place that wintery morning at dawn;

right there in the crack of my ass.

He was a monster, no doubt.

My mother had done the right thing.

By the time I was on my way back home to New York, very early the next morning, my dick had calmed down and my grin had changed from inane to sober, my jaw still aching from all the laughing, though, and my mind active on how I would need to keep this whole crazy episode quiet.

Very quiet.

The last thing I wanted was for Pearl to find out I'd been bound and drugged, especially by Laura of all people.

For one thing, it did little for my manhood. A black-belt in Taekwondo being nearly overtaken by a skinny blonde with a handful of drugs? It made me look like a real pussy.

Not to mention the fact that Pearl wouldn't believe me for a bloody second. Even my own sister doubted me when I told her the story. There was no way Pearl would be convinced.

This winter wedding business was threatening to undo me. It was still only October. The sooner Pearl and I were married, the sooner all this backlog of ex-nutters would be off my case, out of my life and leave me in peace.

Surely they wouldn't hound a married man?

Little did I know, at that point, that Laura's shenanigans were just the beginning.

I found Pearl in bed. I slipped in beside her and needed, oh yes, I really *needed* to be inside her. Her velvet cave was becoming my security. My home. It was where I belonged and where

I constantly wanted to be. I felt secure there.

I didn't fuck her hard, and ravage her as I'd threatened to in our Skype call. No. I held her close, kissing her toothpaste-fresh mouth, my tongue exploring hers with tiny, fluttery movements so I could feel every nuance, every miniscule touch. I entered her wetness, stretching her open, my hands clasped greedily beneath her round ass, bringing her closer with every thrust as she moaned under me.

"Please don't stop, Alexandre," she told me, tears sparkling in her eyes.

"I'll never stop fucking you, baby," I groaned into her mouth. "Never."

She'd got the hang of it, all right. These days, orgasms were coming out of her like a string of pearls. I could feel her now, massaging her clit against the root of my thick dick in a rhythmical rocking movement. I sensed the heat build inside her, her pussy clamping around me, owning me. I couldn't get enough of her. Each time she came, it was more intense, deeper—even more carnal than the time before.

The pair of us were insatiable.

Pearl was truly addicted to me. Couldn't get enough of me. Or my cock.

Or so I thought.

A rude awakening was about to prove me dead wrong.

3

I started noticing the change within Pearl after her first dream. She was crying out in her sleep, tossing and thrashing in the bed, the small of her back soaked with sweat.

"Get off me. You fuck!" she screamed.

I woke up with a start, thinking Rex had jumped on the bed, landing in a painful bound on her breasts (as dogs and cats tend to do), but her eyes were closed and Rex wasn't there—he had his own bed. My hands held her wrists to try and calm her, but it made her yowl even harder and sent her into a kicking frenzy. Her swim-toned legs were strong, crashing against my calves with all her might. *Jesus, what was the nightmare that had caused this?*

"Pearl, chérie, wake up!"

Her eyes flew open. She was panting; beads of sweat were gathered like raindrops on her brow, under her arms, behind her knees.

"Baby, what's wrong? What the hell were you dreaming about?" I asked, holding her close. But she shoved me away, a sneer etched on her lips.

"I'm going to take a shower, I'm drenched." She tried to smile at me but it was obvious I had done something terrible to her in her dream and she hated me in that instant.

"Baby?" I tried again, taking her hand. But she shooed it away, wrestling herself free from the confines of my embrace.

"Please, Alexandre. I just need a shower, I'll be fine."

"What were you dreaming about?"

Her eyes flashed with fury. "Nothing. Really, I can't even remember. I was being chased by a sort of scaly-fish monster or something. Just a typical bad dream, nothing more."

Liar.

Meanwhile, Sophie had suddenly decided that Pearl was marvelous. She was almost obsessed with her, wondering why Pearl was spurning her friendship.

"Because," I said, "you've been a bitch to her in the past and she doesn't trust you an inch." We were sitting at a bar in a restaurant in SoHo, waiting for our table, listening to *Lady Grinning Soul* by David Bowie. It reminded me of Pearl.

"But I'm getting her a bloody Zang Toi wedding gown—it's costing a fortune!"

"If there's one thing you need to know about Pearl, Sophie, it's that she doesn't give a toss about money. She does appreciate the thought, though, but she's suspicious of your motives, and I don't blame her."

"What, just because I called her a cougar?"

"You called her worse, if I remember. And when you came to dinner the other night you were being all bitchy. Pearl noticed, believe me."

"That was not directed at Pearl but at you, dear brother…my jibe about the engagement ring. You could have had *our* diamond if you wanted it so badly, not buy that second-hand gem that belonged to some Russian royalty who fucked horses."

I laughed. "You were guarding that silly Indian diamond like a phoenix, Sophie. And the vintage piece I bought for Pearl and had converted into that spectacular, eat-your-heart-out-Liz-Taylor ring, I would hardly describe as 'second-hand.' It belongs in a bloody museum."

"Anyway, Pearl is an enigma. She makes me…I don't know…I feel—"

I nearly spluttered my beer all over the bar. "Jesus, you don't *fancy* her, do you? Lay off; Pearl's *mine.*" This place made great Bloody Marys but I'd be steering clear of *those* for a while, so I'd settled for an ice-cold beer.

Sophie cackled with laughter. "No, but I do have to say I think she really is very beautiful. She has an angelic face. Really, she looks like an angel in a Botticelli painting. There's an innocent soulfulness about her eyes. There *is* something special about her. I just wish she wanted to be my friend."

"Give it time, Sophie. Pearl's like a cat. You have to let her come to you; not be pushy or she'll run away."

"By the way, speaking of felines, Claudine called me," Sophie told me. "She says she's left several messages and you haven't got back to her. She's very upset. I mean, *really* upset.

Hurt feelings. You'd better get in touch."

Oh no. "What does she want?"

"Well, she split with her boyfriend recently."

"Oh God."

"She's doing well, though. She's just been offered a campaign by L'Oréal. You know, the glamorous older model, the over thirty type of thing. She looks amazing for her age. She's quite a stunner."

"If you're into bones that look as if they can snap in two and skin paler than alabaster, yes, she's a beauty."

"Anyway, you'd better call her because she's been really bugging me about seeing you. She says she misses you and wants to hang out. She sounded very depressed, very doomsday about everything, despite her modeling success."

I could feel my insides churn. Would there never be an end to this slew of exes battering at my door?

"I'm getting married, Sophie. I don't want to see Claudine. Nor Indira, nor Laura. Nor any other beautiful ex that might pop out from under the fancy wood paneling."

Sophie laughed again and said in English, "It never rains it pours. I love that expression."

I felt my lips tighten. *Bloody Claudine. I thought I was off the hook.* "I'm in love with Pearl," I enunciated—to myself as much as to my sister. *I won't be roped into a guilt trip noose about my neck again. Claudine needs to sort her own fucking issues out with men. There is no way I'll partake in any more mercy fucks for Claudine.*

Sophie dabbed her lips with a hint of gloss. "Alessandra will be all over her, I just know it."

"Who?"

"Alessandra will be all over Pearl."

"That's right, you met Alessandra Demarr, that time backstage after we'd been to see her in that play. I'd forgotten about that. What's she like?"

Sophie turned her face away from me and said, "Oh look, our table's ready. I'm starving, aren't you?"

At the time I didn't put two and two together.

The dreaded phone call came the next day.

"How did you get my number?" I asked Claudine. She hadn't even spoken but I suspected it was Claudine because of the weighty silence that I knew I was expected to fill. Responsible, as I was, for her misery. *Not.*

"Alexandre, I'm so down. My boyfriend and I—"

"I know," I cut in. "Sophie told me. I'm sorry it didn't work out but don't lose hope—there are plenty of other men out there who would be delighted to date you." *Delighted until enlightened…to the psycho side.*

"You're the only man I've ever known who knows how to fuck me properly, Alex."

Uh, oh. "You're being dramatic. Don't be silly."

"I've been on a binge. I've fucked eight men in eight days and not a single one of them has gotten me even close to feeling turned on, let alone having an orgasm."

"Claudine, that's not the way to go about things. Men usually don't care if a woman comes or not. They're in it for themselves. That's why you need to develop a *real* relationship with someone. So he cares about your needs."

"I tried. You think I didn't try? My last boyfriend. But it

was a disaster in the end. Even *he* was crap in bed."

I sucked in a deep breath. "Look, I'm sorry but I can't help you. What I can do is pay for you to see someone. A psychiatrist or a counselor—someone you can discuss all this with you in depth."

"All those bloody book boyfriends don't help."

"What?"

"I feel so *inadequate*. All the women in those stories come in thousands of different positions as easily as if they were brushing their teeth. They even come on command. On command for fuck's sake! All the guy has to say is, '*Come* for me baby,' and the woman comes, one point zero seconds later. Just like that! As fast as clicking a finger. Is that even possible for a woman? Because it sure as hell isn't possible for me! I can't come at all, let alone on bloody command. What's wrong with me?"

"Claudine, that's fantasy, not reality. In reality things are more complicated. Don't believe what you read. I know…my mother's into that shit. You think if all women were coming on command they'd be reading those books? No, they'd be busy fucking instead."

"It's not just the novels but the magazines, too. It's all about the men. How to please *the man*. How to be a sex goddess. What about *us?* Why aren't they being taught how to please *us?*"

I thought of Sophie. This was her next business plan—to set up a 'romance spa' as she described it. Very chic. Expensive, where men would be trained to please women—women would be the only clientele—no male clients allowed. The sex workers cum 'escorts' (yes, the word cum is very appropriate here) would be handpicked. Models—really good-looking types who would learn everything from scratch. Have their bad habits wiped clean. Learn how to make a woman come from just a foot massage. How to give her mind-blowing orgasms, even if she'd never experienced one before. There would be sex workers to accommodate gay women too. It would be fantasy haven. But better than fantasy, fantasy made reality.

"Alex? Are you there?" Hell..ooo?"

"Yes, Claudine, I'm still here. I was just thinking about my sister's business plan, sorry. Listen, I'm serious—I'll pay for a shrink or someone you can talk to, but I can't see you myself. I told you I was serious about Pearl. We're getting married."

"But you're not married *yet?*"

"As good as. We're engaged."

"But you haven't got a ring on your finger."

"Claudine—"

"Which means you're still *technically* single."

I took another deep breath and looked at my bare left hand. I wanted that wedding band on my finger more than I imagined Rex wanted a big, fat, juicy bone.

And damn it, I wasn't bloody well going to wait until winter.

4

When Pearl suggested that we go to LA, I jumped at the chance. Her bad dreams had gotten out of control but she wouldn't discuss them with me, just insisted she couldn't remember what had happened each time. Yet I could feel her pulling away. Her desire for me was wavering like a flickering candle. Why all of a sudden? As if something had triggered the bad dreams, which in turn were making her jump when I touched her as she slept. What and why?

I wondered if I was somehow responsible; if I'd been too sexual with her—too dominating, too insatiable. She was holding something back but I had no idea what. So I put it down to the documentary she and Natalie were making on child trafficking. The tales she told me of young girls being raped and beaten were pretty horrific. Selfishly, I was glad that Pearl wanted to take a break from making controversial documentaries and move into something less harrowing:

feature films. Although, dealing with actors' egos could also be pretty tough, but at least her day-to-day work would be somewhat more lighthearted.

So LA would be a breath of fresh air, I thought. We'd go, take a vacation and then I'd leave her there if she wanted to stay on as I had a business trip in Canada coming up. I hoped that it would calm her down a bit—a change of scenery would stop those nightmares. She could tinker with the *Stone Trooper* script with the scriptwriter, as Alessandra Demarr had insisted on changes. Being a Tony award-winning actress, Alessandra had some clout and Sam Myers seemed to be bending over backwards to keep her sweet.

LA was perfect. Sunny, blue sky, palm trees, people smiling incessantly as if they were taking some sort of happy pill. Our trip was made all the more enjoyable by our choice of rental car: a powder blue, 1960 Eldorado Biarritz convertible Cadillac. It had fins and glistening chrome that shone silver in the sunlight. I felt as if Pearl and I were riding on a giant shark, cruising the wide avenues, spotting other vintage cars and California girls as we sped by, the wind catching our hair, the music blasting through the speakers. Pearl looked like a true California Girl herself—tanned and lithe, golden and sun-kissed, so I played the song, *California Girls* by The Beach Boys, and we sang along.

We were on our way to Alessandra Demarr's house in Topanga Canyon and when we arrived, my eyes strayed, not to Alessandra in her black negligee outfit, but to her classic car, a

1962 Porsche 356B, also black. As Alessandra eye-fucked Pearl, roaming her saucy gaze lasciviously all over Pearl's body and suggesting Bloody Marys of all bloody things (yes, I know), I was only too glad to take Alessandra up on her offer of taking her car for a spin.

"She's all yours, Alexandre, the keys are under the mat."

"I can see you can't get rid of me fast enough," I said with a wink.

"Come back in half an hour," she said in her lilting Italian accent, taking Pearl's arm and guiding her away.

Pearl looked like a lamb being led to slaughter. Sophie had been right; beautiful seductress Alessandra was all over her. Funny, we could have been siblings, Alessandra and I. She had eyes my color: fiery green. I guess I was used to looking at myself in the mirror and didn't think about my eyes, one way or another, but on Alessandra they looked predatorily unnerving, as if she were about to literally devour Pearl. I wondered if I looked the same. Like a wolf. Or a panther. Because before Alessandra began her feast, I imagined that she'd lick Pearl all over first and taste every inch of her body. It turned me on, actually, to envision this, and I felt rather wicked for leaving my fiancée in her clutches, but it also amused me.

At first.

The drive was beautiful. I took the car along Pacific Coast Highway, speeding, seeing how the old Porsche could handle corners, as the ocean shimmered on one side and scrubby mountains rose above on the other. I figured that if I got stopped, I'd just show the cops my French license—it usually did the trick. No points off because the paperwork was too much hassle.

When I returned, I found the two women snacking, and drinking their Bloody Marys. I wondered for a second if Alessandra had done a Laura on her, as Pearl was innocently sipping her drink through a straw. Alessandra was wet, had obviously gone for a swim; her pert breasts clinging to her see-through dress, her hand on Pearl's thigh. A vision of them kissing flashed through my head. I closed my eyes to think of something else so my hard-on would go away.

Alessandra looked up. "Hi Frenchie."

"Hi, baby," Pearl said. "How was your drive?"

"Beautiful." I stood there, legs astride, watching the two of them.

"I was just trying to persuade your fiancée to stay on as we need to work on the script."

I knew it. She was going to get her smooth, gay fingers all over Pearl. For a second, I felt a frisson of jealousy tingle through my spine. I stared Alessandra down. *She's mine, bitch-on-heat.* I walked over to stake my claim. I put my hands on Pearl's shoulders and kissed the nape of her neck.

I'd test Pearl, I decided. If she wanted to stay...well then...she'd get seduced and she damn well knew it. She'd have to battle with her inner-gay-goddess all on her own. If she came home with me, then she really was my girl. I couldn't make that choice for her.

"Stay, chérie, enjoy the weather, have some *fun* with Alessandra," I said with a wry grin. "Anyway, I have to go to Montreal for a meeting so you might as well hang out here for a bit."

"I don't know," she wavered, looking at Alessandra and then at me. "I should really get home, but it *is* so beautiful here;

so nice to feel the sunshine on my back."

"You're staying, Pearl," Alessandra barked like the alpha female she was. "I won't allow you to leave yet. We have important work to get done here with the script."

I almost wanted to take the two women at once and fuck them both, there and then. Show Alessandra who was boss. I was also extremely turned on thinking about them together. My heart raced just imagining our threesome, but I knew it would be a very bad idea. Pearl would go wild with jealousy, and anyway, it would feel like incest; Alessandra was too similar to me.

What would happen, I wondered, if Pearl was truly gay, though? If she played around with Alessandra and got converted? The woman was every inch a movie star. She had the X factor, that *je ne sais quoi* that set her apart from the crowd. And she wanted Pearl. I almost felt like calling Ellen DeGeneres to break up the happy party… distract Alessandra, get her away from *my* woman. Insanely, I felt threatened by her. Ridiculous! Being threatened by a she-wolf when I was the alpha male?

I guess that's why I toyed with the idea of Pearl staying on. To prove to myself I could handle it. So paradoxically, by not stopping her and being so blasé about it all, I actively encouraged Pearl to remain in LA for a few days.

The next morning, while Pearl and I were making love—and I say 'making love' because it was far more than just a fuck—she pushed me off her, saying she felt sick. It was sudden. A click-of-a-finger sudden. One second she was squirming beneath me in ecstasy, and the next she was repulsed, looking as if she really *was* about to throw up. Was I going crazy? Was this Alessandra Demarr thing for real? *Jesus. Is my woman a fucking full-on lesbian?*

As the day went on, I still wasn't sure what was going on. Pearl thought she had food poisoning. Then I decided that perhaps she was pregnant. *Hallelujah!*

We were walking along the oceanfront by Venice Beach. I could feel Pearl's coolness. Normal, I decided, pregnant women often push their males away—human nature.

"Could you be pregnant?" I blurted out after a long bout of silence.

"I wish," she said in a sad voice. "No, if I were pregnant my breasts would feel swollen and I would have missed my period by now."

"What's wrong then, baby? I get the feeling that you'd rather I weren't around for a while."

"Just that smoothie I drank yesterday, I think."

I was hoping that she'd say, *Don't be crazy, of course I want you around.* Or, *I'm coming back with you, coming with you to Montreal.* But she didn't. She just clutched my arm and walked ahead in silence, her private thoughts ticking away in her head. Not letting me in. Mentally pushing me out. Everything seemed more interesting to her than opening up to me. She people-watched the assortment of nutters that passed us: a guy on roller-skates with a guitar, a bodybuilder wearing a leopard-print leotard, a woman with huge round breasts that looked as if they would pop any second, a dog wearing shades.

"Pearl, are you sure you're okay?"

"It would be nice to live by the ocean, wouldn't it?"

Ignoring me. "Just say the word and we can buy a house in Malibu. Whatever you want. I could surf and you could walk along the beach with Rex, unless you're brave enough to brace the icy water. Would you like that?"

"Maybe." She smiled weakly. Nothing I said seemed to warm her.

"You don't have to keep working, you know. You can throw in the towel with HookedUp Enterprises any time. Be my kept woman. Read novels and laze about in the sun."

"I've worked all my life; I'd get bored. Anyway, what about you? You said you'd break things up with Sophie and HookedUp, yet you still carry on, even though it's obvious she wants to see our relationship come to an end."

The Sophie issue again. Whatever I said, Pearl was convinced that Sophie was out to get her. I kept my mouth shut. I got the feeling that *whatever* I told her, it wouldn't work out in my favor.

"Alexandre, if you and your life met right now, right here, what would you say to it?"

"What?"

"If you and your life could have a conversation, what would you tell it?"

"Je ne regrette rien," I said with a laugh, quoting the Edith Piaf song.

"Seriously."

"I *am* serious. The only thing I might regret is not having kissed you sooner."

"If you could re-live your life, is there anything you'd do differently?"

I tried to gauge her expression but she wasn't giving anything away. I answered, "I am who I am because of all my choices; the good and the bad. Even the mediocre." I thought of Laura and a shiver of shame crept up the back of my neck. "I mean, thank God things happened the way they did, or I might have ended up with Laura and I wouldn't have met you." The second I said those words I wished I hadn't bloody mentioned Laura.

"Do you still think about her?"

Yes. That she's a fucking fruitcake! And I just escaped a bloody close shave. "She's a friend, I guess. We shared a past, that's all." I felt my face heat up.

"So you don't agonize over choices you made and wish that there were things you hadn't done?"

Pearl was onto me. Somehow, *she knew.* That's why she'd cooled off. *Did she know about Laura trying to fuck me?* Or perhaps she'd guessed about my mother? The way she was staring into my eyes had my solar plexus feel as if someone had swung a baseball bat at my gut.

I tried to sound cool. Unfazed. "Sometimes you don't have a choice, Pearl. External forces choose for you."

"We always have a choice. A choice not to get ourselves into bad predicaments in the first place. At least when we're adults, that is. Children don't get a chance to choose."

And was she now *choosing* to break up with me, or something? Her glass-cold face wasn't revealing a thing.

"Your mother, for instance? She had a choice," Pearl went on.

Jesus! What does she know? Does she know what my mother did? "My father was a monster," I said in retaliation, my teeth gritted.

"What happened to your father, anyway?" she asked, her eyebrows raised as if she had guessed the real truth.

"He disappeared," I said, as casually as I could.

"Oh really?" Her brows did their thing again.

"Yes, really, Pearl. That nasty douchebag just disappeared into thin air."

"Aren't you worried that he may come back and *haunt* you?"

I told her that he had disappeared but she seemed to know that he was *dead*. She used the word 'haunt.' *How* did she know? I said in a cold-fire voice. "He's gone for good. He won't come back. Ever."

5

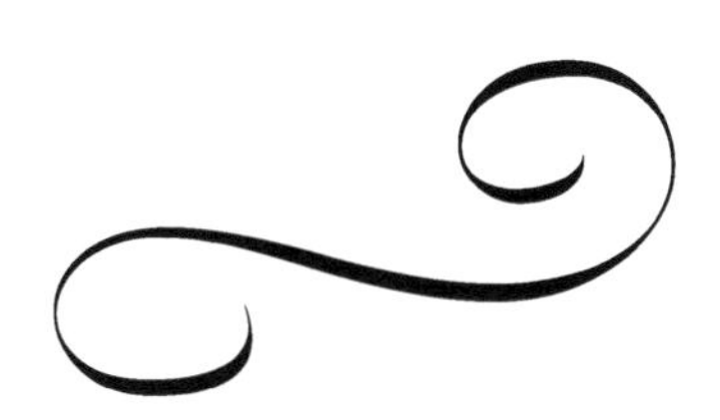

I feel his hands around my shoulders. He's behind me, pressing himself up against my back; his hug tight—he's squeezing the breath from my lungs with his grip. I can smell the whiskey on his breath, like dragon fire, and I wonder what would happen if I lit a match—would his breath go up in flames?

I imagine myself as St. George, piercing this creature—because when he's like this, he IS a creature. Yeah, I could lance this slimy dragon right through his leg. He would roll over in pain. I wouldn't actually kill him but I'd maim him so he could never hurt me again. Because he would truly fear me.

Forever.

I want to move. But I don't. If I move, it'll wake him and he's beginning to snore; the air around us thick with molecules of whiskey, dancing around his smelly mouth. Molecules of hate. And lies. I mustn't hardly breathe. I mustn't make a sound. He'll fall asleep, snoring like a wild hog, and when he's out cold, I'll leave the room.

I want to go to my mother but she's so weak she can't protect me. She can't protect herself. If she cared, she'd do something. Only Sophie cares but Sophie isn't here.

I can hear the snow, softly tapping against the windowpane of my room. I look at the posters on my wall and wish I could escape inside them. Fly in my spacecraft to a different planet and never return. I close my eyes and prepare myself for the cold outside. My parka will have to do. If I walk fast enough, I'll keep warm. There'll be the man selling chestnuts—in a couple of hours. I want to steal some coins from Papa's pockets but he'll hear. Like a bat, he is, even when he's drunk.

Why? The only word now in my head is why.

Why, why, why?

Why does it have to be this way?

I felt something pressing into my back and realized with relief that it was Rex, his paws digging into my shoulders as he stretched out on the mattress, snoring rhythmically. I was about to push him off the bed (when did he jump up?), but a wave of gratitude swept over me, a surge of butterflies swooped about my stomach, knowing that it was just my boy Rex, and I flung my arms about him and hugged him close, kissing his soft ears. I was grateful for every goddamn thing in my life at that moment.

I had escaped. I got away free and clear. Scarred, both mentally and physically yes, but free. Not in a mental hospital somewhere. Not beaten down. Not the speck of dust, the vessel of despair my father wanted me to be. I was a survivor, I *am* a survivor, and like all survivors, we learn the hard way.

I am who I am because of my past. Je ne regrette rien.

However crazy Sophie drove me at times, I thanked her for everything she had done for me. She gave me my dignity back. She told me I was a hero and deserved to be called Chevalier.

She taught me to be strong, and how to fight. She fed me.

I owed her, literally, my life.

I got showered and dressed and took Rex to Central Park. With Sophie on my mind, I called her. I wanted to let her know that Elodie was doing fine; had even been going out with friends, and was dressing less like a Vampire Goth and more like a girl her age. I missed Sophie. We'd been sparring, mostly due to her previous attitude towards Pearl, which, although now over (as far as Sophie was concerned), Pearl was still wary and suspicious. It was going to take more than a wedding gown to patch things up. It was going to take time.

Time…the great healer of adversity.

"Sophie," I said into my cell, as I walked with Rex past Tiffany, casting my eye along the display of jewelry, wondering if I could find a necklace to match Pearl's ring. "How are things in Paris? Have you seen Maman lately?" I don't know why I asked—I knew the answer.

"No, I haven't had time. So many meetings."

"Oh yeah? Anyone I should know about?"

"I've bought a chunk of Myers Industries."

"Myers Industries?"

"Samuel Myers; the one you and Pearl are doing *Stone Trooper* with."

"Well that's a surprise," I said, wondering how this news would go down with Pearl. "What brought that about?"

"He's going broke, Alexandre. He's in dire straits. If someone doesn't bail him out, that movie won't get made."

"Since when have you felt so charitable, Sophie?"

"Not charity, just a good business deal and, you know, looking out for my future sister in-law."

"Have you told Pearl?"

"I think you'd better tell her. Something tells me she might see it as a sort of *coup d'état* if my money's involved in helping produce the movie."

"Yeah, she's proud of her autonomy with this project. I know she wouldn't be too thrilled about you being a part of it. I mean, *I'm* not even involved. I'm not sure how she'll take this, Sophie."

"It's only money, Alexandre. I'm not getting involved in any way creatively. It upsets me that she's so offhand with me. I wish she didn't feel so alienated, so mistrustful. I'd like to be friends. Go shopping, see a movie, you know."

"Just give it time, Soph. Give it time." I moved on, crossed the street and walked toward the park.

"What are you up to right now?" she asked.

"About to go to Montreal. I'm seeing a video games artist there. This new venture could be big, Soph, really big."

"Well, good luck. I know you love that shit."

Despite my reservations about Sophie now being involved with Samuel Myers, I felt a rush of nostalgia pump through my heart—I believed that my sister really did want to make things right with Pearl. It was true; her money would save everyone's ass if Sam Myers really was in a financial bind. "What about you? Are you happy?" The question popped unexpectedly out of my mouth.

"Happy?" Her voice cracked just a touch.

"Well isn't that what life is all about? Finding your slice of happiness? Love? Peace?"

There was silence. I felt bad. I wondered for a second if Sophie had *ever* been truly happy. I had found my little piece of heaven with Pearl. Was Sophie still searching?

"I'm getting there, Alexandre. I'm seeing someone now."

"Oh yeah? Who?"

"We'll see."

"Okay, you don't want to tell me. That's fine. I'm glad you're dating, anyway."

"I'd prefer to tell Pearl, myself—when the moment's right. And I don't want Elodie to know."

"Of course not."

"You know, gay is all very cool and hip, but when it's your own mother? It might not go down so well with Elodie." She sucked in a long breath. "Have fun in Montreal. Is Pearl still in LA?"

"She's hanging out with Alessandra Demarr."

"Hanging out?"

"Tinkering with the script. Alessandra has taken a shine to Pearl—you were right."

"Slut."

"What?" She bloody better not be referring to Pearl.

"Actresses are all the same," she ranted. "Such narcissists. Always seeking attention. Not enough love from daddy or something. They want the world to love them. Anyone will do."

"Pearl's not anyone, Sophie. I can easily see why a gay woman would go potty over her."

"Shut up already!"

"Why does this bother you? You're feeling protective over Pearl?"

"Something like that. Anyway, I must go. My trainer's coming over any minute and I need to get ready."

"Okay. We'll speak soon. Oh Sophie, one more thing…"

"What?"

"This Sam Myers business. You swear it's just your share of money involved in *Stone Trooper*? You promise you won't get involved in the creative side of things."

"I swear."

"Okay, then."

"Bye."

I pressed 'end'. A frisson crept up my spine—a sort of premonition of doom, although I couldn't pinpoint what. I pulled Rex away from the edge of a mailbox—dogs, men, we all want to make our mark—piss on everything; tell the world that this spot, or that, belongs to us. "No, Rex, enough is enough—how come your bladder always has extra to spare? Come on, boy, let's go to the park."

While Pearl was in sunny LA, New York was turning from autumn into winter. Days were passing more slowly; dark evenings were descending more rapidly. Montreal was even worse. The minute I stepped off the plane, I felt the air, icy on my cheeks. Pearl and I had spoken on the phone before takeoff but the line went dead. She said she had something important to tell me—the thing which had been responsible for her nightmares. Finally, she was going to divulge her secret. *We all have secrets and that's what a relationship is all about—finding the right moment to reveal pieces of our past.* Pearl was about to share hers, but I was still hiding my own slithering nest of vipers in a dark pit. It felt unfair and reminded me that she was too good for me.

Her call came through, and I picked up, feeling a sense of relief. Though her voice was shaking, trembling with rage.

"Why didn't you tell me, Alexandre?"

Heat spiraled through my veins. My mother's secret? Laura's Bloody Mary? "Hey, babe, great to hear your voice. What's up?"

The tirade began. Samuel Myers. Sophie. Shit, I'd forgotten to tell her about Sophie coming on board when we'd spoken yesterday.

"Calm down, chérie, I was going to tell you; it just slipped my mind."

"Bullshit!"

"It's just money, Pearl. No big deal. Sophie won't be involved in any way whatsoever—she's just helping out financially."

The conversation dragged on—Pearl screaming at me, which she had never done before. She was usually so calm but her conversation was laced with threats, tumbling from her livid lips: phrases like 'future ex-marriage' and 'our relationship is over.'

I had to act fast. She was hysterical about this Sophie thing. I said in a level voice, "I'm coming to get you now, Pearl. I'm going to cancel my meeting, hire a jet, and fly straight out to be with you and we'll get married in Vegas tomorrow. You can still have your white wedding but let's just stop this waiting game nonsense and get married."

But she wasn't having it. "You're not listening to a goddamn word I've said, Alexandre Chevalier. Once you have split with Sophie, once and for all—gotten out of HookedUp, *then* we have a chance of making our relationship work. Until then, adios amigo, because you know what? The last thing in the world I want right now is a relationship with a cock."

I felt like the dragon being lanced by St. George. So *that* was it…she was gay, after all! She'd fallen in love with Alessandra Demarr and wanted me out of the picture. More fool me. What an idiot I'd been to be so casual about the whole thing. Worse, actively encouraging her to explore her inner bloody lesbian!

"Is that all I am to you? A cock?" I said quietly.

"Men are pigs. Pigs! You rape women. Everything you do is conditioned by your dicks." She went on another tirade…something about rape in South Africa, celebrities shagging mentally handicapped children, and men fucking underage girls. She must have been getting updates from Natalie for their documentaries. But Pearl was preaching to the converted. If anyone knew how sick men could be, it was me.

"Pearl, my darling," I said in a gentle voice. "What's suddenly brought all this on? Is it Alessandra?"

Between her sobbing and hitched voice gulping for air, I could hardly understand a word Pearl said. "Call Daisy," she hiccupped, "she'll explain. I can hardly speak right now I'm so furious about Sophie. I do not want Sophie in my life!" She hung up on me.

So we were back to the Sophie topic again. Pearl was all over the place. The hairs on my arms bristled with chilled fear. I was about to lose my Pearl. My *life*. For whatever reason, she wanted me *out* and she was using Sophie as an excuse to extricate herself from me. But I simply wasn't having it. No fucking way.

I called the videographer with whom my meeting was scheduled, and cancelled him. And I instructed my assistant to get a plane to take me immediately to LA; I required a car and he also needed to book a preacher to marry us in Vegas that very night—orchestra and all—and a jet to take us away to Bora Bora for our honeymoon. I'd nip this nonsense in the bud. Pearl and I would get married and live happily ever after. I'd deal with the Sophie issue at a later date when I'd got Pearl under control. Because she *did* need to be controlled. She was like a racecar spiraling all over the track. She needed me to steady her. If she'd turned gay, I'd simply ease her back again into being heterosexual. She'd loved sex with me before—I'd win her back again. I'd mend her broken wing; the wing someone had damaged in her nightmares.

I was used to hysterical women. Pearl would be no different. And even if she were just as nutty as the rest of them, I didn't care; I wanted her anyway.

I called her back. She would have had time to cool down a little. "I've cancelled my meeting; I'm on my way."

"Well I won't be around when you get here," she said through tears.

"Don't be silly, Pearl, just stay where you are."

"I don't want to see you." *The lance, again...stabbing me.*

"Please explain what's going on, baby. Is it Alessandra? Is it those nightmares you've been having? What's going on?"

There was a long pause and she eventually said, "A long time ago when I was at university..."

Finally the truth. But she stopped mid-sentence.

"Go on, chérie...I'm here for you. I love you. Please share your pain with me. Your pain is *my* pain—I can get you through this."

"No you can't, you're a guy and sorry, Alexandre, but males repulse me right now. I am *disgusted.*"

"I understand, baby. I swear, I do. I agree—men can be pigs. I may be a man but all I want is to love you, protect you, and care for you. Please tell me what happened, my angel. You can trust me. I'm here for you."

The floodgates opened. It all came out. The gang rape at college. The spiked drink (well, Laura taught me about the infallibility of that one). How Pearl felt she'd asked for it because she was wearing a miniskirt. The guilt. The sense of culpability, shame, and then the blackout which morphed into a blank-out—memories better left buried.

Oh Pearl, I wanted to say; *I've been there, too.* But I didn't get a chance. I managed to assure her how it wasn't her fault, how we'd get through it together, but she was so upset she couldn't hear me. She started ranting on about Sophie again, then hung up. I called back but she'd put her cell on voicemail. I left several messages, anyway, telling her to meet me at Van Nuys airport where we would catch a private jet to Vegas. Although, somehow, I knew things weren't going to be quite so simple.

I'd have to be the bulldozer guy. I had no choice. Whether Pearl liked it or not, I was coming to get her. She was falling off a cliff with her broken wing and I was the only person who could catch her.

I dozed off on the plane, planning every move in my head: our flash-lightening wedding, our honeymoon, and how I'd insist on us both taking a break from work—maybe that tree-house in Thailand I'd been fantasizing about would be a good plan. Pearl needed a rest, needed time to heal.

August in Paris. Tempers are raising the thermometers even higher.

We had a picnic by the river today and everything was perfect. Sophie's back home from staying at her friend's. Papa's been on good behavior. Maman loves him with every tiny piece of her heart. Smiles; making sexy eyes, laughing, happy dinners, and happy faces. But I can feel the demon returning. The slimy creature is making its way back inside him and settling in for the night. Sophie says he's okay; that he's taken his medication, but I can feel it bubbling under his skin. I hold Sophie's hand. We're watching TV.

I whisper in her ear. "Stay in my bed tonight."

She laughs. "You're a big boy, you don't need me."

I want to tell her how he rubbed himself up against me—when she was away. When he wasn't taking his pills. He rubbed himself up and down, through the sheets, and I could hear him moan when he stopped. I could feel the wetness. He gripped my shoulders. He rubbed. He cried. He rubbed. He got up and left.

"I don't want him rubbing again," I tell Sophie.

She takes my hand and leads me to her bedroom, away from our parents, who are still staring at the TV screen. Sophie isn't smiling now. "What did he do? Did he touch you here," she asks, her finger pointing to her private place.

"He didn't touch me there. But he breathes in my ear and cries and rubs himself up against me. He tells Maman he's coming to say goodnight to me and read me a story but sometimes he falls asleep in my bed when he's drunk."

"The bastard." Her eyes are looking about her as if she's planning something. "And Maman does nothing?"

I nodded my head. "She doesn't know."

"No point telling her because she won't believe you anyway. But I believe you, Alexandre. I know what he does. I know." Tears are in

Sophie's eyes now. I wonder if he has rubbed her too, but I don't ask. "Are you going to stay at your friend's house again?" I ask with fear.

"No, I'll stay here tonight. If he touches you, call out to me. Okay?"

I nod my head.

I woke with a jolt. The plane was landing. Pearl and I had more in common than she realized. We were both victims. The only difference was that I was a victim who would seek revenge because I'd grown tough over the years. I wasn't that vulnerable little boy anymore. I'd find out who had hurt Pearl and give them what was fucking coming to them.

The rental car my assistant had organized for me was waiting. I was glad to see it was the latest Mercedes—I'd need something speedy because Pearl was really giving me the runaround—not picking up her phone. I drove to the hotel in Santa Monica where she was still staying. But soon found out she wasn't. She'd bloody well checked out without giving any indication of where she was going. Calling her was fruitless. She was obviously in a terrible state and it seemed she wanted nothing more to do with me, until I, literally, handed her a signed affidavit proving that Sophie and I had parted ways. It was crazy—as if that were something I'd be able to do overnight…a multi-billion dollar company? Pearl should have known better, but then I guessed that working in documentaries and film was a far cry from what I did, and she simply didn't have a clue about how many people it would involve—the logistics of doing such a thing. Pearl was morally blackmailing me: wanting me to choose between her and Sophie, obviously still convinced that Sophie was out for her blood. I could see, too, from Pearl's perspective, why it looked like Sophie was being sneaky. What a fucking mess!

The only place I could imagine Pearl being—unless she'd hightailed herself out of LA altogether—was at Alessandra Demarr's house. Of course, Alessandra wasn't picking up either, but I sped along Pacific Coast Highway toward Topanga Canyon, hoping I'd find Pearl there.

What a fucking fiasco. I had never chased a woman like this before in my life. All that talk about letting women come to you like cats or children, and here I was flying along in this Mercedes in hot pursuit of a madwoman. A fucked-up, dys-functional, neurotic nutter, just like every other female in my life.

The only difference was that this time I felt that my world was at stake. I needed Pearl and I couldn't be without her. At least, I couldn't be *happy* without her.

The gods were on my side. I spotted Pearl exit Alessandra's driveway, but because it wasn't the same powder blue Cadillac, it took me a second to register. She'd changed her rental car and was now (I was pretty sure it was her) driving a BMW. I did a screeching U-turn and pursued the car. It sped up—a wild driver was at the wheel and I knew, by that point, it was definitely Pearl. Our cars were careening along the highway as if we were in a Steve McQueen movie—I was racing to outrun her. The Mercedes and the BMW…always had been rivals on the road. I flashed my lights at Pearl but it only made her go faster. This was insane; we'd get pulled over by a cop—worse, this was LA, we might have a gun held to our heads or flung on the ground and handcuffed.

I zigzagged like a lunatic, weaving between other drivers to pin Pearl down.

Finally, she pulled over at a restaurant parking lot. I overtook her, and then screeched to a halt. I got out of my car and pelted towards her, just in case she got it into her head to take off again. She buzzed down her window, and in that moment, I knew that she was not only crazy, but loving the attention, lapping up the drama.

Yes, Pearl Robinson was a drama queen. She was trying to suppress a grin, which stretched across her full, wide lips.

I leaned into her open window. "Nutter. You want to get us both killed?" I couldn't help but smile too.

But, stubborn as ever, she continued her little game. "I meant what I said, Alexandre. I am not going to Vegas with you. I'm going to Kauai to see my dad."

"Oh Kauai now, is it? I don't think so." I opened her door and hovered my lips centimeters away from her face. "Correction. *We* are going to Vegas. *Together.*" I heard my own voice and I sounded so French… *togezzaire.* "We're getting married tonight; it's all arranged. Then we can go to Kauai for our honeymoon."

I *had* planned for Bora Bora, but who cared? As long as we sealed the deal, we could go anywhere. I grabbed the keys from the ignition and scooped Pearl into my arms and then flung her over my shoulder, so I had my hands free. She was kicking like a child, screaming like a little girl.

"Put me down Alexandre! This isn't funny!"

"Then why are you laughing?"

"Because this is preposterous! You're being outrageous!"

I strode over to the trunk of her car and took out her suitcase; a vintage Luis Vuitton, the weight of which was hard to manage with Pearl jiggling and kicking and flailing her arms about and thumping my back. My Taekwondo training certainly helped me manage this little vixen.

"Enough, Pearl. Stop behaving like a child. Or I'll have to spank you."

"Ha, very funny. You are *insane,* Alexandre Chevalier! Let me down! I won't marry you. I won't, I *won't!*"

"Yes, you will. Stop playing games."

"Don't you dare try and control me, you arrogant French shit!"

"Don't tell me what to do, Pearl. I know what I want and it's your crazy ass. You know it, and I know it. You *know* that we're meant to be together but you're just too stubborn to accept it right now. Stop wasting time because in the end, I'll get my way."

"Ha!" she squealed, still laughing. "You can't marry me because you don't have proof of my divorce!"

Pearl had underestimated me. I'd gotten my hands on her divorce papers weeks ago. "All taken care of, baby. All will be quite legal I can assure you."

I practically threw her into the back of my Mercedes and quickly locked the door. Child safety locks. She couldn't get out. She was pummeling the windows and I too, knew that I was behaving like a madman. But I didn't care. I wanted Pearl Robinson—soon to be Chevalier—and I wasn't going to take no for an answer. I drove off. I could see her through my rearview mirror pouting like a ten year-old in the back seat. The Sophie topic came up. Of course. Pearl was convinced, now, that Sophie was out to kill her.

She announced, "Laura called."

Shock horror! The word, 'Laura' made my body flush with heat and nausea. Had she revealed all to Pearl? *Oh, Jesus.* My stomach churned. *What is that psycho up to now?*

"She told me that Sophie is sure to have me killed in Vegas. That she owns chunks of it…hotels, everything; that she's powerful and owns politicians and police and—"

"Nonsense," I interrupted. I tried to sound nonchalant. It was true, Sophie did have important contacts in Vegas…did own hotels there. But the last thing she'd do was hurt Pearl. Hell, she wanted Pearl to be her friend! *Oh Laura, oh Laura, why can't you fucking stay out of my life?*

Pearl pounded her fist on the car seat. "Why are you ignoring me? Sophie will have me murdered—I'll end up in a dumpster somewhere in Vegas, all because you won't take this seriously!"

In that second, I so wanted to come clean. Tell Pearl about Laura drugging me. Assure her that Laura was making this rubbish up. But I knew that it would make things worse with Pearl. She was on the edge. Admitting that I'd had Laura on top of me, naked, would hardly be the right move—no, Pearl wouldn't have accepted that for a second. So I said nothing, just kept driving to Van Nuys airport where the jet would be waiting.

"Sophie's insane," Pearl went on. "She stabbed your father in the groin!"

Something in me snapped. If it hadn't been for Sophie, I'd be in a loony bin by now. I bashed my closed fist on the steering wheel. "Don't you fucking bring my monster father into this!" I shouted.

Pearl was silenced for a while. I could hear her uneven breathing. She really did believe that Sophie was going to have her topped off, but my hands were tied.

I changed gear. "She's jealous Pearl, that's all." What else could I say? *Laura tried to fuck me?* "Sophie will get used to you."

"She won't fucking get 'used' to me because I'm bailing, Alexandre. I value my life too highly. I love you. I'm *in* love with you, but I refuse to marry you with that crazy woman in the picture!"

The truth was on the tip of my tongue again. I wanted to blurt it all out. Assure her Laura was nuts. But if I did that, Pearl would want to know why. No, with the state she was in—her nightmares, her instability—now wasn't the time. So I just said, "I made some calls tonight. I'm selling HookedUp to Sophie, once and for all." It was only half a lie. I *had* discussed it with Sophie but nothing had been set in stone. "Satisfied?"

The truth was I wanted those wedding bands on our fingers, first. Seal the deal. My mission was to marry Pearl and sort the rest out afterwards. Typically male, I realized later. I should have laid all my cards on the table.

But I didn't.

And it got me into more of a mess than I imagined possible.

"Don't try and pussy-whip me, Pearl," I said, ridiculously grabbing onto any excuse, like a child holding onto a balloon, hoping it will whisk him up and away into some fantasy land.

There was silence and then Pearl said in a quiet voice, "I got pussy-whipped tonight."

Then the second set of secrets was revealed. Pearl told me that she found a photo of Sophie and Alessandra in an embrace. So *that* was who Sophie was seeing. *Jesus, the plot thickened.* I looked guilty as Rex with a stolen bar of chocolate. The fact that I had no idea that Alessandra was Sophie's new romantic partner didn't let me off the hook. I hadn't told Pearl that Sophie was gay—that was her private life. Sophie was bailing out Samuel Myers and acting as a silent partner on *Stone Trooper.* Sophie and Alessandra were in each other's panties. Alessandra had also wheedled her way into Pearl's panties, or so it sounded from Pearl's pussy-whipped quip. *What a fucking tangle. All the more reason to abduct Pearl and take her away with me and get that bloody ring on her finger.*

"Interesting," I mused. "Sophie met Alessandra after that play we went to see her in in London." I laughed. This whole scenario could have been some silly sitcom.

"Did you hear what I said, Alexandre?" Pearl was leaning forward, still in the back seat, her angry breath on my neck. "I got pussy-whipped by Alessandra."

"Well I'm not surprised," I answered, coolly. "She was all over you."

"She seduced me and I let her! I have a sore ass. I'm a fucking head-case. Why the hell do you want to marry me, anyway? I'm a quasi lesbian. I can't do a work deal without being screwed. Yeah, I'm screwed in every way you look at it. I'm a mess, Alexandre."

I couldn't help but let a smile curve onto my lips. "I know."

"No you don't! You thought I was perfect!"

"Perfect for me, chérie. Perfect for me. I guess you must have figured out by now that I'm hardly normal myself. And what happened to you in the past has only made me love you more. We need each other, baby. We're both two dysfunctional peas in the same pod. And we won't be able to *dis*-function properly without one another, you'll see. If you try and run away from me, from *us*, you'll come back because we're destined to be together."

Famous last words.

Little did I know that 'run away' was exactly what Pearl had planned.

With the car parked, and Pearl desperate for the ladies room, we went inside the small airport of Van Nuys. She dashed to the toilets.

I waited for her. And waited.

I stood there like a fucking lemon, holding Pearl's handbag. At first I wasn't paying attention because I was so busy talking on my cell, organizing our wedding. What a fucking joke. I called the car rental people to ask them to come and pick up the car key from me. *Hang on a minute…where's the bloody key?* I fumbled in my jacket pocket…no key. *Did Pearl have it? No, why would she?* That was the first alarm bell. When I saw that the coast was clear and no other women were in the ladies room, I snuck in.

"Pearl? Hurry up, baby. Are you done?" She had told me that she needed to change her tampon. Nothing. The place was empty. I peered into all the cubicles. *What the fuck?* Then I saw…I looked up and there was a tiny window, wide open. I dashed out of the room, through some double doors, and onto the tarmac to the spot where I'd parked the Mercedes.

Gone.

She'd done a bloody runner! I looked in her bag and she had even left her phone behind. And her credit cards. She was *that* desperate to escape from me. A woman on the run. As if I were a wife-beater or something—she wanted nothing more than to get the hell away from me. Tears prickled my eyes. *This woman does not want me.* I felt as if a hole had been scooped out of my gut. Now I knew the British expression of 'feeling gutted.'

The jet was waiting.

But without Pearl, I had nowhere to go.

6

That whole night was torturous. I feared that in Pearl's state she'd drive off a cliff or something, so I called the car rental company and, as I suspected, they had a GPS system fitted underneath the car—Pearl could be tracked. I offered them a bribe, or as I liked to phrase it, "a big tip" so that I could keep her under my radar without causing too much fuss. But it was proving to be tricky because I hadn't included Pearl in the insurance policy (how the fuck was I to know that she'd make off with the car?) so I bought the car, instead. It was heading toward San Francisco. Good. She was on her way to her brother's, obviously. My head was like a computer unscrambling data. I couldn't find a solution to my predicament. The only words I heard ricocheting in my brain were, *Pearl doesn't want you Alexandre. Accept it.*

I made up my mind, then and there; I wasn't going to chase after her anymore. I'd take my own tried and tested advice: let her come to me—the bulldozer technique hadn't worked. I remembered a couple of adages—ironically given to me by my father (when he was in one of his kind moods): *What's yours won't go against you*, and *What's yours will come back to you.* Was Pearl mine? *I* certainly felt she was. I'd have to wait and see. Wait and see if she would return to me—be mine. And not only come back to me, but stick with me for good. I had to bide my time.

Having paid for the jet, I thought I might as well use it, so I flew straight to San Francisco and checked into a hotel. I totaled up the amount of hours it would have taken her to drive here, and I called Anthony, knowing that by now, she would have arrived. He denied that she was with him. More proof that she wanted out. I told him I had a team of detectives on the case. I wanted her to feel the gravity of what she'd done. I didn't need a detective; I myself was enough of a Sherlock Holmes to make up for the whole of Scotland Yard. But he believed me, I guess.

After I hung up, I listened to the messages on Pearl's phone. Most of them from me—but then one from Laura. I pressed my ear to the receiver and heard her sickly sweet-butter-wouldn't-melt-in-my-mouth tone:

"Pearl, you don't know me. I'm sorry to bother you like this. I finally tracked down your number. My name's Laura, Alexandre's ex…maybe you know who I am?"

I shook my head in disbelief. This woman was one hell of a piece of work.

"I'm calling to warn you. Sophie's really crazy. She could be out to hurt you. I'm sorry but…" at this point Laura did a nice little acting job; she sniffled down the line and put on a weak, pathetic, poor-me voice. "I had a terrible accident several years ago and could have died." *Wish you bloody had.*

The message rambled on in a Good Samaritan voice, ending with, "As one woman to another I thought I owed you this…"

I heard a guttural roar tear from my throat as I threw the cellphone against the wall and it smashed to the floor.

I was in this Laura shit up to my neck. She was such a good liar that I feared Pearl wouldn't believe me if I told her the real story. So I did what all guilty fools do; I dug myself in even deeper. I created more lies to cover myself. To this day, I will never forgive myself for this: I *lied* to Pearl.

The following afternoon, I waited for Pearl in Anthony's back yard. She came into the garden, her hair wet; she'd obviously been for a swim. She looked so beautiful in a bedraggled sort of way, her blonde hair loose over her shoulders, her eye make-up smudged. She looked as tired as I felt. I took her by surprise, as if she hadn't expected me. What did she think? That I wouldn't find her? I wanted to hug her there and then, take her in my arms, but my voice of reason kicked in and told me that I needed to stick to my plan. *Make her come to me. Don't suffocate her. Give her time to sort out her fucked-up state of mind.*

She stuttered, "Alexandre, I…I'm…I'm sorry, I didn't know what I was doing last night."

My lips tipped into a crooked, ironic smile and I took a step back. My pride kicked in. "Oh yes, you did, Pearl. You seemed to know exactly what you were doing."

"I…I…no, I had no choice—"

"I was standing there with a fucking lady's handbag while you climbed out of a bloody toilet window!" In that second, I almost wanted to laugh, call a truce; the whole drama was risible, but I stayed proud, immovable; I needed to drum it home to her how much she had hurt and belittled me. I gazed into her innocent blue eyes. Those eyes that had ripped my heart out. "Did that mean nothing to you? The fact that I wanted to marry you?" I could read the panic on her face.

She lifted up her arms and let them fall in an exasperated thump either side of her hips. "I still want to marry you, I still—"

"Don't you get it, Pearl? It's too late for that now," I lied.

She scraped her fingers through her wet hair and then covered her mouth with her hand. It was sinking in: the idea that she could lose me forever. Her pain was palpable. *Good. It shows that she still loves me.* But she was teetering on the edge—the edge of indecision. She could have gone either way. Rejection was quivering on her lips—she still wasn't ready to commit to me a hundred percent, and was using Sophie as an excuse. I needed all of her, every last percent. She was still obsessing about my sister, and if I admitted that I knew what Laura had done and that I'd listened to her voicemail, then I would have had to reveal the whole story of what had happened in London. This wasn't the time.

Sometimes in life you make dumb choices. And in that moment, everything I said, everything I did, was unforgivable.

So when Pearl brought up the subject of Laura's phone call, I pretended that she must have misinterpreted what Laura said. Because if Pearl knew what Laura's motives were—that Laura still wanted me—it might make her run from me for good. I couldn't risk that. Panicking, I told her that I'd lost her handbag with her phone and credit cards inside. That I'd reported it stolen. The fact that either of us could have listened to Laura's messages without the phone itself, didn't seem to register with Pearl. Perhaps she was in too much shock.

If I could do things over again, I would not have said what I said. But I did.

Coldhearted.

Bastard.

These were the words to describe me in that instant. Did I subconsciously want Pearl to suffer? Live the agony that I had undergone the night before? Know the stab of abandonment? Feel the desolation of knowing you have lost your other half? Perhaps I did. Because the more I spoke, the more immersed I became in my fabrication of the truth. Perhaps I thought that Pearl's pain was proof of her love for me. Knowing that she gave a shit about me gave me hope for our future.

The words that came out of my mouth showed that I wasn't going to let her off easily. No, she'd need to *earn* me back.

"You know what, Pearl? I'm done," I said, my eyes sharpened flints. "What you did to me last night pushed me to my fucking limit. You demonstrated, loud and clear, that you don't want me and that you're using Sophie as an excuse to run from me."

Pearl's mouth was an O. Her blue eyes round with disbelief. She stood there, shaking, her lips trembling. "I love you, Alexandre. Please, please let's work this out."

"Work what out?" And here, I really *did* mean what I said. I was fed up with this Sophie nonsense—Pearl thinking that Sophie was capable of murder, not believing that she wanted to make amends. She hated Sophie's guts long before the Laura message, and Sophie really had been trying. I went on, "Work what out, Pearl? As long as Sophie's breathing you won't let up. I can't have a relationship with someone who hates my sister, especially when she and I are in business together."

My monologue continued, as I explained to Pearl why Sophie was not her enemy, and culminating with a balm for her wound, I said, "Come here, chérie, and give me one last kiss before saying goodbye." It was if an actor were speaking, not me, and I, the onlooker, from the wings—the audience watching the performance. I was observing a coldblooded, callous bastard who was calculating every move—treating Pearl like an acquisition, not a human being. I knew what I was doing. I was a billionaire businessman and I always got what I wanted. And I wanted Pearl...

To be unequivocally mine.

This was my way of going about it.

"You're breaking *up* with me?" she whimpered.

"No, Pearl. It was *your* choice. You broke us up last night. You broke my heart in two."

"That's not what I want...*at all!*"

I continued my performance. "Say what you like, baby, but actions speak louder than words. Nobody should have to go what I went through. You discarded me like a piece of trash, leaving a waiting jet and a waiting fiancé while you climbed out of a fucking toilet window, like a six year-old playing hide-and-seek. Not to mention the reverend in Vegas, and the surprise I had planned for us after our wedding."

Her eyes lit up. "What surprise?" Ha! I'd piqued her interest. Good.

"It's the past now, baby. Water under the bridge." I leaned

down and kissed her. A passionate, sexual kiss with my hand gripping her ass—to let her know what she'd be missing. I drew her against my thumping heart, and opened her lips teasingly with my tongue, probing, lingering—my cock coming alive with every stroke of my tongue on hers. (I'd piqued her interest—she'd 'peaked' mine.) She yielded to me and then, after I knew I had her attention, I pulled back. If she'd been smart, she would have known my speech was bullshit and that no man can kiss a woman like that when he's not head over heels in love. Not to mention the rock in my jeans.

"Give me another chance," she creaked out, tears spilling from her eyes.

I drew her closer and whispered in her ear, "No." Then I gave her another speech about all the gifts she'd be getting from me: the Mercedes, an apartment in Cap d'Antibes, the Porsche, a new apartment that I'd be renting for her, and HookedUp Enterprises itself. The list went on. Academic, because I knew we'd be sharing all these things in the future anyway. I had no doubt in my mind that she would be my wife. I wasn't going to give up on her—of course not—but she needed to pine for me. Needed to feel what life was going to be without me for a while.

My last words were, "Bye Pearl, baby. Look after yourself." I walked away, not looking behind.

Fuck I was being a bastard.

But it was the only way to win her back for good.

7

Money and power were my obsessions for many years, working around the clock to make HookedUp what it quickly became.

Now I had an obsession of a different nature: Pearl.

Every minute of every day, I wanted to be with her. Hold her. Make love to her, although she still probably wasn't ready for that, after all those nightmares about the college rapists. All the more reason for me to give her time to heal herself, to step away from her; for her to spend a while with her brother and father. She told me she was going to Hawaii to visit her dad.

Pearl and I were talking, but barely. My calls were clipped and businesslike. I sent her a Birkin handbag, replete with cellphone and replacements for her other 'stolen' stuff. She needed a new purse, anyway. The old one I stashed away in a suitcase.

Meanwhile, I waited, like a lonely crocodile in his patch of territory; no mate, no friends (except for faithful Rex), biding my time until Pearl wouldn't be able to bear being away from me anymore. Only then would I make my move.

I had two things to sort out: sell my share of HookedUp to Sophie, once and for all, and deal with the dreaded Laura.

If I wanted to make things work with Pearl, even if she were being irrational about Sophie, I had to extricate myself from HookedUp. Because, seriously, how much money and power does a person need? I'd proved myself—I'd never have to work again if I didn't want to. It was a small sacrifice to pay for a smooth road ahead with the woman I loved.

But Laura...*Jesus,* that was an unquantifiable problem waiting—like a grenade—to detonate.

I dialed her house number. I was hoping to get James on the line, to tell him what was going on—to get his crazy wife under control and keep her away from me for good. But James hadn't been answering his cell so I wasn't surprised when Laura picked up. As I stood in the kitchen in my apartment, I opened the fridge door, wondering what I should snack on, but the moment I heard Laura's voice, I lost my appetite.

"Hello darling" she cooed.

"How did you know it was me?" I asked with suspicion—I'd hidden my number.

"Gut feeling."

I slammed the fridge door shut so hard I heard a bottle smash. "I am not your darling, Laura. I don't ever, ever want to see you again. Your shenanigans with me at The Connaught were bad enough, but what you did to Pearl was beyond imagination. She was terrified. Terrified."

She chuckled. "That was the idea."

"I'm marrying Pearl so you might as well accept it and get

out of my fucking life."

"You won't marry Pearl, Alex my love, when I tell you what I know."

Blood pounded in my ears. "What do you know?"

"I think it's something we need to discuss face to face. I'll come to New York—we can have a little chat."

"No!" And then I said calmly, "I have business to attend to in London. I'm going to Provence to see about house stuff—I'll pick up those books of yours and bring them over to your place. And I'll pick up my Aston Martin from your garage, too. That way, you and I will break all ties and we won't ever have to see each other again."

"So final. So dramatic! Well, Alex darling, if you like a little drama, I can guarantee you that I won't disappoint."

"No more games, Laura—really, this isn't funny."

"I thought our time together at The Connaught was hilarious, and if I remember rightly, you did too."

"The drugs had me laughing, but I can tell you it wasn't bloody funny standing with my dick poking out like a fucking torpedo in front of my sister and Indira Kapoor."

Laura cackled into the line, her breath hitching in hysterics.

"So when I next come to London, I'll bring those books, get my car and sayonara, okay?"

"No, Alex, it's not okay. I'm still in love with you. Surely you must have guessed that by now?"

"What you have for me, Laura, isn't love; it's some sort of sick obsession. If you loved me you'd want me to be happy. Please, I *beg* of you—leave me, and leave Pearl in peace to get on with our lives."

"But I can't do that—I want your baby."

I knew it! *That* was what she was after when she laced my Bloody Mary with Viagra, and God knows what else was in that cocktail. I hung up on her, my stomach coiling with fury. She was beyond insane. When she had her accident and the doctors said she hadn't suffered brain damage, I now knew they'd got the prognosis wrong. This woman was not right in the head. Okay, she had always been highly-strung, demanding and spoiled, but this? This behavior was psychotic.

My cell rang again. I ignored it. Laura, wanting to wind me up some more. But then I glanced at the screen and saw that it was Elodie. I opened the fridge again to get out a drink.

"Elodie," I said with relief, cracking open a beer, "what's up?"

"I'm outside your door. I forgot my key."

"The door's not locked, I'm in the kitchen." I gulped down the whole bottle of beer almost in one go and the fizz prickled my nose—Laura had made me thirsty.

Elodie giggled into the line. "Oh. Duh! Okay."

She came into the kitchen and I took a double take. She wasn't dressed in her usual Goth attire and she looked quite beautiful without all that black make-up on her eyes. She was wearing skinny jeans tucked into elegant, black boots and a pink, scoop-necked sweater which accentuated her delicate neck. But the headphones she was wearing still gave her a street-cool look. She was slim, as always, but didn't look like a scrawny sparrow anymore. I gave her a big bear-hug. I'd missed her. She hadn't been coming into the HookedUp offices much lately, because she said she was getting her art portfolio together.

"I was thinking about making an omelet or something. Are

you hungry?" I asked.

She sat down. "What?"

"Take your headphones off and maybe you can hear me. What are you listening to, anyway?"

She took them off and disconnected her iPod. "She's a new singer from New Zealand, still in high school. This song, *Royals,* hasn't even been released yet, but a friend of mine got her hands on it—knows the producer or something."

"Hungry?"

"Sure."

I narrowed my eyes at her suspiciously. "Really, you're eating now?"

"A girl's got to eat."

"Great. That's great." I got some ingredients out of the fridge, cracked open some eggs and whipped them in a bowl. Elodie watched me with curiosity. I doubted she did any cooking herself. Lucky about the massive choice of take-out in New York or she probably would have starved from laziness.

"You're pretty flashy, breaking eggs with one hand."

"I worked as a sous chef in a restaurant in Paris once upon a time."

"I didn't know that," she said.

"There's a lot of stuff you don't know about me."

"I know that you and Maman left home very young and had to look after yourselves, but she never tells me details. What did she do as a job?"

"She worked as a waitress," I lied. "Hey, Elodie, I forgot to ask you; how's the portfolio coming along? Still taking photos? Still making those angry angel collages?"

"Going okay, I guess, but I need to get away for a while,"

she said, not wanting to look me in the eye.

I lit the gas. "What's wrong? You're not paranoid about being followed again, are you?"

"I need a break but I don't want to go back to Paris. I want to do some traveling or something. Backpack around Asia. I can go with my roommate, Claire."

"You know what? There's a lot to see right here in the United States. There's no need to go schlepping around dodgy foreign countries when there's too much unrest in the world right now. Go to the Grand Canyon or Yellowstone Park, why don't you?"

To my surprise, she replied, "Okay, good idea."

I tore some fresh basil leaves, sprinkling bits into the pan, and suddenly had a thought. "I have a car...well, it's Pearl's car. It's in San Francisco and needs to be brought to New York. Is your driver's license in order? And your friend's?"

Elodie got up and took a couple of beers out of the fridge and offered me one. "Yup. Cool plan. Can we take as long as we like to drive cross-country?"

"Sure. No rush. Just be careful. Don't go over the speed limit—be prudent. Speak to my assistant, Jim—he can get you your plane tickets there, hotels, whatever you need. Maybe you can even stay with Pearl's brother. Anyway, the car's at his place in his garage. I'll call Anthony and Pearl and get it all arranged. I'm sure Pearl won't mind—actually you'd be doing her a favor."

"Why is Pearl's car in San Francisco? I thought you guys had gone to LA?"

"We did, but she stayed on. Went to visit Anthony. Now she's in Hawaii visiting her dad."

Elodie ran her gaze over me, dissecting me, drilling her eyes into my thoughts. "You look guilty, Uncle Alexandre. What's going on with you and Pearl?"

"Nothing." I tried to suppress the heat-rush I felt, by turning on the sink faucet and putting the underside of my wrists under cold running water. A trick I learned in the Foreign Legion. As if on cue, my cell started buzzing. The words LAURA popped up on the screen. Elodie picked up my cell without pressing anything, but saw who the caller was.

She arched her brows. "Well aren't you going to answer it?"

I shook my head. *Fucking psycho Laura, leave me alone!*

"She called *me* the other day, you know. She wanted to know Pearl's number. What's up?"

"Keep away from Laura, Elodie. Don't answer her calls and do not, whatever you do, give her any information about *anything* or *anybody* at all."

"But Laura's nice! She was always really friendly to me."

"*Was* is the operative word. That accident changed her."

"So what's that got to do with Pearl? Why does Laura want to get in touch with her? Why didn't you go with Pearl to Hawaii?"

I switched off the gas burner. "Would you get us a couple of plates and utensils?"

Elodie got up. "Why didn't you go to Hawaii with her?" she asked again.

"She needed space. Needed to sort a few things out."

"I doubt it. Pearl's crazy about you—anyone can see that. It's *you,* I bet, playing games. Playing 'I need space' games. So typical."

"We both need a little break."

"Yeah, right. That's male code for "back off."

"Not at all. I want to be with Pearl...she just needs some time on her own and—"

"Ha! You're just making excuses so that you can behave how you like without any thought for Pearl."

"You've got it all wrong, Elodie."

She sneered at me. "I don't know what you're doing, juggling two women at once. Typical man behavior. As if male babies were born with a mean gene in them. You're all the same—*all* of you. The only difference is, some hide it better than others but the bastard gene is buried into every man's DNA."

She had a point. "That, mademoiselle, is a very uncalled for and rude accusation!"

She put the plates on the table. "I know more about men than you think." She blew air out of her lips—pouting while she spoke.

"Elodie, I thought you were meant to be going to art college this fall anyway, not traveling about and wasting your time." I served up our omelets and sat down.

"Next year."

"Don't procrastinate."

She rolled her eyes. "Yeah, yeah, yeah."

"And cool it with the cocky attitude, okay?"

She gave me a salute. "Okay, sir!"

Elodie was right. I had the bastard gene in my DNA. What was I playing at? All this, *Let Pearl come to me,* was bullshit. I loved Pearl. Damn it, I couldn't be happy without her. I was going to go and find her, whether she was ready or not. I was so in love with Pearl Robinson, I couldn't concentrate on anything else.

We belonged together and I didn't want to spend one more day without her. I'd already wasted enough time.

I'd been tracing Pearl's movements with the tracking device I'd installed on her new cellphone. Guilty. Guilty of obsession, possessiveness, jealousy, and controlling, manipulating behavior of every kind. I convinced myself that all I was doing was keeping a distant eye on her, in case of any emergency; that I could be wherever she was like a knight in shining armor, ready to save her should the occasion rise. Except, my armor was a little rusty, the metal too bulky. Maybe when I was seven years old I'd been a good *chevalier,* a good knight, but now I'd lost the flair. She had been in London for several days. Why? Instead of catching a plane from Hawaii to New York, she'd gone there. Hampstead to be precise. I remember her having told me that Daisy's mother lived there.

By this point, I knew I needed to go and join her.

I stopped off at my house in Provence first. The pool was being fixed so I had a meeting with the builders, stayed the night, picked up those bloody books of Laura's, and left. Technically, a few of the books were mine; gifts from her. I could have taken them to Goodwill, or the French equivalent, but somehow getting them free and clear of my house and giving them back to Laura was symbolic—a fresh start for Pearl and me. Returning gifts to the gift bearer sends a clear, no-nonsense message—*get out of my life; not even your gifts hold any meaning anymore.*

I took a nice, small and discreet room, not at The Connaught, but another hotel, just in case Laura decided to track me down. Annoyingly, when I asked one of the members of staff to wrap some gifts for my mother—some cashmere scarfs I'd bought—they also giftwrapped the bloody box of books. I didn't have time to unwrap it. But the last thing I wanted was for Laura to believe I was showering her with gifts or there was some good, pre-Christmas feeling on my part. No, I wanted to ice her out. I'd go there, give her the books and get my Aston Martin, which James had been kindly looking after for me—it was parked in their garage which I still had the keys to. I'd asked him to run the engine every now and then to keep it tuned. I'd bought the car in England and had hoped to drive it to France with Pearl, but we hadn't had a chance. Right now, the idea of my precious classic car being anywhere near Laura was making me nervous—I could just imagine her dousing it with acid or something, stripping off the beautiful gunmetal-gray paintwork.

I couldn't wait to snip all ties with her.

8

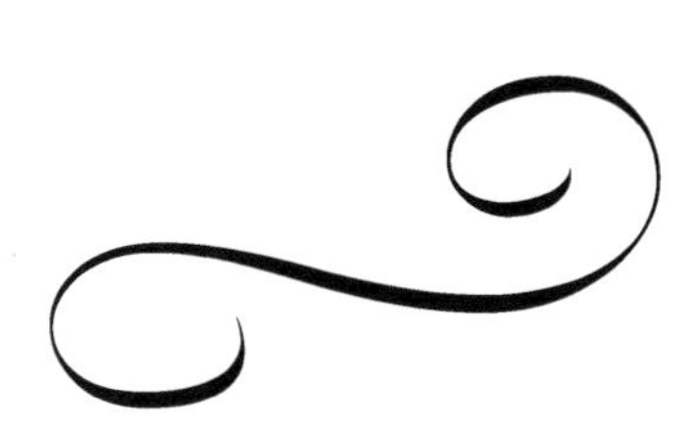

The hotel didn't have a gym so I used one close by. I wanted to expend some of the pent-up, surplus energy I had, which was playing tricks with my brain; making me angry and quietly aggressive. I knew part of the reason was because I hadn't had sex for nearly two weeks. It shouldn't have affected me; I'd been without sex for long stretches before, when I was in the French Foreign Legion, but that was before I met Pearl. She was imprinted on my brain. I tossed and turned at night, smelling her, hearing her sweet voice, feeling that silky soft skin, dreaming of fucking her. Hearing her whimper when she came, the tears that would fall when her orgasm was so intense she couldn't believe it was true.

After the gym, I showered, then checked my cell to see Pearl's whereabouts. A rush of adrenaline spiked my veins; she was at James and Laura's house! What the fuck? Not only was Laura playing games with me, but she was obviously fucking with Pearl, too. Regret washed over me—I should have warned

Pearl—told her how dangerous Laura was. She must have called Pearl again after the 'Sophie is a killer call' to set up some sort of meeting. I dashed over to my hotel to grab the box of books and set off in the direction of Chelsea. Finally, I could deal with the problem in situ. I'd confront Laura with Pearl right there; Laura's lies would be etched across her face and Pearl would believe me. We could be rid of Laura, once and for all; face the music together as a couple. I hailed a cab and jumped in, giving the taxi driver Laura's exclusive Chelsea address.

I thought back to my code; treating women with respect at all times, no matter how unhinged they were. Bad idea. I should have told the lot of them to fuck off a long time ago. Laura, Claudine, even Indira. After the way my father treated my mother, I swore I'd always be gentle with women in every circumstance—the idea of being like him in any way disgusted me. But my kindness wasn't paying off; it had got me in a tangled web with a whole lot of Black Widow spiders out to gobble me up.

"Can you please step on it—don't mean to be rude but I'm in a hurry," I said to the driver who was chatting away in his Cockney accent about immigration.

"No problem, gov. It's those bastard eastern European scum and the like. Vey come 'ere expectin' work, stealin' jobs from decent British citizens. Arf of 'em 'av illegal, dodgy businesses, drugs, prostitution and ve like—vey really are ve scum of ve earf." *They really are the scum of the earth,* I finally realized he was saying.

"Is there a shortcut?" I suggested.

At first he thought I was engaging in conversation so I repeated, "Can we get there any faster? It's an emergency."

He swerved to the right and took a narrow street through the back of Belgravia. "Are you Rumanian, or sumfing?"

"No. French."

"Like a few frogs legs, do ya? Snails?" He laughed at his joke.

Finally we arrived. I shoved too many pound notes in the driver's hand, not waiting for change, and dashed to Laura and James's front steps, rapping hard on the brass doorknocker. Laura came out and grinned at me, flinging her arms about me as if we were two long-lost, passionate lovers. I held the box of books out and pushed my way through the door.

"How lovely, Alex—you brought me a present; how sweet of you."

Once inside the house, I shouted, "Pearl? Are you here?"

Laura started laughing. "She just left."

I dropped the box on the marble floor; it landed with a thud. "Damn! How long ago?"

"Ten minutes."

"Damn," I cursed again.

"She doesn't want to see you, Alex, so I wouldn't get your knickers in a twist."

I wanted to ignore her quip but heard myself ask, "She said that?"

"Yes. She came to England especially to see me."

"Bullshit Laura."

"It's not bullshit. She told me you'd split up and that she'd had enough and was going to start dating other men. That she'd had time to mull things over in Hawaii. She said she didn't have time for silly games and that she understood that you were too immature for her—she wants to go out with someone her own age."

I wanted to believe that Laura was lying but she knew about Pearl being in Hawaii—her conversation with Elodie had been before Pearl had even decided to go to Hawaii. Laura's words stung like little poison darts. Perhaps there was an element of truth to them. I *had* been acting immaturely and it wasn't a surprise Pearl wanted to date a more mature man. Fuck! I now regretted leaving her in tears in the backyard at her brother's. Begging me to give her another chance, I pretended her words were empty. I'd behaved like a total, coldblooded bastard. In that moment—in Anthony's garden—it hadn't occurred to me that Pearl had choices; she could simply dump me. Dump me at the drop of a hat. She was gorgeous—she could get any man. What the fuck had I been thinking?

I stood there, remembering how it was *Laura* that had intensified Pearl's fear of Sophie, with that crazy phone call getting us into this mess. My eyes were pools of ice as they locked with hers. "I've brought your books back, Laura. The hotel gift-wrapped the box by mistake so don't get any grand ideas. I'm leaving now, I'm going to get my car." I strode down the hall towards the garden, which led to the garage.

"Alex, wait!" Laura limped after me with her cane. "Why are you so pissed off? I thought we could have some tea and have a heart-to-heart."

"Yeah, right, Laura. I'm really going to drink your tea, laced with some bloody drug. You behaved like a fucking psycho last time we met and what you did to Pearl was unforgiveable. Un-fucking-forgivable. You should go and get professional help—I'd offer to pay for a shrink but I don't want to be involved with you in *any way, whatsoever*. Is the garage locked?"

"It's unlocked," she said sulkily, as if what I told her was a surprise. "You know where the buzzer is for the garage door and you still have your own keys, I suppose. Alex, don't be a spoilsport—*come* on."

I suddenly thought of something. "You didn't give *Pearl* a cup of tea, did you?"

Laura smirked.

I grabbed her by the shoulders and found myself shaking her. I'd never hurt a woman in my life. *Jesus!* But the temptation to slap her was overwhelming. My heart was pounding, my breath unsteady. I stepped back, sucked in a calming lungful of air, let go of her, and said in a quiet voice, my teeth clenched, "Did you offer Pearl a cup of tea?" If I had been like Michael Corleone—as Pearl so often described me—I would have felt no qualms about having Laura eliminated. But I wasn't. I respected a person's life too much—God knows, I'd been responsible for enough deaths to see me well into the depths of Hell—I didn't want another on my conscience. And however crazy Laura had become, we had shared something once. You can't wipe away your past.

"Yes, I offered her tea," but she quickly added, "she didn't want any, though."

I exhaled a sigh of relief, marched off, swung open the back door and raced towards the garage. My beautiful 1964 DB5 Aston Martin was under a tarpaulin, and when I peeled it back, I was both surprised and delighted to see that it was unblemished. What a beauty! No wonder this model had starred in two Bond films. I got into the front seat, humming *Skyfall* to myself, and inhaled the wonderful aroma of Classic

Car (*they really should learn to bottle this*). For a second or two, the wonder of my car soothed away the fury I felt with Laura. But then I turned the key. Dead. Bloody nothing. My blood rose again. The battery was fucking dead! I got out and saw Laura standing there, her lips quirked into another victorious smile. Had she done this on purpose?

"James is away so hasn't been here to start the engine. *Poor* Alexandre," she said, sarcasm dripping from her languid, snooty tongue. "Anyway, the delay will be perfect—I'll change into something more comfortable while you recharge the battery, then while we wait for it to juice-up, we can have a heart-to-heart."

"No, Laura. I'm off. *Now.* Suresh can come and pick up the car at some point; I don't have time for this nonsense and the last thing I want right now is a cozy chat with you." I slammed the car door shut, sheathed my pride and joy with its cover, then stormed over to the red button on the wall, which I pressed with vigor. The garage door buzzed open. I shot out under the narrow space, as Laura shouted after me, but I legged the hell out of there.

I didn't want to see Laura's brazen face ever again.

9

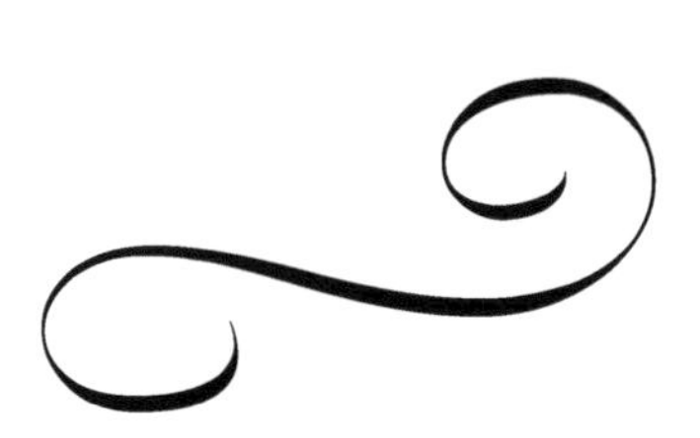

I called Pearl but her cell was off. I wanted to explain the whole Laura fiasco, minus the Bloody Mary incident. I still couldn't bring myself to admit that it ever happened. I felt ashamed of myself being trussed up, hands bound, body numb—as immovable as a Christmas turkey about to be delved into. It made me feel like a real fucking fool. One day I'd tell Pearl—after I'd gotten a ring on her finger, but right now wasn't the time.

I wondered how much longer she'd be staying in London. I debated whether I should go to Hampstead—to Daisy's mother's house—and just wait outside the front door for Pearl until she came back. Then my cell went. I hoped it was her calling me but then it hit home, *Why on Earth would Pearl call me now? She's given up on me. Not interested. Can't be bothered with my stupid games and I don't blame her.*

I pressed 'talk'. It was Sebastian, my new video game partner.

"What's up?" I asked.

"Do you have time for a pint?" I'd forgotten that—the British are always talking about 'pints down the pub.' I weighed my options. I really did want to just get going to Hampstead. Be that stalker.

"No," I answered in a flat voice. "You've caught me at a bad time."

"I really need you to meet our other programmer. Just for five minutes. You know, you can always tell in the first few seconds if you like a person or not. I'd rather you checked him out, personally."

"I trust your judgment, Sebastian."

"He's coming over to the office so I thought we'd pop round the pub just to make him feel at ease."

"The one around the corner from the office?"

"Yeah, The Lamb and Flag."

I looked at my watch. Covent Garden was pretty much *en route* to Hampstead. "Okay but just five minutes."

I hailed a cab.

After our brief pub meeting—the new guy nervous but a good, hard-working type and apparently very talented—I stood outside the pub on the street, amidst the traffic, and tried calling Pearl again. I'd noticed that London had become a fascinating melting pot of foreign bodies, fluttering and weaving about like ribbons of different colored flags through the busy streets. Nobody spoke English here anymore; Brazilians, French, Italians, Germans, South Americans, all having made London their home—was anyone British? (Except the taxi drivers—the opposite of New York City.) The phone rang and rang. No bloody answer. My cell buzzed in my hand—it made me jump. It was Sophie.

"Why didn't you tell me you were in London, Alexandre? I'm here, too. We could have met up."

"What for?" My voice was clipped. Sophie was not my favorite person in the world right now. In fact, *everyone* was getting under my skin since Pearl and I had been parted for the last two weeks. I'd been edgy, snappy and volatile. "How did you know I was in London?"

"That's why I'm calling. Pearl told me. We bumped into each other. She just dropped me off in Hampstead."

"She dropped *you* off? She rented a car?"

"No. She's with my driver. I dropped in to see a friend up here. Pearl and I crossed paths in Harrods. What a coincidence, eh? She confirmed what you told me about Laura's lies. Said she'd been at Laura's and recounted the whole freaky story—that Laura said I'd tried to kill her—that her accident was my fault. Fucking crazy! Alexandre, I don't know what game you're playing seeing Laura still, but Pearl loves you. *Really* loves you. She told me she saw you at Laura's house. Entering her front door. What the hell were you doing there? Are you *fucking* her?"

"Of course not. I was taking those bloody English books back and went to get my car."

"Well you should stay away from that little bitch—she has it in for you."

"Yeah, I'm coming to that very same conclusion. She's insane. Did Laura mention the Bloody Mary fiasco to Pearl?"

"I don't think so—if she did, Pearl didn't mention it. Pearl told me you'd split up, that you didn't want to give her the time of day and that you were dating Laura again. You're not lying to me, are you? It's not true, is it?"

"What do you think? Of course bloody not."

"I didn't think so. We bonded, Alexandre. For the first time ever, Pearl was open with me. She was crying and everything—she's so distraught and brokenhearted. I felt so guilty for having been such a bitch to her. Poor thing, she's really hurting right now. She's so in love with you, Alexandre. So in love."

I felt an ache in my solar plexus. *Poor Pearl. She must be confused out of her mind.* "Well I'm going to hail a cab right now and go up to Hampstead."

"She won't be there now. She just zipped by the house to get her suitcase and say goodbye to Daisy's mother—I told my driver to take her to Heathrow Airport."

"Where's she going?"

"To New York."

"Do you know what time?"

"I do, actually. She'll be leaving about ten thirty. She's flying with American Airlines." All Sophie's information was computing in my brain. There was no point going to Hampstead now. I'd get on a plane myself to New York—get there first and wait for Pearl at her new apartment—the one I'd rented for her. Ha! I even had a spare set of keys. She wouldn't be able to avoid me.

I called the airline and got her upgraded to First class with special instructions to take extra care of her. That was the least I could do.

Thanks to the private jet company I use (yes, I'm really green, really ecological with my great, big, black, carbon footprint), I got back to New York ahead of Pearl and in time to organize a few things.

I had several boxes of groceries delivered, with everything essential for a new apartment, and stocked up the fridge with food. The place was perfect for Pearl; two bedrooms, a smart marble bathroom. Pre-war but sleekly furnished in neutral colors, and with all the mod cons. However, I was now kicking myself. I wanted her to come back home where she belonged: to *my* apartment.

I waited patiently, making a few business calls in between checking her whereabouts. She had arrived at JFK. A driver would be there to collect her but with strict instructions not to let her know that I was the one who sent him—*let her believe it's Sophie.*

I wanted to take her by surprise when she came home. Make it so she couldn't say no.

An hour or two later, I heard the key turn in the lock and I quickly opened the door. Pearl fell into me, landing in my waiting arms, surprised as hell, obviously mistaking me for a rapist or a burglar—and I thought for a second, *That's me, the burglar who wants to rob her independence, steal her for myself.* And a rapist, because all I had been thinking about was fucking her, despite my conscience telling me it was wrong, that she wouldn't be ready, that if I'd been a 'good' person, sex would have been the last thing on my mind.

"Pearl, baby. I've missed you so much. I'm so in love with you—I can't live without you. I've been climbing the walls." My feelings spilled out of my mouth in a torrent. I could feel my nose burning as my eyes misted up. She looked so beautiful; her blonde hair mussed up, her cheeks glowing from the cold night. I gathered her tightly in my arms, bringing her close to my chest and kissing the top of her head to hide my face. I didn't want her to see my wet eyes. Her hair smelled so sweet—I breathed her in. My savior, my life.

"Get off me!" she screamed as she struggled from beneath my amorous grip. "What kind of game are you playing Alexandre Chevalier? You're with Laura now!"

"No, baby. No! I love *you.*"

"Why are you torturing me? Leave me alone."

I couldn't help myself. I started to kiss her ravenously, licking her lips, forcing my way in; anything to quell her suspicions, to wipe Laura from her mind. My cock was rock-hard against her belly, pounding in my pants. I loved Pearl but my insatiable need for her after being apart for so long was overwhelming. "Please baby, believe me, I am so *not* with Laura."

"Don't lie! I saw you entering her front door! I saw you with my own eyes!" Pearl pushed me away, rapping her fists against my chest.

I quietly closed the front door. Her suitcase was still outside but I feared the whole building would be woken with the noise. For the next few minutes the banter continued; Pearl's accusations and my defense. Yet I could hardly concentrate on the conversation: my eyes hooded with longing, my groin raging. All I wanted was for us to fuck and forget this Laura nonsense, but I had to calm Pearl down first. I could see it in her eyes too—she wanted me urgently but her head was telling her to protect her heart. Yet right now, her heart was telling her to make love to me. I could read it in her gaze, her tweaked nipples. She was hungry for me. Fucking ravenous.

I stepped close to her again and took her flailing wrists. "Pearl, my darling—please, please let's just be close. I've missed you like crazy."

"Bullshit! You haven't even called me!"

"I did call you. Today actually, but your cell was switched off."

"Big deal! *Finally,* after all this time making me suffer, making me plan my life without you, you call. You call when you feel like a fuck! You want to be with Laura but you're using me. For sex. Laura was right, you're only in 'lust' with me—all your marriage talk was bullshit."

Yeah, a waiting jet and a huge rock of a ring is bullshit. I realized this Laura thing had taken over her mind. Not letting her see coherently. "NO! Pearl, I *do* want to marry you."

"Oh, so you can have little wifey waiting for you at home while you go off and have affairs! I'm not that kind of girl, Alexandre. Maybe there are plenty of women out there who would stand that kind of marriage for the luxuries you can provide, with all your money, but I don't *care* how rich you are! I just want a faithful husband; a man who sees *only* me." Her eyes flashed like warning lights, the blue a deep, glimmering ultramarine.

I kissed her hand. I dared not do more—her wrath was impressive; her fire blazing. "I only see *you,* Pearl, I swear. It's been hell for me. I've missed you like crazy—I've been obsessing about you night and day. I've been going around with a hard-on for two weeks—please calm me down, chérie—I feel like an animal. I need you. I need you baby." Bad little speech that one. It made her rage all the more—it sounded as if I only wanted her for sex. The whole 'books in the box' saga was dredged up. More explanations while Pearl raised her eyebrows at me with suspicion and disdain. I explained the gift-wrapped box, the fact that I'd gone to Provence, first, and why I hadn't sent it by mail. I finally thought I'd won her over. But no.

Not even close.

"That doesn't explain how Laura knew so much about me. She said you'd called me a "loony with a slutty past." Pearl pushed me away again and tossed her head in disgust. "You told Laura my secrets, things about my private life. About Alessandra, because Laura just happened to know *everything!*"

I had been able to explain my movements and reasons up until now, but not this. How *did* Laura have all that information? Sophie hadn't spoken to her, and Elodie didn't know that stuff. I thought back. Had Elodie listened in on one of my private conversations with Pearl? No. *How the fuck did Laura know all this?* The argument between Pearl and me went on, back and forth. Pearl not believing me. A bolt of rage shot through me.

I shouted, "I don't fucking *know* how Laura knew that stuff but I *love* you, I want to marry you and I don't want Laura fucking well *near* me! You *have* to believe me!" I roared so loudly that the sound echoed through the fresh, newly decorated apartment.

Finally Pearl was silent. The drama had appeased her. I saw her breathing was erratic, her lips parted and her gaze flicked down to my crotch and then to my eyes. *Her look said, Please just fuck me—I can't take this mistrust.* Make-up sex. I couldn't wait a second more. I had to get my tailored pants off—my dick was wedged uncomfortably beneath the fine wool fabric like a massive steel rod. I closed in on Pearl, pinioning her wrists above her head with one hand as I slowly unzipped her jeans with the other. She let me, as she nipped her bottom lip between her teeth and moaned quietly. I eased my hand inside her panties and felt her oozing moisture trapped there, waiting to explode.

I growled into her mouth as I kissed her, my fingers entering her liquid warmth, "That's it, no more drama games Pearl—you want this as much as I do."

I gathered her in my arms, carried her into the bedroom and threw her on the bed. Being a gentleman was not the first thing on my mind in that moment. The scene that ensued was hectic, wild, both of us like savage beasts. We ripped off our respective clothing, both acting like a pair of jungle cats in heat. Pearl spread herself out like a starfish—wanton—on the bed. I lay on top of her, no time to lose. But ever the little actress, she then squeezed her thighs together, trying not to let me enter her, meanwhile kissing me frantically, her slick pool beckoning me to stretch her wide open. She wanted me to ravage her. Play the dominant.

"Don't pretend you don't want this," I said, my hips pumping into her as I fucked her dripping wet clit. "You want me to despoil your tight little pussy?" The crown of my cock was going to detonate any second. I kept the rhythm up, sliding my length up and down her slit, the pressure of her tight, worked-out thighs like vices around my dick, not letting me in. This game was really arousing me—Pearl's thighs squeezing the sides of my cock as she whimpered and moaned beneath me.

"Oh baby, fucking you is like flying on a cloud straight to Heaven." I grabbed the mane of her hair as I fucked that nub relentlessly until she couldn't hold out any longer—she opened her thighs and I slipped right in. Deep. Cramming her full. *Oh fuck!*

"This wet, hot pussy can't deny me, baby. Whatever your brain tells it to do, it has a mind of its own." I slammed into her hard and she cried out. I made little circular movements, my hips grinding round and round as I found her G-spot—her already sensitized clit was swollen like a ripe fruit.

She opened her thighs even further, maneuvering her body and hooking her ankles around my neck, bucking her hips up at me, as she clawed her nails into my ass and started shuddering beneath me. Usually she screamed, but this time she started weeping. "I'm coming, baby," she whimpered through tears, "I'm coming so hard."

My button was pressed. My thick cock expanded even more as I felt her pussy contract around me, sucking me in, gobbling me up with its avaricious grasp. I thrust back and forth mercilessly and she started screaming, as I exploded inside her, my scorching seed shooting into her womb. I sucked her neck like a vampire needing blood. I had to have her taste on my tongue; I needed to mark her. As I pumped my orgasm into her, she climaxed again. I accentuated my thrusts with each word. "I. Love. Fucking. You. My cock thinks about you. All. Day. Long. All. Fucking. Day. Long. Your. Wet. Pearlette. Always. Ready to be fucked by my....Big. Hard. Horny. Cock." More of my cum spurted inside her as I moved my mouth from her neck to her lips and lashed my tongue on hers, sucking, licking, locking together. The rampant carnal fireworks between us were insane.

"Are you cured of your cock phobia?" I asked, knowing

the answer as she moaned into my mouth.

"Oh yeah, oh God Alexandre, as long as it's you. I'm still coming, baby...*oh my God!*"

There was no way we could stay apart anymore. We were addicted to each other. We had to fuck like this every day. We had to satiate each other's craving for one another.

For the next twelve hours it was intermittent sparring, followed by make-up sex. Then Pearl would get suspicious again; the cross-questioning *Homeland*-style would begin once more, with me trying to explain. Then I'd fuck her again, and so on. Was it the drama that turned us on so much? Pearl getting me wild and emotional with her cool games which got me simmering with pent-up irritation and desire? It seemed she loved playing cat and mouse so that I would then ravage her, dominate her; fuck the coolness out of her—make her crumble beneath me. Sexually, she was a natural submissive and this was bringing out my bestial instincts. It worried me and excited me. I didn't want to fight; I wanted a smooth ride but I asked myself if the kind of ride Pearl desired was more of a roller coaster. Or perhaps she was just testing me to see if I was worthy of her love.

But I couldn't blame her suspicion about Laura. The question still remained unanswered. How the fuck *did* Laura know all those intimate things about Pearl? I sure as hell hadn't let anything slip. Had someone betrayed me?

10

Pearl's resolve to keep me on my toes continued for the next couple of weeks. The chill of the winter air seemed to match her emotions. She refused to move back in with me. Daisy and Amy took up residence with her in her new apartment, which meant I didn't have her all to myself. Daisy had split with her husband who had cheated on her—all the more reason why Daisy was acting like a guardian phoenix—always on the lookout, scrutinizing me with quiet reserve to see if I behaved well; if I did right by Pearl. Yes, I was on probation; all female eyes monitoring my every move, even little Amy who was only five years old.

Pearl had been trying to get in touch with Laura. She wanted a direct explanation from her. How, she wanted to know, did she have all that personal information? I sure as hell wanted to know too, and at that point—considering my line of work and now knowing how scheming Laura was—I stupidly hadn't put two and two together. What a dunce.

As for Pearl, she just didn't trust me—about Laura, about the history of my father—no she didn't buy my tale that he'd just 'disappeared into thin air,' and would slip it into the conversation every so often. I so wanted to reveal my secret, be honest with her, but it wasn't my call. I was protecting someone who had sworn me to secrecy.

I wanted to be as close to Pearl as possible but I felt that she was only half mine. We were still having sex, but somehow the situation was very confusing to me. She had discovered a newfound joy: sex without full-on commitment. It was as if she were twenty-two again. All those wasted years in her twenties and thirties after the rape—some of those married years (when she had been emotionally and sexually blocked), were given a new lease on life—her inner 1960's-sexual-revolution-babe had been unleashed. She'd become like a young Jane Fonda. I could hardly complain, but I was wondering if our marriage would *ever* go ahead. Pearl had what she wanted: me at her beck and call, 'servicing' her, filling her up' but without binding herself to me. She even had a nickname for me: the Exxon Guy. I laughed at her joke—what else could I do?

Talk about an odd juxtaposition of roles; it was as if she were my age and *I* was forty. All I could think of was getting rings on our fingers, while she stalled me with excuses. The bottom line was her wavering mistrust.

And just as I thought that there was a beam of light at the end of this tunnel (yes, the word tunnel could sound crass), an earthquake separated us as if we had been standing on the San Andreas fault line itself—Pearl and I seemed doomed. Just when I thought that I, the frog, had a chance of becoming Pearl's prince by finally getting that magical, proverbial kiss,

Laura chucked parts of me into her bubbling cauldron, stirring me in with her poisonous ingredients.

> *Eye of newt, and toe of frog,*
> *Wool of bat, and tongue of dog.*
> *Adder's fork, and blind-worm's sting,*
> *Lizard's leg, and owlet's wing,*
> *For a charm of powerful trouble,*
> *Like a hellbroth boil and bubble.*
> *Double, double toil and trouble,*
> *Fire burn and cauldron bubble.*

Shakespeare's lines—which I'd once learned at school—reverberated in my brain. I was busy shopping at Dean & DeLuca when Laura caught me by surprise. I had been eyeing up delicious Stilton cheeses and Christmas cakes and cookies but now I felt like throwing up.

"Darling," Laura purred into the line like the *Macbeth* witch she was, "so glad we're going to finally get a chance to chat."

My mouth was a thin hard line, my teeth clenched like clamps. "I have nothing to say to you, Laura, I'm going to hang up."

She quickly replied, "If you don't want your mother to be arrested for murder, you'd better hear me out."

I felt like a cartoon character being steamrolled. I looked down at my feet and saw that I was still in one piece but my body was experiencing a strange flattening sensation as if I were actually part of the floor itself.

I did a fake, raucous laugh. "You have a great imagination, Laura."

"Alex, I'm not in the mood to play your beating around the

bush game. I've given you so many chances to make amends with me—nothing has worked so now I'm going to have to get tough."

"I don't have time for this nonsense, I'm hanging up." But I didn't hang up. I couldn't. I stayed on the line, my brain desperately trying to find a way out. I cast my gaze furtively around the store to see if eyes were on me but people were too busy shopping for holiday treats to notice. I said nothing more, just waited to see what would come next.

She went on, "I mean it. I have evidence. You were a fool to leave hip replacement parts hidden in that bookshelf. You supposed, I'm sure, that nobody would have known what they were. Well I *did.*"

Jesus! It had simply slipped my mind! "I got those bits of junk from a *vide grenier,*" I said with a weak chuckle, knowing she wouldn't buy my lie. As if I would buy hip replacement parts at a yard sale.

"Traceable, Alex, and you know it. Because if the patient has trouble after an operation—years later—the prosthesis needs to be traced to the manufacturer. Same thing with the teeth that I found stuffed inside a chopped out encyclopedia. Dental records, Alex. And just like the hip parts, I'd say those teeth belonged to a man. A man that I would also say, quite definitely, was your own father."

"You're insane, Laura," I croaked out, my mouth dry as desert sand.

"Scotland Yard might not think I'm so insane. We all watch CSI. Things are very state-of-the-art these days with forensics."

"I have no idea what you're talking about."

"I have proof. Has your mobile phone been acting up a

little lately?"

Duh. How had I been so dumb? In my line of work, especially! She'd bloody listened in on my calls or seen a text message. I knew that it was possible these days. Without even touching someone's cell you could eavesdrop on a conversation. Calls, text messages—everything could be monitored by the intruder, even if you weren't actively talking on the phone. Spyware had become so advanced the cell could act as a recording device—as if the listener were sitting right next to you. I thought of a call I'd made to my mother back in the summer, telling her...what *had* I told her? I couldn't even remember but whatever it was, Laura had cottoned on. She'd been eaves-dropping on Pearl, too. That's how Laura knew all those intimate details about her shenanigans with Alessandra. *What a dunce I'd been not to preempt that!*

"Alex? Are you still there?'

"Yes, I'm still here." I couldn't do any more denying. "What do you want, Laura? Money?"

"Don't be silly! What I want money can't buy."

"Most things have a price. What's your price, Laura?"

"Happiness."

"You *have* happiness: a very kind husband, a stunning house, money. Your health is back. What *more* do you want?"

"Simple. I want you."

"You know that's impossible."

"Your choice. Either your mum ends up rotting in jail or you be nice to me."

If only Pearl hadn't done a runner! We'd be married. A wife can't be forced to testify against her husband. We'd be a team. I stood there in silence in the middle of the store, amidst the beautiful display of gourmet foods. I was speechless. My fist was clenched in a ball while the other hand clawed the receiver of my cell. I had to sort this shit out. Now. I had visions in my head of a bus mowing Laura down, or her choking to death on a fish bone.

I heaved out a long breath and said, "I'll come and see you in London and we can talk this through."

"Good boy. I knew you'd see the light. I'll expect you by latest tomorrow. No stalling, Alex. Can't wait to see you, darling. Bye, bye."

I bought an apple juice, glugged it all down in one go and called my mother, letting her know I'd be coming to Paris.

Christmas was around the corner. Pearl and I had ordered a tree and bought hand-made glass decorations to adorn it with. She had even found a special red silk ribbon for Rex. Everything was on the brink of perfection.

Until now.

I stood on the sidewalk and noticed my hand was trembling. I needed to call Pearl. This news would be the nail in the coffin for me. For us.

I was totally fucked. *Merdre!*

Her cell number was ominously out of order; a voice message saying it was no longer valid. I called her landline in hope.

In dread.

She finally picked up. "Pearl, baby," I said quietly. I could hear the tremors in my voice. "Your cell isn't going through."

"That's because I changed my phone number. It was hacked. By Laura."

"I know."

"What? You *knew* this? Why the hell didn't you warn me?"

"Because I've just found out myself. I'm sorry, I've been a

fucking idiot; I can't believe I didn't think of that one, especially in my line of business. I'm so sorry, chérie."

"This is monstrous," she said, her voice cracking. Little did she know the monster had gotten even more out of control.

I swallowed. The lump in my throat barely giving me airspace. "Baby, I've got bad news. I have to go away for a week or so. It's an emergency; I have to see my mother."

"Oh my God, she's not ill, is she?"

"No, nothing like that."

"Are Sophie and Elodie okay?"

"Yes, everyone's fine. Look, I wouldn't be going if it weren't an emergency."

"What, Alexandre? Why aren't you saying what the emergency is?"

"When we're married I'll tell you." As I said those words I realized it came out wrong. Like some sort of moral blackmail. Pearl latched onto that immediately, chewed me out, and then added:

"But what about the holidays?"

"I know, I'm as disappointed as you are."

"Disappointed? That doesn't even begin to describe how I feel, Alexandre. I'm fucking devastated." Pearl rarely swore. "It's our first ever Christmas together."

"I'm in a real bind, baby. A real mess. I need to see my mom. I don't want to lie to you, chérie, so please don't ask me any more questions."

"You're going to London, aren't you?" Her voice was an ice pick.

"I have no choice."

"We always have a choice, Alexandre. Only abused children or animals, or women who are locked up in a basement somewhere, with their passports taken away from them working as slave prostitutes for their sick pimps, or starving people in Africa—they don't have choices, but us? You and I do have choices because we're the lucky ones who live in wealthy western civilizations. We *do* have choices, so don't lay that shit on me."

I listened to Pearl's rant. A knot tightened in my throat. *A choice with a price to pay so high, I'd never forgive myself.* My mind flitted to Pearl being gang raped at college. She didn't have a choice then, although I knew that she was still blaming herself. Those fuckers would get their comeuppance—one of them I'd already tracked down. I thought of Laura again. How she was fucking up everyone's lives. I said in a low voice, "External forces are trying to pull us apart."

"Laura, you mean," Pearl said flatly. Just hearing that woman's name made the apple juice I'd drunk rise in my throat.

"Yes," I admitted, shame caught in my vocal chords.

It was all my fault. That bloody evidence had been sitting happily in a drawer at my mother's in Paris. I brought it to my house in Provence to make sure my stepfather would never find it. To protect my mother. To make her safe. What a fucking joke!

"Laura," Pearl repeated. "You're going to see Laura?"

My internal voice pattered on in my head: *I should have chucked the teeth and hip parts in a river but my mother wanted to keep them as a souvenir to remind her that he was dead. Really dead. My instinct begged me to destroy everything. And I didn't fucking listen.*

"Laura," she said again, annunciating the L.

"Yes," I whispered.

Pearl hung up.

11

If you asked me to describe Christmas with my mother, or my trip to London to see Laura, or anything about that dark period, I couldn't. It was a gauzy haze of nothingness, like white noise on an old TV screen. I do remember my mantra, *What's yours will come back to you,* and I said this to myself over and over, truly believing it. If Pearl and I were meant to be together, then all this Laura business would somehow sort itself out.

But all that happened was that things got worse.

Laura had stashed the evidence in a safety deposit box at an undisclosed bank. Or so she told me. With a letter saying that if some strange accident befell her, that it would be murder. Names cited. Namely me. She didn't admit to this in so many words, but that was the gist of it. Meanwhile she wanted us to get married.

Or else.

I didn't tell Sophie any of this, and my mother was so distraught that she lay in bed reading romance novels, eating pretzels and drinking white wine, pretending she had the flu, begging me every day by telephone to find a solution.

I called Pearl but of course she never picked up. It seemed she now went about without a cellphone—normal, why would she want Laura tracing her calls? Or me, knowing her every movement? So every now and then, I had a chat on her landline with Daisy or Anthony, who had come to visit her for Christmas. She was fine, they told me, but had no interest of having anything to do with me as long as Laura was in the picture.

I didn't pursue Pearl. How could I until I had a plan up my sleeve? I watched her from afar, though, as she stalked Rex when he went for his walks to Central Park with his 'nanny' Sally. I was stalking her and she was stalking Rex. Ironic. That was what gave me hope. Pearl, Rex and I were a little family unit. We belonged together. I knew that we had a chance when I observed her excitement every time she saw him. I followed her like some sort of detective in a hard-boiled Raymond Chandler novel—keeping my distance, ducking into alleys, lurking behind corners and trees. All I needed was a Fedora hat to complete the look. I had taken to wearing a long, dark, wool, military coat. I wondered what war hero had played his part in it. Did he die on the battlefield or come home triumphant?

I was in my own mini battlefield right now.

An emotional battlefield.

I had become a recluse in my apartment in New York, sporadically going to visit my mother in Paris, or Laura in London, trying to convince her to put an end to her blackmail. She wanted me to father her child. Insane. I was going to give it one more go, I decided. One more go to convince her that her scheme was crazy; that I could never love her child—that the only child I wanted was Pearl's. I had even fantasized about taking Laura heli-skiing, deep sea diving; on some dangerous, life-defying vacation where an accident could happen and nobody could prove a thing. But every time, my mother's face would loom before me, her misting eyes wide, her plea pitiful. She had finally found some peace in her world. I needed to protect her, and the letter Laura spoke of in that safe-deposit box, coupled with the evidence, made the risk too great, although my instinct told me she was bluffing.

The morning was icy and crisp; showing New York City at its most beautiful. Snowflakes drifted through the air as if in slow motion, and an orange glow of sun was casting warm gleams onto the white landscape of Central Park. Dogs were loose, playing and rolling about with each other; their tails up, their owners proud. The dog world going on in the park amused me; the one place where social classes of all ranks could mix happily because they all shared something in common: canines. Park Avenue heiresses and blue collar workers all eyed up their babies, talking of nothing but their dogs' vets visits, eating habits, and quirks. I watched as Pearl and Sally exchanged dialogue and observed Rex, who trotted happily off with Pearl into the depth of the park. I didn't like it the way Pearl was so nonchalant about her own safety. Into the depth of the wood she went, into the Ramble, alone, where some people prowled for anonymous sexual encounters, attracted by the thick cloak of vegetation, serpentine paths, giant boulders and meandering streams.

I followed her, my breath white in the chilled air, my collar up, my boots squeaking on the powdery snow. It made me think of something Pearl said once, and I laughed. "Love is like snow," she told me. "You never know how many inches you're going to get." Inches, in more ways than one, I thought, feeling myself expand inside my jeans the second I set eyes on her. It was insane; just seeing her from afar could get me aroused. And I couldn't deny it now; I was plagued with the idea of never fucking her again. It was driving me to distraction. I couldn't concentrate on work, she was in my dreams, my daydreams—all our lovemaking sessions, both rampant and gentle, were playing and rewinding and playing and rewinding in my sexually deprived, love-obsessed brain. All Laura's talk about my getting her pregnant had done only one thing: make me obsess about getting *Pearl* pregnant. Father her child. The idea of even *touching* Laura was abhorrent to me.

My inner animal was awoken as I watched Pearl now; wearing her little wool hat, her blonde hair peeking out, spread over her shoulders as she held her head up, catching snowflakes on her pink, fresh tongue. I had to kiss her. I wanted her hand to alleviate my aching groin that held so much seed, only for her. Like the park perverts, I stalked her into the wooded area, in hope that she would speak to me—my fantasies had me fucking her against a tree. My cock flexed again, imaging how sweet that would be—I could feel that rod of mine pining for attention, eager to fulfill its biological role.

I was the prowler and Pearl my prey.

"Pearl!" I shouted after her. She carried on walking. Rex

was darting in and out of scrubby groves, chasing squirrels. "Pearl, stop!" I hurried up to her and closed my hand around her coated elbow. I pulled her towards me and wrapped my arms around her. I rested my head against hers and breathed into her mouth, my breath hot, my desire scorching. She pulled her face away from mine and shot me a disdainful look.

"Why are you following me like this? What do you want?" Her eyes were darts.

She knew what I wanted, and she wanted it too, although her head was telling her to disbelieve her heart. I needed *all* of her, every single inch of her: her mind, her body, her sweet, kind soul. I pulled her into me again and could hear a growl rumble from within myself. I wished I had more self-control. I pressed myself up against her, holding her hips into my hard groin with one hand and her shoulder with the other. I began to kiss her all over her face, the melting snowflakes soft on my lips, the smell of her skin like honey as I inhaled her scent. I maneuvered her so she was up against a tree, my tongue parting her mouth as I probed my own inside, flickering it, letting it tangle with hers. She moaned and I imagined her wet pussy pulsating with yearning for me. Another wave of desire surged through me, coupled with visions of fatherhood, and I groaned into her lips.

"Leave me alone, you bastard," she breathed into my mouth as she whimpered through the kiss. "Oh, God, Alexandre, why can't you leave me alone?"

"I need you, baby," I whispered, rubbing my groin against her. All she had to do to make me come was brush her hand against my crotch—I was that horny, but she didn't. I took off my glove on my right hand and slipped my palm through her coat, around the flesh on her waist, forcing it down her belly and down into her panties. I slid my finger along her slit and felt the oozing wet warmth—but only for a second before she pushed my hand away with a thud. I slipped it behind, onto her ass and up to the small of her back. I wanted to feel those little dimples there, but she slammed her butt back against the tree, trapping my hand.

"Fuck you, Alexandre Chevalier, who do you think you *are* molesting me like this?"

"You're mine," I growled, clawing the ass that belonged to me. "I have to have you, I can't stand this anymore. You and I belong together, Pearl. Every waking moment, every sleeping second, I'm thinking about you, baby, dreaming about you. I'm so crazy and obsessed with you, it hurts."

"You just want to fuck me and go back to Laura, that skinny 'asparagus stick', as Sophie so brilliantly described her. Keep away from me, Alexandre—stop torturing me with your games!"

But her protestation was fruitless as her frail arms tried to beat on my heaving chest. I kissed her nose, her eyes, her chin, her hair, then back to her full, soft lips. I murmured into her mouth, "I love you Pearl, I love you more than you can possibly know; my life is an empty shell without you. It means nothing without you by my side."

"You want to have your cake and eat it too," she objected into my kiss.

"You're—" I trailed my tongue along her lips— "the only cake I want, I swear. The sweetest cake there is." It was true—she smelled delicious; her skin more fragrant than ever; not perfume but her own Pearlish scent that was indescribable. It sent shivers of lust and love right down my spine, pounding into my dick—all a mélange of beautiful, confusing chaos of love.

The drama carried on, the banter about Laura as I tried to protest my innocence in vain. I told Pearl that Laura had something I needed, which only blew her fire to flare up into a full-on bonfire—I could not slake her fury. There was a new, defiant look in her eye as if she were protecting something more than just her pride. I wasn't going to get my way, although I was trying damn hard.

"You and Laura deserve each other," Pearl hissed, her breath a mist that caught my tongue mid-sentence.

"Pearl, please, we—"

"You two," a voice from behind me yelled. "No sex in public, it's a felony." It was a police officer, strolling toward us, half amused, half serious. I stepped back; Pearl ducked from under me, slipping from my grip. She ran off, trammeling fresh snow, Rex racing after her, his deep paw prints testament of his adoration for her.

Even Rex was against me or he would have stayed loyal by my side. I felt wrath swell in my heart—the kind I experienced in the Foreign Legion, because I felt a sense of hopelessness; that the world was outside of my control. Destiny taking its own pigheaded course. I needed to expel the pent-up energy spiraling though my veins. I needed sex to calm me. That obviously wasn't going to happen.

So I needed to fight.

That rapist fuck had had it coming to him for nearly twenty years.

Payback time.

12

The muscle memory was about to kick in again. In a trance, I drove to Mystic where one of the guys who'd raped Pearl lived on weekends. His house, where he was cozily ensconced with his wife and kids, was pretty plush. I'd had him tracked down; and found out everything I needed to know. Revenge was bubbling, like Laura's cauldron, in my hot veins. It was my way of showing Pearl how much I loved her, although I wasn't going to reveal my violent side to her. No, this 'escapade' would be my secret.

I followed him to his drinking hole by the waterfront and took him by surprise. It felt good to scare the living shit out of him, even though I did it with a fake gun; one of those cigarette lighters. He had raped my girl, albeit eighteen years ago. He had defiled her with his stinking dick. I hated mankind. Man, not kind. Man—so often a fucking piece of shit. Pearl and Natalie were right to expose all those fucks in their documentaries—merciless nothings who were ruining women's lives in such a cavalier way. I felt so proud of Pearl. She had that all-consuming sense of justice. She was a fighter. A warrior. She wanted to right the world. This was my chance to help her.

Few people have guts to do what she did for a living. Everyone is so busy trying to seek approval, be popular, be 'liked' on Facebook or HookedUp. Pearl didn't care about being liked. She cared about integrity. She was on a mission to defend others through her job as documentary producer, but somehow, she hadn't believed that she, herself, needed shielding. This was my way of protecting her, albeit too late. I enjoyed laying a few punches into this overweight, ex-football-playing cocksucker, swinging my leg hard into his chest—letting him know that he had fucked (literally) with the wrong person.

He'd fucked my girl. In the nastiest, most despicable way. Which meant he'd also fucked me.

Revenge is a dish best served cold. And this revenge had been on ice for eighteen years.

I remember two distinct things about that night in Mystic: the cold. And the man's expression on his milky white face when I told him he'd have to part with two month's salary—a hundred grand to be wired to a charity I'd set up in Pearl's name. In 'Jane Doe's' name. With a ten percent discount if he revealed all his rapist buddies' names—each and every one who participated in the gang rape that fateful night. Of all the punches and kicks, the financial punch was the most painful to this pathetic man; hit 'em where it hurts most—in the wallet.

It gave me momentary satisfaction.

But it reminded me of Pearl's vulnerability. She needed to be protected. She needed me by her side, whether she knew it or not.

I couldn't stand to be without her a second more. Despite my promises to my mother, I'd have to tell Pearl the truth because I was dying inside.

I left Mystic and drove back to New York, singing along with the car radio to the Kinks, *You Really Got Me.* I had to make Pearl mine, whatever it took. *You got me so I can't sleep at night*...so true.

Sleep...it was hitting me now. I pulled the car over. I felt spent and needed five minutes shut-eye before I continued driving—I didn't want to have an accident through tiredness. The image of Pearl had me needing to jack off—to expel the heat I felt inside after the fight. I had blood on my knuckles, a bruised lip; the idea of her kissing it better made my cock swell with longing. I came fast and hard, her tits and ass on rewind and play, rewind and play, as I raced myself to an intense orgasm. Better this way—I needed to see her and didn't want to behave like a feral animal, the way I had in Central Park. Now I was less frenetic. I closed my eyes, calmer now, reclined the leather seat, and drifted off into a brief but heavy catnap.

"Don't fucking move." One hand is clamped on my neck. His breathing is heaving fast and furious, his nails like bear's claws digging into me. His other hand is pulling down my pajama bottoms. Am I dreaming? I open my eyes wide and try to roll forward but he's got me in a tight grip. I jab my elbow backwards and it whacks into his shoulder but I can't escape. Maman is in the hospital for the night. Because of him. Yesterday, I attacked him, trying to protect her, and he left the apartment, saying he wouldn't ever return, muttering under his whiskey breath as Maman lay in a pool of blood on the kitchen floor. I dialed the fire brigade because the ambulance is always too slow.

I didn't hear him come in tonight. I didn't bolt the door from inside, in case Sophie came home late. Stupid me. I'm all alone. He's naked. He smells of sweat and whiskey.

"I said don't fucking move or it'll hurt." I hear him grab his bottle and slug down the booze. I take the moment to slither out from his grip but it makes him roar. "Why can't you just let me love you, goddamn it? You're my son; I love you."

I hop to my bedroom door—my pajamas are around my ankles so I can't move fast—I can't open the door in time. He chases me, tackling me like a rugby player. We both fall with a thud to the ground.

"Papa, please, you're drunk. Let me go!" I crawl up on my knees. I'm panting hard but he pushes me down on the floor again. My teeth smash against my lips. I'm bleeding. "Please, Papa," I beg, my face crushed on the black and white tiled linoleum. I thrash like a snake but he holds me down. My pajamas are still caught around my ankles like a net. He's sticking it in and it hurts. I scream out in pain and manage to get to my knees so it slips out.

"Stop jiggling about, Alexandre Dubois—stop disobeying your father!"

I roll on my side. I'm on my back now. I take his arm, bring my mouth up to his shoulder and bite into it with all the power I have.

"Ah! You fuck!" he cries out in a blood-curdling yell. He gets up and staggers towards his whiskey bottle, grabs it and races at me, swinging it wildly. My hand is on the doorknob and I turn it. The door is ajar; it's open. I stick my barefoot in the gap but I'm too late. He smashes the bottle against the door. I shove my head through—whiskey spills all over my back. I feel a thump on my bottom and see blood pooling on the floor. My bottom is stinging as the whiskey trickles between my crack. It's my blood I see. He jams the broken bottle inside me, twisting it like a corkscrew and I'm screaming in pain now. Shards of glass, whiskey, blood—my blood—all over the floor. I hear a noise. I look up and see

Sophie rushing towards me. She's clutching a kitchen knife—

I sat bolt upright with a jerk. Jesus! I was lying on something sticking right into my butt. My wallet. I let out the breath that I had been holding in without realizing. That memory hadn't been around for a while. Why now? I thought of the guy's blood tonight in Mystic, pooling around his ears after I struck him with my ruthless kick. I remembered my own blood, the glass, the metallic taste in my mouth, my chipped tooth, my father with the knife stuck in his groin, and how Sophie and I ran and ran and never returned.

Maman had a choice and she chose *him*. After everything, she betrayed us. I sat there now in the rental car, my head slumped on the steering wheel and choked back the lump in my throat. *I will not be broken. I will not be broken.* Finally, I had my chance at happiness with Pearl but I was jeopardizing it all for a woman who had not protected me, who had not put me before her own desires. I couldn't shoulder her weight any longer. I needed to be honest with Pearl. Or I would lose her. I *had* lost her. But maybe, just maybe, I could win her back. If.

If I told her the whole story.

She needed to know who and what my mother really was.

I slipped into Pearl's rental apartment—I still hadn't handed over my set of keys. Daisy and Amy and Pearl would probably, I deduced, be asleep by now, and I didn't want to wake anyone. But Pearl was wide-awake, a tub of ice cream in one hand and one of Amy's toy cowboy pistols in the other. I fell in love with her all over again. It was proof that we had to be together; that we were soul mates. Both wielding toy guns in the same night?

It was a *fait accompli.*

She was standing there in her pajama bottoms, her tits voluptuous, her nipples erect in her little tank. But sex was no longer on my mind. I was too broken up that night.

"Why are you doing this Alexandre? Why are you here? Back to torture me?"

"Love the toy gun," I said with a faint smile. "You and I have more in common than you think, baby." But it wasn't funny anymore. I crumpled to the ground, my resilience in fragments, my barriers gone. A tear plopped onto the floor, landing on the slush of snow pooled next to my big black boots. "I can't stand this anymore, Pearl. I really can't." I looked up at her like a puppy waiting for a clue from his mistress. I had no answers. I needed help.

This was the moment in time when everything froze like a snowflake floating in midair; unique and perfect. I gave in to Pearl. Completely. I threw myself into the arms of Fate. If God gave a fuck, he'd sort this Laura shit out for us, but nothing was now going to stand in the way of the goddamn truth, my mother included.

I took Pearl home, just as she was, in her pajamas. We didn't make love but we did make promises. I told her everything—each tiny, gruesome detail, leaving nothing unsaid. She embraced my truth, swore she'd stand by my side, no matter what. We were a team, she said, and nothing could break that.

Recounting how my mom murdered my father in the bathtub, by throwing a live electric heater into the water, somehow alleviated me of the black weight I had been heaving over my shoulder for so many years. Just saying the words made me a free man.

I kissed Pearl's knuckles on her ringed hand and said—the diamond glittering in my eyes as I spoke—"Pearl, I know you and I know myself. If we don't spend the rest of our days together we won't be truly happy. We'll go around half dead. Without you, my flame is snuffed out. Without you, I am only half a man. Without you, my life will be running on empty." Maybe I sounded like a cliché—an actor speaking his lines—but it was unrehearsed and how I truly felt.

I came clean with Pearl that night. I revealed all to her. My past. My mother. The lot. And then Pearl told me *her* big secret. The best damn secret known to man.

She was pregnant with my child.

13

I won't go into detail about all the trials and tribulations that Pearl and I endured over the next month or so because of Laura. Suffice it to say that there was enough madness and intrigue to make a long movie (that would have seemed too far-fetched for most intelligent beings) *and* a TV spin-off of several seasons, to boot. Laura had us running around in circles, doing cartwheels, backward walkovers, and nosedives, suffering several near coronaries and many sleepless nights. But the difference now, was that Pearl and I weathered the storm *together*. And knowing that she was pregnant made our family unit stronger, all the more invincible. A tiny voice inside my head assured me that we would pull thorough.

We had to.

We had a thousand nutty plans to out-fox Laura. Her latest scheme was to use me as a sperm donor for her brainchild baby-to-be, generously letting Pearl 'keep' me for herself, Laura having finally given up on actually marrying me. It was bordering on laughable her plan was so outlandish.

Our last 'encounter' was at Laura's house in Chelsea. She was threatening my mother again and I found myself on a plane to London to put an end to her blackmail, once and for all. However, in an unexpected twist, Fate and Irony got their first.

Laura had an accident—another fall, this time tumbling downstairs in her own house, her head cracking open, and her heart—which had erroneously believed it loved me—finally stopped beating.

Her husband James (emerging like a dormouse from a long winter) had been in rehab for several months—all this I found out during the bizarre scene that followed.

Pearl had been imagining all that time that Laura had topped him off. James was one of those high-class heroin addicts (able to afford the best) and had spent time at The Priory—a sort of British Betty Ford equivalent—to kick his habit. Although, I didn't find all this out until we were both embedded in a drama that made us both look like murderers.

James and I found ourselves in an almost comical situation—murder suspects as we were—as we both observed Laura lying, dead as a smashed mosquito, at the bottom of the staircase in their London house. We arrived at the scene of the 'crime' simultaneously.

She had a serene smile on her lipsticked lips as if the accident really had taken her unawares. I still remember the color red, vivid and dramatic—the pool of blood, the crimson of her silky negligee, her shiny, vermillion-painted lips. Both James and I looked guilty as dogs who had raided the trash—I had just come in through the back, via the garage door (with my own set of keys), and James suddenly emerged from the front door. Which one of us was a victim of circumstance, and which one a murderer? We fixed our gaze, first on Laura, and then one another.

"She must have careened down the stairs like a sled," I said to James as we continued to size each other up. We then looked back down at Laura's corpse, each silently accusing the other. "Her feet must have slipped forward, and her body slanting backwards, bashing her head on the bottom step." *Jesus, it sounds as if I know too much.*

James cast his glance at one dainty-heeled slipper on Laura's left foot and then looked about to find its pair. It was lying a few feet away. He bent down and touched her pale cheek and I thought, "Fuck it's *him*; *he* did it." Laura looked all tarted-up; make-up, a sexy, skimpy little outfit—for my benefit? James obviously thought so, and by the look on his face he suspected his wife and I were having an affair. *He killed her out of jealousy and rage*, I thought.

I locked my eyes with his.

"You fucking cunt," James shrieked at me. "You sneaky fucking bastard." He laid his palm across his wife's breast to double-check if she was as dead as she looked. "You bloody well killed my wife!"

"James, no! What are you saying? That's *crazy*. I just *got* here, at the same time you were coming through the front door. I swear. This is just as much a surprise for me as it is for you."

James looked up at me with his odd, angular face, a sneer etched on his thin lips. He raked his bony hand through his blond hair and said in his British, upper-class voice:

"What I don't understand, is why. *Why,* Alexandre? Did you try to kill her last time, too? When she had that supposed 'accident' and she ended up in a bloody wheelchair? I mean, it's obvious she fell down the stairs. One push, that's all it must have taken. You fucking bastard!" Spittle sprayed as he spoke.

I knew he wasn't the type to lay a punch. English aristocratic men are usually pretty cowardly (too polite for their own good), but I flinched all the same, and wiped his spray of angry spittle from my face. My stomach churned with sick dread as I thought of my father's teeth and hip bits—evidence in that safety deposit box. Laura dead was all I fucking needed.

I shouted out, "Okay, James…this is just great. You accusing me of murder? How about I accuse *you*? Where the fuck have you been for the last couple of months? Eh? Suddenly appearing like this. Perhaps you *knew* that I was coming over. Laura knew. I called her. Maybe it was really bloody convenient for you to bump her off and then blame me."

"I'm going to call the police," James spluttered, his eyes wet with emotion. Real emotion? Fake?

The word 'police' sent a hammer to my heart. I thought of the evidence. Laura's note stowed with her lawyer revealing everything if she ever had an accident. My mother rotting in a jail somewhere. And I'd be accused of her murder, on top of it all. Fuck!

James traced his finger along Laura's once-determined jaw. "Laura wouldn't just fall down her own stairs in her own house now, would she?"

"It is possible, she had those heeled slippers on," I answered.

"How the fuck did you get in, anyway?"

"Through the back, from the garden," I said. "I still have your garage keys."

James nodded. "That's right—your Aston Martin. I'd forgotten about that."

Now I looked even guiltier. My Aston Martin excuse wouldn't wash because it wasn't fucking there anymore! Suresh, my driver, had moved it to France. I had no reason, *whatsoever*, for coming through the back door. I quickly added, "Actually, I moved my car a while ago. I knocked on the front door but there was no answer, and Laura didn't pick up the phone. She was expecting me. So I came through the back."

"Nice excuse, Alex. Tell that to Scotland bloody Yard."

That particular TV episode was a long and complicated one—the finale to an outrageously elaborate plot, peppered with an element of black humor. I must have had 'killer' written all over my face, because I could not deny the onslaught of fatalistic fantasies I'd had in the run-up to Laura's death. I do think I willed it to happen. I really do. The power of imagination is awesome. And when I say 'awesome' I mean it in the true sense of the word.

In my mind I had killed Laura. Perhaps James had too; who knew the anger that had been building inside him. Here we were, staring at each other open-mouthed, dumbstruck that she really was gone for good—each accusing the other of murder. It was as if the screenwriters in our TV serial spin-off had Agatha Christie in mind, because what ensued, after we had both been arrested on suspicion of murder, was that Laura and James's housekeeper, Mrs. Blake, came forward.

As I sat at the local police station, wondering how I would burrow my way out of my Alice-In-Wonderland rabbit hole,

Mrs. Blake—my fairy godmother—waved her magic wand: waxy polish on the stairs, coupled with Laura's kitten-heeled slippers, were both the murder weapons and the murderers rolled into one. It was confirmed by forensics that there was polish all over the soles of Laura's shoes.

Finally, Pearl and I were free.

Or so I thought.

Because Laura—even from her *chaise longue* in Hell (she was probably having cocktails and flirting with the Devil himself)—had other plans for our future.

14

Our long-awaited wedding was a fairytale. It took place in Lapland—yes, Lapland really does exist—on St. Valentine's Day itself.

Pearl had done everything to make it extraordinary, including reindeer with white velvet ribbons tied around their antlers, to pull us with sleds. She had told little Amy that they were on loan from Santa Claus and even I believed her. It really was a dream winter wedding. Pearl was the Ice Queen and I her King. She looked resplendent in a floor-length, ivory-colored gown. It was silk velvet, and caught the light as she glided through the wedding ceremony, the long train trailing behind her. Beads of 'ice crystal' blossoms cascaded off one shoulder. Elodie and Amy were her bridesmaids, both dressed in pink. Elodie looked like a movie star, the derriere of her gown low and scooped, caught at the back with pink silk roses, and Amy, taking her role very seriously, was dressed in a pink, baby-doll, organza number with a wreath in her hair.

The chapel was made of real ice, sculpted from the frozen land. Dozens of artists had arrived from across the globe to carve the ice interiors. Each year, they told us, the designs were completely different and would melt in springtime. Nothing but our memories and photographs would be testament to our magical day.

I stood there in my tails, nervously waiting for Pearl as she walked quietly down the aisle. Everybody was entranced. Sophie was misty-eyed; both her husband and Alessandra by her side—he still had no idea, and thought Alessandra was just an old friend from Sophie's 'acting' days. My mother stood tall and proud, my stepfather holding her hand. Anthony and Daisy were blatantly blubbing into handkerchiefs. And Pearl's father winked at me as if to say, *She's yours now, don't fuck up the way I did.*

No, I wasn't going to fuck-up. I had fought hard for this prize.

I locked my eyes with Pearl's and let out a sigh of relief. She was about to be mine. All mine. I thought back to how she bolted from me at Van Nuys Airport and wondered, just for a split second, if she would run from me now. But her gaze remained steadily on my face, a faint smile on her lips. Concentrated. Determined. She wanted me. All of me. The bad me, the okay me, the me that knew that we would be together as long as we both lived.

A dysfunctional match made in Heaven.

No, she wasn't any more perfect than I was—in fact, she really was a pretty wayward character, but she was perfect for *me.* She broke out in a huge smile and I beamed at her in return. We giggled nervously like schoolchildren at the excitement of it all. Then I mouthed silently, "Pearl Chevalier," as she walked slowly towards me, her eyes glistening, twinkling with emotion.

And then she was by my side as we did our wedding vows. At the end, after we'd exchanged rings, the pastor asked everyone to affirm our matrimony.

"If you believe that Pearl and Alexandre are made for one another, say yes!" he cried out, and everyone shouted back in unison, "Yes!"

"Say it louder!" he demanded, and they did. It was an unorthodox touch on his part, no doubt planned ahead, but it took us both by surprise, and something about that big 'Yes' made us snap out of the surreal dream of our fairytale wedding, and into a shocking moment. Shocking because this was it. Forever—the Yes giving us strength for our future. They all believed in us, just as much as *we* believed in us. Words are powerful when spoken by many at one time. Especially with conviction.

It was comforting to know that our twins were also part of the ceremony, even if only in Pearl's stomach. The family I had always dreamed of was almost complete.

Our wedding bands were made of 22 carat gold and each had the other's name inscribed inside. So not only was *PEARL* engraved on my heart, but on my finger, too.

The celebration continued all night, everybody doing their own thing—sled rides, vodka drinking, feasting, and general jovialities all round. I just wanted to be alone with Pearl.

I helped her down from the sled onto the powdery, glittery snow, as snowflakes fluttered onto our faces. Reindeer and sled dropped us off at our remote log cabin where a glowing fire awaited us inside. I glanced skyward, soaking up the spectacle.

The Aurora Borealis—the Northern Lights—swooped above us. Five fingers of sweeping green light, like a giant's hand, raised itself towards the Heavens. God's hand? Pearl thought so. If ever there was a moment when I felt that there was a Higher Power, this was it. I had it all. The woman I loved by my side, pregnant with twins, and a sense of freedom and relief as I had never known before in my life. The old world was behind me and I was starting afresh. We were a mountain together, Pearl and I.

That night, we fucked for the first time in months, so it really did feel to me as if it was new to us. Okay, we'd had delicious sex in many other ways, but no penetration—doctor's orders in case Pearl suffered a miscarriage. It had happened to her twice before during her marriage to Saul and we didn't want to take any risks. So this night really was our wedding night in every sense. She was my virgin bride. I felt reverent towards my new wife, but I also couldn't wait to enter her. Deep. Profound. I needed that union. It had been far too long. As beautiful as her wedding gown was, I had visions of what lay beneath—and I couldn't wait.

I observed Pearl quietly as she lay on the bed before me. Horny as I was, I didn't want to rush a thing. This was a moment to be savored for the rest of our lives. I could hardly breathe I had so much love overflowing from within me; a pumping surge which took my body by surprise. I could now know *for sure* that she belonged to me. No more ifs or buts. No more cat and mouse.

"Pearl Chevalier," I said, rolling those sweet words on my tongue. "Madame Pearl Chevalier, tu es magnifique." The golden light of the fire highlighted the curves of her nude body and glowed on her beautiful face. "Je t'aime," I added with pride. I could feel myself get hard. "Do you realize how I've been longing for this moment? Counting down the days, the hours?"

"Well, that's how they had to do it in the olden days. The groom had to *wait* for his wedding night," she said.

I remained stationary, drinking in the incomparable image. The image that I wanted imprinted on my brain until the end of my days, so when I was old, gray and doddery I could remember this moment.

"Do you know what I'm going to do to you?" I murmured. She bit her lip and spread her legs a touch. My cock flexed again. I slowly sauntered towards her, my eyes locked with hers. Her blonde hair had grown in the last few months and was spread like silky bands across her shoulders.

I bent down and kissed her. I inhaled in her sweet scent, and a feral moan rumbled from my throat. She opened her lips and her pink tongue, fresh and eager, darted out to meet mine. She whimpered and I knew how wet she'd be, even though I hadn't even touched that part of her yet. "Pearl Chevalier," I said again, and winked at her. "Mrs. Pearl Chevalier. Madame Pearl Chevalier."

"Oh don't be so sure, I might decide to be Mzzzz," she teased, "or mademoiselle. I might keep my maiden name."

"No more games, Pearl," I said, nipping her pussycat lip, "you're mine now."

"Prove it," she moaned into my mouth.

"Oh, I will."

Her nipples were tweaked with desire and her tits full and round from the pregnancy. I trailed my tongue over her lips, and my fingers grazed across her taut breasts and I pinched and rolled one nipple lightly. "Oh God," she groaned, her eyes fluttering.

I pinned her beneath me, my knees either side of her hips, my cock rock-hard against her curved belly where Louis and Madeleine—we had just come up with the names a couple of hours earlier—were growing stronger day by day. I almost felt wicked, knowing I was about to defile their pure mother. But it also made me all the more ravenous for Pearl, knowing that the seed inside her was growing into two special little beings, who would talk and walk and have their own opinions about life. *We* had created them together. Through love. And lust.

She traced her fingers over my pecs and ran them slowly down to my abdomen, letting her fingers dip into the ridges, scanning my torso with her guileless, approving eyes. "You're beautiful, Alexandre," she told me.

I leaned down to kiss her again, letting our lips rest quietly together. We were united and about to be joined even closer. I needed that proximity. I needed to be deep inside her. I edged further down until my cock rested on her slick wetness. Desire pooled low in my gut and blood pumped hard and fast into my groin. I was huge and worried that I might hurt her, yet the need to fuck her was stronger than ever. I could feel every nuance of her soft, liquid heat and I slid in just a millimeter. *Fuck!* It felt out of this world. "Is that okay, baby? I don't want to damage you."

"Help me," she whimpered.

"Am I hurting you?"

"Please fuck me, Alexandre. *Please.*" I pushed in another inch, using my arms to control my weight on her. Her eyes flicked to my biceps and she bit her lip. She bucked her hips up at me to get closer but I carried on controlling myself. "Your muscles are so defined," she whispered. "You're so incredible—every part of you."

I made small circular movements so she could adjust to my size. I could feel myself throbbing, and the sensation of her tight pussy, like a warm glove, had my sensitive cock ready to plunge into her. Fuck her hard. But I counted to ten and remained steadily, gently thrusting, only a couple of inches in. I had to control myself.

"So. Juicy. So. Fucking. Beautiful." My dick punctuated each word.

She clawed my ass with her nails and drew me in closer but I wouldn't give in, in case I hurt her. Her ankles clamped my calves and she pumped herself in rhythm with me. "Oh my God, this is incredible," she moaned. "I'm going to come soon."

Our foreheads were locked together and our breaths in unison as if we were one being. I pulled out and let my cock slide up and down her clit—she was on the edge—so this was a way to both bring her back down and also to drive her wild. I wanted this to last longer because I was in a sort of spiritual, lovemaking bliss. She was too. Long gone were the days when I had to work hard to make Pearl come—that challenge was over. I slipped back inside her and resumed the mini thrusts, just my crown teasing her mercilessly as she arched her back, groaning for more of my thick, solid cock.

"Remember to…Love. Honor. And, Obey. Your. Husband," I growled, half jesting. I could feel her contractions gripping me, sucking me in—she was coming hard. I couldn't hold it any longer. I pushed myself in a little more and exploded, my seed probably joining the twins.

Pearl's tongue was all over mine as she murmured almost incoherently, "I'll obey you, Alexandre. I'll do anything for you. Anything—every inch of me belongs to you."

We were climaxing together in an emotional rush of trust, lust and love.

"Anything?"

"Oh God I'm still coming....anything, baby," she moaned, her fingers were gripping my ass.

"Stay with me forever, my belle Pearl."

"I swear," she said, kissing me again.

15

Pearl and I settled beautifully into married life. After the twins were born, she became more of a woman and less of a girl; so much so that I would goad her sometimes to be more frivolous and less responsible. Perhaps I missed that foolish character that jumped out of the ladies' room window and got me running round in circles—a little bit anyway. I understood that our wayward paths had been the right ones, and nothing we had ever done in our lives could—or should—have been different, including the 'fuck-ups.' If they had been, we wouldn't have felt so lucky to be together.

Pearl became quite a mover and shaker with HookedUp Enterprises and began to spread her wings. I was so proud. Those wings which had been damaged when I first knew her, were now helping her soar to great heights. She had so much more confidence being married and a mother.

One evening, as we sat by a roaring fire in our apartment, I came clean about the Bloody Mary incident—it had been eating at me. I didn't want to hide anything. I went into detail about how I was trussed up like a Christmas turkey, hands bound with electric cable, 'marinated' by the drug-spiked Bloody Mary, with Laura poised on top of me, my dick ready for lift-off. Pearl thought it hilarious—in retrospect—but admitted that I'd done the right thing not to tell her at the time. We had no secrets from each other now. I reveled in my newfound freedom of not carrying weights upon my shoulders; secrets so heavy that they made you stumble through life—what a relief. Both Pearl and I were free and it felt fucking great.

I had become a sort of househusband, being able to work from home, with the twins on my lap, or crawling about the floor while I 'tested' the video games in my new company, or made calls—I'd also bought up a chain of boutique hotels to add to my portfolio, which I needed to manage. Sally had become nanny to the children as well as to Rex, so we were a busy, bustling household. We were making ridiculous money with our video games, my new partner and I, and it was more creative than HookedUp, which Sophie was now handling pretty much solo. I still owned shares but was out of the day-to-day grind of it. Sebastian's and my new video game was a work of art, with high concept character building and role-play. Meanwhile, Pearl and Natalie went from strength to force with HookedUp Enterprises and had branched out into magazines as well.

The evening of the New York premiere of *Stone Trooper* had

finally arrived. Originally, Pearl had said that I needn't bother accompanying her, but then she changed her mind. She had assumed I agreed but I was getting so into the househusband thing, I had other ideas. I lay on the sofa with my toddlers crawling all over me, their sticky fingers in my eyes and hair.

"Alexandre, you *have* to come," Pearl pleaded, standing at the doorway. Her blonde hair was swept up in an elegant chignon—the hairdresser had been in our apartment all day. Her make-up was sultry and darkly seductive. She looked stunning.

"Sorry, babe, I really don't like doing red carpet—you know that," I mumbled, a set of baby fingers in my mouth.

"But this is different."

"Still red carpet. I like to keep my anonymity. I already did the first premiere in LA. One's enough. Sophie will be with you. Natalie, Alessandra, Elodie. You really don't need me as well. Besides, someone has to stay home with Louis and Madeleine, and Sally's busy tonight."

"You told me Sally would be here," Pearl grumbled. "You're so stubborn, you know that? So *tetu*, it's unbelievable!"

"I'll stay home, order Chinese, and hang out with the twins."

She walked towards me slowly, letting her ivory silk robe fall open. My eyes grew greedy observing her beautiful nude body—freshly moisturized—she smelled of peaches or something sweet and edible. Her tits were still big from breastfeeding. I felt myself go instantly hard. I'd fuck those tits later. Maybe now even, while she was all perfect—I'd ravage her—*women hate it when you mess with their hair and make-up.* I winked at her.

She raised her brow. "Alright, fine, don't come. Don't blame me if guys come on to me tonight. Don't blame me if Mikhail what's-his-face eyes me up and flirts his ass off."

She had my attention. "That Russian arms dealer fuck? What's he doing coming to our premiere?"

"Oh, it's suddenly *our* premiere, is it? A moment ago I was on my own."

"Seriously, who invited him?"

She exited the room with a *Wouldn't-you-like-to-know* look on her face.

I got up from the sofa, Louis in one arm, Madeleine in the other. Their eyes followed Pearl too, and Louis gurgled, with a grin on his face as if he found the whole scenario hilarious. I called after her, "Who invited him?"

I took out my cell and arranged a babysitter, there and then. Jeanine, in fact, who worked at HookedUp Enterprises with Pearl. She was a big fan of Louis and Madeleine. She said 'yes' immediately. I called Sally for backup and when she said no, I made her an offer she couldn't refuse.

The *Stone Trooper* premiere was less of a flashy affair than LA, but still, everyone seemed to want to be there to be seen, rather than to see.

Not Pearl, though. She was in professional mode, politely chatting to everyone who was congratulating her as we made our torturously slow way up the red carpet, toward the open doors of the movie theatre. She had on a floor-length silk chiffon gown that trailed and shimmied behind her—a sort of pale gold that made her angelic, although she was unaware of how dazzling she looked. It was amazing how fast she'd lost the post-pregnancy weight. Swimming, I guessed. Except for her breasts—no weight lost there. It unnerved me to know that others might see that too. As we ambled on through to the screening—she glided, I ambled—Elodie came up behind me, her eyes flashing with anger.

She clutched my elbow. "What the fuck?" she seethed in a hoarse whisper.

I had the twins on my mind and was on autopilot, nodding politely at people but not paying attention to what anyone said. "What? Did someone tread on your gown?" I asked absent-mindedly. But Elodie wasn't wearing a gown. She was back to Goth mode. She wore spiked black heels that could poke out an eye, and skin-tight leggings with a see-through top. Luckily, she had on some sort of bra underneath.

"She's gay, isn't she? She's fucking well gay!" She shot a look at her mother, who was walking by Alessandra's side, her hips pressed close to her girlfriend. As was often the case, Elodie's father was absent. Maybe he was having an affair too. He was rarely around for events, or if he was, he had an air of invisibility.

"Your mother?" I said. There was no point pretending otherwise. I was amazed it had taken Elodie so long to work it out.

She pinched my arm. "Thanks for warning me. Thanks for hiding it from me for all this time."

"Elodie, this isn't the moment. Come over tomorrow and we'll talk about it."

"Oh crap, that's all I fucking need," she sneered. I looked

over to her line of vision and saw the Russian. He was making a beeline for us.

I turned to her. "You know him, Elodie?"

"You could say that."

For a second, the man looked as if he were about to slit my throat in front of the whole crowd, but then he suddenly smiled as if he recognized me.

"Alexandre Chevalier," he said, his accent very pronounced. "What a pleasure." He held out his right hand. I felt some cameras flash.

I didn't reciprocate. I replied coldly, "I'm sorry but we don't know each other."

Elodie rolled her eyes. "Uncle Alexandre, this is Mikhail Prokovich, Mikhail, my uncle, Alexandre," she said in a bored drawl.

His eyes were menacing as he raked his gaze over her. He said in French, "You can do better than that, Elodie, my darling. Especially considering I'm your date."

"*Va te faire foutre*," she retorted, storming off towards the doors to go inside.

That's right, va te faire foutre—fuck you, asshole! My heart sank into my stomach. My *darling?* Her *date? What the hell?* My eyes locked with his. "You *know* my niece?"

He smirked at me and answered cockily, again in French, "I more than know her. I'm *fucking* her."

Before my brain was even aware of what I was doing, my fist—as if it had a will of its own—punched the man's face. He tumbled backwards. My leg swung in a high arch, landing on the side of his chest in a hard thud. But he didn't fall. I could hear gasps and women squealing with fright. The fuck shook himself off like a Spanish bull and came toward me, hurling his full weight at me. He was as tall as I was and strongly built, his chest wide, his arms thick—even though he was wearing a suit, I could tell he worked out.

Pearl screamed, "Alexandre, stop! What are you doing?" *Good point,* I thought. *What am I doing?* My limbs seemed to have their own agenda.

"I told you I don't do red carpet well," I said—a James Bond quip if ever there was one—as I dodged to the side, managing to avoid Mikhail Prokovich's heaving torso lunge right at me. "Step back, Pearl," I urged her, realizing this was so not the time, nor the place, for this fiasco—that I should have kept my cool.

But it was too late. The guy twisted his body at the last minute and caught me in a vice, his arm clamped about my middle. He was a tough fucker, seemed to have been trained in some sort of martial art like I was, because he had some sneaky moves—I'd met my match.

"She's only nineteen, you fuck!" I hissed at him as we wrestled, both trying to overpower the other, without making too much of a scene. But we *were* making a scene. And how. The next thing I knew, Pearl was beating him on the head with her purse. I pleaded, "Pearl, you must step *back*, chérie, you'll get hurt," although my love for her at that moment swelled, not only at her bravery, but because of her loyalty.

A bright flash blinded me for a second. The paparazzi were at it in full swing now—snapping away at the spectacle: two grown men fighting in public. And then the Russian's large knee jerked up and smashed me in the balls. I winced in pain, doubling forward. Prokovich jabbed me in the back with his sharp elbow. I used my crouched position to my advantage and, bending down even further, I hooked my fingers about his ankle. My opponent lost his balance and fell backwards to the floor, landing unceremoniously on his shoulder.

"You fuck!" he yelled up at me. I wiped my forehead—fighting in a suit was not the most comfortable option, and perspiration was gathering on my brow.

I leered down at him as he was getting up. "Leave my niece alone you arms dealing asshole!" I roared. There was another collective gasp from the crowd. People were filming now—Smartphones out in droves. No doubt the scene was already Tweeted to the hilt and it wouldn't be long before it would be live on YouTube.

I heard hushed whispers of 'arms dealer,' jostling bodies gasping behind the cordoned off ropes, and VIP guests in shimmering, diaphanous gowns or crisp penguin suits, oohing and aahing; some vying for a closer view, others trying to get the hell out of our arena, and Sophie's voice screaming, "Arrete! Stop, you two."

Two hulking, balding men with earpieces suddenly came up either side of me and pulled me back. Prokovich's bodyguards. It hadn't even occurred to me to have *my* bodyguard on call. In that second, I knew what was about to happen as the Russian rose to his feet. I was going to be his punching bag while these two meatballs held my arms captive. As he came at me with a sharp left hook aimed at my gut, my leg shot higher than a Moulin Rouge can-can dancer—muscle memory kicking in (literally). I clipped him under the chin with the toe of my shoe. He flew backwards, his hand clutching his jaw in agony, blood flowing. Pearl flung herself at me, loyal to the last, screaming at

Prokovich's bodyguards.

"Let my husband go, you monsters!" She was using her body as a shield to protect me. I couldn't stop her; my arms being pinned back by the meatballs.

Elodie came rushing up, too. I expected her to shout at me but she stopped at my bleeding enemy, as he was cursing in his own language, sprawled out on the velvety red carpet. She yelled at him in French, "You ever touch my uncle again and I'll fucking *kill* you!"

I couldn't help but beam inside, a faint smile flickering on my lips. My faithful ladies with me to the bitter end. The fact that I struck first didn't matter to Elodie. *Blood is thicker than water, you Russian fuck!* My team of women, including Natalie, was screaming at the bodyguards to let me go from their beefy clutches, and soon enough, the movie theatre security arrived and the bodyguards let me free. Prokovich got back up on his feet and shook himself like a lion, his blond hair dripping with sweat; he even flashed his signature, billion-dollar smile, tinged now with scarlet blood, as our bemused audience observed us with fascination. Fitting, I thought—a bloody smile that has been bought by other people's war-zone misery.

The theatre's security team surrounded us, confused as to know what to do, asking if I was alright. They wondered if anyone wanted to press charges. They offered the same courtesy to Prokovich—but both of us pretended that our skirmish was a minor blip. As if it were a little show, put on for the crowd's entertainment. I knew I'd have to watch it from now on, though. He'd be the type to seek revenge.

Everybody straightened their ties and jackets and snickered with embarrassment, pretending, seconds later, that all was quite normal. Pearl held my hand and then Elodie also came to my side, hooking her pale, skinny arm about my elbow. She shot her lover a look, loaded with both pain and threat.

Then Pearl said coolly, "Let's go in and find our seats."

I was about to turn and walk away from the theatre but then I changed my mind. *This is Pearl's night. She has stuck by me. I'm not going anywhere.*

"Good idea, chérie, let's find our seats," I agreed, adrenaline still pumping through my gut, heating my veins. Elodie gave me a pleading look as if to say, *I'm sorry, I'll explain.* I winked at her, yet my face remained impassive. *Yes, we'll discuss this later,* it said silently—*you bet we will.* But she was still only a child in my eyes. Whoever was at fault, it wasn't Elodie. Prokovich should have known better, messing with a vulnerable teenager. He was a man of the world; she was just a fragile bird, learning to spread her wings.

There I'd been, naively assuming Elodie was a virgin. More fool me.

She couldn't have picked a bigger asshole than Mikhail Prokovich.

She had a lot of explaining to do.

I was so distracted that I had no idea what *Stone Trooper* was about. All I could think of was Elodie and how the fuck she ended up getting involved with the last man on Earth with whom I would have associated her. In my peripheral vision, I observed him scrutinizing her throughout the screening. He was a man obsessed. His eyes greedy, all-consuming, commanding. It was as if he wanted to swallow her whole. He was sitting on his own, though—she had spurned him as her date for the night. Why Elodie? Okay, she was beautiful and charming, but he had his pick of any supermodel. How had they become involved in the first place? I watched Elodie, her nostrils fuming like a young racehorse. I could tell that the betrayal she felt at her stepmother's cheating on her father was eating her, and whatever Prokovich had done, or not done, was making her hate him. Hate or love? The two emotions could be so intertwined.

There was a standing ovation at the end of the film. Alessandra had, no doubt, done a good job. Maybe even Oscar-worthy. Sam Myers was there in the front row, twiddling his porky fat fingers as if counting out his profits already. The movie would do well. Pearl would make a fortune. Sophie, as usual, would make a fortune. I turned to see Elodie's reaction as Alessandra took a little bow.

But Elodie was gone.

Prokovich was still there, his eyes roaming the theatre. He too, clocked her disappearance.

I whispered to Pearl, "I need to find Elodie."

"Go," she agreed. "I'll get a ride home with Sophie and Alessandra. Get out of here before you end up in another fight. I love you, even if you are a hotheaded, proud Frenchman who causes scenes."

I kissed her hand and dashed out while the audience was still clapping and cheering. As I made my exit, I passed Prokovich who was still standing, his eyes scanning the theatre. I called Elodie on my cell. No answer. But seconds later, it buzzed with a message from her:

I'm fine. Had to get out of there. C U at yours.

I'd been expecting her to run—take a flight to Paris or

something. She was going to my *apartment?* I felt white heat on my face and when I looked up, I noticed a thousand cameras flashing in my face. News reporters were all over me, shoving microphones up against my lips. A woman, whom I recognized from TV said, "Mr. Chevalier, can you explain why you and Mr. Prokovich came to blows earlier this evening?"

Another reporter shouted at me, "Are either of you pressing charges? Suing for damages?"

"We're European," I answered, "so we're not into suing." Then I realized my wry joke may not have gone down too well and I wished I'd kept my trap shut.

Someone else yelled over the crowd, "Does your animosity with each other have anything to do with professional jealousy? You're both the same age. Which one of you two is richer?"

"No comment," I said briskly as I weaved my way between a sea of bodies.

I tried to hail a cab but it had started to drizzle. Barcelona and New York—two cities with a dearth of taxis the second rain threatens. I started jogging. It would be faster for me to simply run home through Central Park than mess about with either hailing a cab or calling my driver.

I needed to get to Elodie before Prokovich sent in his Rottweilers.

16

I slipped quietly into the living room and found Elodie staring at the TV, sitting between Sally and Jeanine, all of them eating popcorn on the sofa. They were glued to the news. Rex was also watching the news, his ears cocked when he saw my face on the screen, and heard my words, "We're not into suing."

A newsroom reporter happily sang, "In a surprising turn of events, two of the wealthiest young men in the world came to blows tonight on the red carpet at a New York screening of the blockbuster movie, *Stone Trooper*. French Internet mogul, Alexandre Chevalier, and real estate magnet, Mikhail Prokovich, who hails from Russia, threw a few punches and kicks, before the HookedUp billionaire's wife, Pearl Chevalier, intervened. Apparently, the two twenty-six year old men laughed it off afterwards, Mr. Prokovich telling news reporters that they were 'just practicing a few black-belt moves as a joke.' He says that the two of them are close friends and are even discussing a future business deal together."

"Business deal, my ass," I said to the TV. "Close friends…yeah right. Don't believe what you hear, ladies."

Jeanine turned her head, and with a bewildered look on her face said, "Oh, hi Mr. Chevalier; didn't hear you come in."

"You know to call me just Alexandre, Jeanine. Are the twins asleep?"

"They were angels all evening. Didn't cry once. And yeah, they're fast asleep."

Elodie shoved a handful of popcorn into her mouth as if to prevent herself from speaking. Surely she had a lot to tell me. A whole damn lot.

"How was the movie?" Sally asked me.

"I don't know, I wasn't paying attention because something more important was distracting me. Elodie, tell them what you thought of *Stone Trooper.*"

"It sucked," she said. "Alessandra Demarr is a crap actress."

"That bad, eh? Ladies, feel free to go home; I can take it from here." I could tell they were dying to ask me questions about what happened but my stony face had both of them rise from the sofa. Elodie continued stuffing popcorn into her mouth, every now and then offering Rex some.

"I need to get going," Jeanine said with an embarrassed smile.

"Me too," Sally chimed in. "I'll be back at seven for Rex's walk tomorrow." Rex got up too, his tail spinning like a windmill, the middle of his torso wiggling with excitement. Pretty girls, sofa, popcorn, his dad on TV—what an exciting evening he'd had.

"Night, girls, and thanks so much for looking after the twins."

"Sure." Jeanine smiled awkwardly at me.

"Don't worry, Sally, I haven't forgotten our deal." An all-paid vacation in Venice, Italy, for a week. *An offer she couldn't refuse.* Sometimes, it was really fun to be so wealthy—to 'magic' people every so often. Give them treats they could never afford themselves.

The two women left, and Elodie sat cross-legged on the couch, still eating popcorn.

"So?" I said.

She arched a brow. "So."

"Aren't you going to fill me in?"

"What is there to tell?" she said in a morose, fuck-you tone.

"If you don't tell me, I'll guess and my imagination is probably wilder than reality."

"I doubt that very much," she answered enigmatically.

"How did you meet?"

"Maman and I were having lunch in Paris and he was there. He came over to our table."

"And then what?"

"He became obsessed. Started pursuing me relentlessly. Wouldn't take no for an answer."

"But he's very handsome. And rich. Girls love men like him."

"Like I really give a shit about money."

"You're a headstrong girl. You could have told him to fuck off."

She gave Rex another handful of popcorn. "I did. But he wouldn't listen. It made him want me more."

"So you started sleeping with him?"

"I don't want to discuss my sex life with *you,* you're my uncle. It's weird." She kept her eyes on the TV. *The Vampire Diaries* or something.

"He didn't seem to have a problem with blaring it out in public. It was tacky and crude what he did, telling me he was fucking you like that. In public, for everyone to hear. Even if he said it in French."

"He *is* tacky and crude. He can drink anyone under the table; he fights like a boxer." And she muttered under her breath, "He's insatiable."

"So why did you ask him as your date to the premiere?"

"I don't know."

"Are you in love with him?"

"I hate him."

I turned the sound of the TV down with the remote. "That wasn't my question. Are you in *love* with him?"

"I got hooked in."

"How long have you been seeing him for?"

"On and off."

"So that's why you asked to borrow my bodyguard a while ago?"

"Yeah."

"And why you took off traveling across America in Pearl's car?"

"I wanted to get away from him."

"But you came back to him?"

She said quietly, "I couldn't stop myself."

"Why?" she didn't answer. "Why?" I repeated.

"Because."

"Because?"

"Because I couldn't keep away from him even though I knew it was all wrong…alright? Satisfied now?"

I read between the lines. "There's more to a relationship than just sex, Elodie."

"Oh that's rich, coming from you!"

"What are you talking about?"

"You and Pearl. You're obsessed with each other. You're relationship is so physical."

She'd stabbed me in the gut with her words. "That's so not true. It started off that way. Partly. But we're soul mates. It's a feeling that can't be explained—can't be rationalized. Pearl and I were made for each other and the physical part of it just enhanced that. It's about trust. Trust made the physical bond more intense. Without trust everything else is temporary."

Elodie seemed to listen to what I said, mulling my words of wisdom over in her mind. She then told me, "I came here so I'd be safe from Mikhail. I can't go back to my apartment in the Village."

"You did the right thing. Stay here. Stay as long as you like—you can even help us look after the twins."

"He'll be out there waiting for me. Obsessing about me. He won't rest until he has me. All of me. He told me so."

I knew this sort of stuff was an aphrodisiac for many women. My mother had succumbed to those sorts of promises with my father. Abuse dressed up as love and passion when, really, it was all about control. Hell, my mom's fictional boyfriends were probably full of that kind of talk. I feared that Elodie would be swayed by Prokovich's amour, even if it was more about possession than real love. "Well, you'll just need protection, plus a strong will to keep away from him."

"I *mean* it this time. I don't want him in my life. He's not a good person."

"How do you know he's not a good person?" *I know, but how does she know?*

"I've heard him make deals on the phone. I know who he is."

"He doesn't worry about you being party to all that?"

"No. He likes it. It makes him feel powerful. He wants me to fear him."

"And *do* you fear him?" I asked.

"D'you know why I decided I didn't want to see him anymore? Why I couldn't love him?"

"I can think of a million reasons not to love a man who makes his money selling arms," I said, taking in her little heart-shaped face and her innocent gaze, which was breaking me up.

"Governments do it," she said by way of an excuse. "He's no worse than a lot of politicians."

"I know, Elodie. We live in a pretty fucked up world. But you deserve better than a man like that. What was it then, that finally made you decide you didn't love him?"

"He told me he strangled a cat when he was a boy. I felt sick when he said that." She blew air from her lips and added, "I wish he'd get blown up by one of his own land mines. Or someone would fucking shoot him with one of his AK-47s."

I fixed my eyes on her wide brown eyes. "Don't do anything rash. You hear me? Just keep away from him."

"Hey guys, you all look very serious." It was Pearl, swishing back from the premiere in her heels and shimmery gown. Rex bounded over to her but luckily didn't jump up. "Glad you're here, Elodie," Pearl said. "Anyone for a snack? I'm starving."

"You relax, chérie, I'll check on the twins and make us some sandwiches or something."

"I already took a peep. They're out for the count; Louis has a little grin on his face and Madeleine's pouting in her sleep, dreaming about something serious."

I left Pearl and Elodie together and snuck into the babes' room and observed them in their cots. It was true what Pearl said about their little expressions. We'd been lucky; neither of them were screamers. Sometimes babies come into a world with everything just right. Others have a battle. I was one of the battle fighters. I'd had colic, apparently. Then whooping cough—I had a rough ride. But Louis and Madeleine had two parents madly in love with each other and seemed to be living a stress-free existence. It showed in their faces and in their jolly demeanor.

As I slipped out noiselessly and walked past the living room, I couldn't help but hear a snippet of Elodie and Pearl's hushed conversation.

"He became more and more dominant, you know. He made me play games with whips and stuff. Tied me up. Blinded me."

"Blindfolded you, you mean?" Pearl corrected.

I did that to Pearl, even though all I did was 'whip' her with a feather. But still. Shit, maybe I'm just as fucked up as Prokovich.

"Yeah," Elodie went on. "You know, at first it was…well, it was kind of fascinating and I wanted to please him. But it got more and more crazy. Then I left him and he promised he'd stop but when we started dating again, he wanted to do the kinky stuff and I got scared."

"You mustn't see him if he scares you, sweetie," Pearl advised her.

"He told me that we're meant to be together, that he can't live without me. That I'm his life, his breath, his moon and stars."

"Fancy words coming from such a tough man."

"He's crazy about me."

"*Crazy* sounds like a good word to describe him. You're in love?" Pearl asked.

I moved on to the kitchen. I didn't want to intrude anymore. I fixed us all some sandwiches and drinks but as I came back towards the living room with the tray, I heard more. I stopped in my tracks.

"You know, each time I cut myself, it makes me feel better. Like a relief."

"You need to see someone about this, Elodie. You could wind up bleeding to death."

"I stopped. I'd stopped for ages."

"But you started again?" Pearl asked softly.

"Just that one time."

"Honey, you need to stay here with us. Sort yourself out. See a therapist, you know; we need to find you a professional to talk to."

I stood there, wanting to come in but I was hesitant about interrupting their heartfelt conversation. If I budged, they'd know I was there. I remained motionless, hoping they'd move onto another topic and I could make my entrance. Then I missed a bit as they were talking in such quiet voices. Then Pearl asked:

"So you told your mom about the rape?"

"No, never."

"Why not?"

"Because I was so young—I thought if I didn't talk about it, it would go away."

Pearl's tone was gentle but ominous. "It never goes away, not even if you have amnesia."

That's when I came into the room. "Who's got amnesia?" I said lightheartedly. "Rex? Forgotten he's already had a load of popcorn and is now after our sandwiches?"

"Thanks, honey," Pearl said, helping me unload the tray. "I could eat…I was about to say 'a horse' but I guess with the French eating horses, that isn't such a great expression."

"Yeah, yeah, yeah," I sang. "Very funny. I'll have you know the other day, in some 'health food' takeout restaurant, somewhere near Washington Square, they were serving up kangaroo meat, so it's not just the French."

"That's gross." Elodie winced.

"We should all be like Leonardo da Vinci," I said. "All be full-on vegetarians, then we could feel blameless."

"Apparently lettuces scream when you pull them up," Elodie told us, but then she shifted her eyes mournfully to the Jim Dine painting on the wall that I'd given Pearl for her engagement gift: the multi-colored heart. Elodie's look said, *I wish I could find that kind of love.* "I'm going to bed. Let you two love birds be in peace."

"Don't you want a sandwich?" I asked.

"No, I'm good. And it's so late. So Parisian, to eat at this hour. Night. See you in the morning."

"Night, sweetie. We'll talk some more tomorrow." Pearl blew her a kiss and sank back into the sofa. She tucked her legs under her, and spread out her beautiful chiffon dress.

We delved into the sandwiches. Five minutes later, I couldn't contain my curiosity any longer. "I know it was a private girls' talk but I did overhear a bit of your conversation."

Pearl shook her head. "Eavesdropper."

"I know. I'm sorry. But I *worry* about my niece; I want to help her. If I'd known what her problems were, perhaps she wouldn't have fallen into the arms of the wrong man in the first place."

"She's young and impressionable. Mikhail Prokovich is handsome, rich, charming. He dates supermodels. And he made a beeline for her. She must have been very flattered; very swept off her feet. It's not surprising she fell for him."

I bit into a corner of my cheese sandwich and realized that cheese wasn't the best choice so late at night. Perhaps we'd be awake for hours. "I heard the word 'rape,' I admitted.

"Elodie told me that in *confidence,* Alexandre."

"I still overheard. What happened? And when?"

Pearl dabbed her lips with a napkin, rested her hands on her mouth as if considering whether she should divulge another person's secret. I looked at her expectantly. Then she sighed and finally said, "It was her best friend's older brother. She thought it was her first kiss but he went further and forced her to have sex with him. She'd had a crush on him for years and was crazy about him, but in an innocent, sweet way. But he took her against her will. Apparently, he was a real brute about it. She was only fourteen. He was much older—nineteen. Worse, he wanted nothing to do with her afterwards and her best friend abandoned her, so she felt totally betrayed all round."

I scrunched up my brow. "Six degrees of separation. But from rape of some kind. It amazes me how many people have been affected directly, or indirectly, by abuse. Join the fucking club. Poor thing. About the same time she started dressing like a Goth and wearing spiky heels."

"Exactly. Her defense mechanism."

"I also heard the word 'cut,' " I said.

Pearl grimaced. "Unfortunately, she's a cutter."

"You sound like you're familiar with that term."

"My brother, John…you know, he also cut himself. Sadly, it's quite common."

I screwed up my face, imagining a slicing razor blade. "Ouch."

"Elodie's thing is words. I noticed a scar on her stomach a few weeks ago and tonight I asked her about it. It seemed the right moment as she was confiding in me."

"What do you mean, *her thing is words?*"

"She carves words into her flesh. She cut the word JAMAIS into her hip."

"The word 'never'. Never what?"

"She said it made her feel better. And in control."

I raked my hands through my hair. "Jesus. Poor girl. She needs to see a shrink or a therapist."

"She says she *is* already seeing someone."

I let out a lungful of air which I didn't realize I'd been holding in. "Is this what we're in for, for the next twenty years? Fucked-up kids who carve themselves and end up playing bondage games with ruthless arms dealers? Maybe becoming parents was a bad idea, Pearl."

"Oh, so I guess you heard that part of our talk too?" Pearl

raised her brows. "You caught that part of our *private* conversation? About the kinky stuff?"

"I told you when we met, I think girls Elodie's age are too young to get wrapped up in sexual games like that. Yes, I heard your conversation. I have ears like Rex—sorry but I can't help it. *La Legion* made me that way. I hear everything. See everything, whether I like it or not."

"You're right about her being impressionable—she said she was playing along to please him but he got out of control. And that she became scared of him."

"He better stay the fuck away from her."

"And what if she doesn't want him to? She's an adult; we can't control her life. She has to choose for herself, Alexandre."

"I'll talk to her again tomorrow," I said.

17

But I didn't get a chance to talk to Elodie the following day because she disappeared before I'd even gotten out of bed. She left her phone behind so I couldn't call her. I stood in the spare room—Elodie's clothing and make-up scattered all over the floor. I had no idea where she had gone. Out for breakfast? Would she be back any moment? I was contemplating contacting Sophie but my sister got there first. I answered my cell.

"What the fuck," Sophie began, her voice a pack of ice.

I knew what she was referring to. I couldn't resist an, *I told you so*. "Well, if you hadn't been so gung-ho about having meetings with that shifty bastard in the first place—"

"Yeah, yeah, it's all my fault. And now Elodie hates me because of Alessandra."

"You should have talked to her a long time ago about all that. What did you expect? Elodie's an adult now; she had a right to know. You betrayed her by not trusting her and keeping her in the dark. So yes, you've got a lot of work ahead of you to repair the damage."

Sophie groaned into the receiver. "Thanks for the vote of confidence, dear brother."

"Sophie, you need to come out of the closet. It's not fair on anybody, least of all Elodie. Not to mention your poor longsuffering husband."

" 'Poor, longsuffering husband' has been having affairs for years. Neither of us asks the other any questions; we lead separate lives."

"Fine, but Elodie shouldn't be piggy in the middle."

"Where is she? She won't answer her phone and I want to talk to her. She told me last night she'd be staying with you. I was thinking of coming over but thought I should call first."

"She's not here. She's upset. Upset with you, upset with having got involved with Prokovich, upset with shit that went down in her past."

"What shit?"

"That's for her to tell. It's not my place."

"She's been confiding in you and not me?" Sophie's voice cracked—it sounded as if the floodgates were about to open.

"Not exactly. Look, I'm not going to discuss Elodie's private affairs with you. Ask her yourself," I said.

Sophie gave out a loud sigh. "She told me she didn't want anything to *do* with me."

"She'll come around—just give it time. Look, I've got to go. I can hear the babies waking up."

"Wow, you're taking fatherhood so seriously."

"You bet. I want to be the father I never had myself."

"Talk to Elodie for me, will you. Please get her to call me."

"I'll try my best."

"Anyway," I said later, in an angry rush, while Pearl and I were up on the roof terrace having lunch in the conservatory—my eyes fixed on Pearl as if it were all her fault. "What the fuck happened with your documentary on exposing arms dealers? You even had dinner with the bastard, why haven't you told the world what an asshole he is already?"

"I wish it were that easy," Pearl replied calmly, deflecting my rage with a flick of her wrist.

"Well what's the fucking problem? His name is all over the news now. He and I are more notorious than ever. Grab him while you can!"

"He's a slippery fish, Mikhail Prokovich—you know that. There's no proof, as such. You can't go around accusing someone of something *that major* until you have the guilty package all wrapped up with a nice big bow. The more famous they are, the more delicate the situation."

"Well hurry up about it, baby; I'm losing patience."

"Oh, we're working on it, believe me. The research is complicated. *He* is complicated. Clever. It's hard to link him directly to any shady dealings. If we attack at this point, we could lose everything—all our hard work up till now. We need to be patient. Plus, he's connected to governments and big businesses. We're in cahoots with 60 Minutes and the BBC's Panorama, because we need clout. HookedUp Enterprises can't do this alone. We could get our asses sued if we aren't careful. And despite your little quip about Europeans not suing, I'm sure we'd have Prokovich's lawyers jumping down our throats, crawling all over us, the second they could."

My fists were clenched in tight balls while Pearl coolly sliced a piece of homemade quiche for us both and served us each a small portion of green salad. She carefully poured us each a glass of Pinot Grigio, the crisp white wine—as chilled as she was.

I had married a headstrong woman who complimented my character in every way. She wasn't riled by things when it came to her career. It seemed she had everything managed, including me. Her presence calmed me.

I had certainly chosen the perfect woman to be my wife.

"Anyway," I concluded, "that fuck has some heavy karma coming his way. By hook or by crook, he'll pay for being such an asshole."

Pearl started laughing.

"What's so funny? Are you laughing at my accent, Mrs. Chevalier? The fact that I don't pronounce the H?"

"Not your accent but I love it when you use expressions like 'by hook or by crook.' Do we even know where that comes from? Crook, as in crooked? Hook, as in a shepherd's hook or something?"

"It's probably derived from some obscure village in England called Crook or Hook. Anyway, right now, my focus is on Elodie. I'm worried about her. Obviously she left her cell phone behind on purpose so I can't find her."

Pearl frowned. "That means you can't track her down with the GPS, right? The way you did with me."

"Thanks for that, you make me sound like a real stalker."

She winked at me. "Well you are, Alexandre Chevalier. You

stalked me all the way to the alter."

I 'crooked' my finger at her and patted my lap. "Come here, you sexy wife, sit on my knee. Where are the twins?"

"Having their nap. I've got the baby monitor on. Modern spyware. See?" She showed me her Smartphone. "Sleeping like angels."

"Where's Rex?"

"In the park with Sally."

"Patricia and the staff?"

"It's her day off. The rest of the staff left for the afternoon."

"So we're alone?"

Pearl looked at her Reverso watch—a gift from me. "Maybe for an hour or so more."

"Fuck lunch—it's you I want to eat," I said, lust glittering in my eyes, not breaking my gaze from hers. "You looked so beautiful last night, chérie, in your elegant gown. And I can still smell whatever you put on. Or maybe it's just your natural scent. Whatever your secret is, it has me intoxicated. Get your ass over here."

Pearl smiled and swept her hand over her golden locks, pushing her hair away from her face. She got up and sat on my knee. I was instantly hard. Fuck, even after giving birth and all the intricacies that came with child rearing and a household to run, she had me on red alert. She nuzzled her butt into my groin subtly and I could hear a throaty growl which surprised me as my own. I burrowed my nose into her elegant neck and smelled the Pearl Elixir that had me permanently mesmerized.

I kissed the nape of her soft neck. "Do you remember when we had our first bath together? I read you poetry and you slipped in the oily lavender water and the book flipped out of my hands and sank?"

"I most certainly do," she said. "I thought I'd spoiled the moment but you laughed—your first edition Baudelaire ruined."

I nipped her lobe and she shuddered. I saw goose bumps rise on her flesh. "And then we discussed the power," I whispered in her ear, "of smell and how two people can be attracted to each other for no other reason than pheromones?" I inhaled her sweet essence and a rush of desire surged through my torso, hammering in my groin.

"And I wondered if it was the lavender oil alone which had me hooked on you."

"I'd never felt so at ease with a woman before. I'd never had that intimacy before," I murmured.

Pearl sounded surprised. "Really?"

"Really," I said, my hand cupping her succulent ass. "You know when you're listening to an old vinyl record and it jams? That was my life before. In a rut. And when you came along, the needle jumped forward into the right groove and forced me to move ahead. Finally I could hear the melody—it flowed beautifully, and I knew the way it was meant to sound."

She turned her head and smiled. "I'm a melody? I'm music to your ears?"

I gripped her thigh. "The best melody ever. You have the perfect beat, Pearl, the perfect rhythm. You soothe me. You enliven me. You make me dance. You help me sleep. Yes, you're my music, chérie." I sneaked my fingers between her legs and felt her moistness through the thin fabric of her panties. The fact that I caused such an instant physical reaction in her body made my cock ache with need. We hadn't fucked for nearly a week—that's what having children did—and it felt like a lifetime. I lifted her sweater and snaked my other hand around her smooth waist. "How do you keep so fit? So trim?"

"Trade secret," she answered, nestling her butt into my solid, pounding erection. I spun her around and moved her soft thighs either side of my legs so she was straddling me. I cupped her chin with my hand and pulled her beautiful face towards mine. I didn't kiss her straight away. I wanted to look into her eyes and really *see* her. Those guileless, big blue eyes that could have belonged to a little girl. I breathed her in.

"You're sniffing me again, aren't you?" she teased, her arms closing tightly around my shoulders. "You're worse than Rex."

"Caught me," I said with a laugh.

"What do I smell of?"

"Of Pearl."

"What *is* Pearl?"

"It's unique. The pure essence of love. A secret potion. There's no smell like it in the world—it's deep and nuanced and…fresh. With a hint of sunshine. It makes my head spin every time. If I could bottle it, it would earn me more money than all of my enterprises combined. But then again, I wouldn't want to share your elixir with anybody."

I rested my lips on her mouth, my breath a tease, and with the tip of my tongue explored her Cupid's bow. Such a pretty mouth, that belonged to a woman of another era, like one of Rossetti's Pre-Raphaelites. My hand, still on her jaw, slowly traced down her neck to her shoulder. And then to the curve of her breast. She gasped. I could feel her hardened nipple through the delicate cashmere of her sweater. I trailed more light kisses around her mouth, stroking my tongue across her bottom lip and she moaned, edging her crotch up against me, and her hands moved to unbutton my jeans—my rock-hard cock, pounding with desire, sprang up against my abdomen. Fuck I felt horny.

She couldn't take my tormenting kisses any longer—her lips parted and her tongue flicked out to touch mine as she held my thick erection in her grip. Chills ran through my body at her carnal touch.

I licked into her mouth and, gripping her hair, tilted her head back. "You're mine, baby," I growled—my sound vibrating in her mouth as she played with the tip of my crown, smoothing the pre-cum around my swollen dick—as massive as a cobra. I felt like I was about to explode the kiss was so erotic, and I couldn't wait to enter her. But this foreplay was too beautiful to rush. We were fucking each other with our mouths, our tongues in a wild, wet tango, nipping, biting, stroking, rimming. I kept hold of her hair, not letting her go; my possessive nature a fire, stoked by her love for me.

"Your kisses are my food," Pearl whimpered into my mouth as I consumed her whole. And it was true; we were nourishment for each other. It was as if I were eating her with my lashing tongue—sucking her, tasting her essence. Feasting on the Pearl Elixir.

I needed her so much.

"Sit on my cock, baby," I murmured. "Slide yourself onto me." My hands moved down to her ass which I grasped voraciously—my emotions and desire in a frenzy. I heard a cry, timorous and panicked—for a second, I thought it was Pearl.

She shifted herself away from me and leaned down to grab her cell. "It's Louis," she told me, staring at the screen of her Smartphone. He never yelled that way—I could see why she jumped to attention. "I'd better go downstairs and see if he's okay."

"I'll come with you." I let out a sigh. Fatherhood. A full-time job.

Pearl took Louis to the pediatrician, and I stayed behind with Madeleine, just in case what he had was contagious—two sick babies wouldn't be the greatest, although it was the first time they had ever been separated and I felt badly for them. I coddled her in my arms, rocking her gently. I put on a Vivaldi cello concerto and swayed with her about the apartment, which made her coo and smile—her toothless grin a joy to behold, which sent a rush of butterflies, circling my stomach. I nestled my face against her pearly, soft skin—she too exuded a secret elixir: the baby elixir that was almost as intoxicating as Pearl's.

I kept my eye on my cell, hoping that Elodie would call any second. My instinct told me that she'd be alright. But there was nothing I could do for now. She'd told me she wouldn't be going to her apartment in the Village, but I called her roommate anyway. Nothing.

Women always complain about how tough it is to be female but shit, in that moment, I was in turmoil. Worried about Elodie, my twins, my belle Pearl. Feeling an overwhelming urge to protect them all, but not knowing how.

A few hours later, Pearl and Louis were back home from the doctor—what he was ailing from was just a very bad cold. I felt a huge sense of gratitude. I realized that this was to be a constant feature in our lives as parents: nerves on the edge with worry. And I needed to develop a more *laissez-faire* attitude about my kids or I'd drive myself, and everyone around me, nuts.

But just as Louis had finally settled and was completely calm, and I was finally enjoying a beer, my cell went. It was Elodie. At last. It was well after midnight.

Elodie asked me to meet her. She told me that she was in a brownstone on the Upper East Side and gave me the address; but then we got cut off. I knew the building well because I'd thought about buying it once, when it was up for sale. Obviously someone outbid me. Outbid *me!* Whoever it was, had stupid money. Prokovich himself? Surely not. Elodie said she wanted to stay clear of him and he'd hardly be inviting me over to his house. I imagined it must belong to the parents of one of her friend's, and that they were away for the weekend.

I exited the delivery door of my apartment building, just in case any paparazzi were waiting to take a snap at me out front. Fuck, I hated being newsworthy. As I waited for my driver a block away, I wondered what I was going to do about my niece. It dawned on me that, although I had always envisioned her as so innocent, she was a wild card. But still a damaged bird. Those bloody damaged birds—Pearl included—that had me running around after them, trying to fix their wings, when they were probably perfectly capable of looking after themselves.

I thought of Pearl and our unfinished business at lunch. I had her on top of me in my mind's eye, or my cock in her luscious mouth—her big blue, childlike eyes looking up at me. Like a child with a tasty lollipop. Damn. Images of her sucking me off kept flitting through my one-track mind—it was on replay. I knew now what it must be like to be fat and on a diet, constantly craving treats you can't have. I wanted Pearl at all times, but lately, something always intervened. Namely: kids.

And now, Elodie.

My cell buzzed. It was Elodie again. "Where are you?" I said urgently. "I mean I know where you are—I'm on my way—but whose place is it?"

"In someone's house."

"Obviously, but whose?"

"I'm in trouble. Bad. Really bad."

"Stay where you are, I'm on my way, I won't be long," I promised.

"There's blood everywhere," she whispered.

"Blood? Jesus, what happened? Are you hurt?"

"I'm fine. It's him. He's hurt."

"Okay, stay calm. Who's 'him'?" I knew who *him* was but I wanted to hear it from her lips.

Silence.

"Elodie, who is him?"

"He's lying in a pool of blood."

"Is anyone trying to hurt you? Can he hurt you? Is anyone else there?" I whispered hoarsely into the line.

"I think he's dead." She sounded unfazed. Very matter-of-fact.

"How much blood?"

"He's in the bathtub."

"Did you bind the wound? Get a shirt, or something, and tie it tight about the wound. He might just be injured; did you check his pulse? Elodie, are you listening to me?"

"It's too late for that now."

"Jesus," I said, my heart pounding with blood-soaked images in my head. What had she done? Attacked him with her killer heels? Although with Elodie being so tiny, I couldn't imagine her getting very far. "Who knows you're there?"

"Nobody. I've locked the front door. There's no doorman here or anyone. Nobody. I didn't do anything wrong but please don't tell Mom."

"Of that you have my word. Elodie, stay where you are. Do not open the door to anyone, is that clear? I'll be there ASAP. Do not let anyone in that house."

"I won't."

If I'd been an upright citizen I would have gotten Elodie to call 911, or call them myself. But who knew what mess she'd gotten into? I couldn't risk it. Better Prokovich dead from bleeding than Elodie in some American women's penitentiary with big butch dykes fighting over whose bunk she'd be sleeping in at night.

I called Suresh, my driver, and cancelled him, and hailed a cab instead. There was only one person I could trust with this. He was not dissimilar to the actor, Joe Pesci. Just as nuts as him—or at least the roles he plays. Small. Aggressive. Touchy. Chip on his shoulder type of guy. My man was a 'cleaner,' trained in forensics. He could make traces of blood, fingerprints, clothes fibers, et cetera…vanish. Make the body, *itself,* vanish, if need be, and if he wasn't available, he had someone who was. I called. He answered on the second ring. He was obviously used to emergencies. Strike that. His work, his trade *was* emergencies and emergencies only. Death. Blood. Emergencies of every kind. Sophie had used him once. I needed him on standby, just in case Elodie had incriminated herself. I told him to wait for my call when I knew more.

The New York traffic was full of sirens, as usual, pulsing and frenetic. People crossing the road, buying flowers from corner shops, couples arguing on the sidewalk, people walking their dogs. Saturday night, New York—a city that never sleeps.

I jumped into a cab and tried to make the driver understand where I was going. He'd been in New York for only two days and hardly spoke English. He was from Pakistan. Normally, I would have given him an interview on the spot, asked him a million questions about his country's state of affairs from his bird's eye view, his religion, and what was really going on out there—things we didn't hear about on the news. But I didn't want him remembering me, remembering my face and my destination. Just in case. Who knew what awaited me, and what shit I was going to have to clean up, courtesy of Elodie. What I did know was that trouble was on the horizon—I just hadn't added blood and guts into the equation.

I got the driver to drop me off a block away and I dashed into an all-night shop to buy a hoodie. There were none for sale so I grabbed a plastic rain poncho and a baseball cap. I put them on, once I was out of the store. With me being on the news for the last twenty-four hours, I couldn't be too careful. I imagined Mr. Square-Jaw probably had a state-of-the-art surveillance system surrounding his property.

As I climbed the steps to the brownstone, I kept my head down. What a fuck-up. I suppose I wasn't really thinking straight: I just wanted to get Elodie out of there. She came to the door. Heels off. No make-up and wearing a floaty silk dress. She looked like an angel. Except, she had bright green washing-up gloves on. Had she been watching too much CSI? She opened the door gingerly and I stepped into a very monochrome, but chic, bachelor pad hallway. The lights were off, save a faint glow coming from upstairs.

"Who's seen you here?" I whispered with urgency.

"Nobody." She looked me, and my mad attire, up and down. "His cameras are switched off, don't worry."

"How do you know?"

"Because he always disables them when he's, you know—"

"No, I don't know, Elodie. What the fuck's going on?"

She looked down, ashamed.

"Where is he?"

"Follow me. He's up here."

She led me upstairs to a bedroom. It was huge. Dark red walls, sleek, antique Asian furniture. The blinds were all drawn, but a small light in one corner cast a beam across the room. My eyes scanned the bedroom. Prokovich was not lying in a bath, at all, nor was there any blood. He was on his bed, spread out. Naked, except for two bound silk scarves noosed about his neck, hooked up to bedposts either side. There were burgundy-colored blotches about his neck; he'd been strangulated by the scarves. He had globs of dried cum around his hand and genitals. He'd been masturbating, obviously. I turned my eyes away from his private parts, but bent down to take his pulse, just to double-check. He wasn't breathing. Dead. I looked up and stared at my niece.

"I told you there was blood because I thought it was the only thing that would make you come here," she told me sheepishly. "It sounded more urgent."

"Of course I would have come, silly—you didn't have to make that up."

"I'm sorry, I—"

"And the bath?" I asked, wondering what insane part of her imagination conjured up that particular image of him, lying bleeding in a bath.

"I thought you'd be relieved. No mess."

I had to remind myself that Elodie was still a teenager. I tried to stay levelheaded, not lose my cool. I drew in a lungful of air. "Let's begin at the beginning, shall we?" I sounded like one of those nursery-rhyme readers on the radio that I listened to when I was a child. *Let's begin at the beginning.*

Elodie bit her lip and said nothing.

"I need to make a decision, goddamn it, Elodie. There's a dead man here and I have to know what the fuck's going on! Did you do this?"

"He did it to himself."

"He rigged all this up, *himself?*"

She flushed and looked down at the floor. "I helped him. He wanted it tighter."

"So you planned all this?"

She raised her eyes and looked me in the eye, defiantly. "It was the only way I knew to get him out of my life for good."

"So you played along, pretending you were up for it?" She nodded. I knew what had happened. Apparently, cutting the oxygen supply off to the brain during orgasm causes heightened pleasure, a sort of hallucinatory ecstasy. I had read somewhere that between five hundred and a thousand deaths occur each year in the US, alone, from autoerotic asphyxiation gone wrong. *So this was the shit Prokovich was into and had Elodie running from him.*

Her mouth twisted in disgust. "I hated his sick games. But then, I was also hooked in. Is that wrong? All I wanted was to get away from him. But he kept luring me back. I thought if he was dead, he'd leave me alone, once and for all. Stop stalking me. Leave me in peace."

"So you *did* do this? Was this your idea?"

Tears were falling silently down her milk-white cheeks. She nodded.

Clever girl, I wanted to say, *A+ for imagination.* "And he was up for it?" I asked.

"He thought it was the best idea he'd ever heard."

"Where did you learn to tie that sailor's knot?"

"Remember when we went sailing once with Laura?"

"But that was years ago."

Elodie closed her lids and shook her head. "I never forgot that knot she taught me."

"And then what happened, after you helped him tie himself up?"

"I put some music on. Turned down the lights, lit a scented candle, got him in the mood. Got him going, you know, till he was really into it. Played along; did a striptease. Then I left just as....you know. I went downstairs and poured myself a glass of wine. I did some washing-up to distract myself. When I came back...I didn't expect that it would have actually worked. I thought he'd stop, that he'd…"

I inspected the tight sailor's knot and the whole crazy set-up, but making sure I didn't touch anything. It was obvious that the guy had had an accomplice, or someone who'd helped get him into that position. The last thing I wanted was Elodie implicated in this dirty scandal and one of his Russian aides swooping down on her in revenge. Or, worse, some psycho ex girlfriend, or current girlfriend—the guy fucked around—plotting retribution.

"Did any neighbors hear anything? Did he make a noise?"

"They're all away for the weekend in The Hamptons."

"How do you know?"

"Because he told me. He said he loved staying in New York when everyone else was out of town because it was quieter."

I dialed Joe Pesci's doppelganger. He'd need to make it look as if the Russian had done all this alone; an accidental, autoerotic 'suicide.' He'd need to wipe the whole place down for prints, hairs, anything incriminating. I spoke quietly into my cell, giving him instructions and the address, telling him I'd leave the front door off the latch, not that that would have been a problem; the guy could pick any lock. I pressed end.

"Pin your hair back, Elodie. Get a hat or a scarf out of his closet and hide your hair. Here, use this," I said, fishing a silk handkerchief out of my jacket. "Don't put anymore washing-up glove fingerprints anywhere. You'll need a hat to hide your face. We're going to walk out of here with our heads down and hope to hell that nobody saw you come in. What time did you arrive?"

"A few hours ago."

"So when did he....pass out, exactly?"

"I killed him, didn't I?" she said, her lips twitching with remorse.

"No, Elodie, you did not." I held her by the shoulders. "Get this into your head: You. Are. Not. Responsible. For this son of a bitch's downfall. He had it fucking coming to him. Is that clear?"

"But I helped, it was my—"

"No buts. All you did was speed up the inevitable. Help him do to himself what Karma had planned for him all along. This bastard was responsible for millions of innocent citizens' deaths all over the world. You did the world a favor by helping him reach Hell a little faster."

"Please don't tell anyone. Don't tell Maman."

"Come on, let's get out of here." I peeled the rubber gloves off her delicate hands, rolled them into a ball and put them inside my jacket pocket. I held her hands. "Elodie, you and I are peas in a pod. We both have a darkness that lives inside us. And that's okay. I've been responsible for a few deaths, myself. I'm *here* for you. Always and forever. I understand you. What you did *had* to be done. This is *our* secret, no one else's. I swear, I won't tell a soul. Not even Pearl—who'll be delighted, by the way, when she reads in the papers that this bastard has snuffed it." I drew my niece to me, my arms tight about her tiny frame, and let her sob against my chest.

18

Elodie left the country two days later. Our choice of destination was South America. She'd been clamoring to go backpacking for ages and this was her chance. Art school could wait. We needed for her to lie low for a good six months.

The news was full of Prokovich. Just as I suspected, one of his girlfriends discovered his body the following day. Luckily, nobody mentioned Elodie. Not seriously, anyway. One reporter did call, asking why they were chatting together at the *Stone Trooper* premiere and I said she'd met him once with her mother. I was worried I'd be a suspect in people's eyes after our skirmish on the red carpet, but my man had done such a thorough job in Prokovich's brownstone, that forensics had unequivocal 'suicide' as the cause of death. Sophie had a contact at the NYPD who filled her in. We were free and clear. Elodie was safe. Still, I didn't want her in New York, just in case she let something slip. I encouraged her go backpacking like a hippy. She'd be far, far away from a world of red carpets, bondage and billionaires. She could go surfing along the coast of Peru and Ecuador, eat *ceviche* and study *The Lonely Planet.* Maybe find herself a nice, simple surfer boyfriend who cared about waves and a nice cold beer at the end of the day, not some fucked up control freak, world-playing megalomaniac who'd once strangled animals to death and had no respect for human life. Elodie needed a salt-of-the-earth type. Armed with a Smartphone, she'd be fine. And I realized now that she didn't need looking after. Not one bit.

She was an enigma. Dark like me. Luc Besson's *La Femme Nikita.* They recruited women like Elodie—she had what it took to be a mercenary. She had a ruthless streak. Intelligent. Savvy. She was a schemer, a planner, a loner by nature. She'd be alright, I decided.

Life went on uneventfully, except that Pearl was working very hard with HookedUp Enterprises and Rex got married to a stunning black Labrador who gave birth to six glorious, silky black pups. We took a house for the month of February in The Bahamas, and Pearl managed to do business from her laptop on the beach. The Smartphone was used minimally—why? Because she was pregnant again! Five months and counting. I hadn't even imagined we'd be blessed again with another pregnancy.

We were lying on the beach, the waves lapping gently—a pale turquoise water shimmering and glittering us with its welcome. The sand was almost white and squeaked beneath our feet. Pearl lay under an umbrella, and Louis and Madeleine were happily playing. A new nanny (Sally had her hands full with all the dogs, who were in New York—too hot here for them) had come with us so we didn't have to worry about having eyes in the back of our heads.

"What are you laughing at?" I asked Pearl. She was stretched out on her towel, reading *Vanity Fair.* HookedUp Enterprises had just bought the magazine.

"This interview they did with you in Paris. You're such a liar!"

I narrowed my eyes. "Which bit are you reading?"

"You told them we were living in a tree-house in Thailand."

"I like my anonymity, you know that. Let them send their paparazzi out to Thailand and leave us alone peacefully here. What else does it say?" I asked, looking up at a cloudless blue sky.

"I'll read it out loud and you can hear for yourself what a bull-shitter you are."

"Go on then, I'm all ears."

"**INTERVIEW WITH ALEXANDRE CHEVALIER FOR VANITY FAIR.** By Stacey Black," Pearl began.

'It's 4pm and I'm waiting nervously in the lobby of the George V in Paris to meet one of the top five richest men in the world. That, in itself, is impressive enough, especially considering this man is a renowned philanthropist and gives a percentage of his income to

> *charity. But the fact that he is only twenty-six years old and looks like a movie star makes most people quiver at the knees, including myself. His name? None other than Alexandre Chevalier, CEO of the billion-dollar Internet phenomenon, HookedUp, bigger than Twitter and Facebook and with an offer on the table from Google, poised for a historical buyout that is bigger than most nations' national yearly budgets.'*

"Sounds like this Stacey Black has a major crush on you, darling," Pearl teased.

I grinned. I couldn't deny I liked keeping Pearl on her toes. "Read on, this is interesting."

> *'Finally, Monsieur Chevalier saunters into the lobby. He is wearing dark glasses – very Hollywood. My stomach flips. I shouldn't be so in awe. But I am. This man is power personified. He is dressed in a sharp, obviously hand-tailored, charcoal-gray suit, contrary to how he is usually described; favoring T-shirt and jeans, even for business meetings. I stand up and he smiles at me. Sadly, the smile is kept in check. This is a married man, after all. A man famously in love with his wife. He shakes my hand in a professional manner and takes off his shades. Two searing green eyes greet me. Alexandre Chevalier is devastatingly handsome. But enough of that…I'm here to do an interview.'*

"Yes, she definitely had the hots for you, Alexandre."

"Read on, chérie."

> 'A.C. Sorry I'm late. I got held up.
>
> V.F. It's so great to meet you and thank you for doing this exclusive interview.

A.C. You're welcome. Shall we go through to the restaurant or bar? We can have some tea or something. I lived in London for a while so I picked up a few British habits. Nothing like an afternoon cup of tea to get the brain back on track.

Brain back on track? I doubt it. As well as being an astute businessman, Alexandre Chevalier is known for his brilliance. Self-educated, he started HookedUp with his sister, Sophie Dumas, with no more than 15,000 Euros—a loan from their stepfather. It wasn't long before this French sibling team took the social media world by storm.

We sit down and are presented with a menu. I ask him to choose. My French is not up to much. Besides, hearing him speak his native language is a treat indeed. A waiter comes up to our table and hovers there reverently. Everybody knows who Alexandre Chevalier is, it seems. He orders us Lapsang Souchong tea and some petits fours. I start with my questions.

V.F. Is it true, Mr. Chevalier, that you're retiring?

A.C. (He laughs.) Probably for a nanosecond, and then I'll stick my fingers into some other pie. I am selling HookedUp. Rather, my sister and I are selling. By the way, call me Alexandre—I hate formalities.

V.F. Is it true that you have been offered ten billion dollars for your company?

A.C. I never discuss money unless it's with my accountant or lawyer. *(He narrows his eyes at me.)*

V.F. Okay, well, there is something else that people are dying to know. Rex, your dog, has become a household name since you and your family were all photographed in Central Park together by the paparazzi. Is it true that your dog has become a father?

A.C. Yes, his wife/girlfriend, whatever, has just given birth. I'm glad to say that she's had six very healthy puppies. *(A trace of a smile makes it evident that he is amused by my question.)*

V.F. And is it also true that Rex gave his lady-dog a diamond collar that is worth hundreds of thousands of dollars?

A.C. *(He laughs.)* Never believe what you read.

Pearl stopped reading and burst out laughing. "Sally bought that for Bonnie. It was a cheapie thing from one of those accessory stores. So funny. Sorry, I'll continue."

'V.F Sorry, I couldn't resist. May I ask you why you have agreed to do this interview with us? This is a first, isn't it?

A.C I think you know the answer to that question.

V.F. *(I look blank.)* Err…actually…no.

A.C. My wife has bought your magazine.

V.F. She reads *Vanity Fair*?

A.C. I mean, literally. She has bought you. Out. She owns you now. Well, not you personally…*(he laughs).* The deal was sealed this morning. My wife, CEO of **HookedUp Enterprises**, is now your boss. She owns *Vanity Fair.*

V.F. So **HookedUp Enterprises** is not part of the Google buy-out?

A.C. No, its not, it's a separate entity. But you'd have to ask my wife the details. She's the businessperson now.

I'm just her dogs-body. You know...around to make her a coffee if need be, hand out a bit of advice if she asks me. I'm going to be a kept man from now on. *(The curve of his lips makes me know he is being ironic.)*

V.F. Somehow I doubt that very much! So what will you do with all your spare time?

A.C. We've had a beautiful tree house built for us in a jungle in Thailand. It's hidden away in complete privacy on a private island. The jungle's surrounded by the ocean. I like to cook, you know, simple stuff like fresh fish I've caught that day, and Pearl reads novels. Meanwhile the twins putter about collecting seashells.

V.F. That sounds extremely romantic.

A.C. Romance is what gets me out of bed every day. Romance is what makes the world go round. Without romance one might as well not breathe.

V.F. So you and your wife are very in love?

A.C. I speak for myself when I say yes, absolutely. Now what's going on in that pretty head of Pearl's is anybody's guess.'

Pearl stopped reading and tittered to herself. She put down the magazine. "I thought I was an open book."

"Not at all," I said. "Sometimes you play it cool and I have no idea what you're thinking."

"I wear my heart on my sleeve—it's *you* who has everyone guessing. You're the trickster. You made me believe that it was over between us that time at Anthony's when I was blubbering in his back yard and you gave me all those 'goodbye' gifts. Bastard. Is there still a Coke in the cooler?"

"Coming right up," I said, snapping the ring, pouring the

brown liquid into a glass and handing it to her. "Oh wait, let me give you some ice cubes. And a squeeze of lemon." I dressed up her drink and took a sip. "Delicious. Finish the article."

She squinted her eyes at me. "Why have you got a guilty look on your face?"

I took in a deep breath. Sometimes there are things that niggle your subconscious, even when your conscious mind has wiped it clean. This was one of those things. "Because there's something I never told you," I said tentatively. "Something I hid from you." The blood drained from Pearl's face. "Don't panic," I added, "it's nothing terrible—I'd even forgotten all about it, but when you mentioned the 'goodbye' gifts and so on; it came back to me."

She sat up. "Okay, come clean."

"I still have your old handbag. The one I told you was stolen. The old iPhone I smashed in a temper when I heard Laura's sneaky message telling you that Sophie was going to bump you off."

She raised an insolent brow. Uh oh, the whole Laura topic was about to be dragged out of the muddy mire. But Pearl answered coolly, "I know. When I was looking for an extra suitcase last year, I found the old purse stashed inside, at the back of one of your closets." She winked at me.

"How come you never let on?"

"Because I enjoyed having the last laugh. I loved the idea that you thought you had me out-foxed but, in fact, it was the other way round." Her lips tilted into a self-satisfied smirk, then she closed her eyes and lay back down. "Besides I got a forty grand Birkin bag out of it, so how could I complain?"

"How do you know it cost that much?" I asked. "You weren't meant to know the price!"

"The second Laura and her antennae saw the unusual color of the bag, she knew it was an one-off, custom-made piece of art. It was Laura, herself, who enlightened me; that dreaded time when I went to her house in London to confront her."

Please don't remind me of Laura. I squeezed Pearl's thigh. "So you weren't pissed at me, then, for holding out on you? For not being honest?"

"It was…what, a year later? Laura was dead. You were mine and everything had worked out just as it should have, so no. I was mildly miffed, but not angry. In fact, you probably did the right thing under the circumstances."

"You minx," I said, kissing her hand, "hiding all your inside knowledge."

"It takes two to tango, Chevalier." She opened her eyes—as blue as the ocean before us—and grinned.

"And we tango so beautifully together."

"Yes, we do. Speaking of finding stuff, I forgot to tell you. I found my great grandmother's diary in a box of my mother's that I had in storage."

I remembered Pearl telling me about her. She was a lady's maid, had an affair with the lord of the manor, and they ended up fleeing to America. "The racy one?" I asked. "The English one who eloped with the duke?"

She took a sip of her Coke. "That was pretty scandalous stuff in 1923."

"So what did the diary say?"

"I haven't read it yet. I'm savoring it for when I'm holed up in the hospital, giving birth."

"I doubt you'll be able to concentrate on reading, chérie. Remember the labor pains last time? The *last* thing you'll want to do is read."

"Funny how women have amnesia after giving birth. How we forget the horrible part of it."

"You were designed that way on purpose. If you remembered what a rough time of it you had, you might not go through with it again."

"You're right.

"Finish reading me the article," I said.

Pearl picked up the magazine again and leafed through it until she found the right page:

> *'Just as I am preparing my next question, a woman comes up to our table. At first, I think it is Charlize Theron (No surprise there, so many famous people stay at the George V.) But then I see it is none other than Pearl Chevalier, herself. She is stunning. Even more beautiful in the flesh than in photos. Her skin smooth and golden, her eyes a sparkling blue/gray. Her blonde hair is pinned up in a messy chignon and she's wearing a loose, flowing, floral coat that looks as if it might be vintage Christian Lacroix. I notice her swollen belly. It is evident that Pearl Chevalier is pregnant again.*
>
> *Very pregnant indeed.'*

"Sounds as if she had a crush on *you*, more like," I teased.

"Charlize Theron? Well, that *is* flattering, I have to admit"

"You're more beautiful than any movie star."

Pearl adjusted her weight, trying to find a comfortable position to accommodate her taut, round belly. "Love the touch about the jungle. I don't think a jungle is quite my scene.

Something Elodie might like, though. Have you heard from her lately?"

"She sent me an e-mail. What I said about hooking up with a surfer? Guess what? She has. His name's Lucho and he's Columbian," I told Pearl.

"From the frying pan into the fire."

"I don't think so—he sounds like a nice guy. He's only twenty-three, or so. No money, just his surfboard and a good heart."

"Good luck to her, dating a surfer—if he's anything like my dad."

"He sounds very committed to her. He has no idea who Elodie is, either." The words flew out of my mouth and I stopped. *No idea who Elodie is*...Who *was* Elodie? Not even I had the answer to that question.

"You mean, he has no idea she has a control-freak, powerful, billionaire mother and an uncle who pretends he lives in a tree-house in Thailand?"

"She's just a student with a backpack as far as he's concerned."

Pearl let the magazine drop onto the sand and stretched her arms out. "Smart girl. Or she'd end up paying for his lodging and food for the next few months."

"I don't know—it sounds as if he's very keen on her."

"Well, anything's better than Mikhail Prokovich. I still can't believe he got his slimy hands on her. By the way, any more news on him? It seems so odd what happened. I just don't *get* how someone can kill themselves that way...surely survival instinct kicks in at the last moment?"

"Karma," I answered quickly. "It was meant to be. He got

his just desserts."

"After all that work Natalie and I did," Pearl mumbled.

"Yeah, but you still exposed all his aides; all those dodgy people in high places who were making a mint because of the loopholes in the law."

"True." Pearl pondered what I'd said. "Alexandre, can I ask you a favor?"

I hesitated, hoping the conversation wouldn't go any further. "Sure. Anything."

"Will you rub some sunscreen on my back? I want to turn over." *Phew,* I thought. She maneuvered her body so she was now lying on her front, taking care to not squish her tummy.

"I'll try," I said, getting the cream out of her beach bag.

"What do you mean, you'll *try?*"

"Tall order," I said, squeezing some onto my palm and edging up to her towel. I placed my gooey hands over her shoulders and started to massage her smooth back. Within seconds I was as solid as a rod. I wanted to fuck here there and then. "Jesus, what is it about your skin?"

She turned her head; her eyes scanning down to the bulge in my swim shorts and laughed, her teeth bright against her tan. She rolled over onto her back again, exposing her swollen belly once more. "Okay, do my tummy then if it's getting you so horny."

But her stomach didn't deter my ardor. Her pregnancy really turned me on. I began to rub the cream in gently—my eyes straying to her beautiful, big, full breasts. My cock started pounding; throbbing with desire. "I have to fuck you, Pearl. Please don't torment me with this." I leaned into her face and kissed her. "Please, chérie, let's go inside for a while. It's siesta time."

She looked over to where the nanny was making sandcastles with the twins, and sighed. "Poor Joy, we can't just abandon her."

I straddled her, my swim shorts tented with my raging hard-on. "Yes we can." I leaned down and breathed Pearl in. Sun. Coca Cola, sun cream, the Pearl Elixir. My eyes were hooded with lust. "I have to fuck you," I whispered into her ear, "but first I'm going to flicker my tongue between your legs and in every orifice you have—sweep my tongue all over you—make you scream out my name."

"Sold," she said. "But not here in public."

"That fast? Boy, that was easy."

"Well, what can I tell you, Alexandre Chevalier? I'm an easy lay."

I laughed, our lips touching "Not usually," I murmured into her mouth. "I have to earn my time with you these days."

"Let's go inside. I've had too much sun, anyway, for one day. I'll just let Joy know."

Our house was vast, a restored British colonial with polished wood floors, beamed ceilings, wood-lined walls and multiple, large, shuttered doors. From the ocean side we could whale-watch early in the mornings over a cup of coffee, observe the great creatures dive and splash in sun-glinted waves. Or from the bedroom upstairs, listen to the morning tweet of birds, and catch the view of both the sea and Salinas—there used to be a burgeoning salt industry here once—as sensual, tropical trade winds breezed through the open windows, always keeping us cool. I remembered the year before, trudging through the snow in Central Park, desperate to reunite myself with Pearl whom I feared I'd lost—longing for fatherhood and to start a family with her, and now here we were together. Parents. Basking in the warmth of family love, with another one on the way.

I was the luckiest man alive.

"Lie on the bed, Pearl, I'll continue that back massage I started." She'd just come out of the shower, naked, her golden tan glistening wet, her blonde hair dripping over her shoulders.

"I never say no to one of your massages." She lay herself gently on the bed, less able every day to lie on her stomach. "Even though you know I want a whole lot more than just a rub down."

With her on her front, I straddled her without putting any weight on her and began to knead her shoulders gently. It was tempting to fuck Pearl straight away but I got a thrill out of making her so relaxed, so wet, that by the time we had sex she was practically in tears she was so horny. In the past week, her pregnancy hormones had her wanting me more than ever.

"That feels wonderful," she groaned. "Just amazing."

I traced the tips of my fingers along her spine and down to the crack of her smooth ass, cupping her curves, massaging her buttocks. "This is a part of the body that gets ignored so often," I said. "It needs attention." I explored my fingers around her little dimples in the curve of her lower back, bent down and whispered kisses all over her. "I love you, baby," I told her, my breath hot on the nape of her neck.

"When you say 'baby', do you mean me or…we still haven't come up with a name, have we?"

"I mean both of you," I replied, drawing a slow circle around her dimples as I felt my cock stiffen up against my abdomen. "Don't worry, the perfect name will come at the perfect time."

"I need to turn over now," Pearl said in a bossy voice.

"Not yet, just relax." I trailed my hand down her back again, enticingly, as my fingers crept between her thighs. She was already soaked—I tapped her lightly there.

"Oh God," she moaned. "I need you to fuck me. Now."

"Sshh, chérie, I'm going to take my sweet time."

"Please, Alexandre, I need you inside me."

"Like this," I said, slipping my finger into her liquid heat, and sliding it out again.

"Oh please, don't torture me."

I tasted her on my finger. Delicious. I rolled her body over so she was on her back and pulled her down the bed. She loved being manhandled by me, loved it when I took control of her. I had her so she was on the edge of the bed, her legs dangling over, almost touching the floor. I nudged her thighs wide apart and got down on my knees. First, I kissed her inner thighs so lightly, knowing that all she could think about was her core; but I wanted to give her lots of anticipation. Then I leisurely stroked her glistening pussy up and down with my tongue, tasting her delectable nectar, darting it every now and then at her clit, then circling it. She was writhing and meowing.

"This is incredible. I love you, Alexandre. Oh God."

I always knew when Pearl was being driven wild because she brought God into her moaning pleas. It amused me. I slid my thumb inside her and continued with my tongue, pressuring it on her clit, hooking my thumb so it rested on her G-spot, moving it in a circular motion. She bucked her hips at me—she was in a blissful stupor. Keeping my thumb inside her, I moved my face away and turned my attention to one of her hard nipples and sucked. Jesus it made me horny. My dick was pounding. A low growl emanated from my throat. The feral sound made her grip my head and run her fingers passionately through my hair.

"I'm so wet, you're driving me crazy, Alexandre. Please fuck me."

"You want me to fuck you?" I teased, a smile tipping the corners of my mouth.

"Please…oh God, please. I need you inside me."

I pulled her back up the bed so she was more comfortable and took in my view. My woman with her swollen stomach. My seed, which was growing daily into a special being. "You're beautiful," I told her. "You've never been more beautiful."

She spread her legs even wider and I licked my lips—her pussy was like a split open fig—ripe and lush, smelling of the sun. I wanted to taste it again—go down on her once more. She notice my gaze, fixed between her legs.

She whispered, "I know what you're thinking but I need you inside me, baby—I need your lips on my lips, your breath on mine, your chest against my breasts; I need you close so there's no space between us."

Her words made me shudder. I lay over her; my weight propped up by my elbows, and dipped my broad crown into her wetness. She cried out. She flung her arms about my shoulders and gripped me with her thighs, raising her hips and hooking her ankles around my ass. I felt myself plunge into her velvet warmth and I groaned like a wild animal, thrusting, sliding deeply back and forth—our worlds united as one.

"I. Love. Fucking. You. Pregnant," I rasped, now tantalizing her with mini thrusts, as I rammed my crown along her clit, over and over, her erotic zones stroked and stoked by my thick cock. She slid her tongue into my mouth and sucked on my tongue, ravenous for every part of me. She couldn't get close enough. I plunged in deeper, really fucking her now as her silk walls clamped around me.

"You feel amazing," I said, her kiss devouring my words. And she did. Pearl had a mélange of sweet innocence, coupled with raw sexuality; a heady cocktail that always sent me spinning. I had never been loved so much by anyone. Ever. My heart was thumping with love—waves of it crashing into her and leaving me breathless. I was weak with tenderness. But my aura was also on fire—light and heat circling our bodies like a parade of invisible angels looking on. Pearl had summoned God earlier with her cries, and a Higher Power—the Light—a Divine Flow, whatever you want to call it—was with us.

Everywhere.

I'm not a religious person, but if I had died in that moment I could have gone to my grave knowing, and having lived the ultimate definition of Paradise, because when Pearl and I climaxed together we lived inside one another's bodies for an instant. It is hard to explain, but it was a gift.

A parting gift to make what was about to shock our world, easier to bear.

19

The Bahamas boasts some of the best diving in the world, but of course Pearl couldn't do that, being pregnant. She was able to snorkel, though, and was happy working from her laptop, being mom, and reading novels.

I, however, took advantage of the incredible underwater world here. There are seven hundred different islands and cays but just forty-nine inhabited ones, so the place is replete with marine life, including dolphins, black tipped sharks, rays, and turtles, with protected, dropping reefs, deep as cliffs. It is a veritable diver's paradise and that was one of the reasons Pearl and I came here. We both needed a break from city life and I had been longing to really explore. We hired a cook and had Joy to help look after the twins, so we were incredibly spoiled and enjoying every minute of our extended vacation.

The early morning dive brought a plethora of underwater creatures going about their business. A Caribbean reef shark came alarmingly close to my flippers but swerved off in another direction. I saw spotted eagle rays, hawksbill turtles, an enormous grouper with its unhappy, turned-down mouth, and horse-eyed jacks in glittering silvery-blue with phosphorescent yellow-green fins, and all sorts of other brightly-colored tropical fish that I didn't know the names of. Fish—disguising themselves as sand, fish—in glaring yellow or with orange spots. I felt bad for a Lionfish, its red and gold stripes shimmering in the rays of the sun which were penetrating the deep blue of the water, because any second now, the other diver who had accompanied me would spear or net it and it would end up on somebody's plate. Through no fault of its own, this Lionfish was born into the wrong sea—not indigenous to these waters, its ancestors having made their way from the eastern coast of Africa to a Miami pet shop. Some blame it on the owners tossing them into the ocean when they started devouring their other fish in the tank, and others on Hurricane Andrew in 1992, smashing an aquarium tank, letting them loose. Here the creature was now, its dagger-sharp, venomous spines creating a sort of mane—an exquisitely beautiful specimen, condemned to death because it was threating the eco-system here, an invasive species, feeding on juvenile reef fish and threatening the population of scores of marine creatures.

The water felt like silk against my skin, and it would have been easy to stay here all day but I wanted to get back to Pearl and the twins. I didn't want to become a dive-nerd. I'd seen some people suffer from that—so obsessed, they left their real lives behind. I'd left Pearl sleeping and promised (a whisper in her ear) that I'd be back before lunchtime. She groaned quietly with a little smile on her lips which both said, *Leave me to sleep and shut-up* and, *I love you*. Which, I wasn't sure, but then she did mumble, *Love you, babe,* so I went out feeling buoyed by the perfection in my life.

Those were her last words.

I came home from the dive, my head full of excitement with all I'd seen, bursting to relay all of it to my family, but as I walked up to the front door, Joy rushed towards me, her hand covering her face in panic. My instant reaction was that something had happened to one of the twins.

"Mr. Chevalier, it just happened five minutes ago. She was fine, just fine and then—"

"What? What's wrong? The babies?"

"No, your wife. I tried calling you but your cell was off. I've alerted the doctor—maybe Pearl had a sort of seizure. I called the doctor," she repeated.

"Well done." I rushed inside and Pearl was lying on the sofa stretched out, her lids closed, her face alarmingly pale—compared to the healthy-looking, tanned girl this very morning. My heart started hammering—fear and adrenaline spiked through my body into my fingertips, numbing me. "What the fuck is going on?" *My Pearl….my belle Pearl…*

"She's not responding but her heart's beating," Joy said, trembling. The cook was there with the children and everyone stared at me and then back to Pearl. I leaned down and felt Pearl's pulse. It was normal. Well, 'normal' wasn't the right word. Something was ominously wrong but I wasn't a medic so I had no idea what.

"What happened?" I demanded. Madeleine began to cry at the sound of my shrill voice. Joy swept my baby up into her arms to placate her and said, "Pearl tripped and fell down, walking upstairs a few hours ago. Bumped the front of her head. Not long after you'd left. But she was fine. She even laughed about it afterwards. She didn't even have a cut. Nothing. Then about half an hour ago she said she had a headache and went to lie on the couch. I went to make her a cup of tea, I heard a sort of groan, and when I came back she was out. At first I thought she was sleeping, but she wouldn't wake up."

"Did she hurt her stomach when she fell?"

"No, I don't think so. She slipped and bashed her head but she didn't think it was anything to worry about."

I felt a shockwave of fury surge through my veins. Laura was fucking haunting us. First Elodie, miraculously being able to tie that sailor's knot and kill a man, and now Pearl, falling on the fucking stairs, repeating history. I could hear Laura now, manically laughing, thinking the whole thing was hilarious as she pulled her marionette strings from her armchair in Hell.

I looked at Joy. I was stumped. Horrified. *This isn't happening!* But not only was it happening, it had already fucking *happened.* "You called the doctor, you say?"

"She's on her way. Luckily, the number was on the fridge."

I smoothed my hand over Pearl's brow and noticed the swell of a bruise and discoloration there. It looked as if she had a concussion. I lifted her body up a touch to see if she'd react; if her muscles would clench, but she was as limp as a rag doll. She didn't stir. *Jesus, surely she couldn't be in a coma…could she?* I got out my cell.

"Pearl doesn't just need a doctor, she needs a fucking ambulance. No, she needs a helicopter." I called 911.

The next fifteen minutes were a blur. The doctor arrived,

and while we waited for the helicopter, she took Pearl's blood pressure, pinched her nose, shone a light pen into her eyes and pricked her arm. No reaction from Pearl. The doctor confirmed the worst.

I heard Joy mumbling to herself, "Like that famous actress—what was her name? She tumbled while skiing on the beginner slopes—didn't have a bruise on her—she sent the medics away, saying she was fine. She die—"

I cut her off, "Pearl. Will. Be. Okay," I enunciated, glaring at her. "I can hear the helicopter now."

The medics rushed inside and laid Pearl on a stretcher. While they worked they asked us what had happened and words, overlapping, came tumbling out of our mouths at once; all of us trying to accept that what was taking place before our eyes was real. That was the irony of it all; a silly fall had gotten her into this unimaginable state. They always say accidents happen close to home but this was absurd! I had never seen Pearl so immoveable. Her skin was now looking marbled—it was as if they were about to carry away a valuable Greek statue that needed to be restored.

I put my hand on the shoulder of one of the paramedics to catch his attention—he was so involved in his task; putting an oxygen mask on Pearl, and then hooking her up to a drip, that it was an effort for him to even speak to me, let alone explain. All I knew by their manner, was that this was one hell of an emergency.

He said, "They'll need to access your wife's neurological status—her Glasgow Coma Scale to predict her ultimate outcome."

"What's normal?" I demanded.

"The score ranges from three to fifteen. Fifteen is normal, three is…" He didn't even finish his sentence.

Score—what a shit choice of words; as if someone in a coma had won something. "She's in a full-blown coma then?" I asked, double-checking. "This isn't just a temporary concussion?" I had been hoping that the doctor had somehow made the wrong diagnosis.

"Your wife has suffered head trauma and yes, she's in a coma."

"But it was just a silly fall!" I exclaimed, as if we could rewrite the past, as if my outburst could make a fucking difference.

"We're used to dealing with dive accidents, even golfing accidents, here in The Bahamas, but this really *is* unusual."

"Will the baby be okay?"

"I wouldn't like to say; they'll run tests."

At least he was being honest, although it was the last thing I needed to hear. "How can she be in a fucking coma from a little fall?" I persisted.

The medic adjusted Pearl's oxygen mask. "Often a person's immediate injury is not what does the most damage. More often than not, there's a secondary injury to the brain that can occur hours, even days, later. The patient, as in your wife's case, is unaware may not even feel pain. Internal bleeding. That's why she suddenly had a headache."

I looked at him blankly. Not because I couldn't understand but because I felt as if I were floating through some surreal nightmare.

He took my vapid expression as miscomprehension and added, "The brain moves around in the skull, causing damage to nerve fibers and blood vessels. It causes the brain to swell which, in turn, blocks the flow of blood, causing tissue death."

Death. The word caused a rush of nausea to wash over me. "Not allowing oxygen to get to the brain?"

"Exactly, sir. That's why your wife is in a coma—it's the body's natural defense mechanism."

"So what now?"

"In all the cases I've seen like this, the patient needs intervention as soon as possible."

"Intervention?" My accent sounded more French than usual. Normal—I was out of my mind with fear.

"I'm 99% sure your wife's injuries are neurosurgical but the neurologist will determine her prognosis and the best course to take. Our job is to stabilize her and keep her alive until we get to hospital; I can't say what will happen next." *Keep her alive?* The reality was sinking in fast. If it weren't for them she might be dead by now, all from a goddamn stupid fall. *Things like this do not happen! Why pick on us for this freak-statistic-one-in-a-million kind of an accident?*

Before I could say another word, they rushed Pearl out through the doors to the helicopter, which was waiting on the lawn for them like a giant wasp, chopping up the wind.

I ran after them.

I had envisioned Pearl in the hospital—giving birth—but not this. I had been by her bedside now for ten hours straight. She'd been in OR and had come out still alive, so I was hopeful. Joy and the twins were in a hotel nearby.

The neurosurgeon—apparently one of the most talented in Miami, and even in the whole country, had done his best. Now all we could do was wait. I observed Pearl's face. She looked like a beautiful doll, although she had plastic tubes connected to her nose and mouth; the wheezing ventilator puffing in and out, ominously sounding like Darth Vader, feeding her oxygen, helping her breath, saving her *life.* Wires also ran all over the place and electrode pads on her chest, monitoring her heart. I stared at the green lines on the cardiac monitor in a trance.

I looked away and conjured up a vision of my Pearl, the Pearl who laughed so hard she'd wipe a tear from her face. Or scream at me the few times she got angry, or smother the babies in kisses from their heads to their toes, singing or chanting nursery rhymes. And then I'd look back at the statue of her. Still. Serious. Expressionless, and my eyes filled with burning tears.

Why? Why Pearl? Why not some schmuck who has it coming to him? Or someone who doesn't have the will to live? Why Pearl, of all people?

As I was wallowing in the injustice of it all, the nurse came by to give Pearl a sponge bath and set her IV pumps, saying she wanted to show me how to massage her. Up until now, I was scared of even touching her too much, as if by one wrong move I could cause her to stop functioning. The nurse had no extra news from the surgeons, other than that Pearl and the baby were 'stable' (e.g. alive). The neurologist, she assured, was on his way to talk to me. The last time we spoke, I hardly took in a word he said. All I knew was that Pearl had made it.

For now, anyway.

"Don't be nervous about massaging her," the young nurse

insisted, as if reading my mind. "She's not made of glass."

But she is!

She took Pearl's slim arms in her fleshy brown hands and in a soothing voice said, "We need to keep her body supple so her muscles don't waste or her limbs might get locked into one position. It's important. The medical term is muscle atrophy—we don't want that to happen. Here, give me your hands." She took my large, awkward hands and placed them on Pearl's legs. "Go on, give her a good massage." But all I could do in that moment was bury my head in her thighs and weep. The Pearl Elixir had been replaced with a clinical, medical aroma—the odor of cleanliness and iodine, or whatever they used to swab her down with before she went into surgery.

"I'll be back in a minute," the nurse said discreetly, leaving me to my inner-turmoil.

I stayed that way for a good five minutes but then sat up with a jolt. *Get it together, Alexandre!* I believed that coma patients could feel and hear, despite what they told me, and I didn't want Pearl to sense my anguish.

Even though I rarely prayed and never went to church, I was brought up a Catholic and that shit sticks with you, whether you like it or not. Suddenly God was getting my undivided attention. I'd felt furious with Him (Her?) all day but I reckoned I needed to be a little more amenable if I were to receive any special favors.

So I took a big breath and prayed. I prayed my fucking heart out.

"Please bring Pearl and our beautiful baby back to me. I'll do anything you want."

Anything.

The neurosurgeon came by on his rounds, ten minutes earlier than I expected, and woke me up from a doze. He was cool, professional—a tall, almost gangly man, with a gentle stoop. I guessed he must have been about fifty. Although I knew he would have done everything possible, it unnerved me that this was just his day job. It wasn't his *life*. If Pearl didn't make it, he'd feel bad, would have tried his darned best, but it wouldn't *destroy his world.* I wanted everyone to feel my pain, my fear, my anguish. I wanted everyone here to be as invested in Pearl as I was. But when they got home after work, they had their own lives to lead, their own families and problems. Pearl was not their number one priority. They were mere human beings. What if someone fucked up?

My face was a mask as the surgeon explained the operation. How a substantial amount of blood was removed because the tissue had swelled against the inflexible bone. How they had to relieve the pressure inside the skull by placing a ventriculostomy drain to eliminate excess cerebrospinal fluid. He was trying to speak in layman's terms so I'd understand. I was grateful for that; right now my mind was holding too much fear to think coherently. He told me how they'd removed a tiny piece of skull to accommodate the swelling, which they'd re-implant at a later date. He talked about measuring pressure, inserting valves, and a dozen other medical procedures.

"What about the baby?" I asked. "Won't the anesthesia have harmed the baby?"

The man was calm. I didn't know whether to feel grateful

for his cool, professional demeanor, or furious. Good, he was in control of the situation. Bad, he was dispassionate, as if Pearl were just another patient. Because, let's face it, she was…*just another patient* to him. His patients were his profession but were they *his world? His life?* His Universe would not come tumbling down if Pearl didn't live.

He looked down for a second, took a breath, looked me in the eye and then said succinctly, "Obviously, our first priority is with the mother, with Pearl, but there is no evidence that babies born to mothers who had surgery during pregnancy have a higher incidence of birth defects. We adjusted the dose accordingly—our anesthesiologist is the best in his field, don't worry. We're doing all we can." His last sentence spoke volumes. *We're doing all we can.* And I detected a glint of sympathy that flickered in his gaze. The last thing I fucking needed.

I looked away because I didn't want him to see that tear fall. The tear that told him I was almost a broken man. I turned from him, wiped my face and focused on a huge white bunch of lilies that Sophie had sent. The sweet cloying aroma was wafting about the room and for a second, it made me feel appeased. Pearl loved white lilies. Our engagement cake when I took her to the Empire State was garnished with fresh white lilies. She loved the smell of them, the elegant shapes they made.

I needed to be strong. For Pearl. For my children.

For myself.

20

It was early in the morning when Daisy slipped into the hospital room as noiselessly as a cat burglar. I sat up from my recliner with a jolt. At first I didn't recognize her—she looked taller than before—but on a double take I noticed that she must have lost weight, and her extra height was just an illusion. Her fiery red hair had lost some of its wildness, too.

"I came as soon as I could," she whispered. Her eyes were swollen and red, her eyelids enflamed. But her expression now was brave and her attitude chirpy as if everything were quite normal. *Nice try, Daisy.* Still, I appreciated the effort.

"Billy's getting us some coffees from the vending machine."

I looked at her blankly. "Billy, Pearl's dad?"

"Yeah, he'll be here in five minutes."

"You came together?"

Daisy moved quietly over to Pearl's side and took her hand. "Yes, we flew from Hawaii." A tear slid down her English-rose cheek.

"Your living in Hawaii now?"

"Moved there a couple of months ago."

"Where's Amy?"

"With her dad in New York for a few days. You know, we're getting a divorce but it's still great for her to see him when she can." She managed a limp smile.

"You're living in Kauai?" I repeated, glad to have some distraction from my motor-mind. You came all this way?"

"Of course I did, Pearl's my best friend."

For the next five minutes, I told Daisy all I knew about Pearl's condition, rattling off, in a monotone, every piece of information I gleaned from the neurosurgeon. I was on automatic pilot, my sensations numbed, my body felt as if it were stuffed with cotton wool. The neurologist, who was working alongside the surgeon, had also given me an update, earlier this morning. Pearl was stable but there was no improvement. He didn't look hopeful, at all, but he wouldn't give anything away.

Daisy said brightly, "I've prepared an iPod for Pearl. All her favorite songs. I thought she could have a listen in between siesta time." We both tried to laugh at her joke but then she burst out crying and I tried not to let the lump in my throat morph into a full-blown sob. Daisy wept as we clung to each other, our bodies shaking, gripping each other for dear life, because that's what it was…what it *is…Dear Life.* Even when staring death in the face in the French Foreign Legion, I had never appreciated the fragility of life as I did in that moment.

A freak accident, tripping on the stairs—that's all it took for Pearl to be animated and extraordinary one minute, and the next, three hours later, a ghost of herself.

That is what life can do. Life can take away life from anyone, at any second. We cannot take it for granted. We cannot control it. We cannot expect it to dance to our tune.

I was looking at Pearl's ghost now and it terrified me, mainly because I felt responsible.

"I feel so guilty, Daisy. If only I hadn't had the stupid, fucking idea for us to go to the Caribbean. What a fool! We should have stayed in New York. Or Paris. Or somewhere that had state-of-the-art hospitals five minutes away, that didn't involve a fucking helicopter ride."

"We all know that's not true, Alexandre. Accidents can happen anywhere. *Catastrophes* can happen anywhere, even right on your doorstep. 9/11 is a perfect example of that. You cannot prepare yourself against Fate's cruel blows. If you live that way, you are only half a person."

"But I should have been more careful. I should—"

"It's not your fault, Alexandre. It was a freak accident. The damage occurred in the few hours between her fall and when she fell into a coma. Even if Pearl had been on the doorstep of any hospital in New York City, knowing her, she would have laughed it off and said she didn't need a doctor, that she felt fine. It was a one in a million thing. She was just fucking unlucky."

Her words were kind but didn't alleviate the hatred I felt for myself. All my fury I'd had the night before for the medical team, was now directed at myself. What kind of shit husband takes his family to a fucking island, when his wife is five months pregnant and his children are toddlers?

"I mean it wasn't as if you were in some third-world country," Daisy went on, as if she could read my thoughts. She pulled away from me and looked at me steadily in the eye. "The Bahamas are safe, Americanized. What happened to Pearl could have happened anywhere. Besides, it was her idea to go off to the Caribbean and take a long break."

"Yes, but she did it for me."

"Bollocks, Alexandre, she did it because she wanted to. Pearl is headstrong, she does what she wants." Daisy looked down at her feet. "Sorry, 'headstrong' wasn't the best choice of words."

I tried to smile. "Actually, it is the perfect word to describe Pearl and it gives me hope. She'll get through this, Daisy. I promise." I kissed Daisy's brow lightly and felt comfort with her being there; knowing she was going through the same sort of pain as I was. She could identify. She understood.

"I brought coffee and doughnuts." I looked up and saw Billy with a tray. He set it down on a table and came over to shake my hand. Then he laid an arm around Daisy's shoulder. Were they dating? Just friends? From the way she shifted her body a touch away from him, it looked as if he had one thing in mind and she another. He pointed to the coffees. "These two have cream. The other's black."

I took one of the paper cups. "I'll take the black one if that's okay."

"Pearl drinks black," Daisy said. "That song, *Black Coffee*—the All Saint's version, not the Julie London version, is on the mixed tape. On her iPod, I mean. I've tried to have mostly upbeat songs, you know. Perk her up a little. *Wake Up Little Suzy* is on there, too. Apparently, music can nudge people out of comas, especially if it's a song they recognize and that means something to them."

Perk her up? I looked at Pearl. *Sleeping Beauty.* Maybe I was enough of a French frog to get her to wake up if I kissed her. Or did she have to kiss me back?

Daisy wrung her fingers through her thick red hair. "I made a promise to her once and I'll need to speak to the staff about it."

"A promise?" I felt nervous. What kind of promise? *To get them to pull the fucking plug?* To donate her organs? My eyes were darts, but Daisy just shook her head and smiled.

"Don't look so horrified, Alexandre."

Funny, this woman can read my thoughts.

"Once, Pearl and I were joking around, and she made me swear that if she ever ended up in a coma or was a vegetable, unable to move, that I'd make sure her beauty regime was taken care of. You know, hair-care, leg waxing and stuff. It was a *joke*—I never thought it would actually bloody *happen*, but a promise is a promise."

I heaved a sigh of relief.

Silence sliced through the air like a razor. We looked at each other, Billy cast his eyes at the floor—maybe to stop himself from breaking down, and everybody felt speechless. Except Daisy started chatting again; obviously wanting to fill the awkward void.

She inhaled the bunch of flowers. "These lilies are beautiful. Pearl's favorite. Well, I guess you know that already or you wouldn't have chosen them."

"Sophie sent them," I said.

"How is Sophie?"

"Fine, she'll be here tomorrow," I told her.

"You sold HookedUp, then?"

"Yeah, we did." *Shut up with the small talk, Daisy.*

"Anthony's on his way, right?"

"Yes, he'll be here in a while."

"Oh God, I nearly forgot!" Daisy said, reaching into her purse. "The last time we saw Pearl she let Amy try on her pearl necklace, you know…Amy had been obsessing about it for over a year…so for a special treat, we let her, and wouldn't you know it, Amy went off with it! Naughty magpie."

Daisy carefully brought out the Art Deco necklace I had given Pearl—the lucky one with eighty-eight pearls, the number of infinity of the Universe, the number of constellations in the sky. She laid the necklace about Pearl's pale neck and fiddled with the diamond clasp for what seemed forever. I felt a lump choke up my throat.

"There…these pearls can work some magic, maybe," Daisy said, and then lowered her voice to a whisper, "The nurse will probably say she isn't allowed to wear them, or something, but worth a try, eh?"

The shimmering pearls looked exquisite, lustrous; myriad tones of pinkish gold and honey. I looked away—I thought I'd break into pieces.

"You know what?" I said, hardly able to speak. "I think Billy might want to be with his daughter for a bit. Have a chat." *Hint, hint, Billy—let Pearl know you're sorry for being such an absent father when she needed you most.* My anger was surging back again. At Billy, at myself. Pearl looked so beautiful in the necklace that I could no longer bear to look at her. I needed to get the hell out of this sterile hospital room for an hour or two so she didn't feel my negative vibe.

"I'm going to my hotel to clean up, have something to eat and see my kids," I told them. "I'll be back in a bit. You've all got my number. Call me if anything, you know…happens. I'm five minutes away."

Billy's tall frame stood and sadness was carved across his weather-beaten face. He was a handsome man, with his loose, sandy-blond hair, and looked younger than his fifty-something years. But right now he looked like shit. I guess we all did.

Being back with my children temporarily eased me somewhat. I lay on the floor, which was carpeted wall-to-wall in a thick wool pile, and let them crawl all over me as if they were puppies. I told them how much their mother doted on them and that there was another baby on the way, trying to convince myself that everything would work out fine. But I felt haunted by what Daisy told me; that Pearl had asked her to make sure her legs got waxed if she ended up in a coma. Did she have a premonition? Sometimes, a voice speaks to you. Your subconscious, your gut, your instinct—call it what you will. Perhaps Pearl *knew* this was going to happen.

I played airplane with Madeleine, which she adored, lying on my back and balancing her on my feet while holding her hands. Louis was more grounded. He didn't want to fly or play wild games. He wanted to be quiet and look at picture books or play with colored blocks.

"I've ordered room service," Joy said, standing at the doorway. I turned to look at her and saw she'd been crying too. We were all pretending to each other to be brave but inside we were mush. "I thought you needed some nourishment before you went back to the hospital." She retied her ponytail so her dark hair was scraped against her scalp. I'd become a bit obsessed with scalps, heads and brains in the last twenty-four hours. They'd shaved part of Pearl's head. With my babies, I was always so careful when I held them, afraid to drop them, but a grown woman, who would have known such a thing could happen?

"Great." I didn't even bother asking Joy what she'd ordered. I didn't care. Eating right now was an aid to help me function, nothing more. A way to fuel myself. The neurologist told me that they'd run more tests, but he didn't want to put my hopes up.

As well as talking to all the medical staff, I'd done research. That's all I did, in between massaging Pearl, reading her poetry and stories, and talking to her. But I hung on to Hope, Faith and fucking Charity. I reckoned for all the shit I went though for the first half of my life, I was owed one.

When I got back to the hospital, Anthony was there. He was dressed in a bright yellow shirt and pink pants, his head on Pearl's cheek, crying his heart out. Daisy had put the ear buds on Pearl and the iPod switched on. I thought I heard the tune, *Unchained Melody* and it made my eyes smart. Another nurse—an older woman, this time—waddled in, adjusted Pearl's IV bags, double-checked settings and the cardiac monitor, and left, leaving our motley party to get on with it.

Anthony didn't even notice me. Billy was quietly reading a

magazine. Daisy looked up at me, her eyes even more puffed than before, her mascara smudged. She took me aside and mouthed silently, "Bruce is also in the hospital. Anthony's freaking out."

"Bruce, his boyfriend?"

"He's had another aneurism. Obviously Anthony's torn in two. Guilty if he didn't come here, guilty now he *is* here. He'll be flying back to San Francisco on the red-eye."

"Poor guy. Any change in Pearl?" I whispered. I didn't want Pearl to hear us, even though they assured me she was out of it.

"Not a peep," Daisy murmured back. "And that's another reason why Ant is freaking out. He overheard one of the neurologists talking about Pearl's condition. But Ant is such a drama queen, I don't know."

"But I spoke to Dr. Bailey earlier. He said it's too soon to make a definitive prognosis—that we need to wait."

"That's what I hoped too. But they won't speak to me because I'm not family."

"You *are* family, Daisy."

"Thanks for that." She wiped a tear from her eye. "Anthony said that—"

"I heard the doctors discussing Pearl earlier," Anthony piped up, his lip trembling, his body shaking uncontrollably.

Billy put his magazine down and gathered a measured breath. "We need to speak to Dr. Bailey directly, Ant. What you heard was hearsay." His face was gaunt and drained, his eyes empty with fear.

I came over to Anthony and laid my hand on his shoulder and gave him a pat as if to say, *There, there, now.* I felt ridiculous—I didn't know what else to do—the man was a blubbering mess. I didn't want him to say anything in front of Pearl but he couldn't be stopped.

He blurted out, "They were talking in a lot of technical, medical jargon, you know. Cerebral edema, sub-something-or-other bleeding, cervical spine fracture. They said that her frontal lobes and parietal lobes are irreparably damaged, and that when the anesthesia wears off they can establish brain death. Something about Doppler flows and oh yes, of course they want to get their greedy hands on her kidneys." He started wailing, braying like a donkey, tears spilling from his inflated eyes. "Why me? Why is it all happening at once?" he yodeled.

I squeezed his shoulders. "No, Anthony. Dr. Bailey wouldn't be so unprofessional. He's one of the most respected neurosurgeons in the country. And the neurologist, too. They'd let us know something like that, straight away. There's the baby to think of, as well. You must have misheard."

Anthony gulped air. "It's the weekend. He probably wanted to go fishing or something…you know, couldn't face getting into some heavy family drama, so thought he'd wait until after the weekend to tell us the bad news."

I didn't want to argue about this with my brother-in-law, out of his mind with upset, so I let it pass. I had an urge to throttle Anthony, choke some sense into him, chuck them all out of the room, Daisy included, and just lie there quietly with Pearl. Alone. But they, too, had a right to be with her.

Yet Anthony continued, as he wrung and twisted his fingers through his hair and cried, "I'm sorry, call me a coward but I am *not* going to stay here and watch my sister die! I mean, she is dead, right? Technically *dead,* being kept alive by machines? Her brain isn't functioning!" His pale blond eyebrows shot up. "All they have to do is yank out the tubes and that'll be it!"

"Enough, Ant," Billy barked, trying to remain calm. His fists were clenched though; the tension in his body was raw, his Adam's apple bobbing in his throat, his jaw tense. "If you need to leave, then just go. Nobody is judging you—we all will deal with this on our own terms."

"That's right, Dad. And my terms are shattered to pieces! My terms are…fuck, I don't know…I can't even think straight, but I cannot and *will* not watch while they fucking pull that plug. Bruce needs me. Pearly isn't even aware that I'm here!"

"I dispute that," Daisy said quietly. "She knows. She knows in her soul and in her heart—which, even if her brain *is* supposedly… 'dead,' is still beating, by the way." She whispered the word dead. "She *knows,*" she added, "how much we love her." Daisy buried her face in her hands and then rushed out of the room, crying, into the corridor. I followed her, nearly crashing into a man hobbling along with an IV pole. I needed to find the nurse, call the doctor on his cell or find someone who knew what the fuck was going on.

Pearl's brain had to be alive and functioning. Who was to say someone was 'brain dead,' anyway? There were miracles, weren't there? Misdiagnoses? She *had* to pull through.

She just had to.

Or I'd wander through life nothing better than a grain of dust.

PEARL'S EPILOGUE.

His hands were music to me all day long. His touch so full of love, so perfect, that I drifted in and out of a blissful dream. We were making love and he was telling me that I was the most beautiful woman he had ever known. Were we making love? I don't know, because every time I woke up it was just the movement of his hands and the song of his voice. Poetry. Stories. Tales of Madeleine and Louis. Laughter filled my ears.

And here I am. In a strange world of non-being, yet feeling so alive! So alive with love. I've lived. I've done everything I've ever wanted to do. Some people will tell you that living is the most important thing. But I say it's true only if you are living with life in your *heart*. Otherwise you're dead.

I can feel myself drifting away to *Utopia*. I don't care that I'm leaving Life behind. Because I have loved. I'm in love and have *been* loved. And nobody can ever take that away from me. Someone special—Alexandre—has given me his all. I am full. Literally.

I see a light and it's smoothing itself all around me like a warm sea. I'm bathed in shimmering gold luminosity. I'm weightless, floating. I can see Mom and she's laughing.

She's beckoning me to join her, calling my name.

ALEXANDRE'S EPILOGUE.

Six months later.

The memorial went beautifully, thanks to Ant who organized it all. White lilies adorned the little church on the hill and the view below was breathtaking. Rolling hills and green valleys patch-worked over the land, with houses dotted here and there. I knew that Pearl loved country-side like this. Her dad stood there, his hands behind his back, standing tall and proud, and I wondered if he minded that Daisy hadn't chosen him, after all.

Louis and Madeleine were scampering about, squealing with delight. Only children have the privilege of being so uncouth; blissfully unaware of the turmoil going on in grown-ups' heads, I thought. But Ant had been brave today and hardly shed a tear. The pastor read some lovely prayers and Anthony read a Walt Whitman poem—one of Pearl's favorites, in fact.

I was wearing a suit, the same one that I'd worn on our wedding day. I felt a lump in my throat, remembering the beauty of the falling snowflakes, Pearl's exquisite face, and I was grateful to have that memory—indeed *all* the memories of our wonderful life together.

I felt an arm slip under my jacket and snake it's way around my waist. I looked down at my wife. "So, what did you think?"

"I'm sure Bruce would have loved this," she said.

"Well, I never met the man, but the service was beautifully done."

I peered down into the carrycot just to check on little Lily. Her smooth, delicate face looked so peaceful and her heart-shaped, pouting lips so content.

"Don't worry, she'll be asleep for a while now," Pearl said, nestling her head against my shoulder.

"Shall we go back to the hotel and make another?" I asked with a crooked smile.

"Another baby? You're a fast worker, Alexandre Chevalier; I think I'm babied-out for a good long while. But if you're *careful,* I guess—"

"Let's go back, right now. I feel like hanging out with only you, all afternoon."

"What about those two rascals?" Pearl said gesturing over to our two runaround tornadoes on the loose.

"Joy," I said, "is not called Joy for nothing. She can take them to see the Golden Gate."

"You're on," Pearl agreed.

"That easy?"

"I told you I was an easy lay," she said, and laughed.

"I wish," I answered, taking all of her in my arms. I squeezed her tight and breathed in the Pearl Elixir. "For forty-eight whole hours I thought I'd lost my rare Pearl," I murmured into her soft blonde hair. "My belle Pearl."

Yes, those couple of days when Pearl was in a coma was the worst time of my life. But it turned out that the conversation between doctors that Anthony overheard was about another patient altogether, not Pearl. It was a good thing he returned home to Bruce, because Bruce died two days later. His family organized the funeral, negating the fact that Anthony was his boyfriend—refusing to have anything to do with him at all, so Anthony got this memorial together, six months later. We were now all saying goodbye. It was a poignant moment for me because, although it was sad, I couldn't help but feel that one life was lost and another gained.

Pearl survived.

Daisy was right. *Wake Up Little Suzy* jolted Pearl out of the coma. Her recovery was not immediate, obviously. It took her a long time to get back to complete normality and she spent most of that time in the hospital, due to her pregnancy. I didn't want to take any risks. But the birth went beautifully and she hardly suffered any labor pains, this time around. When little Lily popped out completely healthy, with all her fingers and toes, I thought I'd burst, I was so happy.

Since then, Pearl and I have been taking it easy. With HookedUp out of our lives and more money than anyone needs for several lifetimes, we don't have to work. Natalie has taken over HookedUp Enterprises, and Pearl just acts as consultant once in a while. She sold on *Vanity Fair*—she realized that running a magazine was very different from reading one—in fact, she spends a lot of time reading, and is working on a book based on her great-grandmother's journals. She's a full-time mom and I'm a full-time househusband. The best job I've ever had. After the scare—thinking I had lost Pearl forever—I realized that there is nothing more important than family. Nothing.

Even Sophie has chilled out. After the Google buy-out, she saw the digits of her bank account and nearly fainted. She decided to take a year off and travel around Europe with Alessandra. (Who was nominated for an Oscar for *Stone Trooper* but didn't win.) Sophie finally got a divorce, and her husband married his mistress: a young woman who had been his personal assistant. What a cliché.

All my exes finally accepted that Pearl was the only woman for me and they gave up their pursuit. Indira even sent flowers to the hospital when Pearl came out of her coma, and Claudine sent her a get-well card. Other than that, everything trundles along as it was, except Sally has her hands full with three dogs; we kept one of Rex and Bonnie's puppies. People still believe Bonnie's collar is made of real diamonds.

As for Elodie, she's still traveling about South America, searching for her vocation in life. I have a feeling she has a long and fascinating story to tell. Time will tell. She's a dark horse, that one.

And as for us? Pearl and I have never been happier. I treasure each moment that we have together, each second, each minute, each hour.

We are inseparable.

Pearl Playlist

Can't Get Enough Of Your Love Baby – Barry White

Let's Stay Together – Al Green

Sex Bomb – Tom Jones

Can't Help Falling In Love – Elvis Presley

Sex Machine – James Brown

Feeling Good – Nina Simone

Can't Take My Eyes off You – Frankie Valli and The 4 Seasons

Wonderful Tonight – Eric Clapton

Mission Impossible Theme

Personal Jesus – Johnny Cash

Miss You – The Rolling Stones

Je T'aime…Moi Non Plus – Jane Birkin & Serge Gainsbourg

Manhattan Serenade – Jo Stafford

Frozen – Madonna

Belle Pearl Playlist

Un Homme et Une Femme – Francis Lai

Lady Grinning Soul – David Bowie

California Girls – The Beach Boys

Je ne Regrette Rien – Edith Piaf

Royals – Lorde

Skyfall – Adele

You Really Got Me – The Kinks

Cello concerto in D Minor – Vivaldi

Black Coffee – All Saints

Unchained Melody – Righteous Brothers

Utopia – Gold Frapp

Wake Up Little Suzy – Everly Brothers

To listen to the soundtrack, go to:
http://ariannerichmonde.com/music/belle-pearl-sound-track/

Thank you so much for coming along on Pearl and Alexandre's emotional journey with me. I owe so much to you, my readers, and without you none of this would have happened.

I have more stories to tell, and I hope you will come along for the ride. So please sign up (ariannerichmonde.com/email-signup/) to be informed the minute any future Arianne Richmonde releases, go live. Your details are private and will not be shared with anyone. You can unsubscribe at any time.

The Pearl series:

The Pearl Trilogy bundle (the first three books in one)
Shades of Pearl
Shadows of Pearl
Shimmers of Pearl
Pearl
Belle Pearl

I have also written *Stolen Grace*, a suspense novel.

Join me on Facebook
(facebook.com/AuthorArianneRichmonde)

Join me on Twitter
(@A_Richmonde)

For more information about me, visit my website
(www.ariannerichmonde.com).

If you would like to email me:
ariannerichmonde@gmail.com

Printed in Poland
by Amazon Fulfillment
Poland Sp. z o.o., Wrocław

57902982R00231